# NOT IN A BILLION YEARS

CAMILLA ISLEY

# B
Boldwood

First published in Great Britain in 2023 by Boldwood Books Ltd.

Copyright © Camilla Isley, 2023

Cover Design by Alexandra Allden

Cover Photography: Shutterstock

A CIP catalogue record for this book is available from the British Library.

Paperback ISBN 978-1-83751-941-5

Large Print ISBN 978-1-83751-942-2

Hardback ISBN 978-1-83751-940-8

Ebook ISBN 978-1-83751-943-9

Kindle ISBN 978-1-83751-944-6

Audio CD ISBN 978-1-83751-935-4

MP3 CD ISBN 978-1-83751-936-1

Digital audio download ISBN 978-1-83751-938-5

Boldwood Books Ltd
23 Bowerdean Street
London SW6 3TN
www.boldwoodbooks.com

*To all women entrepreneurs...*

# 1

## BLAKE

When I said it was okay to go on the record, I wasn't trying to pick a fight with sexy billionaire Gabriel Mercer, I swear. But as my number two is kindly pointing out, that might be what I'm about to get.

Evan pulls his blond hair, saying, "Did you really have to slander our biggest competitor in a national newspaper?"

I lean back in my chair and grimace at my second in command. "Slander? What I said wasn't *slander*."

Evan brandishes a printout of *The Wall Street Journal* article that came out today to celebrate my new gym opening and quotes my words back to me. "*I wouldn't call receiving an ivy-league education debt-free along with all the connections certain schools bring, and having your start-up money handed to you on a silver platter, being self-made.* You basically called him a spoiled brat."

"But I also said very positive things about him..."

I ask Evan for the printout and search for the right passage. "'*Gabriel Mercer,*'" I read aloud, "'*is a skillful entrepreneur,*' he said." I pause for a moment, puzzled. "Oh, a typo, they've turned me into a man. Can you call the paper and have them rectify it?"

Evan grabs the sheet of paper from me. "He, she... must be the most common typo in the book." His eyes frantically scan the rest of the text. "You're a she everywhere else. Readers will get that you're a woman."

"I'd still like the online version to be corrected."

"Will do, chief. Anyway, being turned into a man isn't the problem. You picking a fight with Gabriel Mercer is."

"I only said he isn't self-made, which is factual."

"Still, Gabriel Mercer won't appreciate being called a rich boy in the press. Why did you have to go on the record stating it?"

"I run my mouth, okay? I made a mistake. When the reporter cited him as an example of a self-made entrepreneur, I just lost my marbles that she'd call someone with so much privilege, so much access, self-made. And then she wouldn't strike the comment no matter how many times I asked, so... spilled milk."

"Should we post a retraction?"

"No."

"Why not?"

"Because it's true and because that would bring even more attention to it. Maybe Mercer won't even read the article."

"I promise you, that man has a Google alert for his name."

"Then so be it." I throw my hands in the air. "I don't have time to deal with potentially hurt, fragile male egos, I have a cardio class to teach in less than one hour. But I want to go over the Apex pitch first."

Apex is the largest producer of fitness watches and trackers in the country and they're looking for a new sponsor partnership. I want it.

Evan plonks onto the chair opposite my desk. "I've updated the presentation; our social media growth is exponential and our reach unparalleled."

I bite the top of a pen, taking in Evan's gloomy face. "But?"

"But if you shrink down the numbers to the US market only, they're not as impressive. And I've heard their marketing director is more of a traditional—"

"Dinosaur?" I finish the phrase for him. "Let's launch a new campaign to improve our domestic numbers, bring Cara in on this," I say, referring to the head of marketing. "Have her come to me with a few ideas. Anything else we can do to juice ourselves up for Apex?"

"Unless you plan on becoming a fifty-year-old white male with 2,500 physical locations, I don't think so."

Shed twenty years off that description and he's basically described Gabriel Mercer.

I frown. "Is Power Training in the run for the bid?"

"Bidders are confidential, but we can assume Apex has reached out to them. And now you've given Mercer an extra reason to crush us."

"Then let's make sure our pitch is airtight." I drop the pen to avoid chewing on the back out of stress and stand up. "I have to go change now or I'll be late for class."

I round my old desk in the new office, which is sitting above my first brick-and-mortar fitness center. The glass-wall new development is surrounded by a mix of older red-brick buildings, former factories, and warehouses designed by famous architects. A more soulful vibe that I preferred to the glass-and-steel forest uptown to set the new location of my company's headquarters. NOHO ("North of Houston Street"), with its cobblestone streets and vibrant, artistic community, felt like the perfect place for my business to thrive.

The view always puts a big smile on my face. Contrary to my COO, who, while also contemplating the sunny June day, still looks frowny and troubled.

"Relax, Evan." I walk up to him and pat his shoulder as he

stands. "What's the Mighty Gabriel Mercer going to do, anyway? Send me to bed without dinner? Bring it on. I'm all for the intermittent fasting."

"You're being brazen if you think making an enemy of such an influential man won't come back to bite you in the rear end. Mercer has ties to a lot of real estate deals in Manhattan and beyond, and could make it difficult for us to expand."

"As you smartly pointed out, his core business is real estate. I wouldn't even call him a competitor. It just so happens that most of the properties he owns are fitness centers."

"Yes, but we already had to buy this property on the hush-hush to keep under his radar; now you've put us front and center in his field of vision." Evan drops his arms to the side. "Doesn't that worry you?"

"What are you suggesting? That he's so powerful he could buy all gym-suitable buildings in America? Mercer is not omnipotent. And he could never take the internet away from us. We're a crowd. Business has been democratized. Didn't you get the memo?"

Evan purses his lips tighter than a kitten's ass. "Don't say I didn't warn you."

"All right, Taylor Swift, I won't." I give his trapezius a gentle squeeze, the muscle tightly knotted under my touch. "Please go take a yoga class. This level of stress isn't good for you."

I leave him to brood alone in my office, hoping he'll heed my advice and blow off some steam with a little controlled breathing, or at least take a sauna.

I reach the ground floor and greet various patrons on the way to the women's locker room. The chit-chatting almost makes me late for my class, but I make it a point not to be short with anyone despite being pressed for time. I didn't gain twenty million Instagram followers by being aloof and unattainable.

Not the style of the competition, as Evan calls it. The Mighty

Gabriel Mercer—MGM, I rename him in my head—has exactly zero Instagram followers because he has no Instagram, Facebook, or any other social network on the planet.

What a snob.

The only thing more annoying than his looks—dark, handsome, groomed to perfection—are his self-celebratory statements on how he turned a one-million-dollar loan into a ten-billion-dollar empire. Heck, if I had a million dollars to start with, my company would be a hectocorn by now.

Not that I'm judging. But in the male-dominated business world, size counts. The competing little pricks have even designed a scale for their appendage-measuring contest. A start-up is proclaimed a unicorn when it reaches a billion-dollar valuation— that's where I'm at. My company is a rare, magical creature that has beaten all the odds. But I still have to contend with the behemoths that dwarf my worth. The decas, or decacorns, aka the corporations that have hit the ten-billion mark—that's where MGM's at. And above that is the ultimate goal of a hundred-billion market cap, reserved for the likes of Google, Apple, and Amazon —they were start-ups, too, once. Becoming a hectocorn is the pipe dream of every new entrepreneur. Mostly unreachable, to be fair. Especially for someone like me: a woman with no money and no connections who had to start from zero.

But I'm not interested in dwelling on what I don't have or can't ever attain. I prefer to count my blessings for everything that I've achieved and still strive to achieve. For his sake, I hope MGM is the same. That he's too busy making piles of money for himself and his investors to care about little old me and my press releases. He probably doesn't even know I exist.

I change into a neon-pink sports bra, black leggings, and pull my hair up in a high ponytail.

With a bright smile stamped on my face, I cross the gym and

enter my HIIT class shouting, "Morning everyone, who's ready to pump the heat and grind some positivity into their lives?"

## 2

### GABRIEL

"Are you sure you want to blow a million dollars on an old car?" Mila, my executive assistant, asks me as we get out of the meeting room. The deal with Apex Watches is not in the bag yet, but their executives seemed pleased with our proposal to install display cases for their fitness tracker in all of our 2,400 gyms.

"Don't call it an old car, it's a 1960 Aston Martin GT Zagato," I say as we pass by the cubicles of my employees, most of them young and fresh-faced, working away on their computers.

"Yeah, but the wheel isn't even on the proper side." Mila stops when we reach the elevator. "Couldn't you find a less expensive toy to play with, James Bond?"

The elevator doors swish open and we step in. Mila uses the key around her neck to unlock access to the top floor—*my* floor.

I cross my arms, leaning a shoulder against the metal wall, and grin at her.

"Nuh-uh, don't give me that," she chides. "The cocky bastard act doesn't work on me."

I chuckle. "One reason I hired you. Anyway, this time you don't have to rein me in. I want that car."

A ding announces we've reached our destination. As the elevator doors part on the executive floor, the sun bounces off the glass-and-metal walls of nearby skyscrapers, blinding me. I squint at the view of the tall buildings interrupted only by the splotch of green that is Central Park—its majestic trees small compared to where my office sits above the rest. I stride toward my door, Mila close on my heels.

"You're the boss." Mila sighs, resigned. "How high should I bid?"

"Every other loser will bid at around one, but I don't want to take chances, let's go for an even 1.2 mils."

"You got it, boss." We stop at her desk, located just outside my office. "Any other extravagant purchases you want me to make on your behalf today?"

"Nah, thank you, Mila, that'd be all."

She sits at her post, and I walk into my office, taking in the city below from the expansive wall of windows.

Gosh, this view of New York City never ceases to amaze me. Manhattan stretches out before me, a vast glass-and-steel tapestry where everything is possible. Like always, I feel a surge of excitement at being here, in the center of it all.

I take off my suit jacket and drop it onto my chair. Just as I'm about to sit at my desk, my phone pings with a new Google alert. The email links to an article in *The Wall Street Journal*.

I frown. I don't remember giving them an interview and can't fathom why they should do a piece on me now when they didn't bother to give me the cover when Mercer Enterprises made it to decacorn.

I settle in my chair and forward the link to my computer to read it on the big screen.

The article is about a new gym opening in NOHO.

Ah, the *supposed* competition.

It amazes me how most people—even experts—still consider my company a fitness empire when the core of the business is, and has always been, the real-estate deals that gravitate around the fitness centers.

You don't build an empire off a one-time $42,500 franchise payment and a 5 per cent royalty on $39.99 monthly membership fees.

You build it by owning the land upon which the gyms are placed.

My entire business model has been to amass plots of land to then lease to my franchisees, who, as part of their agreement, are only allowed to rent from me.

This guarantees me a steady, upfront revenue stream. Before a single shovelful of dirt is moved, the cash starts to roll in. Also granting me greater capital for expansion, giving me the firepower to acquire more land, which in turn fuels more growth.

Real estate... That's where the money is.

I went into fitness only because that happened to be the commercial activity that made the most sense for my first big plot acquisition.

Still, if an article about a new gym cites me, I want to know what they have to say. I read the opening.

Blake Avery, Instagram fitness sensation, seals the dream with the opening of a new, state-of-the-art fitness center in up-and-trendy NOHO, Manhattan. Now fans—at least the ones who live in New York—will be able to attend in-person sessions with the most popular personal trainer the internet has ever seen. And if you don't live in The Big Apple, despair not, each training session with Blake will be streamed live on Instagram, Facebook, and TikTok. Times will vary to accommodate different time zones.

I'm dealing with a circus monkey, then. Don't even get me started on what I think about social media, influencers, and internet celebrities. I conduct my business under the radar. Professional to a T, as it should be done by anyone with their sanity still intact. Shaking my head, I read the next passage of the article.

"Blake, after over a decade of inspiring people all over the world to be more healthy and fit, you'll finally be able to do that vis-à-vis. Are you excited?"

A decade? How old is the dude? I don't read his reply and skip to the next question.

"Your company is what in the start-up circles is known as a unicorn. What does that mean?"
"It means our latest valuation went over the billion-dollar mark. For a start-up, something as rare as finding a unicorn."

I scoff at that. Try making it to *deca*corn before you boast. Loser.

"You don't come from a wealthy family, do you? How does reaching the status of unicorn make you feel?"

The article is a mile long and, frankly, I don't have time for a rags-to-riches sob story. I save a PDF version of the editorial and search the new document for my name. The question that brings me into the picture makes little sense on its own, so I back up a few passages and read the entire exchange.

"The world of fitness seems to be full of self-made entrepreneurs. Do you think it's because the fitness community is so inclusive?"

"Yeah, I've never found a more supportive group of..."

Blah, blah, blah... I don't read the full apple-polishing response.

"And you're the second one of these remarkable self-made entrepreneurs to become a billionaire—"
"Pardon me, who was the first?"
"Gabriel Mercer, who else?" Blake slightly scoffed at the mention of the competition, so I prompted, "You seem to disagree?"
"No, sorry, Gabriel Mercer is a skillful entrepreneur," he said. "But I wouldn't go as far as calling him self-made..."

The skin at the back of my neck heats. To get to where I am, I bent over backward. Nothing—*nothing*—enrages me more than people assuming I'm sitting in the top chair because I was born wealthy. In my fourth year out of college, I took a one-million-dollar loan—not from my father, but from a venture capitalist, going through the Series A, B, and C funding ropes like any other startupper—and turned it into a ten-billion-dollar company through my hard work.

So, no, I don't take lightly to insignificant nobodies slandering my name. I read the next paragraph, already knowing it's only going to enrage me more.

"Why not?"
"Well, I wouldn't call receiving an ivy-league education debt-free along with all the connections certain schools bring, and having your start-up money handed to you on a silver platter, being self-made."

That's it.
I slam my laptop shut and stand up. This Blake Avery chap

seems to know a lot about me—at least the swellhead thinks he does—and I know exactly nothing about him.

Time for a meet-up.

I grab my suit jacket from my chair and storm out of the office.

"Call my car," I bark to Mila.

She scrambles up from her chair, phone already in hand as she texts Tobias, my driver. "Where are we going?"

"*I'm* going—alone."

"Ooooh." She gives me a coy look. "I'm intrigued. I left you not fifteen minutes ago in a peachy mood, and now you're as amiable as a broody Mr. Darcy forced to attend an unsophisticated country ball. Did someone prompt you to dance with a not-handsome-enough young lady?"

I only grunt in reply.

"Come on, boss, what got your panties in a bunch?"

"Not in the mood for jokes."

"Now I'm even more curious."

Still, I give her nothing.

"Can I know where you'll be in case I need to track you down for something urgent?"

I mumble a non-committal, "Lower Manhattan."

After that, we wait in silence by the elevator until the doors swish open and I get in, alone. I push the lobby button and, just as the doors are about to close again, Mila asks, "Should I wait up for you?"

# 3

## GABRIEL

The company black SUV is waiting for me outside the building. Tobias, my driver, is holding the door open for me. I get in with a confident stride, but the moment the door closes, I clench and unclench my fists, trying to control the panic. Fighting to keep my hands steady as I fasten my seatbelt.

Deep breaths.

The moment the SUV pulls off, panic still lurches in my chest. I squish it down, hating that I have no control over my reactions. That I didn't even notice how my hand went to clench on the door handle and is still gripping it, knuckles white with the effort. It's been fifteen years since the accident, and I still hate being inside a car I'm not driving.

But I won't let fear dictate my actions. I can master it. I can sit in this car without having a fit. I have to; no self-respecting CEO drives himself to business meetings. In my free time, I enjoy my luxury cars—I have no problem with fast rides when I'm the one at the wheel, the one in control, but not when I'm on the clock.

Besides, I usually use the time in the backseat to work, which in turns helps to keep me distracted from the fact that I'm inside a death trap. Win win.

Another deep breath and I take out my phone, intending to find out more about this Blake Avery, but the screen lights up with an incoming call from Thomas, my brother.

He wants to drop by my office later—never a good sign. I try to pry out of him what the ask is going to be—usually, something family-related that would remind the world of my belonging to the Mercer dynasty—but Thomas doesn't budge, leaving me in the dark.

We hang up just as my driver pulls up in front of the address cited in *The Wall Street Journal* article for the new gym's grand opening.

As I take in the artistic, friendly neighborhood out of the blackened windows of the company car, I have to concede this Blake character knows what he's doing—at least real estate-wise. The gym is placed in a high-profile new building. A modern glass box that sits on the corner of two of the most trafficked streets of the neighborhood. Impossible to miss or ignore.

Any passer-by will at least glance at the shiny architecture and wonder what's inside. Not that the twenty-foot banners of a sweaty woman and muscular dude working out will leave any doubt. Nor will the first-week-free offer spelled out in bright print.

Another spike of irritation prickles my neck. Gyms might not be my core business, but the fact that I knew nothing about this property being up for grabs infuriates me. Avery must've secured an off-market sale, which makes him alarming on top of being a nuisance.

Tobias opens the car door for me and I'm half tempted to reconsider. I know nothing about this man who so lightly dropped judgment on me in the press, and I rarely walk into a meeting unprepared. But, in the article, he pushed all the wrong buttons, hitting on the sort of prejudice I've had to deal with at every start-up event since I set out to build a business of my own. As if I didn't belong with the other entrepreneurs. As if my surname took away the right to get funding outside my family's wealth. To be free of all the strings that would've come attached to a loan from my dad. Free to make my own path, my own money.

But I did make it on my own, and no one should question that, let alone in one of the most read business papers in the country.

I get out of the car, exhaling a sigh of relief at being on solid ground again, and ask my driver to wait nearby—no, I'm not sure how long it'll take me.

I cross the street and enter the building, sidelining the reception as if I'm a patron who knows where he's going. This is a good, old-fashioned ambush. I don't want Blake Avery to be alerted to my presence and have time to prepare. That scumbag doesn't deserve a five-minute warning. He already has the advantage of knowing more about me than I do about him.

The article stated the gym will also be the new headquarters for the umbrella corporation that goes by the ridiculous name of Bloominghale. I don't know how Bloomingdale's still hasn't sued them. I'd gladly help.

Out of view in a corner where I won't attract much attention, I study my surroundings. The inside space is as neat as the outer layer, everything one would expect from a luxury gym: pristine, modern, and high-tech. The equipment visible from the reception is state-of-the-art, the best there is. A trendy juice bar is stationed just outside the locker room's entrance to the left. And a yoga studio where a tall, blond dude is perched in the most precise headstand I've ever seen completes the picture.

My gaze locks on the glass-and-steel staircase leading upstairs to what looks like office space—bingo! I dart in that direction and jump up the steps two at a time, hoping to remain undetected.

Maybe not the best move since I'm winded once I get to the top—part physical exertion and part anticipation. Out of breath is the last look I want to project once I finally meet this bigmouth face to face, so I take a few steadying breaths and navigate the upper corridors blindly, again acting as if I belong. I don't know where I'm going, but if I were the big boss at this dubious establishment, I'd want my office to sit in the corner. I head that way.

And jackpot! The big office is right where I expected it to be. The name and title—Blake Avery, CEO—are etched on the door.

The desk outside the office is unmanned.

Fortune favors the bold.

I smirk.

Or carelessness disadvantages the lax.

Mila would never leave my flank open like that. True, her job is made easier because my entire floor has restricted access, but even so, she'd never abandon her post and leave me at the mercy of unexpected enemies.

I close the distance to the unguarded office and grab the knob, ready to make a grand entrance.

I'm not sure what I was expecting upon throwing the door open... perhaps a fit dude all brawn and some brain, mid-thirties to mid-forties if he's been at this for ten years.

What I wasn't expecting was to find a young woman, back turned to me, shaking her booty in a stellar execution of a fast feet drill. She's wearing a neon-pink sports bra and black leggings. Her midnight black hair is up in a high ponytail and she has headphones on, working out in time to an unheard tune.

After the fast feet, I expect her to transition into a predictable lounge or squat combo. Instead, she jumps, throwing her hands up in the air, eyes closed, shaking her body and head in a maniacal way that wouldn't fit half bad in a *Flashdance* remake.

I cross my arms over my chest and lean against the doorframe, enjoying the show. With all the moving and spinning, I can't get a proper look at the woman's features—only guess that she must be beautiful.

The dance exhibition continues for a few more minutes until the woman turns toward me with her eyes open and freezes in place. And, hell... I'm struck by a bullet to the chest as her electric blue eyes meet mine. A deep color, but so bright it's staggering against her thick black lashes.

She's quick to recover, though. She takes me in with a not-so-subtle once over and, in a second, her charged gaze shifts from shocked to hostile.

Yep, beautiful. No, not friendly.

She removes the headphones from her head and unceremoniously drops them onto the desk. "Uninvited guests usually have to pay a ticket for the show," she says.

Not exactly the opening I'd expected. Beautiful and feisty. Pity she's a little too young for me. With her cheeks all red and puffed up from the workout, she looks barely old enough to order a drink.

"Is this a regular gig, then?" I make an attempt at a light rebuke, but seeing how she remains unmoved, I change tactics. "Sorry to intrude." I flash her a grin, one that I've been told leaves no prisoners. "I wasn't sure how to grab your attention over the music and the dancing."

"What can I do for you?" she asks flatly.

"I'm here to see Blake Avery," I say candidly, entering the office properly. "Do you know where I may find him?"

Her eyes narrow. She's about to reply, when the missing secretary—presumably returning from a juice break too many—barges into the office out of breath, panting, "I'm sorry, Miss Avery, I left my post only for a second; reception didn't warn me someone was coming up to see—"

The pathetic excuse-giving is silenced by a raised hand from

Angry Blue Eyes. "It's okay, Tilly, I can handle this myself. Please close the door on your way out."

Confident despite her young age. I like it.

The secretary backtracks, leaving the two of us alone in the office.

"You're an Avery," I accuse, some of my indignation coming back. The dance show got me momentarily distracted. Blake Avery must be more in the forties age bracket, then, if he already has a daughter in her twenties. I mean, she must be his daughter.

Angry Blue Eyes leans back against her father's desk and crosses her arms over her chest. A move that she must intend as unfriendly, but that props up her assets already showcased by the sports bra, making me struggle not to lower my gaze away from her spectacular eyes. The way the generous amount of skin on display is covered with beads of sweat doesn't help either.

"And who are you?" she asks, unaware of my interior struggle to maintain eye contact.

"Your family is in the fitness arena and you don't know who I am? First rule of business, always study the competition."

She raises an eyebrow at me in a way that seems more mocking than chastised. "Second rule of business, don't walk into other people's workplaces without an appointment, perhaps?"

"Touché," I say, and since the sins of the father shouldn't be laid upon the children, I offer an olive branch. "Gabriel Mercer," I introduce myself, and for good measure, I add, "owner and founder of the Power Training franchise." My revelation seems to leave her deeply unimpressed, so I continue, "I'm here to see your father."

"My father?" Her tone is mutinous.

"Yes," I confirm, pointing at the surrounding glass walls. "The owner of all this."

She's a wall of blue steel. "Why do you want to talk to my father?"

"An article came out today in *The Wall Street Journal* where Blake Avery made a few statements that didn't sit well with me. I'd like to straighten out a few facts."

"And, just to be clear, you want to discuss the article with my dad not with me?"

I nod, irritated. "Why would I want to discuss it with you?"

Her mutinous stare flares with cold fury but then her expression morphs from angry to teasing. "I'm sorry, Mr. Mercer, but my father is a busy man. I'm not sure he'll have time to receive you. Anything else I can help you with?"

"Well, he'd better *make* time."

"Or else?"

I don't want to waste the morning on childish games. "I own the fitness game, in case you're not aware, Miss Avery—I didn't catch your name, by the way."

"I didn't offer it."

Bratty and rude. "Suit yourself, but unless you want me to make things difficult for your father, you'd better tell me where I can find him."

The flash of a challenge passes through her electric gaze, but soon, her blue eyes widen in fear and her entire demeanor changes. She becomes accommodating, almost to the point of being obsequious.

"I'm so sorry, Mr. Mercer. Don't mind me, what do we women understand about business and contracts, anyway?"

I don't contradict her. Not because I agree with her, but simply because I don't care to embark on a gender equality debate. Some of my most valued collaborators are women. In fact, I prefer to work with women as a general rule. Less posturing, more dedication.

But maybe *this* woman is still too young to care about her family's enterprise. Heck, at her age, I, too, was more into chasing girls than deals. So I let the comment slide.

"I didn't mean to offend such an important person as yourself." She puts her hands forward. "Please believe me."

The deference act is growing old quickly, so I ask the only question I really care about. "Are you going to tell me where to find your father or not?"

She bites on her lower lip, looking undecided. "I didn't lie when I said my daddy is a busy man, totally self-made, you know?" What's the obsession of this family with being self-made? "But..." she continues, then halts again. Appearing even more torn, she rounds the desk to grab a Post-it block and a pen. "I mean, for a man of your caliber... I'm sure Daddy won't have a problem if I give you this address." Angry Blue Eyes scribbles something on the piece of paper and picks up the note.

She strides toward me, locking that fiery blue gaze on me—a little of her personality coming back. She walks right up to me, getting too close for anyone's comfort, and neatly attaches the Post-it note to my jacket's pocket. Not content with the already too intimate gesture, she smooths a finger over the glued section, making sure it perfectly sticks to the fabric.

A slow current flows from where she's touching my chest to the organ behind my ribcage. I'm not sure what her game is, but I can't shake the sensation she'd rather give me a heart attack than seduce me.

"Anything else I can do for you, Mr. Mercer?" she adds, voice low and honeyed.

Her tone is deferential, but I still can't help but feel as if I'm being made a fool of somehow.

I also don't appreciate the way my breath hitches in my chest when she stares at me so directly. I take a step back. She's definitely too young for me to be thinking what I'm thinking right now —how bad I want to drag a thumb across her cheek and wipe the small droplets of sweat dotting her skin. Yep, I'd better back off.

I give her my best business smile and the most professional answer I can muster. "Nothing for the moment, thank you."

"Any time, Mr. Mercer." She winks, and I swear my insides clench. "Feel free to stop by in the future."

"I don't think that'll be necessary."

"Oh, I don't know. I've got a feeling we'll meet again."

Her smile is the last thing I see as I leave the office and once again enter the gym.

Outside, I stop in the midday sun and think for the first time of checking the Post-it. For a lightning-fast moment, I become convinced she hasn't given me a proper address but has written some sort of joke or jab. Why else would I want to come back to see her?

But when I check the note, I find an actual address for some place in Queens.

Blake Avery, it looks like we're finally going to meet.

# 4

## BLAKE

MGM finally leaves my office, taking his extra-large ego with him and leaving me more breathless than after my HIIT class.

Up close, the man really is something. An annoying, entitled, overbearing—ignorant, I should add ignorant—six-foot-four beefcake. Broad-shouldered, muscular-chested, and arrogant. The nerve of him to come onto *my* turf with no idea of who he was supposed to deal with and lecture me on knowing my competition.

"First rule of business, always study the competition," I repeat in a mock dude's voice.

*Maybe you should take your own advice, scuzzball.*

I don't know why I'm so worked up. Probably because he took one look at me and dismissed me as a silly girl who couldn't possibly be the one in charge, an equal. No, of course he had to assume I was just a frivolous brat playing in her daddy's office.

I'm about to mentally rant some more when Evan crashes into my office. He's changed into yoga clothes, but looks even more agitated than when I left him a little over an hour ago. "Please tell me that wasn't Gabriel Mercer storming out of the building."

I'm not in the mood to receive a second lecture. "Don't worry, I dealt with him."

Evan brings both hands to his face, pulling down his cheeks. "Oh my gosh, what did you do?"

"Nothing," I say, flashing an innocent smile and batting my lashes.

"Should I call the lawyers? Get ready for a lawsuit?"

"Not unless the man is even more of a twit than I already think he is." I shrug and sit on the silver Pilates ball in my office to do some hip stretches. "Or that he has no sense of humor."

"He came because of the article, didn't he? What did you tell him? Did you two get in a fight?"

"Mr. Mercer wanted to discuss the fine print with my father... so I told him Daddy wasn't available and he left." I shrug. "That's it."

Evan frowns. "Your father? Why would he want to discuss the article with your father?"

"Because like the entitled baboon he is, the thought that I—that Blake Avery—could be a woman, never even crossed his mind. He marched in here uninvited and assumed I was having a dance in my daddy's office."

"I take it you didn't correct him?"

"Oh, nooo." An evil smirk stretches my lips. "And what would I pay to be there when he realizes what a fool he's been. But enough about Gabriel Mercer." I shift my hipbones forward on the ball to lie my back on it for a spine stretch. "I already spent half my day talking about him, and the man surely doesn't deserve that much of my time."

I close my eyes and drop my head back on the ball, the phantom of MGM's scent still clouding my brain. He smelled like privilege and danger. The personification of the ruthless corporate alpha who dominates every boardroom. Sticking that Post-it note to his chest wasn't my best idea. Now his scent is registered in my receptors and it'll be hard to shake off. Same as the feel of his toned pecs under my fingertips.

"Earth calling Blake."

Evan's voice startles me, and my lids flutter open.

My friend and colleague blinks at me. "Where had you gone?"

To a dark place I'd better not return.

"Nowhere. I was just relaxing for a second." I straighten back up on the ball. "Did you speak with Cara about Apex?"

"Yeah, the marketing team is brainstorming, they'll have pitches for you by the end of the week."

"Good." I stretch my arms over my head. "And where are we on the IPO?"

To open more locations and bring my company to the next level, I've decided to take Bloominghale public in the fall.

"The investment bankers are still working on the due diligence. They're combing through our balance sheets of the past ten years."

"Anything they need from us?"

"We should start thinking about the S-1 Form."

The first step in going public is the filing of an S-1 Form with the SEC. This includes providing detailed information about our company, the proposed stock offerings, and their pricing structure.

"They want me to write it?" I almost fall off the ball at the idea. "You know I'm not good at that kind of stuff."

"Not the technical aspects, but they want your input on the vision."

"I'll dig deep into my mission-statement wisdom." Gosh, I hate doing this part of the job. "Is there anything else we need to do before lunch?"

"Not if you're sure Gabriel Mercer isn't about to go to the mat with us."

"Death and taxes are the only certainties in life. If there's nothing else you need me to sweat on, I'll go shower."

My COO still doesn't look happy with me, but he lets me go without further comments.

Forty-five minutes later, I'm seated at an outdoor table at one of the quaint neighborhood restaurants overlooking a cobblestone street when my best friend calls me.

Marissa and I met seven years ago at a start-up boot camp in Silicon Valley, a weekend event where various incubators, VCs, and angel investors were giving seminars on how to make it as a young entrepreneur. I was nineteen and fresh out of high school. She was twenty-eight and already working at WeTrade, an investment app that makes trading stocks super easy even for the most technology-averse users, and with no fees or commissions.

Despite the age gap, we clicked immediately and since we got back to New York—she lives and works in Brooklyn—we've been in each other's lives.

I finish chewing on a bite of seared wild salmon and pick up. "Hey, you."

"I've made a decision," Marissa says without preamble. She's a tech nerd to boot and sometimes forgets common social rules, like greetings.

"Okay. What decision?"

"Not over the phone. We need to talk about it in person—on one condition," she quickly adds.

"Shoot."

"You won't try to talk me out of it."

I'm definitely curious now. "Okay, where do you want to meet? Dinner out, in?"

"Can we decide later? I'm not sure how late I'll be at the office and if I'll have time to cook."

Which means we'll probably eat out. Marissa is the only person I know who works longer hours than I do.

"All right, text later?"

"Sure, love you."

"Love you, bye."

I stab a rhubarb pickle with my fork and bite the top half off. Today turned out to be a far more interesting day than I'd expected... I smile to myself, wondering how MGM's lunch break is going.

# 5

## GABRIEL

After half an hour spent in traffic where I got stuck in another business call, which at least prevented any panic attacks, my driver drops me off in Queens in front of a nondescript pizza joint—Joe's. I double-check the address on the Post-it note, but it confirms I'm in the right place.

Looking at the storefront with its faded striped awning and flickering neon sign, I wonder if being here is the best use of my time. But I've come this far, I might as well satisfy my newfound grudge. Besides, now I want to meet Angry Blue Eyes's father and see what's his deal.

Tobias makes to get out of the car to open my door, but I stop him. "Stay."

The driver nods at me through the rearview mirror. "Wait for you around here, sir?"

"That'd be perfect, thanks."

I exit the car and pause for an extra second in front of the restaurant—more of a diner. Definitely a weird hangout for a billionaire. But maybe Avery is a Bobby Axelrod fan and conducts his most secret dealings out of a greasy spoon.

I shrug and push my way in.

The interior has seen better times but at least seems clean. A mix of scents—tomato sauce, basil, and fresh dough—fills the air. The tiny place is lit with fluorescent bulbs strung across the ceiling. Above the cash register, the menu is written on a chalkboard behind the counter next to a massive wood-fired brick oven. Takeaway boxes are stacked against the oven in one corner.

The place is small but packed. In fact, I sit at the last available booth, still looking around me, trying to surmise who among the patrons could be Blake Avery. I scan the tables. A tall, skinny dude in the far corner is too skimpy to be my mark. The table next to him is occupied by teenagers, and one table over, there's a group of men who look like they're employed in a blue-collar job. The last table before mine is taken by a flock of loud women having a social lunch.

I should give up and google the son of a gun. I'm taking out my phone to do just that when a man in his mid-fifties—salt-and-pepper hair, straight back, jovial expression—steps next to my table. "What can I get for you?"

I glance in passing at the blackboard menu where my options are spelled out in white chalk: Regular – 5.95, Pepperoni – 6.95, Day's Special – 7.95. But I'm not here to get lunch, am I?

I study the man a second longer before I say, "I'd like to see Blake Avery."

"Blake?" The man seems surprised. "She hasn't worked here in years."

*She.*

The cogs in my brain spin with the million ramifications that simple pronoun prompts.

"Blake used to work here?"

"Yes, but not since her internet business took off," the man continues. "Are you one of her fans?"

"No, I'm..." What am I? A fool, apparently. "We have some business to discuss. I'm sorry. How do you know Blake?"

"I'm her father."

The echo of a conversation plays in my head, and I silently groan.

*And, just to be clear, you want to discuss the article with my dad?*

Despite myself, I smile. She got me. Oh, she got me good.

"You have an exceptional daughter, Mr. Avery," I say. "I'll take a regular pie and a Coke, please."

A man has to eat.

"Great. I'll be right back with your drink."

With him gone, I'm finally at liberty to check *Miss* Avery's online presence.

First, I go back to the *WSJ* piece, confirming that the only part with a he/she typo is the one I read and that from the rest of the article, it is clear Blake is, in fact, a woman.

Inner groan.

Next, I google her. The first result at the top of the search page is a string of pictures of Angry Blue Eyes in various sporty outfits closely followed by several articles on her start-up and ascent to Instagram fame. That's how she kept out of my notice for so long; I don't follow online trends—fitness related or not. My business model is rooted in the traditional use of the land. What properties will gain the most value over time. Which neighborhoods have the best gentrification potential. What's the best risk-reward opportunity for each new development.

By the time my pizza arrives, I've learned plenty about Blake. She started her business as a teenager shooting workout videos in her childhood home garage. She was only sixteen when she began posting videos of herself doing ballet tutorials, dance routines, and more streamlined workouts. Her Instagram handle is @blakehale.

Blake is a self-proclaimed introvert and says that vlogging, recording herself, and talking about fitness and workouts are the perfect way for her to share her passion for fitness, dancing, and a healthy lifestyle, and to interact with her followers. She has over twenty million of them.

She's an only child and very attached to her family, especially to her father, whom she credits with all her success for teaching her hard work and always encouraging her to follow her dreams.

According to the gossip columns, she isn't married or dating anyone at the moment. And she is twenty-six, not barely twenty-one, as I guessed this morning.

I won't pretend that knowing she's single and of a dating-appropriate age leaves me indifferent. It is rare for me to have the rug pulled out from under me or for someone to impress me, and she's managed to do both in just a few hours.

The last person who managed to do that was my ex-girlfriend. My last serious relationship imploded the year after college. But before that, my ex and I had that academic rivalry that would spice things up in the bedroom and prompt us to strive to always best the other in class. After that ended, I've never been able to replicate that spark. True, for the past decade I've been a workaholic without much time for a personal life. I don't date women I work with. And most women I meet at social events have been too accommodating or too bland to ignite a real fire in me—maybe also why I'm still single at thirty-three. But I've got a feeling Blake would be neither accommodating nor bland.

"Anything else I can do for you?" Blake's father asks after placing the pizza plate in front of me.

"Actually, I wouldn't mind asking you a few questions if you're free, Mr. Avery."

"It's Joe, we're a family business. We don't like formalities here." Blake's father takes a look around the restaurant and, after confirming that all other customers are taken care of, he sits in the booth opposite me. "I might have a few minutes. What is it you wanted to discuss?"

"You said Blake used to work here?"

"Yep, never seen a kid working harder. She used to help me and her ma out in the evenings and weekends, go home to study and do her homework, and then get up at dawn to shoot her workout videos in our garage or in the backyard in the summer."

Each new statement makes me feel a little smaller. At sixteen, I didn't even have a summer job. I took my first internship at Dad's firm the summer after I graduated high school and only because I wanted him to pay for a two-month backpacking trip to Europe. Now, I see why Blake thinks her and my brand of "self-made" are two different stories.

Joe continues speaking as if he was reciting a slogan. "*You can always wake up half an hour earlier and squeeze in a twenty-minute workout,* used to be her motto. Anyway, once she graduated high school, her business was already taking off, and she didn't have time to come round here to help anymore. Blake started working full-time at Bloominghale and put herself through college, taking evening and weekend classes. She's a smart kid, that one. I couldn't be prouder of her."

And I've shrunk further. I've always thought of myself as an overachiever, but admittedly my hard-working days didn't start until *after* I graduated college—as Blake kindly pointed out, debt-free.

The group of blue collars in the back stands up, and one of them calls out, "Joe."

Blake's father gets to his feet. "Sorry, Mr...? I have to go."

"It's Gabriel." I stand as well and offer him my hand to shake.

Joe takes it and jerks his chin toward my plate. "Eat your pizza before it goes cold, Gabriel. You don't want to waste such a good pie, trust me." He winks at me and goes to take care of his customers.

I've been so absorbed in his tale that I'd completely forgotten about the food. I grab a slice of pizza and take a generous bite.

Mmm.

Joe wasn't kidding. This has got to be the best pizza in New York. Well, at least I got a good meal out of the morning's woes.

* * *

"You're late," my brother points out as I stroll into my office some two hours later after getting stuck in another horrible traffic jam.

Thomas is sprawled on my leather couch casually browsing his phone. He's wearing a light-gray tailored suit, hair combed back in a five-hundred-dollar haircut, and his signature captivating smile pulling at the corners of his mouth. The perfect image for the heir apparent to Mercer Industries. He's the good kid. The one who followed in our father's shoes without ever making a fuss about being independent and creating his own fortune. I love my dad, but I could never bear to work with him —*for* him. It'd drive me nuts.

I'm glad Thomas took the burden upon himself. Otherwise, my father would still be pestering me to join the family business.

"Thomas, always a pleasure to receive one of your spontaneous, selfless visits," I say in our usual bantery, sarcastic tone.

I'd forgotten about the appointment and the pile of dung my younger brother is surely about to unload on me.

Thomas gets up from the couch. "I don't even deserve the benefit of the doubt?"

I throw my suit jacket across my desk and rake a hand through my hair as I sit.

My brother settles in the chair opposite me, spending a few moments appraising me. He takes in my wrinkled shirt and disheveled hair, asking, "Rough day?"

"Just..." I allow myself an instant to pick the right adjective. "Unexpected."

He raises his eyebrows. I'm not a man who gets easily surprised.

"Do you have Instagram?" I ask him point-blank.

Thomas's expression becomes even more baffled. Everyone knows I hate social media.

"Yeah?"

"How many followers do you have?"

"About a thousand, give or take."

"All people you know?"

Thomas grips his chin. "I'd say it's an eighty-twenty split. Why?"

I ignore his question. "Is it hard to get followers?"

"Depends on what numbers you're talking about."

"In the millions."

"Well, not necessarily if you're some kind of celebrity, I guess."

"And what if you're just a regular person shooting videos out of your garage?"

"Then I'd say it's pretty damn hard."

*Thought so.*

Thomas leans his elbows on my desk. "Why are you suddenly asking all these questions about Instagram followers? Are you about to make a social media play?"

Hell, spare me. Although, I signed up for a dummy account on the way over and stalked Blake's feed the entire time I was in the car—another good distraction from impending death.

"Nope," I reply.

"Then why the sudden interest?"

"Just something I came across this morning."

"Care to share that tale?" Thomas asks.

"I'd rather not."

As if talking to thin air, Thomas asks, "Mila, do you have any intel?"

The intercom on my desk immediately buzzes to life. "Only that he left on a secret quest this morning, I suspect because he didn't like what a certain Instagram-famous business lady had to say about his origin story," Mila says. "If I had to guess, I'd say the meeting didn't go as he planned and he got his behind handed to him. Then he went to have lunch at a pizza place in Queens—for totally mysterious reasons—and came back looking as ruffled up as you found him."

"Stop listening to my private conversations," I bark.

"You pay me to listen to your private conversations," Mila's voice comes back from the interphone.

It's true, I do. In case I need a second opinion, last-minute info, or on the off chance that I've missed something important. No one has an eye—or *ear* in this case—for detail like Mila.

Thomas looks up at me, making puppy dog eyes. "Please, I'll give you anything you want to hear the full story."

"Anything? How about you get me out of whatever it is you came to ask?"

Thomas grins. "Anything *but* that."

"No deal."

"I'll give you my season ticket to the Knicks."

"Got my own and in a better seat."

"Yeah, you're right. I'll give you an IOU valid for everything except today's favor. Non-expirable."

"Nope."

Thomas hesitates before sighing. "I'll give you my signed Michael Jordan basketball."

"You mean *my* Michael Jordan basketball..."

I lost it in a stupid bet years ago and have wanted it back ever since, but Thomas never put it on the table again. Still, I shake my head.

"Ooooh," Thomas hollers. "It must be truly awful if not even the MJ card worked. Sorry, brother, you leave me no choice. Mila, is this business lady hot, by any chance?"

"Yep." The intercom buzzes.

"What's her Instagram handle?"

"@blakehale."

Thomas gets his phone out and repeat-mutters the handle as he types, "@blakehale."

A heartbeat of silence passes, and then a low whistle.

I peek over my desk, but I can't see what he's doing. "What are you doing?"

"Just followed her. Mila, do you think Blake reads her DMs?"

I've no idea what DMs are, but it sounds ominous enough.

"Someone from her staff sure does, and if they saw a message from a Mercer, they'd probably respond."

"What do you say, Millicent," Thomas says, using his nickname for my assistant. "Should I invite her out and ask for her side of the story?"

"Don't you dare," I say.

"Then out with it."

I drag a hand through my hair. "I should've said yes to the Jordan ball."

Thomas's smirk is merciless. "You *so* should've said yes to the Jordan ball."

"First tell me what it is you want from me on top of a full confession."

"Challenged Athletes Charity Gala, this Saturday. Dad has bought a table but can't go—last-minute withdrawal, no explanation given. Dad wants someone from the family to be present, but I can't go."

I hate those evenings almost as much as I despise social media. I'm happy to donate to charities for various causes, but please don't ask me to penguin up and spend a night making meaningless, polite conversation with middle-aged folks and socialites I've nothing in common with.

Before I can refuse, Mila chips in from the intercom, "Before you say no, boss, you should know that Blake Avery is being presented with an award at the gala."

I'm almost afraid to ask. "An award for what?"

Mila replies as if she were reading from a program of the night, which she might very well be doing. "For her outstanding involvement in the impaired athletes' community. Apparently, she sponsors a girls' sitting volleyball team, and her workouts include several variations catering to trainees with a range of physical disabilities."

Thomas chuckles. "This day is getting better and better. Here I came thinking I'd have to grovel, while instead, I'm basically doing you a favor by sending you to the party. You're welcome, brother."

I'm not going to lie, the idea of seeing Blake again so soon is tempting. I was already trying to come up with ideas of how to accidentally-on-purpose bump into her and the perfect one just fell into my lap.

Thomas seems to read my mind because he smiles, satisfied. "I'll send you the details." He fidgets with his phone, probably forwarding me the invite as we speak. "It's a black tux gig, which makes me kind of curious to know what dress Miss Avery will show up in."

*You and me both.*

Thomas shakes his phone at me. "Guess I'll find out from the after-party Instagram post, while you lucky dog will get the live show." My brother knocks on my desk. "Now that's settled, please tell us how you made an ass of yourself today."

# 6

## BLAKE

"You have a new follower," Evan says, strolling into my office, eyes glued to his phone just as I'm about to leave to meet Marissa.

As expected, my best friend and I are going out. But, in a twist of fate, she's asked to meet at my dad's restaurant, claiming she needed the carbs to have this conversation and that if we were going to have pizza, we might as well get the best.

I don't live in Queens anymore, haven't for a while. But I'm happy to make the trek tonight—and not just for the pizza. I'd be lying if I said I'm not curious to know what went down when MGM realized I sent him on a wild goose chase.

"Just one follower in all of today?" I ask.

That's way below my average.

"No, I meant one new person of interest."

I stuff my laptop in my messenger bag, collecting my things before I leave. "Oh, who?"

"Thomas Mercer."

"As in...?"

"Yep. None other than Gabriel Mercer's brother."

I hook my messenger bag over one shoulder and round the desk, leaning in to look at Evan's screen. "It could be a fake."

"No, I checked. The profile is legit. It's his brother."

Evan scrolls through Thomas's feed on his phone.

The resemblance is uncanny, even if minor details are different, making Thomas a slightly fairer version. His hair is a lighter brown, a color that must easily turn blond at the tips in summer, and more styled, less tousled. The eyes, instead of the warmest brown, are more of a hazel green. The broad shoulders are the same, but Thomas is smiling in most of his pictures. And while his persona also screams old money and privilege, his vibe is friendlier, less arrogant.

"Mr. Mercer Junior also liked all your most recent posts and left various emoji comments," Evan continues. "Smiley faces, winks, and a hawt emoji on your sexiest pics."

"Which one is the hawt emoji?"

"The one with the red face sweating and tongue dangling out. One post even earned you a chili pepper."

"Mmm. What do you think it means?"

"If news of the meet-cute already reached the family, you must've made an impression."

"I'd hardly define what happened this morning a meet-*cute*."

"Why, what happened? You still haven't told me."

I get up from the desk and head toward the door. "That is a story for another day, my friend."

"Why?"

I pause on the threshold. "Because I still don't know how it will end." I wave at him. "Go home and relax. You work too much."

"Yes, Pot."

"Night, Kettle."

I leave Evan behind and hop down the staircase. The gym on the lower floor is still buzzing with activity: late-night classes for patrons who prefer to or only have time to work out in the evenings, runners training on machines, and even people relaxing at the juice bar. We've been open for ten days, and after the first-week-free trial, customer retention has been exceptional.

I push past the entrance glass door, unable to suppress a thrill of pride. I made all this. Built it from the ground up, with no one's help.

Down the street, I flag a cab and give the driver the address to my dad's restaurant. On the journey over, I can't help but wonder what it means that Thomas Mercer followed me.

Well, for sure it means that MGM now knows who I am... and he's talked about me with his brother. To say what? Thomas's approach seems pretty cool, friendly even. Could that mean MGM is not a total sourpuss and can recognize when he's made a blunder?

Would that change my opinion of him? Not much. He'd still be a spoiled rich boy with whom I've nothing in common.

The driver pulls up in front of Joe's just behind another cab, and Marissa and I get out of our respective rides at the same time. We hug on the curb outside the restaurant.

"Hey, beautiful," she says, glancing at my flowy maxi-dress—I spend most of my days in tight-fitting clothes so when I go out I prefer to let loose. "Looking good."

"Thanks." I return her smile. "You, too."

Never seen a hotter nerd.

With sea-foam-green eyes, chestnut wavy hair, and a dusting of freckles that makes her look several years younger, Marissa is a total knockout. If someone spotted us on the street right now, they wouldn't be able to tell I'm almost ten years her junior.

"I'm so glad you were free tonight," Marissa says.

"I'm always free for you." I give her another mini-squeeze and let go. "How are you?"

She's never asked me out to have mysterious conversations about life-changing decisions before. When we're together, we mostly talk about work. Men occasionally, but not that often as we're both too busy with our careers to properly date. But I have a hunch tonight's conversation isn't going to be job-related. Men-related? Maybe. But her earlier stipulation that I can't talk her out of it, sort of rules the boys talk out. Unless she's decided to join some mysterious sexual cult—I highly doubt it. "Is everything all right?"

Her smile is warm. "I'm okay. Stressed, but okay." Marissa squeezes my arm and looks at me with intent. "But I really need to talk to you."

I place a hand over hers. "Should I be worried?"

"No." She smiles. "It's a beautiful thing." She jerks her head toward the restaurant. "Talk inside?"

We head in arm in arm. Joe's is buzzing like usual. In fact, all the tables are taken. Luckily, there are free stools at the counter, so we head that way.

Dad is taking orders in the far corner, but when he comes back and spots us, he breaks out into a huge smile.

"Blake! What a wonderful surprise."

I kiss him on the cheek. "How are you, Pa? You're not working too hard, are you?"

I've begged him a million times to retire. I know he's still young and has a lot left to give, but running a restaurant mostly alone for two turns every day is tough on his back. But he won't have it. Claims he'd get depressed without his work. But at least Mom and I convinced him to hire a manager for the weekends so he can rest and they can enjoy more life together.

"I'm fit as a bull," he reassures me, then turns to my friend. "Ah, Marissa! So good to see you, too."

She gives him a hug. "Hey, Joe."

"What can I get you, girls?"

"What's the day's special?" Marissa asks.

"Prosciutto."

Her bright smile makes her look even younger. "I'm sold."

"Me, too."

He doesn't ask about drinks because we've been drinking Coke with our pizzas since the first day I brought Marissa here seven years ago. "I'll be right back with your orders."

Dad gets behind the counter, and I hear him scream, "Tim, three regulars, one pepperoni, and two day's special."

I lean on the counter, facing my friend. "What's the big secret? I've been dying to know all day."

Marissa's eyes sparkle as she prepares to speak. But my dad arrives with the Cokes and a basket of French fries, stalling her.

We both take a sip and wait for him to be gone again before Marissa joins her hands together and announces, "I'm having a baby."

I spit half the sip of Coke back into the glass to avoid choking on it. "You're pregnant?"

I didn't even know she was dating someone.

"No." Marissa shakes her head, still smiling. "Not yet, at least."

"Okay, explain."

"I'm almost thirty-five, Blake. I don't have a husband, a boyfriend, or even the shadow of a man in my life. If I have to wait to fall in love to become a mother, it'll never happen. I want to get pregnant with IVF."

I don't respond right away. The topic is serious, and I need a moment to collect my thoughts.

"I know I said not to talk me out of it, but please say *something*."

Our pizzas arrive, giving me a few extra seconds to think before I speak. "I won't say I don't see where you're coming from, but have you considered all the consequences?"

"Like what?"

"Let's put some carbs into our bodies and then I can grill you."

We eat the first slice of pizza in silence, then I ask, "Have you thought that if you do this, it'll be even more difficult to find love?"

"Why?"

"For starters, you'll have less time to date, and not all men are happy to take on the extra responsibility of raising a child not of their own."

Marissa wipes her mouth with a paper napkin. "If someone doesn't want to date me because I'm a single mom, I'd rather screen them out right away."

"Fair point. And what about work?"

"What about it?"

"I don't know if you've noticed." I pointedly stare at the wall clock mounted behind the counter that's reading 9.30 p.m. "But your hours aren't exactly motherhood friendly. Especially single motherhood."

"Shonda will cover for me. I covered for her when she had Lo, and now that her daughter is three, she's back on full-time."

Shonda is her CEO. They're the team at the top.

"Okay." I finally let myself get infected by her enthusiasm. "Guess I'll be an aunt soon, then."

Marissa hops off her stool and pulls me into a tight hug.

When she lets go, I ask more questions. "Do you already have a clinic?"

"Yep, the best in the city."

"Have you chosen a donor?"

"No, I still have a few months."

"Months? How long does it take to get pregnant?"

"I have to do some preliminary tests first, check that everything is in order down there." She points at her nether regions. "Then the clinic wants me to meet with a psychologist to make sure I've truly considered the physical stress and emotional impact motherhood will have on my life."

"They're very thorough," I say between bites.

"Told yah, they're the best. And even when all that is taken care of, they prefer for their clients to sit on the decision for a couple of extra weeks before taking the plunge."

I smirk. They don't know who they're dealing with. Once Marissa sets her sights on a goal, she's relentless. If she says she wants to have a baby, she'll be pregnant by the end of the year.

The restaurant is slowly emptying, and with no new customers to serve, my dad comes back to talk to us.

"How's everything, girls?"

"Spectacular as always, Joe," Marissa says, then turning to me, she adds, "I'm going to miss prosciutto."

"Why?" I ask.

"Pregnant women can't eat curated meat," she explains.

Dad raises an eyebrow. "Who's pregnant?"

"No one, Dad," I reassure him.

"Oh, okay. By the way, Blake, a friend of yours came by at lunch."

I can't help but perk up on my stool and notice how Marissa's eyes narrow at the gesture.

"Really?" I ask in a voice too shrill to pass for casual. "Who?"

"Nice fella, tall, elegant, handsome..."

The profile matches MGM to a T, even if I'm not positive about the nice part.

"Gabriel," my dad continues. "You know him?"

"Sort of," I say noncommittally. "What did you talk about?"

Dad shrugs. "He asked me a few questions about you, had a pie, and then left."

"What questions?"

"Oh, you know, general stuff."

"Like what?" Marissa presses.

I throw Marissa a grateful look for asking. I didn't want to interrogate my dad and sound too eager, but I'm dying to know what Gabriel and Dad talked about.

"The usual. What Blake was like as a girl, how she started her business."

"And what did you tell him?" I ask, not able to restrain myself. I need all the deets on that conversation.

"Only the truth. That you're the most hard-working kid I know, and I'm very proud of you, baby."

I groan inwardly. Maybe sending MGM to meet my father wasn't my smartest moment. I showed him too much of who I am. To grant an enemy such an unfiltered view into my background was a mistake. But today's was an impulse decision. My blood was boiling from his prime display of male arrogance, and when I see red, reason flies out the window.

A few customers get in line behind the cash register.

Dad knocks on the counter. "I'll be right back."

Marissa turns to me with a foxy grin. "Tall, handsome who?"

"Doesn't matter," I say dismissively, hoping my cheeks aren't flushed.

"Your face says otherwise."

"I don't even know him, really. Met him this morning, and I'd rather forget about him. The sooner the better."

Marissa pinches her brows, staring at the ceiling as if hoping the answer will be magically spelled there. "Gabriel, Gabriel, Gabriel... do we know any Gabriels?"

"No, exactly my point."

"Does the guy have a surname?"

"Sure he does."

"Come on." Marissa widens her arms. "You're not going to make me beg for it."

"Mercer," I mutter with my mouth still full of pizza.

"Come again?"

I swallow. "Mercer. Gabriel Mercer, are you happy?"

"*The* Gabriel Mercer of Mercer Enterprises, son of Nolan Mercer of Mercer Industries?"

"Yep," I say, staring at my plate.

Marissa taps her chin with two fingers. "His *Insider* profile last year showcased unruly black hair, dark eyes, a jawline to die for, and an impressive set of shoulders. Hmm... handsome indeed. Something I should know?"

"Nope."

"I don't buy that."

After some more badgering, Marissa convinces me to give her the full story.

My friend smirks when I'm done. "Is he as good looking in person as he looks on business magazine covers?"

"That's irrelevant. I'm not interested. Not in someone like him, never again."

Marissa's face turns serious. "You know, not all men are like Justin," she says, referring to my dung beetle of an ex. "Just because he's rich, doesn't mean Gabriel Mercer would gaslight you or try to control you. In fact, he's so rich he'd never try to steal your business. He doesn't need to."

I push the shame of my breakup with my ex into the dark box at the bottom of my chest where I locked it so long ago. Love made me stupid, careless, naïve. I almost lost everything because of it. And the fact that I realized what a gross piece of work my ex was only by chance still smarts.

Repressing the humiliation is the only way I can bring myself to even speak about the fact. "Well, forgive me if that relationship left me with a few trust issues." I push a lock of hair behind my ears. "And it's not even about that. You should've seen Mercer today, Mari, he was so cocky, so entitled. And the way he looked at me and saw nothing more than a backup dancer; I'm tired of being underestimated by older men."

"Who are you calling older? He's younger than me!"

"But you don't suffer from testosterone-induced egomaniac tendencies."

Marissa smiles again.

"You find the situation funny?"

"No, sorry, I was just picturing you doing the "Maniac" routine from *Flashdance* in front of Gabriel Mercer."

"You know I use that song to de-stress."

"I bet he enjoyed witnessing your relaxation techniques." She waggles her eyebrows.

I throw a French fry at her. "You're a horrible friend."

"Just calling it as I see it. Trust me, he didn't dismiss you as a backup dancer; he probably wanted to be your Nick Hurley," she says, referencing the romantic interest in the movie.

"Yeah," I scoff. "Not in a billion years."

# 7

## GABRIEL

The night of the gala, I pull up on Fifth Avenue earlier than I would've planned if tonight were only a family obligation. I drop off my keys at the valet parking service, steering clear of the main Met entrance. I might be a willing partygoer for once, but I didn't completely lose my mind. I'm not going to walk the red carpet.

Outside of business circles, I'm anonymous, except for a few appearances on celebrity gossip sites like Page Six that I try to keep to a minimum. I can get away with a low-key entrance from a side door. The valet gets in the driver's seat and I watch him drive away my car—a classic Porsche 911, not the vintage Aston Martin GT Zagato I'd hoped to drive myself in. Sadly, Mila informed me earlier today that we lost the bid. The auction was private and I've no way of knowing who the lucky bastard enjoying my ride is.

I step onto the curb, buttoning my tux jacket, and stare up at the museum entrance. On the stairway to benefits heaven, the bleachers are in place, the red carpet is rolled out on the front steps, and spotlights pierce the heavens aided by a thousand flash-bulbs busy capturing the newest celebrity. No matter the cause, a gala in New York at the Met always attracts the rich and famous.

I skirt the hot perimeter and text my contact on the inside, waiting by a service entrance. The door magically opens for me not two minutes later. Jared, a tall, brawny security guard, holds the door open for me and steps aside to leave me room to enter the narrow service hall.

"Evening, Mr. Mercer," he greets me.

I step in and hand him a few hundred-dollar bills. "Jared, always a pleasure doing business with you."

The security guard nods and, after a quick check of the street outside, closes the door, resuming his post behind it.

"See you next time." I wave at him, making my way down the hall. I've used this route enough times to orient myself around the maze-like interiors of the Metropolitan Museum of Art like it was my house.

"Enjoy the party, Mr. Mercer." Jared's parting words bounce off the narrow walls as I go.

Once inside the museum, I grab a flute of champagne from a passing tray and position myself strategically by the wide windows overlooking the main entrance. I don't want to miss Blake's arrival. I'm not sure if she's the type who'll enjoy being in the limelight or if she would've preferred a low-key admission like me. But I know she won't have a choice. It took me years to gain my privileged access.

I lean against the cold glass and keep my eyes on the scene below. Each arriving limo is greeted by a throng of fans, as ever more famous celebrities walk the red carpet, making the cameras and crowds grow wilder with each new arrival.

After a while, I lose interest and hope Blake will be next. She could already be inside. I came early, but maybe she beat me to the punch again. I'm about to walk away, but stop dead in my tracks as the name "Blake Avery" echoes over the PA system. There she is.

Miss Avery is wearing a simple slip dress that drapes over her toned body like the Devil's cloth. The fabric is silver with a metallic shine. Under the spotlights, with the flashes of the cameras bouncing off the textile, the dress looks radiant, as if it were *made* of light.

Simple is not synonymous with plain. Miss Avery has taken the less is more factor to the next level. The high rise of the slit on Blake's left thigh is enough to make my blood sizzle. I roam my eyes over the rest of her body up to her face, and it's a strike to the chest again. Only this time, instead of a single bullet, I'm hit by a full volley straight to the heart. I worry I should start wearing a bulletproof vest whenever I'm around her.

The neckline of the dress is low and it pairs perfectly with the diamond necklace strung around her neck. Her hair is let loose in a silky curtain that hangs as low as her solar plexus. Unconstrained on one side and pulled behind her ear on the other to showcase a diamond ear cuff that circles her entire outer ear.

An irresistible urge to bite the piece of jewelry clear off her takes me over. I look away. Not that focusing on other parts of her helps. Blake's lips are painted in the same red as a rose petal. She's angled toward the cameras so I can't see her eyes from up here, which is probably a good thing, seeing how those two sapphires are her most striking feature.

One last smile for the press, and the woman struts down the red carpet in her sky-high heels as tall and confident as if it were a catwalk. She looks like she was born to do nothing else.

I've been to many events, but I've never seen a woman so gorgeous, breathtaking, and mesmerizing. Blake strides down the red carpet as if she were about to accept an Oscar, hands down the most beautiful woman of the night.

Several well-known journalists attempt to interview her. Whatever the request, Blake politely refuses, parading the remaining length of the carpet without stopping until she disappears inside.

It's only when the door shuts and she's gone that I realize I've been holding my breath.

I down my champagne in one gulp as my throat closes. A tight knot forms in my stomach, and my chest feels as if it were on fire.

All I can say is I'm glad the only accessories she's donning tonight are sparkly ones. If she'd come on the arm of some coxcomb, I might've broken something. And everything around here is pretty expensive—not to mention extremely rare. So it's a good thing she came alone.

Gossip columns can be trusted from time to time.

I don't care how much crow I'll have to eat from Miss Avery; I'm going in after her. She won round one, but I'll make sure round two goes to me. I push off my window perch and go mingle.

# 8

## BLAKE

Inside the museum is a sea of fancy people. Whenever I come to one of these soirees, I feel like a fraud, sure someone is going to call me out as the kid born on the wrong side of the tracks and kick me out.

If not fully ready to play the part emotionally, at least I'm dressed for it. The ruse seems to work. Everyone I pass greets me with polite smiles and nods, unaware a nobody from Queens just entered their midst. I don't make a secret of my background, shout it to the winds, actually. But, usually, the people at these events take inventory of my appearance and assume I'm one of them. At least until they casually drop into the conversation how they're related to a robber baron. When I can't boast any family ties to the Vanderbilts, the Rockefellers, or the Astors, *then* their noses wrinkle.

I'm proud of my upbringing, but besides making me lose faith in all men, my ex also made sure I'd never feel adequate among New York's old money. I may have the bank account to match now, but I still can't shake the feeling that they're part of an aristocracy of sorts and I'm the nouveau-riche filth.

To avoid any such interaction, I compile a list in my head of which of the celebrities present used to come from nothing like me. Was Rihanna poor when she grew up?

Then I see my true crowd, the athletes we're celebrating tonight. With a big smile on my face, I'm about to head that way when I'm stopped by a deep voice calling my name.

"Blake."

A single word rolled out in such a husky tone that it almost startles me out of my designer dress.

I wait for a heartbeat longer before I turn around, steadying myself for the man standing behind me. Gabriel I'm-Too-Sexy-For-My-Suit Mercer.

But no amount of waiting could prepare me for the appearance of MGM in a black tux. Damn, the man is a sight for sore eyes —or more the reincarnation of a Greek god so handsome he has the power to make a dead woman's heart beat again.

His hair is swept back tonight, making the resemblance with his brother even more evident. His chiseled jaw is shaved clean. Dark eyes on me. Full lips curled up in a cocky grin.

The man is a work of art, and if he were to be assigned a label like the rest of the pieces exposed in the museum, his would read: Alpha board member specimen of the twenty-first century, known for his power to melt the underwear off women with a single stare. Believed not to be used to hearing the word no.

I steady my racing heart and flash him a bright smile. "Ah, Mr. Mercer, I see you've had time to conduct some research on the *competition.*"

I stress the word competition sarcastically, barely stopping myself from making air quotes.

MGM arches a brow in a dangerously attractive way. "You don't believe me to be the competition?"

I take a step toward him. "Please, our businesses may overlap, but we both know you're not really in the fitness game. More into the walls that contain it."

He stares at me for a long second, all the humor gone from his gaze. What's he thinking? Those dark, penetrating eyes are making me too uncomfortable to bear the stretching silence, prompting me to talk again. "So, Mr. Mercer, we meet twice in a week. Just a lucky coincidence?"

The smirk is back. "My brother usually attends these events. I'm only here as a proxy."

A passing server offers me a flute of champagne and I gladly take one. MGM does, too.

"Your brother, Thomas, right?" I ask after a quick sip. "He's become quite the fan recently."

MGM's eyes widen, and he seems to have trouble swallowing his bubbly.

"I take it you told him about our previous encounter." I can't suppress the evil little smirk curling the corner of my mouth. "Only good things, I hope?"

"Of course. By the way, I need to thank you for the other day..."

"Oh, and for what?"

MGM unleashes a smile on me that's sinfully charming. I should turn on my heels and run. Run as far away from him as possible. But my stilettos, for as little surface they have in contact with the floor, seem glued to the spot.

"For introducing me to the best pizza New York has to offer," he says.

So the man has a sense of humor and can take a joke. This new tidbit of info is more alarming than reassuring. As is the silly smile now pulling at my lips.

"Go figure, a pretty face and possessed with self-irony."

He places a hand over his chest. "Only pretty? I'm deeply wounded."

Ignoring the comment, I raise my glass to him. "You're welcome, Mr. Mercer."

"You can call me Gabriel."

Nuh-uh, even his name is too darn sexy. "I'll stick with formal titles."

"Why?"

"Less risk of confusion. If you'll excuse me." I point with my glass to the main room. "I have some friends I'd like to say hello to." A total lie. I barely know anyone at this party. But it's a self-preserving move to get away from the six-foot-four wall of testosterone in a tux.

MGM has other ideas. He gently grabs my wrist, causing a wave of molten lava to flow through my spinal cord from my nape to my tailbone. "Leaving me already? I was looking forward to having a more even conversation with you."

"Even how?"

"One where we know each other's names."

I regain control of my hand, not without consequences. The brush of his fingertips on my skin as I pull away makes *both* my arms break into goosebumps. "Ah, Mr. Mercer, I'm sure you're used to having women fall at your feet, but I'm not interested in furthering our acquaintance. I wish you a wonderful evening."

I clink my glass into his and make my way down the hall, leaving him standing behind me like a lump.

## 9

### GABRIEL

After Blake oh-so-politely brushes me off, the night becomes point-a-revolver-to-my-temple-and-pull-the-trigger boring.

I don't know what's worse: that she's avoiding me or that she's having fun in the meantime. She has a warm smile for everyone she speaks with, while I'm banished behind a wall of wariness. And can I blame her after the stunt I pulled the other day?

Despite my best efforts, she's as hard to track across the museum as a rogue snowflake in a storm. Everywhere I go, she seems to be there at a different moment.

So I do what I do best.

I watch.

And I wait.

And try to avoid all the ancient chatterboxes who all seem more than eager to share with me their hip-replacement horror stories. I retreat to a less crowded room—hide would be a more appropriate word—to be left alone with my thoughts. Relentless, they revolve around the woman who's been on my mind since I first laid eyes on her the other day. Not the girl I thought I'd met in her father's office. But the grown woman with killer blue eyes and an attitude problem.

I'm considering whether I should just give up and leave when I catch a streak of silver pass before the door. I follow it like a hound with the scent of prey in his nostrils and find Blake confabulating with a security guard who, after they're done talking, nods and blares instructions into his radio—probably alerting the valet to bring her car around.

Miss Avery is trying to sneak off early. Suits me just fine.

I drain the last dregs of champagne in my glass and drop it on a white-clothed table.

Party's over.

I catch up with her outside, midway down the grand steps. The previous crowd has dispersed and no cameras are waiting for the departing guests. But even if the scene were as busy as before, I'd only have eyes for the woman in the silver dress.

All the cars for this event have been parked at least half an hour away in a separate parking facility, something she probably didn't know, or she wouldn't have come out already.

"Leaving so soon?" I ask, approaching her from behind.

Blake jolts, turning toward me. Blue eyes zeroing in on me and delivering the by-now-familiar punch to the gut.

"Mr. Mercer, we meet again. One may start to believe chance had nothing to do with it."

I ignore the jab. "Waiting for your driver?"

"By gosh, no." She laughs as if genially amused by the question. "I might be rich now, but I'm still getting used to all the..." She pauses for a second and points at our surroundings. "Bubble wrap."

"Says the woman wearing a five-thousand-dollar dress." I tilt my head. "Give or take."

"An eye for fashion. Any other hidden qualities besides the obvious?"

I raise my eyebrows. "You mean my pretty face?"

"No, I didn't. I was referring to the effortlessness of someone who's always been used to having the best of everything."

"Do you resent rich people, Miss Avery?" I ask, sticking to her stupid rule of using our surnames. "Because in case you haven't noticed, you've joined the club."

"Yeah, I just want to give to Caesar what belongs to Caesar."

"Meaning?"

"Well, you read the article."

I didn't come here to argue, but my jaw tenses all the same. "Here we go again. Just because I went to an expensive school and didn't have to pay for it, it doesn't mean I never had any struggles. A top-notch education was a rare privilege, I agree with you. But everything that came afterward I earned with the sweat off my back."

Blake blinks at me for a second. "You're joking, right?" At my morose expression, she theatrically inhales. "Oh my gosh, you're not."

When I still say nothing, she takes it upon herself to continue the conversation. "Listen, I don't take pleasure in dragging other people's names through the mud. When the reporter asked me that question about you, I responded without thinking. I requested to strike the comment afterward, but she told me I'd agreed to go on the record and she could publish our entire conversation with no further permission on my part. No do-overs in traditional media, it's not like shooting a TikTok. So there you have it. I'm still getting to grips with this new world of interviews and benefits and whatnot, and I still haven't learned not to say the first thing that passes through my mind."

"Clearly," I mutter between gritted teeth.

She flares her nostrils. "I'm sorry if I offended you, but I said nothing but the truth. I still didn't wish for the comment to be published, but I'm not taking back what I say. You're a brilliant entrepreneur, but you're not self-made. You come from money, Mr. Mercer. Old money." Blake points at my persona as if it disgusts her. "It's written all over your stance, your air of entitlement."

"I might come from money, but my company is all me. I didn't ask for a handout from my family. I earned everything I have now."

She crosses her arms over her chest. "You really want to do this here?"

"Don't know about you, but I don't have anywhere else to be at two in the morning on a Saturday."

"Okay. Where did you live when you moved to Silicon Valley after college?" Blake fires the question at me without preamble.

"An apartment," I say, not seeing her point.

"How did you pay for rent?"

Oh, I see what she's getting at. "It doesn't matter. I could've been living under a bridge and I still would've worked myself into the ground to reach my goals."

"I think what you meant to say was, 'My trust fund paid the rent.' At least if we're being honest. You might consider rent money trivial, but not everyone who launches a start-up can afford the luxury of moving to one of the most expensive parts of the country and not stress about how they're going to pay for a place to live or to buy food." She's not sparing blows. "But let's say for the sake of argument that rent didn't count. Where did you get the money to fund your company?"

Before I can answer, she halts me with a raised hand. "I'm not talking about your first VC investment. I'm talking about the actual money to buy the laptop you were making your business plan on, or how you paid for the graphic designer to do your logo, your website... how much did it cost you? Ten, twenty K? It might be loose change for you, but for some people, it's all they can save in a lifetime."

"Just so we're clear, I worked for a few years at an investment bank right after college, saved the five-figure end-of-year bonuses, and used them to pay for rent in Silicon Valley—where I shared a house with five other smelly dudes—and made the initial investment in my company."

That shuts her up, and her expression softens.

"Okay, then I partially misjudged you," she concedes. "I'm sorry. What I was trying to explain to you," Blake continues, "is that for the longest time, so many doors stayed closed to me, and I had to break them open kicking and screaming. While you probably found a butler in white gloves, welcoming you and offering you a cup of champagne for your trouble."

"I can assure you it was no easy feat to get my A-round investment; I had no help from my family whatsoever."

A shadow passes over her face and she looks away, no comment. So I push. "Can I get at least a partial retraction on my start-up money being handed to me on a silver platter?"

Again, she avoids meeting my eyes. "Sure."

I walk down a step so that we're now sharing one. "Why do I feel you're holding out on me?"

"It's just a rumor I heard."

My nostrils flare. "What rumor?"

She waves me off. "I'm sure it was just nonsense."

"I'd still like to hear it."

Blake looks at me undecided, but she eventually speaks. "That Fidelity Credit Union financed your A round because your father made them the unofficial partner for all of Mercer Industries' dealings in the West."

The accusation shakes the very foundations of my being.

A slow heat creeps up my neck. Dad would never... we had a deal that he'd stay out of my business.

Blake takes in my dismay and offers me a small smile. "Sorry to ruin the corporate fairy tale for you. I'd imagined you would've connected the dots a long time ago."

The truth is that after securing that first loan, I went into tunnel focus and didn't pay attention to anything happening outside my start-up until we reached the breakeven point. And a cloak-and-dagger deal like that wouldn't have been publicized. It'd take years of analyzing each of Mercer Industries' transactions in the West to reach that conclusion.

"Who told you that?"

She hesitates. "My ex works in finance."

I'm about to counter-argue when the roar of an engine distracts me. I turn my gaze toward the sound, and my mouth gapes open. The 1960 Aston Martin GT Zagato of my dreams just pulled up in front of the museum.

I watch with a slack jaw as the valet jogs up the steps and hands the keys to Blake, saying, "The keys to your vehicle, miss."

A roar of laughter bursts out of me as I shake my head.

Blake floors me with a stare. "Something the matter?"

"Oh, you had me fooled Miss Still Getting Used to The Bubble Wrap. You seem very well adjusted to it."

"Excuse me?"

"That's a 1.2-million-dollar car you're taking home."

Her eyes narrow. "You an Aston Martin fan? That was an almost perfect appraisal."

"How much did you pay for it?" The question is crass, and I wouldn't normally ask it, but I want to know by how much I lost.

Blake's red lips curl in a wicked smile. "One million, two hundred and five thousand dollars. The owner told me the second highest bidder came in at a clean 1.2 mils. It must've been a man."

"Why do you say that?"

"Men can be so unimaginative sometimes." She nods at me and, turning away, finishes descending the steps.

The valet opens the door for her, and she gets in from the side closest to the steps. As Mila kindly pointed out, this is an original British model with a left-hand drive.

As Blake settles in the driver's seat, the slit of her dress rides sinfully high, making my mouth go dry.

She pauses a second with her hand on the car door, saying, "Goodnight, Mr. Mercer."

Her lips still curved in a small smile, she closes the door, puts the car into gear, and speeds away into the night.

I shove my hands into my pockets and roll back on my heels as I watch the car zoom through the streets until Blake turns a corner and disappears from sight.

Lost the car.

Not gonna lose the woman.

# 10

## GABRIEL

Sunday brunch at my parents' house is as inevitable as fireworks on the fourth of July, the Macy's Thanksgiving Day Parade, or sparkly lights during the holidays.

Unless equipped with a valid medical excuse, my brother and I are expected to attend. Fifty-two weeks a year—no justifications accepted when on Manhattan soil.

So after a night spent tossing, tormented by images of blue eyes, red lips, and silver cars, I drag my sorry ass to my parents' Upper East Side penthouse.

I'd walk, except the day is already sticky at ten in the morning and the last thing I need is to arrive to brunch looking like a zombie and smelling like a locker room. Nothing I can do about the zombie part. But at least I can make sure I'm not a sweaty mess.

When I got home last night, I made the mistake of opening Instagram before going to bed, and I don't know how Blake managed it, if she has a team working round the clock on her social media, but her profile already featured a post with multiple photos of her on the red carpet plus a few of when she accepted the award, a video story of her entrance, and most disconcerting of all, a reel where some sort of grand angle camera zoomed in on her in slow motion as Blake was smiling with a flirtatious look. Then she twirled on herself, her silky hair fanning in a curtain around her and, when she landed back from the turn, she blew a kiss to the camera. The caption read #Glambot.

Not sure what a glambot is, but that kiss haunted me all night. Hence the zombie status.

I take the Porsche, and when I pull up in front of my parents' building I don't even have to open the door because the building's valet is already there, ready to collect the keys. I step out and we swap places as he gets in the driver's seat.

The doorman, Darryl, is also waiting to greet me. The man is an institution. He knows each family living in the building better than even their members know each other and has been working here since before I was born.

"Morning, Mr. Mercer." He welcomes me with a slight bow. "Your brother is already upstairs."

I check my watch. A zombie and five minutes late.

"Thank you, Darryl."

The doorman closes the car door behind me and knocks on the hood, letting the valet know he can go search for parking.

Before I can make it to the main entrance, Darryl is already there, holding the front door open for me.

"Have a nice brunch, Mr. Mercer."

I take in his white-gloved hands and inwardly cringe as a comment Blake made last night grates on me. *"...for the longest time, so many doors stayed closed to me, and I had to break them open kicking and screaming. While you probably found a butler in white gloves welcoming you and offering you a cup of champagne for your trouble..."*

At least she got the champagne part wrong.

The elevator ride to the top floor seems at the same time too long and too short. What Blake told me last night about my dad supposedly pulling strings to get my start-up financed is the flip side of the coin that kept me awake all night. I need to ask him; I'm eager to. But I can't pretend I'm not afraid of the answer he might give me.

The elevator doors open straight into my parents' apartment, which occupies the entire floor. As soon as they swish open, I find a server on the other side in a black uniform, holding a silver tray with a single champagne cup on it.

"Apéritif, Mr. Mercer?"

*Oh, for crying out loud.*

I thank him and begrudgingly grab the glass.

"The others are waiting for you in the parlor. Your mother thought it'd be too hot to have drinks on the terrace today."

And just as well.

I walk through the marble-lined entrance hall toward the parlor. Familiar voices greet me as I enter the room. Dad is sitting on his favorite armchair, a brandy snifter in one hand and an unlit cigar in the other—Mom doesn't let him smoke inside, but he still likes to smell the tobacco with his Sunday drink.

Thomas is sprawled on the couch opposite him, feet on the coffee table, while Mom is trying to get him to take his feet down.

"Come on, Tommy, where did you leave your good manners?" I say, making my presence known.

Mom immediately abandons her quest and comes to hug me.

Thomas drops his feet from the coffee table and, arms draped on the couch backrest, casually flips me the bird with the hand Dad can't see. "Nice of you to finally show up, Gabriello."

While hugging my mom, I flip him right back.

Mom pulls back from the hug but still holds me by the shoulders. "Are you all right, baby? You look a little tired."

"Late night?" Thomas smirks from the couch.

"Boys." My dad's voice booms across the room. "Wait at least until we've had appetizers before you start."

"Start what?" Thomas and I both say, the image of two good boys.

My father shakes his head.

"Hi, Dad."

He nods at me.

I make to move, but Mom is still on my case. "Are you sure you're all right? You look a little pale?"

"I'm fine, Mom, I promise."

Dad takes the last swig of brandy and stands up. "I don't know about you, but I'm hungry."

"Me, too," I say since I skipped breakfast.

Mom pats me on the shoulder. "A good meal will make you feel better."

Both my parents head to the formal dining room. Thomas stretches a hand as if asking for me to pull him up, but I know better than to fall for it.

"Get your ass off that couch on your own, brother."

"Aw, come on."

Thomas springs up and tries to ambush me in a headlock, but I'm prepared and, before he can loop his arm around my neck, I snatch his wrist and fold his arm behind his back.

Thomas taps out, and I let him go.

"Mom is right. Someone is prissy today." He drops an arm over my shoulders and steers me toward the dining room. "Did Blake ruffle your feathers again last night?"

"Nope," I lie.

"Saw the pictures on Instagram. She looked *phenomenal*."

I only grunt in reply.

"Oh, come on, did you move in on that or not?"

"None of your business." I get rid of his arm as we enter the dining room. "And now shut it."

Thomas makes a mocking zipper-over-mouth-throw-away-the-key gesture and goes to take his place in front of me while Mom and Dad sit at the opposite heads of the table.

Except for the white linen tablecloth, the table setting is not your typical Upper East Side style. No fancy china, or thin-stemmed crystal glasses. The plates are in multicolored ceramic, same as the glasses, and an arrangement of tropical flowers towers in the middle.

Mom says the bright colors remind her of home—Cuba.

I've barely sat down when their maid starts a table run, serving salads.

Brunch drifts amidst small talk, my mother expressing her usual concerns that I work too much, and the occasional gossip on boring people I don't care about.

I wait until we're back in the parlor and coffee is being served to broach the subject I'm really interested in discussing. Dad is in his armchair, Mom in the one opposite him, I'm in the middle one and the baby of the family has the couch all to himself as usual.

"Dad," I say, stirring the sugar in my coffee cup absentmindedly. "Can I ask you a question?"

Dad raises his eyebrows. "Sure, son."

"Did you offer to make Fidelity Credit Union your covert partner in the West if they financed my start-up?"

My father's face remains stony as he says, "No, I didn't."

A political reply. He's not lying, but he isn't telling the whole truth, either.

I press him. "So is it just a coincidence that one week after I signed my deal with them, you dropped Wells Fargo for FCU?" After stalking Blake's Instagram last night, I researched the timeline of Dad's biggest operations in California and didn't like what I found one bit. FCU brokered their first big transaction for Mercer Industries one week after my deal was signed, and then nothing ever again after my B-round funding went through.

Dad sighs.

He drops his coffee cup on the small table next to his armchair and, propping his elbows on his knees, leans forward to talk, looking me straight in the eyes. "I didn't ask Fidelity Credit Union to finance your company." Loaded pause. "*They* came to me one week after they'd signed with you and said that either I made them my preferred partners in the West or they'd drop you." Before I can say anything, he raises his hands. "Your company was a solid investment, and you've proved that a thousand times over, but the VC world is small. You get your A-round funding and one week later the deal falls through? Word is going to get around. It would've made it impossible for you to get an investor onboard in the timeframe you needed to lock in your first building." Dad spreads his arms. "I had no choice."

The truth lands on my chest like a ton of bricks.

"And that's why you dropped them as soon as I got my B funding."

Dad nods gravely. "Don't particularly like having a business partner strong-arm me into a deal."

That he even accepted tells me how much he cares about me.

"Why didn't you ever tell me?"

"You wanted to prove a point and you did. I didn't like that you refused to work in the family business, but I've always respected your choices, son. Want it or not, the Mercer name comes with strings attached, but that doesn't mean I can't smooth a few wrinkles for my sons along the way."

I nod at him, trying to process all this new information.

"Where is this coming from, Gabriel?" my father says. "Why

ask me after all this time? It happened what seven, eight years ago?"

"He met a woman." Thomas hides a smirk behind his coffee cup. "She's been calling him out on all his bullshit."

"Oh." My mom is finally prompted to join the conversation. "You met someone? Who is she?"

"No one," I say, staring daggers at my brother.

Thomas flips a folded sheet of paper out of his suit pocket, holding it between his index and middle finger. "So if I called in several favors to get Blake's private number, you wouldn't be interested in me passing it along?" He wiggles the note.

I say nothing. Only try to incinerate him with my stare.

Thomas, not even a little intimidated, shrugs and pockets the sheet of paper. "Guess I'll just ask her on a date myself, then."

Before knowing what I'm doing, I'm lunging for him, flying over the large coffee table separating us and pinning him to the couch. We wrestle and roll onto the floor.

We're still struggling when the blare of a bugle horn destroys our eardrums.

Shocked by the sound, we pull apart and find Dad towering over us with the red stadium trumpet in his hands. "I thought we got over this in grade school."

Mom is still shielding her ears with her hands and now drops her arms. My family is rich but not as uptight as Blake imagines.

I stand up, patting away the wrinkles and dust from my suit. Then, being the bigger brother and bigger man, I offer a hand to Thomas. My brother takes it, but instead of letting me pull him up, he pulls me down while simultaneously working with his legs to cut me off balance.

I land on the couch with a surprised, "Oof."

Before Thomas can get on top of me and resume the fight,

Dad, hands on his hips, threatens, "Boys, don't make me use the horn twice."

The first horn blow is a free pass. Second one? No one wants to be around for that.

Thomas raises his arms innocently. "Just a friendly brawl, Dad."

He plonks down next to me, pushing his disheveled hair away from his forehead, and turns to me with the biggest fish-eating grin. "I take it you're interested in Blake's number, after all?" He offers me the note again.

I snatch it from him and put it into the inner pocket of my jacket.

"Blake?" Mom asks, unfussed by the fight. "Do we know her?"

"Not unless you're a fan of her online workouts," Thomas chirps, making it especially hard for me not to cap him over the head.

Mom's eyes widen. "You mean Blake Avery? I love her!"

"You—you know her?" I stutter.

"Of course, I've been following her forever. Her postural workouts have done miracles for my back." Mom rolls her shoulders backward as if to demonstrate one of the moves.

Did everyone on the planet know about Blake except for me? Apparently, yes.

Mom frowns. "Isn't she a little young for you? How did you meet?"

Thomas is loving this. "Should I tell them the story, or would you prefer to?"

"If you don't shut up right now, you're dead to me."

"Oh, honey, don't talk like that to your brother," Mom chides. "Anyway, I read somewhere she's opened a new gym in NOHO. I've been meaning to check it out and see if she offers some live classes."

And if my mother is ready to trudge eighty blocks downtown just for a gym class, that is saying something. Wait a minute. A light bulb pops above my head.

I stand up abruptly and pull my mom up from her armchair to crush her into a bear hug while kissing both her cheeks. "Mom, you're a genius."

"Why?" Mom asks dazed. "What did I do?"

"I have to go." I ignore the questions. "Mom, Dad, thank you for lunch. Thomas, you're an asshole."

"I love you too, brother."

My Porsche is mercifully parked close by, just down the road. I take the keys from the valet and speed away toward NOHO.

## 11

### BLAKE

On Sunday morning, I wake up sweaty in bed from a sexy dream about a man I've no place fantasizing about. The vision is still so vivid in my mind that for a second, all I can do is blink, lie back on the pillows, and make sure I'm actually alone in my room.

Yep. No six-foot-four-tall walls of testosterone in sight. Nothing out of the ordinary. Since moving into my new apartment in Manhattan a year ago, my bedroom has seen as much action as an icky public restroom at the back of an airport terminal. At least I hope icky public restrooms at the back of airport terminals see little action.

I peel the sheets off my overheated body and decide to take a quick shower before I have to go to work for my 10.30 a.m. class.

Sundays are no rest days for me. I don't do rest days. But since half of my job comprises doing the thing I love the most—blowing off steam with a good workout—I consider myself to be off half the time. It's all the financial planning and meeting with investors that drains me. After Justin, I've wanted to keep the control solidly in my hands. I'm aware I'm overdoing it, that I should delegate more, focus on what I love. But since the man I loved and trusted with all my heart blindsided me so thoroughly, I've had trouble putting faith in anyone else. Hence why I've reserved all the decision-making, and consequent headaches, for myself.

But things are about to change. I won't be able to oversee everything once we go public. I will have a board of directors. Shareholders I'll be accountable to. The company will have to evolve and become more structured. The usual spike of anxiety at the impending change grips me. My head hurts just thinking about it.

To be fair, the mild hangover from last night isn't helping.

I rarely stay out partying until three in the morning. And last night, to take the edge off MGM's looming presence, I drank two glasses of champagne instead of my usual limit of one. The alcohol had already left my system by the time I drove home, but apparently, the headache is here to stay. I turn the water cold and plunge my head underneath to properly wake up.

Twenty minutes later, I'm hurrying out in a T-shirt and a pair of leggings. I grab my laptop, remember at the last minute to drop the towel around my head, grab my purse, and dash out of my apartment. At least now that I live in Manhattan, the commute is super short and I can walk to work. The road from Queens to NOHO has been long. I first moved out of Queens to Brooklyn five or six years ago. But I crossed over the East River a year ago when the renovation works on the first Bloominghale fitness center started.

Short commute or not, I'm running more than walking as I dart through the front doors, making a beeline for the juice bar—thank goodness for it, or I would've had to skip breakfast.

"Irie," I yell to the barista. "Emergency protein shake."

From the mini-fridge, Irie pulls up my already prepared order and slides it over the counter toward me. "Coming your way, boss."

"Gosh, you're a life saver, I love you."

The barista blows me a kiss, and I hurry up the stairs, taking two steps at a time.

I barely have time to drop my laptop into my office, suck the shake dry from the paper straw in an unhealthily long, single draw, and rush back down to the group classroom.

At least my first lesson of the day is Zumba: high energy, low strength—much fun.

\* \* \*

For lunch, I order a salad from the juice bar and consume it in my office. It's a hot day outside and I don't have the energy to take a stroll around Manhattan at midday. Despite the light lunch, my lids feel heavy once I'm finished. The office couch calls to me.

I have a gazillion things to do. Upload my story of the day to Instagram, make a silly TikTok, reply to about a million emails... Evan has sent me a list of required SEC forms for public companies I should familiarize myself with: 10-Ks and 8-Ks and 10-Qs and 8-Qs. Insider transaction forms 3, 4, and 5. Just looking at the list makes my eyes cross. I should really get started on this, but another yawn prompts me to opt for a power nap instead.

I kick off my gym shoes and stretch on the couch, grabbing a decorative pillow that I tuck under my head. I'm asleep in minutes.

My phone is ringing. My eyes fly open and I jolt upright, causing the phone to tumble off the couch. I snatch it off the floor and move my thumb automatically to silence the alarm.

I blink and check the time.

Oh my gosh, I slept for three hours.

I swing my legs off the couch, cracking my neck and doing a light arm stretch. It's already time for my next class.

When I enter the dance studio on the lower floor, thankfully only a few people have arrived. I'm not late.

While I wait for everyone else to drop in, I sit on the floor in a butterfly pose and stretch my back and neck some more. The office couch isn't exactly ergonomic.

I've just stretched my left leg forward on the floor, keeping the other bent in a modified Hurdler Stretch when, out of the corner of my eye, I catch a pair of large black sneakers walk into the studio.

The shoes are attached to a pair of long, muscular legs dusted with soft dark hair and clad in black shorts. My gaze travels up to a light-gray tee stretched over an obscenely defined chest, and up again to MGM's self-satisfied face.

Our eyes meet.

His gaze twinkles with boyish mischief as he squats next to me.

"Good afternoon."

I straighten up from my hamstring stretch and gain some distance.

Even the man's shins are sexy. I need air.

"What are you doing here?"

"Do you greet all new gym patrons with such hostility?" He smirks. "It can't be good for business."

"What do you mean, new patrons?"

MGM's grin spreads. "Just got my annual membership." MGM jumps up and stretches his shoulders, pushing his elbows out wide.

He got a membership to my gym? It takes me a minute to recover from the shock, so when he offers me a hand to pull me up from the floor, I distractedly accept.

Big mistake. For several reasons.

As soon as our palms touch, I feel like I'm getting grilled. Instead of blood, liquid fire courses through my veins. And once I'm upright, the momentum brings me almost crashing against the brick wall of muscles that is his chest.

Our eyes lock again, and all the merriment is gone from his. Instinctively, I take a step back and drop his hand as fast as if I were holding hot coals.

Note to self: skin contact with MGM is a big no-no. Avoid at all costs.

To enforce even more distance between us, I cross my arms over my chest. "Mr. Mercer, you take the 'know your competition' concept to a new level."

"We're not competitors, you've said so yourself."

"Then why are you here?"

MGM shrugs. "Just wanted to see what all the fuss is about."

It's my turn to smile. "And you're taking *this* class?" I point at the linoleum floor. "It's a pretty advanced one."

"I asked where to find you. They pointed me to this room." He reaches with his left arm across his chest, pushing at his elbow with his other hand. "I can handle whatever course you're teaching." He drops his left arm and repeats the deltoid stretch with the other.

MGM wants to play? Let's play.

With an open-arms gesture, I welcome him into the class. "If you're sure you can handle it."

The smile I give him is borderline evil, considering how MGM just walked into my advanced ballet class.

## 12

### BLAKE

Dancing is how my passion for training started. I could've become a professional ballerina. By the time I was in the tenth grade, I was going to dance school every afternoon for several hours. I wanted to apply to Julliard. But then my mom got sick. She had myocarditis, an inflammation of the heart that arose as a complication of a viral infection and required her to spend several weeks at the hospital. The disease is curable, and we caught it in time. But while she was fighting the illness, she could no longer help my dad at the restaurant. Medical bills were piling up, and the dance lessons were so expensive given the number of hours I was putting in, that I quit.

When Dad asked me why, I couldn't tell him it was because we could no longer afford it. That he needed me at the restaurant while Mom was recovering because we couldn't afford to pay for the treatments the insurance didn't cover on top of ballet on top of hiring help for the restaurant. Instead, I said the first thing that popped into my head, that I wanted to start a business and didn't have the time for dance lessons anymore.

The next day, I recorded my first ballet-for-beginners video. I had no idea what I was doing, or that my amateurish videos would really turn into a business. But I was certain of one thing: no girl should ever miss out on dancing because she couldn't afford the tuition. And that's why all the dance courses on my platform are free.

Ballet lessons soon expanded into modern, then jazz, and then I developed the dance warmups I used to take at the local studio into more complex workouts that also included a bit of yoga, Pilates, and other techniques in the mix.

One reason my workouts became so popular is that they're fast and don't require any expensive equipment. Ever seen a ballerina's body? They reach perfection with the weight of their own muscles and need nothing else. Besides not needing costly gear, my workouts are very accessible, with several variations for beginners.

But not this one. This class is the one exception, the one I don't record or stream because it's too advanced.

Ballet is an art. One that has a steep learning curve and requires years of training. Something I'm pretty sure MGM doesn't have.

The man seems disoriented by my sudden switch to a welcoming attitude.

He turns around and frowns, probably noticing for the first time how the class is entirely made of women. His confidence further deteriorates as the ladies remove their overlarge tees and sweatpants to reveal leotards, sheer wrap skirts, and leggings. I tie my own pastel pink wrap skirt over my black leggings and study MGM's attire.

He looks at me with a slightly panicked expression.

I smile sweetly. "You can drop the shoes, Mr. Mercer. You won't need them for this class." Then, before he can reply, I clap my hands. "Okay ladies... and gentleman," I add, nodding at a now positively terrified man. "Let's bring out the bars."

The ballerinas nod back and bring out four portable bars, positioning them perpendicular to the mirror wall in the front.

I brush past MGM. "You can still quit," I goad him.

His jaw sets. He looks like a man who'd rather cut off a limb than quit at anything.

At the display of male stubbornness, I hiss, "Suit yourself."

MGM kicks off his shoes and takes position at the bar closer to the door between two other dancers. Smart man—this way he can follow the others' movements whatever side we're working on.

Ages vary within the class from late teens to adults up to their mid-forties. What doesn't change is that everyone in this room has had formal ballet training, everyone except MGM.

"Okay, gals, let's warm those legs. We're going to start in second position and do three *grand pliés*." I demonstrate. "One and two up three and four and again, feeling your turnout, seven and eight third time reverse the arm. Two, three, four into the bar. Five and six, coming up, *tendu*, seven and eight. First position. *Demi pliés*, again, *grand plié* reverse the arm on all the *grand pliés* today, six, seven, and eight. Fourth. *Demi, demi, grand, port de bras*, come to fifth, *demi, demi, grand* again. Forward and back and *sous-sus* and balance. All right?"

All the dancers nod except for MGM.

I select the playlist on my phone and relaxing classical music blares out of the studio's speakers.

"On one, two, three."

My ladies begin to move, and MGM does his best to follow the exercise. I start my round at the other end of the class and slowly amble my way toward his bar.

"Your *grand plié* needs a little work, Mr. Mercer," I comment. "Keep your knees aligned with your toes, hip bone tucked in."

He pushes his pelvis forward, getting in a slightly better position while positively glaring at me.

"Chin high, gaze ahead," I reprimand him.

Next, I torture him with a lightning-quick sequence of *tendus* that has him almost falling flat on his face when he tries to follow along. MGM doesn't know his left from his right and he keeps confusing sides.

I give the man a breath of oxygen with a long stretch sequence at the bar, but there's nothing I can do to save him from the center work or the diagonals. At one point he looks like he might throw up. I hope he didn't come to a ballet class after a big lunch.

He finally gives up on the pirouettes and just sits in a corner, drinking water from his steel bottle and shaking his head.

When the lesson is finally over, I clap. "Great job, gals, and please give it up for Gabriel, our newest recruit."

The women all clap and cheer while Gabriel makes a very poor attempt at a *révérence*, curtsying to the girls on wobbly knees and almost falling flat on his face again.

One by one, all the dancers file out of the class until I'm alone with MGM in the studio. He still looks a little out of breath. Admittedly, I didn't go easy on the *sautés*.

"Are you okay?" I ask.

He looks at me, a little disoriented. "I'm fine. Just need a minute."

"Take all the time you need. The next class in this room will be in an hour."

I make to leave, but he calls me back, "Wait."

I turn, raising an eyebrow.

"Don't I at least deserve a juice after all the hard work?"

I play dumb. "Sure, you can redeem your new-membership coupon at the bar."

"Aw, come on, you can't spare me twenty minutes after everything you just put me through?"

"I didn't put you through anything. I warned you the class was advanced."

"Fine." His lips curl in a smirk. "I thought my sweat and tears during all those exercises would have earned me *something*."

I press my lips together, trying to keep from laughing. "You know what? You're absolutely right."

"I am?"

"Come with me."

"Where are we going?"

"To the juice bar."

"Oh, right."

I lead the way out of the studio, hoping an intake of natural sugars will help him recover faster and go away. Still, I won't deny being a little curious about his next move. I never, *ever* would've expected the Mighty Gabriel Mercer to participate in a ballet class. What is he going to pull now?

I sit at the bar on one of the high metal stools and note how MGM winces as he sits opposite me.

"For someone who owns, what, two thousand gyms, you look pretty stiff."

"I mostly do weight training," MGM groans.

I low whistle. "Then I predict you're going to be sore for a couple of days. What are you having?"

MGM stares at the menu and says, "The Regenerator, please."

Irie nods behind the counter.

I smile at the barista. "And I'll have the Detox on the Rocks. Thank you, Irie."

MGM raises an eyebrow at me.

"I don't usually drink," I explain. "And I'm still paying for every bubble of yesterday's champagne."

"A lightweight?" he mocks me.

"Only when it comes to drinking. So, Mr. Mercer, you still haven't told me what you're actually doing here."

He makes a puppy dog face. "Are we back to formal titles? I thought making a clown of myself at least earned me being called Gabriel."

"All right, Gabriel." The way his name rolls off my tongue is pure lust. He must think the same because his eyes darken, our gazes interlocked. And I swear my heart is racing faster than after a million *pas de chat*.

Thank goodness that's when Irie puts our drinks in front of us. I jump at the excuse to look away and take a sip from my smoothie.

When my pulse returns to a slightly more normal tempo, I dare another peek at MGM. "Why did you come?" I repeat.

A smile plays on his lips as he takes a long sip of his smoothie. "I like a challenge."

I chuckle nervously while trying to keep an impenetrable façade. "I hope we're still talking ballet."

His gaze turns wolfish on me. "What else would we be discussing?"

A blush creeps up my neck as I try to ignore the heat emanating from his gaze. "Okay, well, I hope you found the class challenging enough for your tastes."

He leans forward, his voice dropping to a low whisper. "Sure was."

I clear my throat and scoot back on my stool, trying to put some distance between us.

He nods, a hint of amusement in his eyes. "Do I make you nervous, Blake?"

"Do you *want* to make me nervous?" I make a conscious effort to keep my voice level as I ask the question, but it still comes out coarse.

"Do you always answer a question with another question?"

I give up. "Okay, yes, you make me nervous. Happy?" And now I sound unreasonably shrill.

He winks. "Can't say I'm not." With one long draw from his straw, he finishes his smoothie. "Who should I hand my coupon to?" he asks.

I roll my eyes. "This one's on me."

"Thank you for the smoothie and for the workout, then. I'll see you around."

He's leaving? Just like that. He got me to admit he makes me nervous and then he just ups and leaves? Is this just a game for him? A way to prove he can one-up me? Is he interested in me or just in winning?

MGM stands up, confirming that yep, he's going. The move, unfortunately, brings him several inches closer. Alarm bells go off in all my internal systems, but for a moment I can't help but stare into his dark-brown eyes as if hypnotized.

At least until he winks at me again. "Admiring my pretty face?" he whispers.

I frown. "No, worrying about what lurks behind the prettiness." I can't read this man and it's unsettling.

"Only good things, I promise."

He makes to go again, but some perverse instinct prompts me to reach out and grab his arm. My fingers curl over solid granite biceps, earning me another searing electric shock.

For a moment we both stare at my hand resting on his arm, then his gaze moves up to meet mine, and it's a second electric shock.

I let him go. "Take a long bath tonight, Gabriel." My voice comes out an octave lower than normal. "Your muscles will thank you."

He nods and moves on toward the locker rooms without

another word. And I swear I don't even notice how pleasantly those shorts stretch on his round behind.

* * *

Later that evening, I'm lying on my couch eating a bowl of Reese's Puffs with milk and not enjoying the sweet treat as much as I should. Sunday nights are eat-whatever-I-want nights, and since I didn't feel like cooking and I'm out of toffee popcorn, peanut butter corn puffs it is.

I surf Netflix shows, find nothing I want to watch, turn off the TV, drop the remote on the coffee table, and release a puff of air.

What's the matter with me?

*What or who?* the devil on my shoulder asks.

I snort.

Okay. What kind of man goes to the trouble of taking an entire ballet class to then just order a smoothie and leave?

What sort of behavior is that?

I stuff my mouth with another huge spoonful of Reese's Puffs, hoping the deliciousness will melt my sour mood away. But the sugar rush is disappointing. I've already picked off the buttery puffs, and that's why I've had to add the milk.

Sometimes it sucks to live alone. I know it's what adults do, and what many New Yorkers dream of being able to afford. But at times, I miss the old days when I was living with five other girls, all of us working on our businesses. We were a community, what I imagine a college sorority would be like. But then not all of my roommates' businesses took off like mine; when I started making so much more money than them, I could tell some of them started resenting me. Plus, I wanted the big apartment in Manhattan, proof that I'd made it. So now here I am, alone in a glass box.

On a whim, I grab my phone to text Marissa. But the screen

lights up with a text from an unknown number. Then another. And another.

I open the chat with a beating heart.

FROM UNKNOWN NUMBER

> I wanted to let you know again how much I appreciated today's class

> Thanks to you, I can't move a single muscle in my body without hurting

> My male ego is dented

I can't help the smile that pulls at my lips.

My fingers fly over the virtual keyboard.

Only dented? I type, but then hesitate before sending.

I shouldn't text back. The man is gorgeous, has a sense of humor, and can self-deprecate just the right amount. In short, he's very dangerous. And resourceful if he could get my private number. Not to mention, relentless.

MGM is a man who can turn bones to Jell-O in bed and fry brains without breaking a sweat, but break hearts just as easily. Definitely not the kind of distraction I need in my life right now. My life will change too much already with the IPO. Even if Gabriel were a regular dude and not the owner of a fitness empire ten times the size of mine, now wouldn't be the right time to start a new relationship.

And he's probably not even interested in a relationship. I bet he just wants me to prove he *can* have me. That man should walk around with a warning sign strapped across his broad chest.

I erase the reply and close the chat.

Immediately, the phone pings again.

FROM GABRIEL

> Ghosting me, really?

I stare at the screen, still undecided until another text pops up.

FROM GABRIEL

> I can see the three dots flashing

> I know you're there

Damn messaging apps and their lack of privacy.

I wipe the dumb smile from my face and fight an internal battle not to reply.

Ping.

FROM GABRIEL

> If you keep the silent treatment going, you'll force me to send a selfie from my bubble bath

I shake my head again, accepting defeat, and start typing.

## 13

### GABRIEL

Three seconds pass from the selfie threat, and finally my phone pings with a reply.

FROM BLAKE

I hope that bath is full of foam and nothing gross is visible

TO BLAKE

By gross, I suppose you mean my rubber duck?

FROM BLAKE

I don't know. Is your rubber duck gross?

TO BLAKE

We've been together many years, I never got complaints

FROM BLAKE

Is that how you always deal with the competition?

Hijack their ballet classes first, and then threaten them with duck pics?

> TO BLAKE
>
> A duck pic from me would be a gift, not a threat
>
> And we both know I was the only victim in that class

An eye roll emoji pops into my inbox, followed by another text.

> FROM BLAKE
>
> I can't tell if you're flirting with me or just trying to rile me up

> TO BLAKE
>
> If you can't tell, then my male ego is a little more than dented

> FROM BLAKE
>
> I'm sure there's still plenty to go round

> TO BLAKE
>
> I am flirting, BTW

The woman bails on me again. The three dots appear and disappear a million times until I tire of waiting.

> TO BLAKE
>
> I thought we were playing duck, not chicken

I hold my breath until a reply lights my screen.

> FROM BLAKE
>
> That's the thing. I don't like to play games. Neither in my professional nor personal life

> TO BLAKE
>
> Then come to dinner with me
>
> No games, I promise

Radio silence again. Blake is more skittish than a cat in a carrying case en route to the vet. I'm not scary, am I? Okay, our first introduction could've gone better, but I sort of made up for it, didn't I?

What says "laid-back dude" more than a man with no dance experience willing to take a ballet class and make a fool of himself?

But I might be wrong. I'm not used to chasing women; it usually goes the other way around, which is probably part of the appeal. Even more unusual, Blake doesn't seem to be interested in my money or family name—to the contrary, she seems repelled by them.

A welcome novelty. Takes off the I'm-wearing-a-thirty-thousand-dollar-watch edge most women seem to care so much about. But like the best things in life, she's going to make me work for it.

A ping distracts me from my mental reverie.

FROM BLAKE

> Sorry, Gabriel. You seem like a perfectly nice man, but I have to focus on my company now. I don't have time for distractions

Oof. Miss Avery doesn't pull punches.

TO BLAKE

> That was brutal

> I swear no woman has ever given me the 'it's not you, it's me' speech before even agreeing to go on a date with me

FROM BLAKE

> I bet no woman ever gave you that speech, period

True. But I don't comment on it.

FROM BLAKE

And I thought I'd been gentle?

TO BLAKE

Calling me a perfectly nice man?

Come on

That was unnecessarily cruel

My ego is blown to smithereens

FROM BLAKE

Go stand in front of the mirror in a superhero
pose, it'll recover in no time

TO BLAKE

I can't move, remember?

FROM BLAKE

Deep breaths

You'll be fine in a couple of days, I promise

Night, Gabriel

The incomprehensible wish of hearing her say those words to
me instead of reading them in a text—possibly even while she's
lying sated in my bed—takes me over with a violent intensity.

TO BLAKE

Sweet dreams, Blake

PS. Try not to make them about my rubber duck

# 14

## BLAKE

I read that last text and can't suppress a smile. Gosh, MGM is even funny. A deadly addition to his raw sex appeal, brilliant mind, and I-don't-take-myself-too-seriously attitude.

A man like that could crush me. Destroy me.

I shake my head and drop the phone on the nightstand, my pulse still accelerated from the text exchange. I should've ignored his first message and never replied. Darn, I was this close to saying yes to a date with him, which would've been a total disaster. If I dated him, I'd fall in no time. And when he tired of me and left, there'd be nothing left behind.

We're too different. We come from opposite worlds. And even if I'm dabbling into his gilded universe now, we'd never fit. I tried to mix with New York's aristocracy once and still bear the scars on my heart. I promised myself I'd never repeat that mistake and I won't. Plus, he's probably after me just because he's not used to being denied. Once I gave in, I'd lose all the appeal.

To reinforce my conviction, I grab my phone again and google "Gabriel Mercer dating."

A string of Page Six articles pops up featuring MGM at various

galas and social events. Each article features him with a beautiful
—*different*—woman attached to his arm. Carbon-copy blonde
beauties. Each of them so perfectly groomed, they all look like
royalty. These are all socialites born and bred to wear diamonds,
low chignons, and never work a day in their lives. MGM clearly
has a type, and the hustling daughter of a pizza maker from
Queens definitely isn't a fit.

With a frustrated sigh, I drop the phone again.

Pity.

MGM is the first man who's kindled a spark in me in a very
long time. At least since my last—and only—serious relationship
ended in a bruising humiliation. But it's best to kill the spark
before it can spread. The danger with sparks is that they lead to
fires. And if I got caught in a blaze with MGM, all that'd remain of
me afterward would be ashes.

I barely made it out in one piece the last time I gave my heart
to a man who was part of that old-money elite. Never again.

\* \* \*

The next morning, I wake up to the blaring sound of my alarm
clock. Last night, it took me forever to get to sleep thanks to MGM
and his annoyingly charming texts. I groan in frustration as I
throw the blankets away from my body. Maybe I should listen to
Evan and drop at least a few of the classes I teach in person—like
6.30 a.m. Monday Pilates-Yoga fusion.

Nonsense. And what would I do with all that free time? Even if
the breakup with Justin was three years ago, I'm not ready for a
serious relationship. I don't even want to think about dating.
Burying myself in work, especially the part I love the most, seems
like a far better use of my time than wallowing in my non-existent
love life.

I take my phone, ignoring the urge to re-read last night's text exchange, and pull up my motivational playlist as I shower and eat breakfast.

At 6.15 a.m., I jog through the glass doors of Bloominghale deeply caffeinated and eager to get moving.

I drop my bag into my office and go straight to the yoga studio where I wait for the patrons to arrive. Sitting on the floor, I review in my head the plan for today's lesson and adjust the class playlist on my phone accordingly.

Slowly, the class fills. I check the enrollment log and I'm happy to see all the available spots have been filled. More than that, there's already a waiting list for the course. Bodes well for my plan to expand our course offering and maybe open a second physical location next year. In fact, there are a few unfamiliar faces who have joined. A petite woman in particular catches my gaze as she waves at me in a friendly manner. She must be an Instagram fan.

I welcome everyone, clear my throat, and call the class to attention.

"Welcome back to the second week of beginners Pilates-Yoga fusion. I hope you all enjoyed last week's class and are eager to learn more poses."

The woman who appeared to be an Insta-fan a moment ago nods and grins enthusiastically.

"Today we're going to start with some warming-up exercises. Get your mats ready and ease into lotus pose."

I wait for everybody to get into position and start a guided meditation. Most people drop their hands on their knees and close their eyes, but the petite woman in the back is different. She's very attentive and watches my every move. It takes me a few minutes to realize why she looks familiar. And then, in a stomach-dropping moment, it sinks in. She has the same eyes as MGM.

No. I must be hallucinating. The man has scrambled my brain

cells with his easygoing charm, hard muscles, and smoldering eyes, and now I'm imagining things.

I push the idea aside and force myself to look away from the woman, concentrating on the positive energy flowing through the room. I take a deep breath and get into my zone, leading another short meditation break.

"Deep breaths and clear your minds," I say in a soothing voice, never in so much need to heed the words myself.

With our minds cleared, I start with a few cat-cow stretches to warm up and then we flow from sun salutations to a series of vinyasas. Next, I push the pace a little harder, flow into some standing postures, and then we twist, bend, and squat. It's a killer workout, and I don't take it easy on the participants. I want them to begin their day energized, their bodies primed and strong, and with an expression of pride on their faces for their hard work.

The hour flies by and at the end, everyone applauds heartily. I tell them to go enjoy their days and come back next week.

I rest my back against the wall and watch the class leave—all except for the petite brunette who must be an Insta-fan after all. My followers are all eager to meet me in person, and I always dedicate as much time to them as I can spare. I wouldn't be where I am today without the support of my online community and I'm never going to look down my nose at them or act as if they don't deserve my attention.

"Miss Avery?" The woman approaches me with a polite smile.

"Hi," I say, beaming back. "You're new?"

"Yeah, I've been following you for years. Your modified workouts are the only ones that don't make my back hurt." She stretches taller as if to emphasize her words.

I laugh and say, "I'm glad to hear that. If you have any problems with the coursework, reach out to me after class."

"Thank you," she says. "I'll do that."

Then I ask my customary question. "How did you learn about the opening?" I'm always eager to know which of our marketing efforts is working best. "Did you see the announcement on Instagram?"

"TikTok, actually, I've switched over. It's addictive, isn't it?"

"Totally."

"But it was my son who finally convinced me to enroll."

A sense of unease prickles at the back of my nape. "Your *son*?"

"Oh, how silly of me. I haven't even introduced myself, Camila Mercer."

She offers me a hand.

I shake it, unsure of how I feel about meeting MGM's mother. But I sure can't stop the curiosity.

"Gabriel has been talking about me?"

"No, no. He's too private, he would never. But Thomas was teasing him about you yesterday at brunch." My eyes widen in shock; I can't imagine MGM being playfully teased or stick two words in before Camila continues. "And well... Gabriel was getting all riled up." She winks at me. "And our Gabriel doesn't rattle easily."

I hate the blush that immediately goes to color my cheeks, which only seems to make Camila more satisfied.

"Well, it's been a pleasure meeting you in person, Miss Avery—"

"Please call me Blake."

"Blake." MGM's mom nods. "Hopefully, I'll see you again soon."

And I have a feeling she doesn't mean in yoga class.

Ten minutes later, back in my office, I'm cradling my phone in my hands.

I shouldn't text him. I *definitely* shouldn't text him. I barely stood strong enough yesterday to refuse his invitation, and if he flirts with me again, I'm afraid he could not only get me to agree to a date but charm my pants off before we even get to dinner.

Still, I can't resist seeing what the man has to say about his mother coming to introduce herself. I open the chat app and type:

TO GABRIEL

I met your mother today

Not two minutes pass before a reply trills in.

FROM GABRIEL

Oh?

And I hate that I can almost imagine the cute frown of surprise on his beautiful face.

TO GABRIEL

She came to one of my classes

FROM GABRIEL

Yeah, she mentioned she's a fan

Hope you didn't leave her as wrecked as I still feel

TO GABRIEL

Your mom knows her domain

She didn't overdo it

FROM GABRIEL

I sense a jab in those words

TO GABRIEL

No jabs, just truths

FROM GABRIEL

Oh, Mom's calling me

> Guess I'm about to get the full scoop on your meeting

> She probably just wants to gush about the awesomeness of my training skills

> Let me know what she says, customer feedback is very important for us at Bloominghale

I wait a heartbeat, two. But MGM doesn't reply.

Half an hour passes with still no response. Even if the call with his mom was on the long side, it should be over by now. MGM isn't replying, period.

*Customer feedback is very important.* What a lame message to send. I wouldn't reply either.

Or maybe he's too busy managing his multi-billion empire to reply. Right, I also have better things to do myself than wait by the phone like a teenager with a crush.

I slam my phone onto my desk screen-down and power up my computer. I hate the feeling of disappointment that he didn't flirt with me today or that he didn't renew his invite to take me on a date. Another sign that I made the right decision last night. *Not* dating the man is already causing me more stress than getting ready to take my company public. I definitely don't need to get burned right now.

Still, throughout the day, I can't help throwing longing stares at the black screen of my phone, hoping it'll light up with another text from him. Or jump whenever a new notification pops up, trying to fight the sinking feeling of disappointment when it's not from him.

I'm so distracted, I take twice as long to do my usual work. Another point in favor of keeping MGM solidly out of my life. So much so that by 8 p.m. that night, I'm still in the office trying to sort through trainers' CVs to decide who to hire to be a second me when the business side of things keeps me out of the studio. One CV in particular is calling to me. Catalina Morales has over ten years of ballet experience, was a former backup dancer for a few name-drop celebrities, and she's an ex-elite gymnast. And she also has a Bachelor's degree and a Master's degree in Exercise Science —when did she find the time to get those? And she's attained various certifications to work with people with mental and physical disabilities. She's perfect.

I do a quick online search for her. Catalina's Instagram profile is the first thing that pops up: 400k followers. Not bad. As I scroll through a few reels of her doing some basic workout routines, a notification pops up, distracting me.

Thomas Mercer has liked your reel.

Now MGM's entire family is hounding me. How will I ever get him out of my head?

*Shut up and repeat after me*, a voice chants in my head. *We're not into MGM.*

Nope. Not even tempted.

The thought has barely left my mind when there's a soft knock on my door and Tilly sneaks in, whispering, "You have a visitor."

I check the time on my monitor: 8.17 p.m.

Seems a little late for a business call.

"Who? And how many times have I told you not to stay late when I'm here after hours?"

She waves me off. "I was about to leave. Should I let him in?"

"Who?" I ask again.

She points her thumbs toward the door. "Gabriel Mercer. He just walked in and he's asking to see you." She sounds and looks flustered, not to mention the violent blush her cheeks still haven't had time to recover from. I'm not sure if I should laugh or despair.

"He's behind that door?" I mouth-whisper.

Tilly nods vigorously.

I sigh, shaking my head. I can't pretend to be out of the office at this point. And the man is implacable anyway. He would probably just come back tomorrow. Maybe I should change his title to the Relentless Gabriel Mercer. But the truth is, I want to see him. He ignored me all day and it worked. I'm like an eager puppy wagging her tail.

I wave at the door. "Let him in."

Tilly pushes the door wide open and remains at attention to the side. A few seconds later and Manhattan's Most Eligible Bachelor walks into my office. White shirt rolled up at the elbows, suit jacket casually tossed over his shoulder, a paper bag in his other hand. After a long day, he looks slightly less put-together. But even small imperfections work in his favor. The crinkle around his eyes, tingle-inducing. His wrinkled, rolled-up shirt, a window to uber-sexy forearms. The disheveled hair, an invitation to smooth it over.

"Good evening." He unleashes a devastating smile on the room that I'm not sure Tilly can withstand. My secretary is leaning on the door for support, her cheeks back to a flaming red.

"Gabriel, what a surprise. Are you here for a late evening class? Got rid of the lactic acid already?"

He frown-winces in a way that's too cute for anyone's good. "Actually, no. It's still very painful to move."

"To what do we owe the pleasure, then?"

He dangles the paper bag in his hands. "You wouldn't say yes to dinner out, so I brought dinner in."

He's pulling no punches, and I'm not sure how long I can resist the assault.

In her corner, Tilly lets out a low mumble that suspiciously sounds like an aww.

I incinerate her with a stare. "It's okay, Tilly, I can take it from here. And please go home."

She nods, apparently struck mute by the excessive testosterone, and flees the room, leaving me alone with MGM.

Mr. Pretty Face waits for Tilly to close the door behind her before advancing toward my desk and rather arrogantly taking a seat I didn't offer. "Getting rid of potential eye witnesses?" he asks. "Should I be worried?"

I eye his new position. "I take it you're staying for dinner?"

"It's for two."

The paper bag has no logo so I have no idea what he's brought me. "What's in the bag?"

"I found this great tutorial online for homemade chicken skewers with tzatziki sauce."

Coincidentally, tzatziki is the last recipe post I made on my socials.

"Should I believe you *made* me dinner?"

His smirk is infuriatingly sexy. "My chef did, but that's strictly for edibility reasons." MGM rummages in the paper bag and takes out two round paper containers with plastic lids.

He slides one over the desk toward me.

Inside, perfectly grilled chicken skewers are arranged over a bed of greens and prettily cut veggies with a small bowl of tzatziki sauce on the side. It looks like a box of takeout from a Michelin-star restaurant.

My stomach grumbles at the view in an undignified fashion.

MGM chuckles in response. "And it looks like I got here just in time."

I was about to remove the plastic lid, but I stop to study him. "How did you know I'd still be in the office?"

He gives me a long, appraising stare that makes me feel like he can see within the depths of my soul. "Oh, you know, you have that overachiever vibe. I just assumed late nights are par for the course with you."

"Well, you assumed wrong." I finally pull off the lid and take up the disposable bamboo fork—nice environmentally friendly touch. "I try to keep a healthy work-life balance."

A total lie. I'm the worst workaholic and skip meals most days, not to mention the substitute ones I consume from a straw from the juice bar downstairs. But MGM doesn't need to know that or to learn more of my flaws. They'd all be just ammunition that he could deploy against me. To weaken my defenses. This bring-you-dinner-at-the-office gesture is already hard enough to resist.

I have to keep a cool head, because if I let my walls down and let him in, then what would he do?

The same thing Justin did?

I know Marissa is right, and not all men are dung beetles like my ex, but how do I pick apart the good ones from the bad without letting my guard down, without risking my heart?

I can't. My past clearly shows what a poor judge of character I am. No matter that MGM is doing and saying all the right things. So did Justin at the beginning.

I take my first bite of delicious salad and it melts in my mouth.

"So you're not usually here late at night?" Gabriel asks in a sarcastic tone.

"Nope," I lie again.

"Then I guess I just got lucky." MGM holds my gaze, and I almost choke on a turnip.

He's *lucky* I'm not a violent person because he's pushing all my buttons.

"Why do you keep insisting we spend time together?" I ask.

He replies in a cutely perplexed tone, "Why are you so opposed to the idea that we do?"

"The question game again?"

"Just humor me, please?"

I roll my eyes at him and pick up a chicken skewer. "You confuse me."

"Confuse you how?"

I swallow a bite of the most delicious chicken I've ever eaten, and say, "Well, you act like you're determined to make me like you, but the first time we met you were rude and condescending to me."

His voice takes on a serious tone. "I was rude because you'd punched me where it hurts the most."

I raise my brow, not impressed by his logic. "That's a convenient excuse."

"Not an excuse. You must have something that makes you see red, an Achilles' heel of sorts. Being accused of getting everything I have handed to me is mine." I'm about to reply when he silences me with a raised hand. "But we already had this conversation and I don't care for a repeat. And if that was the only problem, you'd have answered my question by saying you don't like me and that's why you don't want to go on a date with me, but you didn't. You said I confuse you. Why?"

"Because the same man who strolled in here exuding arrogance and assuming I was a girl playing in her daddy's office then has enough self-irony to dance through an entire ballet class—"

"And make a fool of himself," he finishes for me. "And what's wrong with that?"

"You seem like a person who'd have no trouble crushing an enemy in the boardroom, but who'd also stop at an intersection to help an old lady cross the street—that is if you ever walked anywhere instead of being chauffeured around."

That cute frown again. "Is potentially helping the elderly cross the street such a bad thing?"

I don't know how else to explain myself. "It makes you a riddle to crack, and I just don't have the time. Plus, let's not pretend that the fact that our businesses overlap wouldn't be an issue. As a woman CEO, I can't date just anybody."

"What's that supposed to mean?"

"That if we became a couple, they'd probably call us the King and Queen of Fitness or something, and most people would assume my success is a proxy of yours." I take a sip from the paper cup Gabriel has included with the meal and smile that it's kombucha—the man's got game. "No one would run the timeline on things, they'd just assume that your wealth gave me the platform I needed to succeed even if we started dating *after* my company blew up."

He sits back in the chair, a smirk smugger than smug on his lips. He looks victorious, and I've no idea why until he tells me. "So you see why I get so worked up when people assume I'm a decacorn because my father is rich."

That momentarily stuns me into silence. I mirror his pose and lean back in my chair, tilting my head to the side. It's like a game of staring and I'm about to lose. I crack and smile. "I'm understanding better where you come from. But you won't get any pity from me."

He makes a mock-hurt face. "Don't my vulnerabilities make me more attractive?" He accompanies the question with a waggling of his eyebrows.

"No." I chuckle. "Just more risky."

He smirks. "I might be human and therefore undatable?"

I push my empty bowl aside and point a finger at him. "You have heartbreak written all over those cute dimples, so thanks, but no, thanks."

"Ah, I see."

"See what?"

"You feel the attraction, but are too scared to put yourself out there. What is it, fear of getting hurt, of not being in control?"

Both and more. Fear of being humiliated again. Of making a fool of myself, of getting my heart broken. Heat rises to my cheeks at the thought that he's nailed me so completely. And I snap.

"How about you choose whatever explanation you prefer as long as you leave me alone?" I ask, all fake sweetness. "It's late and I still have stuff to do."

MGM eyes my empty bowl and stands up. "My job here is done. You're fed."

He grabs his suit jacket. I take in the wrinkled fabric again, how normal it makes him look, and I'm surer than ever that I'm making the right call. If I discovered this man's vulnerabilities, saw his bed hair, or heard his still-groggy-with-sleep voice, I don't think I'd come out the other side alive if he ever ended things with me. I'm twenty-six and my romantic experience can be summed up in one disastrous relationship. I've always been too focused on my career to have time for dating, but the one time I let myself be vulnerable with someone, I promptly got crushed. And Justin wasn't half the man Gabriel is. I can already tell.

MGM isn't someone you just date. A relationship with him would be very *tumultuous*, I suspect. He might not have the upper hand in running a business—I can hold my own, thank you very much—but he sure does with love entanglements, at least if his Page Six profile is to be trusted.

He walks to the door now and pauses on the threshold, leaning against the door frame. "Lovely and charming, by the way."

"What?"

"Is what my mother had to say about you."

MGM winks at me—causing a confetti explosion in my belly —and then leaves as suddenly as he arrived.

I stare at the papers scattered on my desk, not even remembering what I'm supposed to be doing.

I need to go home and perform an exorcism on myself. How do you force your brain to forget crinkly brown eyes and dimples? Think Google has a solution for that?

# 15

## BLAKE

Half an hour after MGM leaves, I peel myself away from the desk. Now it's definitely too late to call prospective trainers about a job interview. I've only waited hidden in my glass fortress for this long to be sure of not bumping into MGM downstairs in case he lurked around.

I grab my bag and let out a puff of air. Gosh, I hate unproductive days.

As I exit Bloominghale, there's no sign of MGM. But the moment I step onto the curb, a man in a black driver's uniform approaches me. "Good evening, Miss Avery."

"Good evening," I reply, taken aback by being greeted so formally by someone I've never met. "Can I help you with anything?"

"Actually, I'm here to help you."

I raise my eyebrows quizzically.

"I'm Mr. Mercer's driver, Tobias. Mr. Mercer asked me to wait for you and offer you a ride home." The man shrugs, offering me a warm smile. "Said he felt like walking home and possibly helping an elderly lady along the way."

I roll my eyes. That man is impossible. My first instinct is to refuse, but I *am* bushed and my legs are as tired as my brain.

Plus, what's the harm in accepting? MGM won't be in the car with me.

I nod to the driver and let him open the car door for me.

MGM might not be in the car, but his scent lingers behind, trapped in the high-end fabric of the seats. His cologne. It smells expensive, seductive, dangerous. Exactly what I'd expect a handsome, powerful, billionaire to smell like.

"Where to, miss?" the driver asks from the front seat.

In a lightning moment of clarity, I predict this to be a plot for MGM to learn where I live, so I give the driver the generic crossroads.

He drops me off at the corner of Broadway and Houston ten minutes later—the same time it would've taken me to walk home. I thank him and wait for the black SUV to disappear into the night before I head to my building.

I don't wear makeup during the day, it'd just melt off in my first morning class, but I still scrub my face clean the second I get home, no matter that I've already showered at the office. Hair up in a messy top knot, I take my time applying moisturizer in front of the bathroom mirror.

*What is it you like so much, Gabriel?*

I shake my head at my own rhetorical question. It's probably just the novelty of not having a woman fall flat at his feet with gratitude for having spared her a second glance. Must be the thrill of the chase. And once I give in, he'll get bored in no time.

I clear a smudge of moisturizer from my forehead and free my hair from the top knot ready for bed.

I've just snuggled under the covers when a text arrives.

FROM GABRIEL

I'll have you know I didn't assist any elderly
citizen on my way home

I shouldn't text back, but the perfect, witty reply just popped
into my head.

TO GABRIEL

I need more. Did you at least litter a little along
the way?

Help kill the planet a bit?

FROM GABRIEL

Sorry, no littering to report either

The next text MGM sends is a string of unintelligible
characters.

FROM GABRIEL

Wbavsyxgwvabx

TO GABRIEL

??

FROM GABRIEL

My cat butt texted you

He's sitting on my chest, competing for attention
with the phone

Of course he has a cat.

TO GABRIEL

I'm allergic to cats

I type and hit send. I don't know why I wrote that, it's not true.

FROM GABRIEL

Latte is a hypoallergenic breed ;)

Every message that pops into my inbox is an assault on my heavily barricaded heart, but the defenses are crumbling. Latte is an impossibly cute name for a cat. And the winky face, even via text, makes my belly flutter.

What am I doing? I'm flirting with danger when I, 100 per cent, shouldn't.

Without even wishing MGM goodnight, I turn the phone off and quickly drop it on my nightstand as if burned.

I might have to change my number.

# 16

## GABRIEL

Twenty minutes and no answer. Wow, I'm really losing my touch. I'm trying to sleep, but I'm not getting very far. The fingers of my right hand strum against the mattress nervously, wondering what it'd feel like if it were Blake's skin under my fingertips.

I'm being absurd. I've never had a problem with women and getting their attention. Before Blake, I mean, the queen of brush-offs.

When she ignores the last text, I try to work myself into a state of rightful indignation, but I can't. Instead, I'm surprised by the ache I feel when I think of her falling asleep without saying good-night to me.

Plan A—to rely on my easy charm—isn't working; time to move on to plan B.

I know what I have to do, but it doesn't make it suck any less.

I put off setting things in motion until the next morning at the office. At my desk, I push the intercom button, then change my mind and lift my finger without saying a thing, second-guessing my decision a million times over.

I do it again now. Only this time, Mila precedes me. "If you push that button one more time without actually speaking, I'm going to quit my job. All the static is making my ears ring. What is it?"

I kick the last glimmer of pride to the side and say, "Can you get me Thomas on the line?"

I love my brother, but I'm usually not the one who gets in touch.

Mila chuckles through the intercom. "Thomas, huh? This should be good."

"Thank you, Mila," I say, closing the communication.

Two minutes later, my private landline blinks red. I pick up. "Thomas, hi."

"Gabriello, my favorite brother—"

"I'm your *only* brother."

"You're still my favorite. What can I do for you?"

I steady myself before I say the words. "I need a favor."

"Come again?" Thomas's mocking tone comes from the other side. "I don't think I heard you right, you... what?" I can almost imagine him pulling his ear.

"Need a favor," I repeat, grinding my teeth.

"Uh-huh. What kind of favor?"

I don't reply.

"Ah." Thomas sighs. "Is this related to Pretty Blue Eyes by any chance?"

I call her Angry Blue Eyes, but... technicalities.

I grunt in the affirmative.

"Sorry, bro, but I don't speak caveman," Thomas says, chuckling on the other side. "You need to give me a few more specifics."

I knew this wouldn't be easy. I close my eyes and explain my plan to Thomas. "Can you do it?"

"This close to the date? It's going to be hard." Thomas coughs to clear his throat. "But for you, Gabriello, I'll make it happen. I won't even ask for anything in return," he concludes, his tone imbued with brotherly sanctitude.

"You mean besides the million favors I do for you on a regular basis?"

"Now, let's not score count. You're my brother, and out of the goodness of my heart, I'm going to deliver the impossible to you."

"Call me when it's done."

"Yes, master," Thomas says in a silly, shrill voice.

We hang up, and I drop my head in my hands. I hope she's worth it.

## 17

### BLAKE

"Now come out of the *port de bras* standing tall." I guide Amita in the move as we finish a livestream of an early-morning introductory ballet session. "And we're done."

I clap, then, staring into the camera of my phone, I add, "I hope you enjoyed today's lesson and if you want to find out more about ballet and dancing, you can check out my website for my free dance courses, the link is in my bio." I take Amita's hand and lift it. "Now give it up for Amita who helped us today, and see you next time..."

I go to the tripod and turn off the livestream.

"Uhf." I let out a puff of air. "That was great, thanks again Ami."

"Don't even mention it." She hugs me. "I would've never gotten into dancing if it weren't for you. I'm happy to give back to the community."

"Yeah, I love how many new recruits we're bringing in."

"Speaking of new recruits." She flashes me a teasing grin. "Is the new guy going to become a regular?"

I don't need to ask who the new guy is.

"He's not," I say definitively.

"Pity, he was kind of sexy." She nudges my shoulder. "So who is he? Your boyfriend?"

"No, nooo. I don't have a boyfriend. I'm single. Totally single, and happy. I'm happily single..." And ranting apparently.

"Okay." Amita smirks. "What a shame, though, he had a really nice butt."

I play dumb. "Did he?"

"Oh, come on, don't pretend you didn't notice."

I blush for no reason. "Okay, he had totally bitable buns." Not happy with just the inappropriate comment, I make a grab-and-bite gesture, and that's when Evan crashes into the dance studio, yelling, "You're still live."

"What?"

He points at my phone. "Camera's still rolling."

In a panic, I pick up the phone and catch a few of the incoming comments:

No one who says how happily, happily single they are is actually happy

Who is this mystery guy? Can we get a name?

Gosh, she really wants to take a bite out of those buns

"Hi again, everyone," I say, trying to keep my voice under control. "Sorry for the mishap."

A million more questions pour in about the mystery guy.

I take a deep breath, trying to regain composure. "Okay, I think that's enough for today, guys. Thank you so much for joining me in this dance class. As for the mystery guy, I'm not going to reveal his identity. He's not into social media and I don't want to invade his privacy."

Rather vocal protests ensue.

I clear my throat. "Um, sorry to disappoint you all, but the new guy is just a friend—well, not exactly a friend." I read another comment. "Definitely *not* a friend with benefits, there are *no* benefits involved. Just an acquaintance. Nothing more. And let's focus on the dancing, shall we?"

Amita shakes her head behind me, clearly not buying my explanations, same as my followers, judging from the comments still rolling in. "All right, folks, I wish you again a great day, byeeee."

I push the end button three times just to make extra sure, and slide down the mirrored wall to the floor, hugging the phone to my chest.

Evan looks down at me with a stern expression. "Who's the mystery guy?"

I shake my head.

Amita pulls on a sweatshirt and, grabbing her bag from the floor, turns toward Evan. "Name's Gabriel if it helps," she rats me out before exiting the studio with a friendly wave.

Evan pulls both his hands through his hair. "*Mercer?*"

I'm getting ready for a new lecture when my phone rings, startling me. I check the number on the screen and pick up. "Mom?"

"Darling, it's your father."

Dread pools in my chest. "What happened, is he okay?"

"Yeah—yes. Sorry, dear, I didn't mean to scare you. It's just his back."

I sag against the mirror, flooded with relief. "What about his back?"

"It's his sciatica, it's flaring up and he's insisting on going to work anyway."

"Can't the weekend manager substitute for him?"

"No, Jerry has another job during the week. I'll go if you just can help me convince him to stay put."

My mom's back isn't much better than my dad's. "No, Mom, I'll go."

"No, honey, no. You're too busy."

I am busy, but not so busy I'd turn my back on my family. But after today, I will insist with Dad that he hires an extra hand during the week as well as weekends.

"Mom, now don't you also be difficult. I said I'll go, I'll go. You stay home and take care of Dad, okay?"

"You're the best daughter. I love you."

"Love you, too."

I hang up and look up at Evan, knowing he won't like what I have to say. We had a financial planning session scheduled for this afternoon. (Can't say I'm sorry to be getting out of that.)

"I know you're not happy with me, but you know my dad. He's stubborn; either I cover for him or he'll kill himself going to work just to avoid shutting down Joe's even for a single day."

Evan sighs, resigned.

"Anything urgent before I go?"

My COO hugs himself. "No. Apex called, though. The sponsorship award is between us and another company; they'll give us the final decision by tomorrow."

I nod and quickly gather my things. "Okay, I'll check my email as soon as I'm done at Joe's. And Evan?" He looks down at me. "Sorry about canceling on you today. We'll reschedule for next week, yeah?"

Evan nods, a small smile on his lips.

I rush upstairs and ask Tilly to have the Aston Martin brought around while I shower. I could take a cab, but I feel like driving today.

* * *

I arrive at Joe's a few minutes after opening time. Tim, the pizza guy, has already let himself in, but the front door is still closed to customers with a small line forming outside.

I street-park the Aston Martin, getting a few raised eyebrows, and strut toward the crowd, greeting the patrons.

"Morning, everyone! Sorry for the delay. My dad had a little health issue this morning, but I'm here now. Let's get started!" I say, beaming at the hungry customers.

I unlock the door and let them in. I enter the kitchen to drop my bag in the back, inhaling the scent of fresh dough and tomato sauce. I put on a white apron while talking to Tim. "Change of plans today; I'll be manning the ship."

I explain the situation with my dad and then ask what the day's special is.

"Sausage."

"Okay, perfect." I tie the apron behind my back and grab a notepad. I can't remember a thousand drink and food orders at the same time like my dad does.

As I start taking orders, I almost feel sixteen again. There's something about the fast-paced environment of a restaurant that is both exhilarating and calming. But I don't have much time to reflect through the lunch rush hour. I have tables to serve, to-go orders to fulfill, while also working the register. Things slow down in the afternoon only to pick back up again toward the evening.

I'm balancing four large pizza plates in my hands when my phone rings in the pocket of my apron. I drop the plates to the right table and just about manage to pick up before the line goes silent.

"Hey, Marissa, what's up?"

"Are you down for a drink tonight? I need a shoulder to cry on."

"Oh? What's happened?"

"Nothing serious, just a bad date."

I shift the phone between my ear and shoulder as I ring the cash register for a couple. "I can't do drinks, but I can feed you. I'm at Joe's." I explain the situation and then ask, "Unless you already ate on the date?"

"No, he skipped town before we made it to dinner. I'll be there in half an hour."

When my best friend arrives, she finds me a total mess.

My once-white apron is stained with tomato sauce, flour, and who knows what else. My hair is pulled back into a messy bun, with strands of baby hair escaping all over the place. Except for the side where I accidentally greased over it with sausage fat while I was cleaning a skillet. It'd make John Travolta's Elephant Trunk hairstyle in *Grease* pale in comparison.

But Marissa doesn't seem to mind; she pulls me into a tight hug before taking a seat at the bar.

I put a regular pie in front of her because I know she doesn't care for sausage or pepperoni, alongside a Coke. "So tell me all about this date from hell."

Marissa groans. "Ugh, it was terrible. He seemed nice enough at first, but then I followed your advice."

I raise my eyebrows questioningly; I don't remember giving her dating advice.

Marissa takes a bite of pizza and explains between chews. "The thing you told me about men not wanting to date single moms."

"How did motherhood even come up?"

"I casually worked my IVF plans into the conversation and the moment the word 'baby' came out of my mouth, he pretended to get an urgent call and left." She licks tomato sauce off her fingers.

"I mean, the phone was right there on the table, dark screen and all. I could see it wasn't ringing."

I pass a hand over my face, probably adding more flour to my non-existent makeup. "And he did a whole pretend call?"

"Yep, took his time, too; must've been a minute of him nodding seriously and uh-hmming before he fake-hung up."

"Oh, gosh, I'm so sorry."

Marissa takes a sip of Coke. "Don't be, your proposed screening method works really well. You should patent it. So that was my day, how was yours?"

I point down at my dirty apron. "This pretty much covers it. Oh, and I became a meme."

I quickly give her my phone, which is showing a GIF of me grabbing and biting air, before going to serve table three their pizzas. Marissa is still laughing when I come back.

"Were you really in the mood for a burger?"

"Worse." I tell her about Gabriel and the ballet class and the live stream blunder.

She chuckles and then gives me a more serious stare. "So you're really into his rear end, but you still won't date him?"

"I can't, Mari. Not with everything else that's going on in my life. I don't have the time or the strength to allow someone new in. Someone I can't trust completely. And after Justin, I'm not sure I'll ever be able to rely upon a man 100 per cent again."

She pulls me into a side hug. "I wish I could say you're wrong. But tonight, I'm with you on this. Men suck."

## 18

### BLAKE

Evan walks into my office the next morning wearing a dark expression.

"What is it?" I ask.

He lifts the phone in his right hand. "Apex just called; we lost the bid."

"Oh, okay." The news stings, I'm not going to pretend otherwise. "Do we know who won?"

A short pause and then... "Power Training."

Heat rises to my cheeks. "Please don't pour salt in the wound," I say. Evan warned me Gabriel is our competitor, that even if he makes most of his revenue from his real-estate deals, he's still a behemoth in the fitness industry. I didn't listen; I let my guard down. And now reality has come to bite me in the ass—quite literally. I think of yesterday's meme and start laughing hysterically.

"Are you okay?" Evan asks, looking at me with a perplexed expression.

"Super-duper," I say. "Apex doesn't want our platform? We'll start our own line of fit watches. Get the product team on it asap;

we'll call it the Bloombeat, make a whole accessory line out of it. Screw Apex and their old trinkets."

"I don't think starting a new product line ahead of the IPO is the best idea."

He's right.

"Sorry, Evan." I lean on my elbows and massage my temples. "I just really wanted to get the deal."

"I get it. And the Bloombeat is actually a great idea, but perhaps next year?"

I nod. "Next year."

When Evan leaves my office, I allow myself a short moment of self-commiseration. Then, pity party over, I should go back to looking at potential names for board members; so far, I only have secured the chairman, Tom Cheney, my first and biggest investor to date. And I will need at least five or six more competent, trustworthy professionals to appoint who also have the time—why I can't pick Marissa. A challenge. I should really get started on this. Instead, I pick up my landline and call my assistant.

"Tilly? Can you have the Aston Martin brought around?"

* * *

The drive uptown to Mercer Enterprises' headquarters is smooth. They even have a guest garage where I can park. And a smiling receptionist welcomes me as I request to speak with the CEO, her eyes only slightly widening at my aggressive tone. I try to apologize for it with a friendly smile, but, given how her lips curl over her teeth in response, it must have been more of a scary grimace.

I have to wait a few minutes before someone gets back to her. She nods into the phone, throwing me even more surreptitious glances until she finally stands up. "Please follow me."

I expect her to bring me to the top floor. Instead, we climb only a couple of floors in the elevator before she gets out, asking me to follow her.

She guides me along a corridor of black walls and swipes her security badge over a security pod at the end of the hall, unlocking an equally dark door.

"Mr. Mercer is waiting for you inside."

I thank her and enter the room, discovering Gabriel seated on a gym bench in the middle of a weight-training workout. He's wearing a black tank top that leaves his muscular shoulders and arms bare. But even more annoying is the grin he's sporting. *Couldn't keep away?* it seems to be asking me.

He greets me with a simple, "Hello, what can I do for you?", not even bothering to stop his workout.

Before I speak, I have to recover from the sight of his sweaty biceps, but then I remember why I came here and that I'm on the warpath.

"Did you know?" I accuse.

Gabriel tilts his head and keeps flexing all those stupid muscles. "Know what?"

I point at his general chest area. "Can you stop lifting for a second?"

His grin widens. "I thought muscles were your bread and butter; you should be used to the sight."

Not when it's him. Not when my body is practically begging me to take those stupid dumbbells out of his hands and have my wicked way with him on that bench. Not when he's the last person I should have these kinds of thoughts about.

I drag my eyes away from his muscular arms and settle on his eyes, not that it helps. "Apex, did you know we were the last two companies in the run to win the bid?"

That finally gets his attention. He drops the weights to the mat and leans forward, resting his elbows on his knees.

"Did you?"

I shake my head.

"Competing bidders were kept confidential; I had no more way of knowing it was you than you had of knowing it was me."

I glare at him.

His features soften. "It wasn't a personal slight, just business. They wanted physical locations and that's why they went with me." He waves at me. "You're too new and shiny for them. And the CEO still can't be bothered to grow their online sales."

I believe him—his appraisal is spot on. And Gabriel doesn't strike me as petty; he wouldn't steal a deal from me on purpose. But I don't know how to respond. I'm not even sure why I drove here.

Gabriel has the same curiosity.

"Did you come all the way up here just to congratulate me?" The smirk is back, as is the flirty tone, and coming here was a mistake because all I want to do now is push him back on that bench and kiss the smugness out of him.

"I just came to reiterate why we cannot date. The Apex deal is a perfect example of why our lives would clash. You have to agree." I sound desperate.

He shrugs. "Sorry, I don't."

"How can you not?"

"For the way you're looking at me right now. No deal is worth missing out on that."

It's not just my cheeks that flare up. My entire body becomes engulfed by flames.

I let out a weak, "Agree to disagree," that comes out more like a squeak, and flee the premises.

"You can't run away forever..." His words chase me down the hall.

And the most terrifying part? I'm afraid he's right.

# 19

## GABRIEL

The days after my call to Thomas, and Blake's surprise visit are the longest of my life. It's like I've been thrown into the middle of a mental tennis match.

I want to text her. I want to call her. Hear her voice, see her face —see her eyes. I'd even settle for another ballet class if it meant I could flirt with her afterward. But I especially can't get out of my head the way she was looking at me in the office gym.

The air between us was crackling with electricity. Blake was staring at me with such intensity I wasn't sure if she was about to whack me over the head with a dumbbell and put an end to my suffering or if she wanted to lay me down on the bench and kiss me to my deathbed.

Given a choice, I would've much preferred the latter way to kick the bucket.

But I know it's best if I keep my distance and give her time to miss my witty texts and pretty face.

Thomas finally calls me back one late afternoon when my mood is as stormy as the dark clouds outside my windows.

The moment I pick up, my brother hollers into the phone,

"Bingo, my man! I've got you two golden tickets to the Chocolate Factory."

"Westwood came through?" I ask, still not sure I can believe him.

"Yes, sir," Thomas continues, exploding with energy. "I made the impossible happen. Now, as for your payment—"

"I thought we agreed there'd be no quid pro quo."

"There isn't. I just want to hear you tell me I'm awesome."

Between gritted teeth, I say, "You're awesome."

"Ah." Thomas gives a contented sigh. "Just so you know, I was recording you, and now I'm going to personalize your ringtone with the audio."

"Whatever."

"Also, saying thank you wouldn't hurt."

"Thank you. Anything else on your wish list? Should I send a basket of muffins?"

"I prefer cupcakes. Chocolate chip cookie dough, strawberry shortcake, and sweet vanilla are my go-to flavors. Mila knows my favorite shop uptown."

"How does she know?"

"Because she's an extremely smart, attentive, detail-oriented—"

"Stop trying to poach my assistant. She's not coming to work for you."

"I don't know how you can stand his grumpy ass day in, day out, Millicent."

Mila, who also listens in to all my phone calls, drops into the conversation. "He pays me very well for my trouble."

"I'll double whatever he's giving you," Thomas offers.

"Sorry," Mila replies. "I'm also loyal."

"You break my heart, Millicent," Thomas says, sounding disgruntled. "Every, single, time."

"If you're done importuning my employees, I have work to do."

"Ah, Gabriello, the usual ray of sunshine. Let me know if you want to ride with me on the jet. I can't wait to spend some quality time with my favorite brother."

I roll my eyes and hang up.

Swiveling my chair to face the window, I stare out at the incoming storm. I know I'm rocking the boat. It won't take Blake long to put two and two together and realize I've interfered. She's going to be mad. But I hope that spending time together will prompt her to finally give in to the attraction she's fighting so hard against.

This is a make-or-break move. And it's too late to back down now.

The bait is set. Will Blake catch the hook?

# 20

## BLAKE

I hit the refresh button one more time, still incredulous. I'm shocked by the unexpected invitation that just dropped into my inbox as quietly as a spam email for a new credit card and toaster bundle offer.

For something as life-changing as this, I thought at least the mail server would've launched confetti out of my computer screen, or played a choir of celestial music.

Instead, nothing. As of two minutes ago, I've been officially invited to attend the annual Billy Conference—the most exclusive, sought-after business conference reserved for the elites of every sector—with no fuss whatsoever.

For the few startuppers who get invited every year, it's like being anointed by the business gods. Whoever attends the Billy will never be passed over by investors again, at least not by anyone who matters in the VC world. The invitees are handpicked. The money and influence needed to attend this highfalutin event are staggering.

I have wanted to go ever since I received my first round of funding. But I'd never really let myself hope to get an invitation.

Now, I have. Or at least I assume the email "Annual Billy Conference" is an invite.

I stare at the subject line for a long time, my fingers chickening out of opening the message half a dozen times.

Finally, I find the courage to click on it.

The message is stylish in its simplicity and lack of over-formatting.

Dear Blake Avery,

Please be advised that given the high quality of your company, you've been awarded a special invitation to attend this year's Billy Conference. The conference will be held in Jackson Hole from 27 to 30 July. We've enclosed your electronic badge, which grants you access to the conference and all its facilities. We hope you'll be able to attend and enjoy the experience.

The world is your oyster,

Billy Westwood, Founder and CEO

I stare at the screen, open-mouthed. I keep re-reading the message. I scan the email, just in case it was a mistake. But no, there's no mistake. I've been invited to the Billy.

My mind is racing a thousand miles per hour. The conference is only two weeks away and I have to RSVP like, right now.

I frown.

The timing seems a little off.

Aren't these invitations supposed to be delivered months in advance? Why am I getting mine only now?

Maybe some crazy person dropped out, and they needed a last-minute replacement. I shrug. I'm okay with not being their first choice. Who cares if I'm their second pick? I'm not about to squander such an opportunity.

I don't have much time to make my decision. I read the email again, confirm all the details, and click yes on the RSVP form. I also click yes on the form that asks if I'd be open to speak on a panel. Then I stare at the confirmation message still in a daze.

Thank you for confirming your participation in the Billy. You will receive another email with the conference program and lodging arrangements.

Heart pounding in my chest, I refresh the page every two seconds until the program arrives. I click on the attachment, scrolling down the list of events: keynote speech, panels, a day-long scavenger hunt in the woods. Not that they matter, most of the conference value is in the fireside chats not listed on any program, where business deals are made, alliances forged, and enemies crushed.

Still, I go over the list of speakers one more time, and my heart positively stops in my chest when I catch my name on the list. I'm on a panel titled The Future of Fitness, Brick and Mortar or Social Media? Heavy Weight or Natural? And I'm pitted against none other than the founder of Power Training, Gabriel, Chief Executive Alphahole, Mercer.

Is this a coincidence? I haven't heard from him in a week, not since I barged in on him working out and made an ass of myself. But it can't be a fluke of fate. Nothing about MGM says he leaves circumstances to chance. But... not even the Mighty Gabriel Mercer can have that kind of sway over Billy Westwood. Westwood is a genius, a gazillionaire, a visionary. Men like him don't owe favors to anyone and can't be strong-armed into doing anything they don't want to.

I stare at the screen, shaken by this unexpected turn of events.

I am not sure what to think.

I try to remember everything I know about Billy Westwood.

He's been one of the youngest entrepreneurs to become a

unicorn and he's the founder and CEO of Silicon Billy, the biggest and most influential venture capital firm in Silicon Valley. He founded the Billy Conference hoping to bring together the best minds of the country, but the conference soon grew into a global gathering of the brightest minds in business, law, and politics.

In his spare time, he's written a few bestselling novels. And his employees love him, adore him, really, at least according to the interviews that have appeared in the press in recent years.

But still... the coolest businessman on the planet or not, it can't be a coincidence that he put me on a panel with MGM. What connection could Billy and Gabriel have that would allow me to attend the conference?

I rack my brain, trying to remember if I've read something about the two of them together. But no. An internet search of the two names comes up equally empty.

And now I'm back to square one. I'm turning my thoughts over and over like a Rubik's cube.

I can't crack the riddle myself. I need a second opinion. I grab my phone and dial Marissa.

She picks up on the second ring. "Hey, honey, I'm heading to a meeting. I only have a few minutes."

"I've been invited to the Billy," I cut to the chase.

The shriek Marissa gives me in response prompts me to distance the phone from my ear. "Oh my gosh, Blake, you've been anointed... you're in the inner circle... you're..." She pauses. "Wait, why aren't you screaming with joy?"

"The invitations should've gone out months ago, and I only received mine today."

"Yeah, but—"

"And I'm on a panel against Gabriel Mercer."

"Oh." Marissa's tone confirms all my suspicions.

"Do you think he's the reason I've been invited?"

"It doesn't sound casual. But do you even care if Mercer is behind a last-second invitation? I mean, it's the Billy, I'd kill to go there. Your invite doesn't have a plus one on it by chance, does it?"

"No, sorry. And, yes, it matters because going to the Billy has been a dream for so long, and I don't want to be invited only as a misguided ploy in the Gabriel Mercer Show. I wanted to get there on my own merits."

"So you're not going?" My friend sounds appalled.

"Of course I'm going. I just need to find a way to make that man regret assuming squaring off with me at the most coveted business conference in the world would be a fun way to woo me."

"What's the title of the panel?"

"The Future of Fitness," I read from the conference program. "Brick and Mortar or Social Media? Heavy Weight or Natural?"

"I get the first part but why ask the second question?"

"Power Training, Gabriel's gyms," I explain, "are all about lifting heavy weights, his clientele is more beefed-up dudes wanting to build mass. While in my system, I try only to use the natural weight of the body to train and make the body lean. They probably want to explore which offer gets the better market share and maybe explore the merits of both."

Marissa chuckles. "All you have to do is show a video of him doing ballet to prove lifting heavy weights isn't the pinnacle of body-mind coordination."

I groan. "I wish I had that class on video. Unfortunately, the cameras were off and those memories will only live in my mind. I need to find another way to crush him."

Marissa stays silent for a beat. "Are you even sure you want to crush him?"

"Yeah, I have to. The way he procured this invite shows he'd be just the kind of overbearing partner I don't need in my life. He's pushing when I asked him not to. Why wouldn't I shut him down?"

I can hear the apologetic smile in Marissa's tone as she says, "Because you sort of like the guy?"

My first instinct is to deny the allegation, but there'd be no point in lying to Marissa—or to myself. "I told you I'm never going to fall for a rich boy again."

"But Justin was an idiot. It doesn't mean all rich men—"

"I won't find myself in that position again, Mari, period."

"Okay, okay. So what's the plan?"

"I'm not sure yet, but I'll make sure Gabriel thinks twice before interfering with my business again."

# 21

## GABRIEL

After the slowest two weeks of my life, I'm sitting in my father's private jet about to take off for Jackson Hole. My stomach is tied into knots, my gaze lost out the window over the wet tarmac, while my fingers drum a nervous beat on the leather seat.

Thomas tilts his head to the side, studying me from the seat across. I pretend not to notice until he talks, and I can no longer ignore him.

"If I didn't know better, I'd say you're afraid of flying. But I know only cars scare you, so it must be the other thing."

"Mind your own business, Thomas."

My brother places a hand over his chest, mock-hurt. "Is this the thanks I get for playing Cupid?"

I glare at him.

"I'm just saying, it's a five-hour flight. No chances of running into Blake while we're in the air; try to relax."

"And you should shut your trap."

"My gosh, that woman really did a number on you. What is it? I mean, sure, she's gorgeous. But you've had beautiful women before." Thomas taps his chin with a finger. "Is it the fact that she can resist you?"

"I don't need a shrink, Thomas," I snarl.

"And I'm not trying to psychoanalyze you."

I sigh, my gaze going back out the window. "I don't even know how I got into this mess."

"You fell for a mysterious woman and asked for my help."

"Which I'm never going to do again."

"Oh, tsk." Thomas shrugs innocently. "So if I knew you might have some competition at the conference, you wouldn't want me to share my intel?"

I level my brother with a stare. "What competition?"

"I might have gathered intelligence that her ex is also attending the conference."

I flex my fingers to avoid crushing the leather cushions in their grip. "Give me a name."

Thomas regards me with a bemused smirk. "I thought you didn't need my help."

"Should I remind you Dad won't be here to blow the horn if I decide to bust you up?"

Nonplussed, Thomas points at the plane's ceiling. "The fastened seatbelts sign is on. I'm sure you don't want to delay the take-off with a brawl."

As if on cue, the plane begins to move down the runway.

"I'm still waiting for that name." Menace laces my tone.

Thomas seems more amused than scared. "Did you forget Mom taught us to always say please?"

"Name. *Please*."

Thomas scoffs. "That was too easy. Love has made you soft."

My eyes widen. "Don't be ridiculous. I'm not in love. I barely know her."

Thomas studies me again, serious for once. "And yet..."

I break eye contact, staring out the window again as the plane takes off. *And yet...*

* * *

By the time we land in Jackson Hole, I've completed extensive research on Justin Trémaux, Blake's ex according to Thomas.

Disturbing fact number one, he's now head of trading at Fidelity Credit Union. And he was already working there when the bank financed my A round and blackmailed my father, explaining how Blake knew about it.

Disturbing fact number two, more of a speculation, really. But from the way Blake is so guarded about even accepting an invite to dinner, I suspect he must've pulled a serious number on her.

There's nothing public about their relationship, and my brother couldn't tell me anything more than that he has it on good authority they dated for over three years. Why the tryst ended and who ended it remain two mysteries.

Disturbing fact number three, this Justin fella looks nothing like me. If someone like him—blond, blue-eyed, clean-shaven—is Blake's type, I'm toast. I mean, the guy looks like such a cliché. I thought Blake would go for someone more interesting...

"Are you disembarking?" Thomas asks, breaking into my thoughts. "Or do you plan to sit there brooding all day?"

I hadn't even noticed the plane had stopped moving.

"I'm getting off," I mutter, shoving the laptop into my carry-on bag. Once I'm on the ground, I'm going to find out everything I can about Justin Trémaux, and then I'll decide if I should shake his hand or break his neck.

I put my shades on and exit the plane.

The sun bounces off the tall mountain peaks in the distance while Wyoming's inland valleys are lush and green even in summer. With the air so fresh it stings my lungs, I feel like I'm taking a breath for the first time in years.

I'm not used to feeling uncertain about myself, and I don't like it. I need to find out more about Blake's past, and try to understand what about me puts her on edge.

I head to the car waiting for us on the taxiway, drop my carry-on in the trunk, and claim the driver's seat. Thomas insisted on not having a driver, professing he would enjoy the private drive across the beautiful mountain scenery. But I know he's just trying to spare me the anxiety of being driven around. He might act like an ass most of the time, but our bond is unbreakable. Our loyalty for each other unwavering.

I just hope the sat-nav works and we won't get lost in the woods somewhere.

Thankfully, we don't, even though the conference is being held in a large lodge in the middle of the forest—code for the middle of nowhere. Us billionaires sure like our privacy. A security detail at the gates of the property stops us, and the armed guards let us in only after carefully checking our IDs and invites. They seemed suspicious of the fact that we were driving ourselves. I wonder what Blake will do with all her claims of not being used to the bubble wrapping. Fly commercial? Catch a ride to the hotel in an Uber?

I park the car near the main resort building, a wood-and-glass structure three stories high with large walls overlooking the valley. Inside, everything is polished to perfection. Natural light filters in from the glass walls facing the mountains. While on the wooden ones at the back, a mix of rustic and modern art gives the place a touch of contemporary mixed in with the classic mountain décor of stag antlers and sheepskins. A large stone mantle dominates the lobby. Lit even in summer, the fireplace is already surrounded by chatting billionaires enjoying a late-afternoon drink of what must be an a-thousand-dollar-a-bottle Scotch.

Thomas and I get in line to check in, and while we wait, I scan the room to investigate if Blake has already arrived. But I spot no luscious black manes in the crowd—only a blond mop of hair attached to the face of her ex-boyfriend that I recognize from online pictures. Justin is laughing with a few pals, at ease in the posh environment as if he were born to be surrounded by luxury.

For all her talk of not liking people with money, she sure has a loaded-looking ex-boyfriend. Or is that peacock the reason why she's crossed off all wealthy men? What did he do to her?

In person, Justin is possibly more attractive than on the internet—at least for a woman appreciative of a boy-band aesthetic. He has the appearance of a good boy, but something about him screams sleazeball to me.

Thomas pushes me from behind, nearly causing me to stumble.

I catch myself just in time, shoving him back. "Watch it."

"Whoa, calm down, tiger," he whispers in my ear. "On edge much?" He jerks his chin toward the reception desk. "It's our turn."

I force my expression to relax and let Thomas lead the way to the check-in desk.

We introduce ourselves to the immaculate receptionist, who verifies our reservation on her computer before handing us our conference badges and room keys.

Not that the resort really has "rooms." Each guest will be housed in private cabins scattered across the woods.

Thomas and I thank the receptionist and head out, following wooden signs to our assigned cabins. The scent of damp earth and pinecones fills my nostrils as we cross the woods. The path is flanked by tall trees and mountains in the distance, while a shallow stream runs to the edge of the forest and down to a small lake. On the ground is a blanket of soft pine needles and green grass. Birds sing among the trees while the needles crunch under our feet.

Thomas and I follow the same path until a fork in the road shows we should split.

"Meet again in half an hour?" Thomas asks.

I nod. Thirty minutes should be enough to drop off my luggage, take a quick shower, and change.

Twenty minutes later, in front of the mirror, I purposely choose not to shave. If Blake likes clean-shaven boys, I'm not the man for her. I mean, I do shave even if not regularly. But my vibe is definitely less polished than that blond fop.

Whatever, I'm giving facial hair way too much importance. I get out of the bathroom and put on a pair of dark-blue chinos, a gray Henley, and a quilted vest jacket.

Thomas is already waiting for me at the crossroads, and we make our way back through the thicket of woods.

Before we enter the lobby again, Thomas grabs my elbow, holding me back. "Be a sport and start mingling. The broody looks aren't good for business."

I roll my eyes in exasperation and head to the bar. I'm not here for business.

I greet the bartender with a nod. He's a young, dark-haired guy with a friendly smile and a nametag that reads "Tony."

"What's your poison?" Tony asks.

"Scotch. Neat."

He pours me a small glass and passes it to me. I take a sip. The smoky liquid lights a warm fire in my throat.

From my vantage point, I scan the room again. There are no official conference events planned for tonight, only a general meet and greet. But everyone knows these informal social gatherings are a priceless networking opportunity, so Blake should already be here somewhere. The schedule for the long weekend is pretty tight. Arrivals today, panels tomorrow—including mine with Blake. I didn't ask Thomas for it, but my dear brother thought it'd add flair to the courtship to pit me and Blake against each other in front of a bunch of CEOs and investors. Me, not so much. Then Saturday is the day of the scavenger hunt—a team endeavor. I've been paired with an old mammoth, but plan to change that. And Sunday, the conference closing.

I take another sweep of the rabble. Where are you, Blake? The women in the crowd are fewer and farther between than the men. Blake should be easy to spot. Still, my eyes come up empty.

I down my drink and am about to order another when my brother leans his elbows on the bar next to me, whispering out the side of his mouth, "Incoming piqued billionairette at your twelve."

I stare ahead of me at the sight of Blake marching our way like she means business, and not the romantic kind.

## 22

## GABRIEL

"Gentlemen," Blake greets us without preamble.

Her gaze is locked on me, delivering the usual jab-hook combo to the heart. She's dressed in business casual clothes. A cashmere golden brown sweater tucked into a black pencil skirt.

"Blake Avery." Thomas fans out the charm at once. "Already a legend in my family."

Her signature angry blue eyes shift from me to my brother. "The other Mercer brother, I assume."

"In the flesh." He gallantly bows at her.

Looking none the more impressed, Blake nods briefly at him and refocuses her blazing eyes on me, hissing her next brusque statement in a low, angry voice. "Are you the reason I've been invited to the conference?"

Direct like a punch. There's no way of wiggling out of answering her with either the truth or a flat-out lie.

I don't even have a drink to take a swig from to stall. Instead, I hold her gaze and say, "Yes."

Her eyes narrow to slits. "How? What do you have on Westwood to force his hand?"

Thomas takes it upon himself to answer. "Nothing shady, I promise. Westwood and I go way back. All my sage, older brother had to do was beg me for help."

"You're being plenty helpful right now, brother," I mutter between gritted teeth.

Thomas theatrically places a hand over his chest. "I live to serve."

Blake's furious gaze shifts from me to my brother twice before she asks, "Who else knows about this?"

Ah, now I'm catching her drift. "No one, I assure you."

She points a finger at both of us. "It'd better stay that way."

Thomas, who never knows when to keep quiet, says, "I'm not sure I understand." He quirks his brows in a picture of innocent bafflement. "Are you upset I got you an invitation to the most sought-after business conference in the world?"

"You bet I am."

"Why? I mean what—"

"Thomas, shut up," I interrupt before my brother can do more damage, but it's too late. Blake is already on a roll.

"I am upset"—she pauses, flaring her nostrils—"because I wanted to get here on my own merits and not as a pretty girl the all-powerful Mercer brothers are trying to woo."

Ah, hadn't thought of that. I'd just assumed she'd get mad I was meddling in her life and business—even if in a positive way.

"Hey." Thomas raises his hands defensively. "I'm not trying to woo anyone. I'm just doing my brother a favor. You know this is the first time in thirty years he's asked me for anything?"

"And now I'm going to ask again," I interject. "Please shut up, Thomas."

Thomas takes a step back. "This is getting all too touchy-feely for me. I'll leave you two happy campers to it." At the glare Blake sends his way, Thomas makes a zipper-over-mouth gesture.

"While keeping everything that trespassed between us strictly confidential."

My brother bows flippantly again, this time also touching a hand to his forehead and then twirling it toward us before he straightens up and makes a beeline for the lobby, leaving me alone with *Very* Angry Blue Eyes.

"You had no right." She goes on the offensive again the moment Thomas has gone.

I'd be scared if not for the fact she looks so cute when she's angry. Better not share that thought since I've already royally messed up and underestimated the impact my actions could have on her self-worth. I get it, I hate it too when someone pulls my strings. But she backed me into a corner, what was I supposed to do? Give up? I don't give up.

I fish for my most contrite smile. "Can you blame a man? I just wanted to see you again."

She doesn't relent or move a millimeter closer to me. "You could have just asked me."

"And you would've said no."

She takes a deep breath as if she's trying to keep from blowing up further. "As is my prerogative."

I smile dashingly. "You're just mad I found something you couldn't say no to."

Gaze of steel boring into me, she huffs. "The conference is the only thing I won't be able to say no to."

Okay, now she's starting to really touch my nerves. I take a step forward, crowding her personal space. "Don't be so sure, Blake. I'm really hard not to like."

She scoffs and crosses her arms over her chest. "I'm finding that pretty easy."

Now I go out on a limb as I lean even closer to whisper in her ear, "Are you sure about that?"

The sharp intake of breath she takes tells me she's not so immune to my charisma. I expect her to take a step back or to push me away.

Instead, she leans in even closer, dropping her hands on my shoulders and raising onto tiptoes. The movement brings the top of her lush ponytail right under my nose. Her hair smells like a warm breeze in the summer and the salt of the ocean. Even though, last time I checked, there are no oceans in Wyoming.

Her voice comes out as a low hiss, sweet as poison, tempting as sin. "I'm looking forward to our panel tomorrow." She lowers onto the soles of her feet again. "I hope you came prepared, Gabriel."

She makes eye contact as my name rolls out of her mouth like warm syrup.

I clench my fists at my sides to avoid doing something stupid like pulling her ponytail down to tilt her chin up and kiss all the nonsense out of her.

As she takes a step back, she frowns as if in surprise and looks down between her legs where a slip of silky pink fabric is slithering to the floor—a scrap of clothing that looks very much like panties.

Her eyes snap up to mine, her cheeks a delicious shade of dark pink.

Before she can move, I bend down and collect her underwear from the floor, brushing my fingertips against her ankle.

When we come back face to face, she still seems too shocked to talk.

"Are you going commando?" I tease.

That jolts her out of her stupor. "No, they must've stuck to the inside of my skirt in the dryer. Give them back."

I pocket the panties. "No."

Her blush intensifies. "Those are mine."

"And where would you put them?" I give her a mock once-over. "You have no bag or pockets."

She gives me one seething look, and without another word, she turns on her heels and storms off. And I would be mad at being ditched like that, if not for the spectacular view her swaying behind and ponytail are offering.

Too soon, she disappears from view, and I sigh. Not that I was expecting a display of eternal gratitude, but I hadn't expected this level of hostility either.

Also, I didn't particularly prepare for our panel tomorrow. The argument for lifting weights versus using body weight is one I've made a million times. I could do it in my sleep even if I'm not particularly evangelistic about it. Market research showed targeting men would bring in more revenues for my gyms. Another study confirmed most men lift weights so that's the direction I took. But now I have to defend the gospel, at least in public.

True, I've never debated the topic with Blake. And she's already shown me she can be as sly as a fox when the circumstances call for it. But what can she really do in front of a room full of people? There are no fool's errands to send me on.

Still, her veiled threat has put a sense of unease in my gut.

I turn to the barman and signal for another Scotch. I've got a feeling this won't be the only drink I'll need before the conference is over.

# 23

## BLAKE

I stomp away from MGM before I do something stupid like kick him in the shins or kiss him—both are equally possible. The cadence of his voice, strong and deep. The brazenness of his expression, the cocky manner in which he tilted his head to the side when he looked at me. Those shoulders, toned and perfect—that I can't stop picturing sweaty and bare. The muscles on those arms stretched tightly against his sleeves. The way he held himself, confident, bordering on arrogant. And the fact that he now holds a pair of my panties hostage in his pocket. It's all too much. I need to steer clear of him—starting now.

Still fuming, I cross the lobby in search of a quiet spot to regroup. My brain is whizzing with the confirmation that MGM is the only reason I got invited to the Billy. The audacity of that man. He didn't even try to deny his involvement. I curse the day I didn't keep my mouth shut with that darn reporter at *The Wall Street Journal* interview. Evan was right on all fronts. Poking the bear was a mistake. Huge miscalculation. I got distracted and dropped the ball on the Apex pitch, landing it straight into Gabriel's lap. I could've worked harder to show the CEO of Apex the upside of a strong online presence, but I didn't. What did I do instead? I became a meme. It can never happen again.

I only wish I could push MGM out of my head—that would help my focus tremendously. But no matter how hard I try, I'm having little success. As I make my way to the fireplace, I bring a hand to my neck where the trail of his warm breath has left a patch of searing, blistering skin. All I can say for myself is that I managed not to shiver and that I stood my ground while he whispered in my ear, the proximity of his lips making me conjure images of what the graze of MGM's teeth against my earlobe would feel like. It took every ounce of self-restraint I had not to tilt my head to the side, angling it upward, when he leaned in to talk to me. It's all it would've taken for us to kiss.

The phantom of his words plays in my ears. "*I'm really hard not to like.*"

What kind of presumptuous peacock says something like that? I hate him more because he can get away with it. Because it's true. The man is hard to resist. But I have to stay strong.

I need to shake MGM off and rid my nostrils of his intoxicatingly masculine scent. An amber haze of mead and whiskey—my new favorite smell. Low and warm, full and husky, laced by wooded undertones mixed with a dangerous spice. Just the memory of it makes my mouth water. Apparently, Eau De Rich Alphahole does it for me.

I hate that he can make me so worked up. Hate that I'm inexorably attracted to him. No matter what my brain says, my body has a completely different mind—one that wants to surrender control to MGM and be ravished. Oh my gosh, now I'm even thinking like a torrid romance novel. I need to get a grip. Keep my focus. I'm here for business, nothing else—definitely not pleasure.

All I have going for me at our panel tomorrow is the element of surprise, and I almost spilled the beans about my plan. I know better than to let my mouth run away with me, but MGM rattles me so easily. And the way I couldn't stop myself from touching him—what is with the man's chest and my inability to keep my hands off it?

Already for a woman in business, especially someone as young as me, it's hard to be taken seriously. I definitely shouldn't flutter my eyelashes at the first pretty billionaire who pays me attention like some schoolgirl.

To banish all sexy thoughts, I concentrate on the ugly painting over the mantle. A huge, dark hound with a fat red tongue sticking out of his mouth is lurking at the edge of a dark cave. Its menacing eyes fixated on a farmer and his daughter are so ferociously intent, I'm surprised the couple hasn't leaped off the canvas to escape the beast.

Same as I should do with my beastillionnaire. Only mine looks a thousand times more attractive than the ugly dog in the picture.

Oh my gosh, will I stop?

I'm not here to obsess over Gabriel "Can't Get His Smell Out of My Head" Mercer.

Right, maybe I should try to mingle. Networking is where most of the conference value lies. I look around and sigh. I came up here expecting the Billy to be a start-up bootcamp on steroids. A place brimming with young, like-minded entrepreneurs where I could make friendships for life like Marissa. The reality is, I'm surrounded by middle-aged, entitled, sure-to-be patriarchy-loving geezers. The idea of walking up to any of them makes my stomach churn. And the way Gabriel got me the invite is sure fueling my impostor syndrome.

Forget it. I'll just go to bed and call the next three days a total waste of my time. I don't have the energy for anything else and I'll need all my strength tomorrow. Yeah, an early bedtime isn't such a bad idea.

Gosh, I so wish Marissa were here. She'd know how to cheer me up. She'd tell a silly joke about monogrammed suits and in no time, we'd be laughing so hard we'd be crying. Or she'd suggest we went out into the woods and cursed MGM. Marissa is totally the witchy type. Just imagining what my best friend would do in this situation puts me in a better mood.

I suck in a deep breath and let it out again. I only have to survive three nights. Tomorrow, I need to be strong and get the panel behind me. Then the next day it'll be the scavenger hunt where I'm partnered up with a man I don't know but who can't be worse than MGM. And then Sunday, I'll finally go home and put all thoughts of Gabriel "Flipping Hard Not to Like" Mercer out of my head. Or I could just leave early, right after the panel. I don't even care about missing the keynote speech from Billy Westwood himself at this point.

*Nighty, nighty.* I mentally wave at the throng of fuddy-duddies crowding the lobby and head for the exit. That's when a hand clasps my elbow, stopping me before I get halfway across the atrium.

"Blake?"

I know that voice.

I close my eyes for a second before I turn around and come face to face with a man I haven't seen in three years, and the last person I wanted to see tonight—or ever again.

"Justin," I say.

## 24

### BLAKE

Justin looks the same. His handsome face hasn't changed since the last time I saw him when he broke my heart three years ago.

He still has those same boyish good looks. The tousled, dirty blond hair and ocean-blue eyes. The memory of the way he used to look at me—hot and wanting—cuts through me like a knife.

I blink. Could this possibly be a dream—a nightmare? How did I miss that he was one of the attendees?

When I first got the invitation, I checked the list of speakers and sponsors, and Justin's name didn't pop up anywhere. But as the star head of trading at Fidelity Credit Union, it makes sense he'd get an invite.

His face-of-an-angel handsomeness used to be enough to knock me off my feet. But now I'm older and wiser to the ugliness that can hide underneath such a flawless beauty—*I hope.*

I can only pray that Justin still hasn't got a firm hold on me. Please, let not all my efforts to forget him, to eradicate his existence from my memory, have been in vain.

"Long time no see," he purrs. His voice is deep, smooth, and as deceitfully kind as ever. "You look amazing," Justin says as he leans in to kiss my cheek.

The gesture is so unexpected I have to control the instinct to jerk my head back. But I have to admit I'm happily surprised when the kiss has no searing effect on my skin. It just feels a little... moist. Ah, ah. Yep. The most hated word in English vocabulary. Take that, Justin Trémaux, you no longer hold a piece of me. You are blown into oblivion, faux Angel-Boy.

I let out a relieved exhale, one I've probably been holding in for the past three years. My chest feels suddenly lighter, and the lightness moves up to my head. I'm almost dizzy for how relieved I am not to feel *less of*, or *not enough of* in his presence. He has no more power over me. He can no longer hurt me.

I study his face a second longer just to make sure there's no wayward zing of attraction left in me, and only smile to myself when all I can think about is that he doesn't have a wrinkle or pore in sight. He's probably had a facial or Botox injections or something.

"How have you been?" he asks, pretending like the last time we saw each other, he didn't totally humiliate me. Must be an attempt to melt my heart with his patented good-boy charm.

*Sorry, pal, not working anymore.*

"I'm good," I say, keeping my tone neutral. I don't want to give him the satisfaction of detecting even a hint of resentment in my words. I'm going for total indifference—the ultimate past-lover slight. "And you?"

*See? I can make polite conversation, even with the scum of the Earth.*

"I've been great," he replies, still with that aggressively charming look in his eyes. "And I've heard great things about you, too. I was so proud of you when I read you'd opened your first physical location."

Proud? Why should he be proud? He had nothing to do with my success. He almost stole my business right from under me first, then tried to sink it when he couldn't get his grubby paws on it all while successfully derailing my mental health after our breakup. That about sums up his contribution: plunging me into the darkest six months of my life where I almost lost everything, including the willingness to fight. I survived only because of my wonderful family, staff, friends, and online community who never ceased to support me even through the dark ages, the people who stayed loyal no matter what. The only thing Justin can take credit for is forcing me to toughen up.

Oblivious to my mental berating of his character, the slimebag continues with his tirade, "I should've sent flowers. And a note. I never got around to it. And I know it's terrible manners. But I was so busy."

Considering we haven't talked in precisely three years, I consider his ignoring my successes a favor.

"Thanks," I manage. I can't trust myself to say more without some of the rancor I still have for him filtering through. And I'm going for a total absence of feelings here.

But apparently, I'm not doing an excellent job of it, because the next thing I know, Justin creeps closer and puts both his hands on my shoulders.

I cringe, looking around myself in a panic, searching for a way to get his hands off me without causing a scene.

"Listen," he starts, all intense, and I do my best not to recoil. "I know I messed up. But—"

"If it isn't Justin Trémaux." We're interrupted by a towering, domineering presence stepping into our small two-person circle. "I've been dying to meet you since learning you were attending the conference." MGM sends a loaded stare my way.

Does he know Justin and I used to date?

How? Has he gone total stalker on me?

A shiver of fear slithers down my spine. Did Gabriel connect the dots that Justin is the one who told me about his father secretly financing Power Training's A round?

Is that why he's here? Or is he coming to my rescue?

And why am I so desperately hoping it's the latter? I shouldn't want Gabriel to come save me. But, gosh, if it doesn't feel good not to have to do all the fighting by myself.

Still, my head spins with exhaustion. This is all too draining. I'm no longer sure of anything. The only thing I know is that if trouble comes, wait for the other. The last thing I need if I want to maintain a shred of professionalism is for two upper-class peacocks to preen their plumage at me. But buckle up, folks, it looks like we're about to witness a cockfight.

## 25

### GABRIEL

*Twenty minutes earlier...*

After Blake stalks away from me, I quietly follow the evening from my corner at the bar. No one will bother me here and all I have to do to keep the drinks coming is raise two fingers at the barman. Suits me just fine.

From my perch on a stool, I have a perfect view of the only two people I'm interested in tonight: Justin Trémaux and Blake Avery.

Blake seems to be having a quiet meltdown by herself near the fireplace. I hope she, like me, is wishing she'd be less headstrong. That she's regretting being so stubborn in denying our attraction and the fact that we could presently be in either mine or her cabin having fun under the sheets instead of stranded in this sea of dullness.

Justin is a whole different story. The dude irks me just by looking at him. He's making brilliant conversation with ever-changing groups of top-drawer dawgs, shaking all the right hands, and apparently, kissing all the right asses.

My research showed that in his role as head of trading at Fidelity Credit Union, he has made millions by making the right deal at the right time. Most of it legal, but not without the occasional shady trade. Not exactly my cup of tea, and not my problem either. The SEC can deal with the likes of him. As long as he stays off my turf, we won't have a problem.

My eyes return to Blake. She's now studying the grotesque painting above the mantel with fascinated horror. What would I give to know what's going through that pretty, bright head of hers?

She scans the crowd next, and her face turns into an expression very much resembling the sad-faced emoji. It doesn't take a genius to surmise she, like me, has had enough of the boring-out-of-our-minds evening and would rather cut off a limb than strike up a conversation with anyone in the room—I count myself out, of course. She's just scared of what talking to me would lead to.

Blake straightens up and, with one last glare at the conference guests, she makes a beeline for the exit.

On instinct, my gaze whips back to Justin, and I catch the exact moment he spots Blake crossing the lobby.

I don't miss the way his eyes widen in surprise at seeing his ex stalking across the foyer or the lewd smile that curls his lips once his brain has processed the visual message. Teeth grinding, I watch him excuse himself from his present company and hurry after her.

I remain calm as he makes his approach. But when I see him wrap his greasy paw around Blake's elbow to keep her from leaving, my blood simmers. What the hell?

I grip my glass so hard I'm afraid it might break.

The dude doesn't know what's good for him because, next, he dares to kiss her on the cheek.

The only thing keeping me rooted to the spot and preventing me from springing into action is the look of faint disgust on Blake's face as his lips make contact with her skin.

I calm down a notch. Justin's attentions seem to fall on the unwanted, back-the-hell-off side of Blake.

*Good.*

But next, he looks at her like he's remembering how she looks naked.

*Bad.*

*Very bad.*

*Awful, really.*

I can't control the surge of jealousy and possessiveness at the thought of those two getting it on. The horrible image is now solidly planted in my head, and I can't think beyond it. Either I intervene or walk away.

I should... walk away... but then again, what's the point of going to all the effort of hauling my derriere across the country to chase after Blake only to let her ex make googly eyes at her? Also, I put her in a situation where she has to face her slimy ex; the least I can do is stick around and see if she needs help getting out.

I take another sip of my Scotch, that's not doing a thing to soothe my nerves, as they keep talking. Or rather, Justin does most of the talking. Blake seems content giving curt, one-lined replies.

Maybe she's just going to shake the pretty boy off and be gone. Getting a good night's rest to be ready to publicly humiliate me tomorrow, apparently.

But my gut clenches when he drops his hands on her shoulders and she cowers away. The Blake I know isn't scared of anything, of anyone. What does he hold over her to cause that panicked expression on her beautiful face?

That's the last drop.

This morning I wondered if when I met the dude I'd shake his hand or break his neck.

It seems it's going to be the second option.

I down the last dregs of Scotch from my glass and go crash the happy reunion.

# 26

## BLAKE

I watch Justin's expression switch from annoyed at the interruption to eager as he recognizes Gabriel "Decabillionaire" Mercer. I can practically see the dollar symbols pop behind his blue irises. How did I not notice in all the time we were together that he was a greedy, unctuous leech, hungry only for money, power, and status? Three things I couldn't help him with when we were together.

He lets go of my shoulders and shakes Gabriel's offered hand. "Gabriel Mercer," Justin says in an oily tone. "The pleasure is all mine."

From the way MGM's knuckles turn white as they shake hands, and from the slight wince on Justin's face, I don't think the meeting is going to be all that pleasurable for my ex.

"Good to meet you," MGM says diplomatically. Then, letting the now-sure-to-be-crushed hand of my ex go, he turns to me. "Blake, I've been looking for you. We should go."

Gabriel looks at me, searching my eyes with a steady gaze. I can't drop eye contact; right now, Gabriel's dark reassuring eyes are the only things keeping me sane.

Yes, Justin no longer has a hold on me, but it doesn't mean seeing him isn't transporting me back to that dark stain of misery and powerlessness in my past. Also, now I'm raging against Justin and the way he took advantage of me back then, only I can't go berserk in the lobby of a fancy resort in front of all the most important people in the country and tell my ex exactly what I think of him.

A few loaded instants pass where Gabriel and I just stare into each other's eyes until I get distracted by a vein in his neck throbbing. MGM is clenching his jaw so hard he might grind his pearly white teeth into powder if he keeps the attitude going. Guess we're sharing the same suppressed rage.

And it comforts me and scares me at the same time that a man I barely know can read me so completely, that he could see from across the lobby that I needed rescuing, that he didn't hesitate for a second to step in.

I wonder what he's thinking as he takes a step closer to me.

MGM wraps his hand around my elbow, and my gaze drops to the point of contact. I don't have to look Gabriel in the eyes to know how much he's enjoying getting to touch me. To stake his claim on me. It's a possessive move, and it should not thrill me as much as it does. But the moment his fingers close on my arm, my senses go into overdrive. My skin hums in response to his touch. I hear the blood rush in my ears. And I smell Gabriel's cologne swirling around me, making my breath lodge in my chest. That darn scent.

I should push MGM away, tell him to mind his own business. But I won't. I need someone in my corner right now. I quietly seethe as I make the admission in my head. MGM has won this round and is about to find out.

I wonder what made him take the gamble I'd let him act like an overprotective boyfriend and play along. I guess Gabriel must know about my history with Justin, and he decided the risk of being publicly rejected was worth the chance to come and liberate me from an unwanted homecoming.

And the scary truth is, I suspect having MGM's solid frame this close to me would feel good even if my sleazy ex weren't involved.

Justin's brows raise in his forehead as he flips a probably-mangled-by-Gabriel's-handshake finger between the two of us. "You two know each other?"

As he asks the question, Justin's eyes turn calculating. Should he make a pass at his now-billionaire ex? Or should he leave the field clear for the decabillionaire to stake his claim on me, score a few buddy points, and possibly open the road for ten times more money and business opportunities?

Not that I care about the outcome of his tally. But it's still somewhat depressing to watch whatever romantic impulse Justin might've had toward me get curbed in pursuit of the almighty dollar. It becomes starkly clear what Justin values more in life when my ex takes a step away from me, leaving a healthy amount of space between us. He has basically offered his belly to the alpha in submission, accepting the female as belonging to the bigger wolf.

Again, how did I waste so much time on this guy?

In response, Gabriel pulls me even more into him until our bodies are so close I can feel the heat of his skin seeping through his clothes, even if we're not properly touching.

The gesture doesn't escape Justin's shrewd gaze.

"I think I've overstayed my welcome," Justin says with a smirk. "We should get together again soon to talk," he says to Gabriel. MGM dignifies the offer with the tiniest nod. Justin turns to me next. "I'll see you around, Blake."

Before I can answer, he walks away.

I shake my head, feeling mostly sorry for myself, and drag my attention back to Gabriel. A shrug of my arm, and my elbow is mine again.

"Thank you for that," I say, adding a joke so as not to let MGM know how truly grateful I am, "oh White Knight in a Shining Rolex."

MGM's jaw relaxes as he weaponizes one of his crooked grins against me. "Jousting for your honor has been my pleasure, m'lady."

I point a finger at him. "You get a pass only because you actually did me a favor getting rid of that sleazebag."

In synchrony, we start walking toward the exit and stop on the outdoor patio just off to the left of the hotel entrance doors.

"So," MGM starts. "Is a pass all I'm going to get for defending your honor?"

I cross my arms over my chest. "Why? What would you like in return?"

"What was it ladies gave to knights before tournaments as tokens of their affection... a jewel? A handkerchief? The promise of a kiss?"

As he says the word kiss, I lose the battle not to lower my gaze to his mouth. His lips are full and luscious and supple. I imagine how soft they'd feel against my own, how perfectly they would fit with mine. I force my gaze back to his eyes—not that their dark intensity is of any help in keeping my cool. "I think kissing among unmarried couples was frowned upon in the Middle Ages."

"Good thing we live in the present, then. You should do more of that."

"More of what?"

"Living in the present."

"What's that supposed to mean?"

"That we shouldn't let our past cloud our future," MGM whispers.

There's too much insight in that simple phrase. Even glad as I am for the rescue, I'm not comfortable with how much of the real me he's seen today. The naïve young woman who could be swindled into almost anything by a pair of pretty blue eyes and a fake smile.

"I should probably go now," I say.

"Should I escort you to your cabin?"

"I can manage on my own, thanks."

"Are you sure? The woods are dark at night and—"

"Full of terrors? You've really gone medieval on me tonight. Thank you, but I'm sure I'll survive."

"Okay then. Goodnight, Blake."

The way my name rolls out of his mouth, like a tender caress, makes my heart flutter. Every. Single. Time. It sends a tingle down my spine. It makes me want to run away to my cabin and at the same time, beg him to bring me back to his and have his wicked way with me all night. But only one option is safe. And since I've no intention of experiencing a repeat of what happened with Justin, I must stay strong. Sex with MGM would be glorious, I'm positive. But it would be both a waste of time and a giant regret on my part once the endorphins dispersed.

Still, part of me yearns to let things go further. But as I'm not willing to risk my sanity on a man again, I can't let my heart—or lady parts—seize control of me. I can't give in to my feelings. MGM is too good at making them come alive.

"Yeah, you have a good night too," I mumble, stepping off the porch and heading down the dirt road in a direction at random.

I'll have time to reorient—both metaphorically and practically —once the impossible man and his stupid pleasant scent are out of sight.

\* \* \*

It turns out that reorienting myself is not that easy. Ten minutes ago, I took off from the resort almost at a run. Like a criminal fleeing the scene of a crime—that of my attraction to MGM. But even as I trudged through the dark woods trying to escape my feelings, my mind was tormented by the vivid image of MGM's chiseled jaw and oh-so-tempting, full lips. I was so distracted thinking about him that somewhere along the way, I must've taken a wrong turn off the beaten paths of the resort because now, I'm standing in the dark, struggling to find a trace of a trail with the flashlight of my phone and not having any luck.

A twig snaps behind me, and I nearly jump out of my skin.

It was probably a raccoon or some other sort of unthreatening animal. Still, my pulse jumps, and a chill runs down my spine. The only weapon I have with me would be a stiletto, and I'm not sure I could best a woodland creature with a shoe. Note to self: next time don't come into the woods wearing a skirt. One, because wayward underwear might get stuck to it and fall into the hands of an annoyingly handsome billionaire. And two, because my legs are getting scratched.

To make matters worse, a few droplets of rain start trickling down. For a second, I wonder if I should just call reception and ask for help. But if word reached MGM, or if a search party were to be assembled, I wouldn't outlive the humiliation. Plus, being the silly woman who got lost in the woods wouldn't be the best business card to present to the very important men and women gathered at the conference.

The only option is to save myself, same as always.

Black clouds obscure the moonlight, casting a shadow over the forest. But in the heightened darkness, I can at least spot a feeble light flicker in the distance about a hundred feet to my left. It must be the porch light of a cabin. If I can reach it, I can find my way back to the beaten roads and home.

A gust of wind, colder than the night, passes by and I shiver. The rain falls heavier. I'm going to be soaked soon in my clothes. Before despair can take over and I start feeling even sorrier for myself, I trudge through the thicket of vegetation toward the blinking light.

I hurry toward it, almost tripping over tree roots blocking my way.

I finally stumble out of the drenched forest in front of a cabin. The outer light is pointed straight at my face, half-blinding me. A man is comfortably nestled in one of the Adirondack chairs furnishing the patio. I can't make out his face behind the glare of the light, only take in his dark silhouette.

"Hello." I step forward. "Sorry, I got—"

The words die on my lips as I finally step out of the circle of light, and the man's features come into focus.

MGM tilts his head and smiles at me, equally infuriating and irresistible as he finishes the phrase for me. "Lost?"

Of course I tumbled right in front of *his* cabin.

## 27

BLAKE

"I'm not lost!"

"Lost or not, come away from under the rain." He beckons me to the porch.

I go to him only because I know when practical should win over petty. The moment I'm under the pergola, MGM stands up.

"You want to come inside?" he asks.

Me, him, in a cozy cabin with a king-size bed and the sounds of the rain and forest as our soundtrack? Yeah, right! Nuh-uh, not gonna happen.

I snort.

"Okay." MGM seems to understand my reluctance without a need for explanations. His lips curl in a little satisfied smirk. He knows I'm saying no only because I don't trust myself to say yes without falling into bed with him. "Let me at least get you a warm towel. You're soaked."

"I'm not soaked, it's barely a drizzle."

Gabriel stares at my feet. "The pool of water at your feet begs to disagree."

He's not wrong. Still, I stubbornly reply, "I'm just a little... humid."

"Well, let's get you less humid."

He goes inside and comes back a minute later with a giant, fluffy towel that he drapes around my shoulders as a blanket. The warmth is amazing, and I can't help but close my eyes and breathe in the scent of clean cotton and the rich sweetness of caramel, honey, and charred wood. Dang, it smells like him and it's heavenly.

My lids flutter open and I find MGM still crowding my space. Okay, maybe the paradisiac fragrance didn't come from the towel. I'm still standing so close to the source, the two mingle. MGM needs to take a step back and take his delicious smell with him.

Instead, he leans closer still as he asks, "If you're not lost, should I be glad you came to my cabin *on purpose*?"

"If I were you, I'd worry I was trying to off you in the woods, where no one could hear you scream."

"You're right." He gives in too easily. "No one would hear our screams over here... be them of pain or pleasure."

His words send a shudder through my body.

MGM's expression is dark, stormy, and fierce, but I also detect a touch of mischief in his eyes.

Gabriel's gaze shifts from my mouth to my eyes, then back again, as if he was about to test his "pleasure" theory. I take a step back and put some distance between us. "You know, when someone threatens to murder you, you should take the warning more seriously."

"Nah, I thought you were going for a public spectacle tomorrow at our panel." He removes a twig from my hair, and I have to muster all my self-control not to purr in response. Gabriel tosses the small branch to the side and continues his teasing. "Wouldn't you rather have a crowd cheer as you annihilate me?"

"You have a point."

"Tell me, Blake." He takes a step closer, reducing the distance between us yet again. "Should I wear protection?"

"Always. Didn't you listen in Sex Ed?"

"My, my." His smile turns wicked. "Cracking jokes." The jerk waggles his eyebrows. "And steamy, too. Happy to see we're making progress."

The only steam here is the one literally evaporating off my clothes under the towel. No matter that I was shivering two minutes ago. Now I'm boiling.

"Keep dreaming," I whimper, taking another step back.

The dance where I retract and he advances continues until my back hits the baluster and there's nowhere left for me to go.

MGM braces his arms on the railing on either side of me. "I'm a determined man. I have a way of not giving up until my dreams come true."

Damn velvet voice.

I swallow. I can't breathe.

"What are you doing?" I whisper; the words are quiet but they grate against my throat like a scream.

Gabriel smiles. "Nothing, just making polite conversation. Something the matter? You seem a little flustered." His voice drops lower as he adds, "Don't you like it when I flirt with you, Blake?"

I'm helpless to stop my eyes from roaming over his face, drinking in his features and details. I'm powerless to prevent my gaze from lingering on his beautiful lips, or the way my heart beats a little faster and my skin warms under the intensity of his stare. And I'm even more helpless to prevent my fingers from inching forward, itching to brush over his very tempting mouth.

I stop my hand midway, suddenly remembering myself. We both stare at it hanging awkwardly between us until MGM leans down the last few inches and cups his cheek with it.

His skin is smooth and warm under my fingers and I can't control the way my thumb brushes over his cheekbone. As I slide down to his jaw, the feel of his stubble on my palm is the most sensual thing I've ever touched. At least until Gabriel turns his face and kisses the sensitive skin of my palm.

I look at him, breathing hard, completely mesmerized. He hasn't kissed me yet, but a few more millimeters and our mouths will be touching.

I want him. I want this.

His lips lower, dangerously close to mine, and my entire body seizes up with fear so intense I drop my hand as if burned and move my face to the side, away from him.

Gabriel lowers his forehead to my temple. "Why are you resisting this? I can see you're attracted to me."

I try to concentrate on his voice and the words he's saying, but the moment his lips brush my ear, I lose all my brain cells.

"It would be a waste to deny ourselves what we both want," he continues. "And trust me, I know you want this. You're just afraid to let go. But you don't have to be afraid of me. I won't hurt you. I'm not Justin."

I freeze. He just said the only word that could sober me up in an instant. *Justin.* No matter that tonight finally confirmed I'm 100 per cent over my ex. The emotional scars he left on me will never disappear. I never want to feel that humiliated, helpless, or power-less again. And the only way to keep safe from all those things is to *not* kiss a man who could hurt me a thousand times worse than Justin ever did.

I push Gabriel backward and wiggle away from the prison of his arms. "Sorry, I can't."

MGM doesn't fight me. He lets me go without putting up a struggle. We face each other from across the patio. His face is tense, his jaw clenched. "Tell me, Blake, am I paying for another man's sins? What number did he pull on you?"

"I'm not interested in discussing my ex with you." I take the towel off my shoulders and hand it to him. "Thank you for this, but I'd better be on my way."

Gabriel takes the towel but blocks my path to the steps. "You're changing into a dry sweater first and I'm walking you to your cabin." His authoritative tone doesn't admit retorts.

"Fine," I say.

I wait for him as he goes inside and returns a minute later with one of his sweaters. He holds it up for me while also keeping the door open for me to go in and change.

"I'll wait out here," he clarifies.

Inside, I remove my sweater and put on his pullover. The thing is ridiculously large for me—I have to roll up the sleeves to fit my hands through the holes—but it's cozy and warm, and it smells like Gabriel.

Once I'm adjusted, I exit the cabin and lift my chin at him as if to ask, happy now?

MGM glares at me, signaling he's far from happy. Taut-lipped, he gestures to the porch steps as if to say, ladies first.

The rain has stopped, but the night is still on the chilly side. I precede him down the dirt trail until we reach a fork in the road.

"What's your cabin number?" MGM asks, rolling on the balls of his feet.

"Three hundred and forty-five," I reply. Then, striving to make conversation, I add, "Aren't you going to get lost?"

After the almost kiss, the atmosphere between us has become awkward.

"Don't worry, I'll spread breadcrumbs."

"I don't see any bread in your hands."

Exasperated, Gabriel shows me his phone. "I put a pin for the cabin position in the map app, I won't get lost."

"Okay."

He now uses his flashlight to illuminate the road and, after what feels like a million turns, we reach my cabin.

I pause before the steps. "Thank you for walking me home and for the sweater." I pull nervously at the fabric. "I'll return it tomorrow."

His only answer is a terse nod, but he doesn't leave right away. He stares at me with a hard look I can feel burning a hole between my shoulders even as I turn away and hop up the porch steps.

I pause at the cabin door, looking at him again. "Goodnight, I guess."

"Goodnight," he says, without moving.

He's waiting for me to get in safely, so I open the door and disappear inside, shutting it quickly behind me.

With my back turned to the door, I lean against it and take a minute to gather my thoughts. I'm torn between relief and regret that we didn't kiss.

But as I get under the covers wearing only Gabriel's sweater, regret takes over.

## 28

---

### BLAKE

The next morning, I wake up groggy and confused. I'm wrapped up in the most delicious scent of caramel and frustrated dreams. I blink and stare at the sky through the skylight window on the cabin's roof.

It feels like I've been asleep for fifteen minutes, but the sun is already rising, meaning it's time to get up.

I sit up straight, rubbing my eyes and trying to shake off the exhaustion. A knot of anxiety wrings my stomach as I remember I'll have to face Gabriel again in just a few hours at our panel. Normally, I'd go for a morning jog to get my head straight, but today I need to preserve my strength.

I pull myself onto my feet and take a quick shower. Then I order room service, feeling slightly guilty some poor server will have to trudge all the way to my cabin to deliver my breakfast. But I'm too on edge to face another chance meeting with MGM—or worse, *Justin*. With my luck, I'd bump into MGM, or his brother, or my ex in the breakfast room, and I could do with a little me time—free of testosterone-supercharged tycoons.

After breakfast, I dress in my armor of jogging leggings and a zip-up running top with long sleeves. I inspect my appearance in the mirror. I look innocuous enough. It's better when they don't see you coming.

There's a slight scratch on my left cheekbone, courtesy of my impromptu stroll into the woods of last night. I consider smoothing it over with concealer but opt not to. It'll be another battle scar to wear with pride.

In the time I have left before the panel, I take out my laptop and go over the talking points I've prepared for the showdown. I've learned them by heart, but I want to sound as natural as possible as I expose my arguments.

I'm re-reading a section of my presentation when there's a knock at the door. I know who it is before I even open it.

And there he is. The laid-back attire of running shorts, tight-fitting black long-sleeved T-shirt, and running shoes, does nothing to soften the blow of his handsomeness.

Gabriel smiles when he sees me, and skipping hello, he says, "I come in peace and bearing coffee." He lifts the two paper cups in his hands.

"What are you doing here?"

He jogs up the porch steps as if I'd invited him to stay. "Last night we left things a little..." He pauses, taking time by dropping the coffee cups on the small wooden table. "...awkward," he concludes.

I scoff. That's a way of putting it.

"But I didn't want to see you for the first time when we have to square off in a public debate."

He's so sweet I want to choke him.

"May I?" He gestures at the two Adirondack chairs on the deck.

I sigh, unable to say no. "Make yourself at home."

The boyish grin of elation I get in response is even more heart-shattering than the peace offering.

I sit in the chair opposite him, the small table in the middle creating a comfortable distance between us, and take a sip of my coffee.

My eyes widen as I taste the exact blend of cream-to-vanilla-to-sugar I like in my coffee.

My head snaps to him. "How did you know how I take my coffee?"

His eyes crinkle. "I have a very good executive assistant."

"Meaning?"

"Assistants trade favors; I guess Mila could get the information from yours."

Mental note: remember to fire Tilly the moment I get home. Of course, I won't. But she shouldn't divulge personal information so freely to my mortal enemies.

"I take it I did a good job?" MGM hides his mouth behind his cup and arches an eyebrow at me.

"It's drinkable," I lie.

MGM chuckles. "I should warn you. The more you make me work for it, the more I like you."

I blush at that but otherwise ignore the comment, which confirms my fear he's only in this for the thrill of the chase, and change the subject. I circle a finger in his direction. "Is that how you're dressing for the panel?"

"No, I'm going to change after I get back to my cabin. You?"

"I've already changed."

"Pity, you looked adorable in my sweater last night."

I give him a side-eye. "Does the teasing ever stop with you?"

"Not if I can help it."

I roll my eyes and look away.

MGM surprises me again by jumping up from his chair. "Glad

to see the air between us has cleared," he says and heads down the steps. "I'll be seeing you at the panel, then."

I watch him leave with a bemused expression on my face, fighting—*and failing*—to suppress a smile.

* * *

An hour later I'm a lot less relaxed as I enter the appointed suite for the debate. Instead of a typical meeting space, I walk into a room that looks like an English nobleman's private studio.

A little mountain-chic décor was expected given the whole vibe of the resort. But this room, with its wood-paneled walls, lustrous rugs, and iron-and-glass chandelier, is taking it to the next level.

Lush leather chairs are scattered around the small stage at the back of the room. Over there, three armchairs upholstered in the same dark-brown leather dominate the scene. The only other piece of furniture on the dais is a stylish wooden coffee table holding a tray with three glasses and a bottle of Pellegrino.

A few guests are already seated in the audience. I avoid meeting their gazes and stroll to the stage to take my seat in one of the armchairs.

MGM arrives next, the sight of him provoking the usual flutter in my treacherous heart. He takes the seat opposite me, winking.

William Westwood III, aka Billy, enters once the room is full to the brim. "Good morning, everyone." The crowd claps, most just ecstatic to find themselves in the same room with a modern-day King Midas who has learned how not to starve while still turning everything he touches into gold. "Every year at the Billy we try to tackle all kinds of business topics from a new angle, giving you a fresh perspective. And today, I'm delighted to take a deeper look at the fitness industry with Blake Avery and Gabriel Mercer."

He gestures to us, eliciting a few more claps from the audience, and then sits in the middle chair ready to mediate.

"Gabriel, Blake, two mammoths in the business who hit success from diametrical opposite business approaches. Gabriel, you attacked the real estate market aggressively from the start. A hard brick-and-mortar approach that quickly made your gyms America's favorite in every state, while keeping the man at the wheel shrouded in a cloud of mystery." Billy concludes his introduction of MGM and turns to me. "Blake, you built your online presence first, making yourself the center and heart of your brand. You now have an army of followers who are extremely loyal to you and would support whatever new endeavor you decide to embark on as the enthusiasm for your first physical location shows." He addresses his next question to the crowd. "Who has the best business approach?"

Gabriel and I discuss the merits of our respective strategies and the debate progresses on a more or less level field. For the better part of an hour, I make a point, Gabriel makes a reasonable counterpoint, I hit him back with another argument, and so on.

But when the back-and-forth lands on the advantages of heavy weight training versus natural body-weight training, Gabriel throws me the perfect assist to finally unveil the ace hidden up my sleeve.

"The only way to achieve actual strength is to use weights," Gabriel concludes. "Blake, you couldn't lift a 200-pound weight."

"Maybe I couldn't, but the real question is, even if you can lift it, how long can you keep it up?"

The crowd snickers at the question, and even MGM raises his eyebrows and smirks at the double-entendre. Poor baby, he doesn't know what's about to hit him. Before Westwood can ask his next question, I say, "Billy, I could spend all morning debating how heavy lifting is only good for short-term strength and bulging biceps, and that to achieve real endurance it is better to train with only the weight of your body..."

"But?"

"But what if I had a way to settle the dispute once and for all?"

"What do you mean?"

I stand up, lifting my arms. "I request a trial by combat!"

# 29

## GABRIEL

I watch, shocked, as Blake stands up and makes the most ridiculous request I've ever heard. I turn to Billy next, expecting him to dismiss the idea as quickly as I have, but he's staring at Blake in a sort of rapturous awe. I check the audience and find the crowd equally euphoric. They're like sharks hungry for blood.

Before I can express my chagrin, Billy asks, "What do you suggest, Blake?"

"If you were standing in a courtyard and had to challenge a friend to a test of strength, what would you propose?"

Billy shrugs. "I don't know, I'd probably bet him I could do more push-ups than him. Is that what you're suggesting?"

The impossible woman nods. "We can make it push-ups, squats, crunches... whatever my opponent chooses." She directs the sweetest, faux-innocent smile at me.

And now all heads turn my way.

"What do you say, Gabriel?"

"That this isn't an episode of *Game of Thrones*."

"Are you saying you reject the challenge?"

I stare at Blake; she's looking at me with a mischievous twinkle in her eyes. Was this her grand plan to publicly destroy me? Put me in a position to either admit defeat or make a spectacle of myself, which she must've guessed is the last thing I'd want. Well, sorry, but she was mistaken. I won't back down. Still, I try one last move to get away. "Billy, I don't think me and the lady are evenly matched."

Blake replies before Billy can, "But that's the beauty of natural body-weight training. Everyone is evenly matched by definition."

Billy turns to me. "I think she got you there, buddy."

Despite not wanting to, I nod and stand up.

"Ooooh," Westwood hollers to the crowd, standing as well. "It seems the Billy is about to have its first trial by combat."

In a matter of seconds, the armchairs and coffee table are removed from the stage, leaving only the three of us.

"What should we make it, then?" Billy asks Blake.

She gestures to me. "I'll let my opponent decide since I'm the one who challenged him."

I look at her body, for the first time clinically as opposed to appreciatively. Of course, she's toned... but how strong is she? She could out-squat me, probably also out-crunch me. But... I take in her lean arms and say, "Push-ups."

Instead of being disappointed, Blake smirks and winks at me.

I shrug off my jacket so that I'm only wearing jeans and a tight-fitting T-shirt. Blake does the same with her fleece, revealing a neon-yellow training tank top that tells me once again this challenge wasn't a spur-of-the-moment decision but a well-planned ambush.

Westwood is now acting like a showman presenting a wrestling match, riling the crowd and upping the ante.

No one is cheering louder than Thomas. I glare at him and my brother blows me a kiss, shouting, "Defend the family honor, oh brother of mine."

Billy assesses that both Blake and I are ready to go and announces, "Rules are simple. The contestants are going to do push-ups as we count; the first who stops loses." He gestures at us to get into position. "Whenever you're ready."

Blake and I drop to the floor in plank pose, and the crowd begins to chant, "One..."

By seventy, I'm a sweaty mess. I dare a side peek at Blake, who looks as fresh as a rose.

By ninety, my arms begin to burn and tremble.

By a hundred, Billy calls, "It seems all we're proving is that both training methods work great."

"How about we make it more interesting," Blake shouts.

Since the audience has stopped counting, I take a second to "rest" in plank.

Billy crouches next to her, and asks, "What do you mean?"

"We could move on to one-arm push-ups."

"Gabriel, do you agree?"

I nod. At this point, I just wish for this to be over.

"All right, it's one arm only from now on."

I lift my left arm and wait.

"One hundred and one," the assembly chorus as one. "One hundred and two."

At one hundred and three, I'm lowering into the push-up when my elbow buckles, giving way, and I all but nose-dive onto the stage floor to the general applause of the onlookers.

"And we have a victor," Billy shouts, helping Blake off the ground and raising her right arm over her head.

All I can do is watch, seated on the floor with my knees bent, trying to catch my breath.

The moment Billy lets Blake go, and the crowd disperses, she comes my way.

I expect her to gloat; instead, she offers me a hand.

I catch it, and she pulls me off the floor, friendly smacking my buttocks as we come level. "Well fought, Mercer, I was a couple of push-ups away from face-planting on the floor myself."

She tries to pull away, but I keep her hand imprisoned in mine, holding both our arms close to my chest.

"How long have you been training for this?"

At least she doesn't deny it. "Been doing a hundred push-ups every morning for the past two weeks."

"How did you know I was going to go for push-ups?"

She extricates her hand from mine and pats me on the chest. "I told you: men can be so predictable sometimes." I must scowl, because she adds, "Come on, don't be a sore loser."

"Pardon me if I'm a little salty about the public humiliation."

"Be salty all you want." She squeezes my arm. "Minerals are good for muscle recovery."

And damn me, no matter that she's just ridiculed me in front of the entire business community, all I want to do is kiss the woman.

She must read the intention in my eyes because she takes a step back. "Don't do that either." A faint flush creeps up her cheeks.

"Do what?" I ask, glad to have the upper hand again.

"Look at me like that."

"Why not?"

She sighs. "You never give up, do you? Haven't you had enough?"

"Of you? Sorry, that is a long time coming."

Her eyes narrow. "At least we agree on something."

"Really? Because last night we came pretty close."

Her flush deepens. "Last night was a mistake."

"It was no mistake for me."

"Well, for me it was."

I shake my head. "I don't believe you."

"Believe what you want. I need a shower and I'm going to go now."

Without another word, she flees off stage.

I go after her.

## 30

---

### BLAKE

My escape from MGM is cut short by his brother. The moment I get off stage, Thomas comes my way and wraps an arm around my shoulders, reserving the same treatment for Gabriel, who apparently was close on my heels. Once he has us in a gentle shoulder-lock he pulls us in, cheering, "You guys, I swear that is the most fun I've had at a business conference ever." Then he turns to me. "Blake, remind me never to make you angry." Thomas studies me for a second. "What you just did to my brother was harsh. Fair, but savage." Then he winks at me. "But it's always a pleasure to see my esteemed, older brother be subjected to a public ass kicking."

Gabriel shoves Thomas's arm off. "I always appreciate a reminder of your undying loyalty."

"As you should." Thomas fumbles in his pocket with the hand MGM just dropped. I free myself from his grip as well and regain some personal space. The younger Mercer finally finds what he was looking for—his phone—and wiggles it in Gabriel's face. "I have the whole thing on video, but, as a sign of my 'loyalty' I won't post your public humiliation on any socials."

At the mention of social media, Gabriel shoots me a panicked stare.

"Don't worry," I say. "I don't have it on video." I give Thomas a side glance. "We're not supposed to record any of the sessions or even *bring* phones to them."

"Oops." Thomas covers his mouth with a hand, his eyes twinkling mischievously. Guess the other Mercer brother is not much of a rule follower.

"And even if I did, I wouldn't post it." I tilt my head at Gabriel. "Your attempt at taking ballet would be far more entertaining, anyway."

Gabriel's eyes widen in panic again, and I smirk—gotcha. "Relax," I say. "I'm joking. I don't have that on video either and even if I did, I'd also never use it."

Thomas follows the exchange with a keen eye. "Wait, wait. Are you telling me he's mystery guy? My brother?"

I blush furiously; the only saving grace about that livestream blunder was that Gabriel hadn't seen it. (I knew he hadn't or he would've given me grief about it.) But, of course, Thomas saw it and now I've given him the missing information to connect the dots.

MGM, still in the dark, looks at his brother questioningly. "What are you talking about?"

"This!" He produces his phone with the meme of me grabbing and biting.

Gabriel's scowl deepens. "What am I supposed to be looking at?"

Smug as a pie, Thomas explains, "Her wanting to take a taste out of your delicious buns." He playfully spanks Gabriel.

Oh, gosh, I want to die.

Gabriel stares at the screen seriously for a few more seconds before he throws his head back, roaring with laughter. When his eyes meet mine again, his grin is ruthless. "If you want to get a taste, all you have to do is ask."

I'm literally dying of embarrassment and cannot talk. Thankfully, Thomas seems to always have something to say.

"So, ballet, huh?" He mercifully puts away the phone and slaps his thighs. "Ooooh, this day is getting better and better. Now I know what to put on our Christmas cards this year. Gabriello, would you prefer to wear a red or golden tutu for the photo shoot?"

"Keep being a smart-ass and you'll be wearing *no* pants to the shoot if I have to drag you there roped up in just your underwear."

Thomas pretends to ponder the threat, then shrugs. "I guess the ladies would appreciate it, and Dad would be thrilled his legacy is assured: elder son in a tutu and me in underwear bondage."

Despite not wanting to, witnessing their brotherly bantering is endearing. It shows me a less intimidating, more human, side of Gabriel, which is so distant from the arrogant dude who marched into my office that first time. Which makes him so much more endearing. Which is bad. So very dangerous. Unwise.

I step back. "Gabriel, Thomas, it's been a pleasure, but I really need to go take a shower now." I point both my thumbs over my shoulders in the general direction of the exit. "I'll see you around."

"Not so fast." Thomas takes a hold of my hand and covers it with both of his. I stare at our joined hands and am not sure what to make of it. Gabriel has a determined look on his face as he glares at his brother in a way that implies, *let her hands go or I'll whack you.*

"Blake," Thomas continues, pretending to be, or really being oblivious to the havoc his actions are making. "Please allow me to invite you to dine with us tonight."

I regain control of my limbs, freeing my hands from Thomas's grip, and frown.

"The formal dinner is tonight," he explains. "And I've put together a group of the least boring people around."

I'm about to politely refuse, when he adds, "Before you say no, imagine how excruciating it'd be to ask a table of strangers if you could join them and spend an entire dinner listening to their useless blabber."

I had actually planned to order room service again and skip the dinner altogether—lost networking opportunity be damned.

I'm about to say that when Thomas continues with the sales pitch. "If you don't want Gabriel to join us, I'll kick him off the cool kids' table if it means we can have you."

I throw my hands in the air. "Gosh, you *both* never give up."

Thomas smirks. "It's a family trait, I'm afraid."

I turn my gaze to Gabriel and his current puppy-dog-eyes expression. "He can come." I sigh. "I don't like to kick a man when he's down."

MGM frowns now, probably remembering his burning defeat.

Thomas grabs my hand again and kisses it. "You do us an honor, Miss Avery. See you at seven in the lobby."

"Seven, then," I say, still not sure how I've just agreed to have dinner with both Mercers.

Two for the price of one girl's sanity.

\* \* \*

I've only brought one dress for the evening gala and now I feel so stupid for selecting the sexy black number that was supposed to be a figurative bird-flipping at MGM in a you-can-look-but-you-can't-touch way. I would've never imagined I'd actually have to sit at a dinner table with him. Now all I can think about is the plunging neckline and how much Gabriel is going to enjoy the view. All. Night. Long.

I could check if the resort boutique has a silk shawl or something that would help me make the dress more modest.

No. There isn't enough time. And I'd be better off owning the dress rather than looking embarrassed in it.

Nothing I can do about my reckless choices now but embrace them.

*Note to future self: always have a wardrobe Plan B.*

I take a step back from the mirror and pull on a long black coat over the dress. Time to go.

When I open the door to my cabin, I find both brothers walking up my alleyway.

Double trouble.

"Good evening," I greet them. "To what do I owe the unexpected pleasure? I thought we said seven in the lobby."

Thomas pats his brother's shoulder. "Tall, dark, and grumpy here suggested you needed an escort."

I meet Gabriel's eyes. He looks so stylish in a dark coat with his hair sleeked back. The only thing I want to do right now is rake my fingers through his black locks, pull him down to me, and kiss the perfection out of him. See him come out of the kiss all tousled and confused and eager for round two.

Ehm. That was wild. Before I start to look like a total idiot, I smile and let Gabriel have this one. "I might've lost my way around the resort maze for a minute last night," I admit. "Thank you for the thoughtfulness."

MGM tilts his head as if to say, *giving in so easily?* And then his dark eyes flash as if wondering what else I could be persuaded to give in to tonight.

Thankfully, that's when Thomas theatrically offers me his elbow. "Shall we?"

I link my arm with his and follow him down the porch steps. I thought dealing with both Mercer brothers would be more difficult. But Thomas actually provides a sort of safety net, a buffer between me and MGM.

In fact, now I can link my other arm with Gabriel's without feeling self-conscious, while still being hyper aware of the man by my side who's silent, but alert and tense.

"You look well rested," I tell him, trying to start a normal-like conversation.

He tucks my arm into him tighter. "You look well elegant."

I purse my lips. Wait until I take the coat off... elegant might not be the first word that comes to mind.

"I don't know," Thomas comments. "He doesn't look all that rested to me. I bet he cried while putting on his suit jacket. Are your arms still sore, Gabriello?"

"I could punch you and find out."

Thomas makes a mock-disgusted face. "How crass to resort to violence." Then he leads us down the path, toward the resort restaurant.

"Cut it, Thomas," Gabriel orders in a menacing tone.

Undeterred by the warning, Thomas turns to me. "Gabriel is not always the easiest to deal with. He has a bit of a temper. But once you get to know him better, I promise he's a soft teddy bear underneath all that corporate crustiness."

"I can agree with the bear thing," I say, staring up at MGM furtively. "I'm not sure about the teddy part."

Thomas opens the door to the resort's vast lobby. "She has a point."

Gabriel grunts in response, further corroborating my theory.

Thomas and I share an amused look, and MGM rolls his eyes.

"Remind me never to go out with the two of you together ever again," MGM says.

I stifle a laugh as we navigate the massive, ballroom-like restaurant and meander through the many round tables until we find an empty one we can occupy for us and Thomas's other invitees to the "cool kids" dinner.

A server is at my side in a matter of seconds. "May I take your coat, miss?"

I nod, and as I shrug the coat off and hand it to the server I can't help but peak from under my lashes at MGM's reaction.

# 31

## GABRIEL

The moment Blake shrugs off her coat, revealing the long, low-cut dress underneath, the air leaves my lungs and contrasting instincts take over. I simultaneously want to rip the dress off her smooth skin to uncover the marvels underneath and put the coat back on her so that no one else will see how beautiful she is.

Blake's skin is spotless, except for the dusting of freckles on her cheekbones and nose. Her hair, straight as a knife blade tonight, shimmers the color of a night awash in starlight, the silky locks tumbling over her shoulders and inviting me to bury my hand in them. Skimming the length of her mane is a mistake as my eyes land on the low-cut V of her neckline, and I have to clench my fists at my side to fight the urge to sweep the hair off her shoulder.

I look away. My gaze travels up from her exposed cleavage to her long neck to finally meet her blazing blues.

Those eyes... they'll be the death of me.

She's looking at me, blushing. I've been caught staring like a kid surprised with his hands in the jam jar.

I'm struggling to find something remotely smart to say when Thomas pounds his fist between my shoulder blades. "If you're going to have a heart attack, brother, tell me now so I can call emergency services."

Blake smirks. "You'd better put someone else in charge of your brother's health, Thomas, since pounding his back would only save him from strangulation."

I don't have a witty comeback to hit her with. I'm still too choked up by the view.

Thomas chuckles. "Why, Miss Avery, you've accomplished the impossible and rendered my brother speechless." He pulls back her chair to help her sit. "You should come to family brunch each Sunday and spare my ears his useless blabbering."

I glare at Thomas. If I didn't owe him for bringing Blake here, I'd give his smug behind a sound kicking.

Thomas takes the seat next to Blake, and I sit on his other side. For once, I don't resent him for sitting next to her. Being too close to Blake dressed like that? I'm not completely sure I could control myself. Just looking at her is torture.

I've barely finished expressing gratitude for my brother in my head, when Thomas pretends to pick up something from the table and hands it to me. "Is this your jaw, brother? I thought you might still need it."

I swat his hand away. "Quit being a jerk."

He unfolds his napkin, places it on his legs, and turns to Blake. "Sorry, what I was trying to say is that you look dashing tonight, Blake. Killer dress. If the push-ups didn't finish the job, your apparel will do my brother in for good." He winks at her. "Call me if you need help hiding the body."

"Oh please," I say, reaching for my glass and taking a large gulp of water to clear the dryness from my throat.

Blake just smiles. "Your mom must've had a blast when you two were kids."

She's not wrong. The "horn" tradition wasn't born for no reason.

"Do you have any siblings?" Thomas asks.

"No, I'm an only child. But I consider my best friend like the older sister I never had."

"Childhood friend?" I ask.

"No, we met seven years ago at a start-up boot camp, but have been inseparable ever since. Marissa Mayer, you might have heard of her. She's COO at WeTrade."

Thomas blinks blankly.

"The low-budget, no-commissions trading app." I smack the back of his head.

Thomas shakes his head. "Sorry, my business focus is very narrow. If it doesn't have to do with steel and I don't have to know about it, I'm not interested."

"So, what are you doing at a business conference?" Blake asks.

"I'm just here for the food." He leans in closer. "And the company, of course."

Blake shakes her head, amused.

Slowly, the rest of the table fills with the other guests Thomas selected. All akin to his level of maturity, apparently. Ten minutes into the meal, the environment feels like the grown-up version of my college parties.

Blake doesn't seem to mind the lighter atmosphere, and I relax a notch and offer the occasional contribution to the free-flowing conversation. Throughout the evening, I catch Blake looking my way more than once. She's quick to look away whenever I discover her, but there's something in those furtive stares.

I guess I'll just have to poke the bear a little more to unleash whatever suppressed instincts dwell behind those pretty blues.

As the night draws to an end, Blake, Thomas, and I make our way out of the hotel together. Close to midnight, the temperature has dropped to the low forties, and the evening breeze has a bite to it.

"Shall we escort the lady back to her cabin?" Thomas asks.

"You two go ahead," I say. "There's something I need to take care of tonight."

I don't know who looks more surprised by my affirmation, Thomas or Blake. And is that a hint of disappointment in Blake's eyes? She's quick to set her features straight, but a man could hope.

Now her expression turns pouty. "I can walk myself home, thank you."

"Please," I scoff teasingly. "We both know you'd just end up on my doorstep ten minutes later, and tonight, you're even less dressed for the trek."

Blake glares while Thomas raises his brows questioningly.

Ever the tension-defuser, my brother takes her arm, and says, "Please, Blake, it's more for my protection."

"From what?"

"Raccoons. Ever since that dirtbag of my older brother set one free in my tent at summer camp, I'm terrified of them."

Blake looks at me as if she couldn't believe I have a playful side.

"Only after he had tried to lure a bear to my tent, coating the perimeter with honey," I clarify.

"But a grizzly never showed up," Thomas rebukes. "You only got a couple of bee stings while I still bear the scars of my encounter with the raccoon. He could've given me rabies."

I roll my eyes at his dramatics. "Sorry, it was the nearest animal I could get to. You should consider yourself lucky 'cause I was really looking for a bobcat."

Blake shakes her head, amused. "Oh my gosh, you two."

Thomas doesn't let her arm go. "This way, Blake. We don't

want to keep you from your beauty sleep, and we should let my brother get to whatever evil he's up to next."

I wave them off. "You'll be fine," I say. "He's all bark and no bite. Join us again for breakfast tomorrow?"

Blake huffs. "Fine. You know where to find me." To Thomas, she says, "Let's get you home safe, Rocket."

Thomas mock-shudders. "Don't joke. I couldn't even watch *Guardians of the Galaxy* with that infernal beast in it."

They both laugh as they walk down the narrow path and disappear into the night.

I take out my phone, ready to bring my next move into play.

# 32

---

## BLAKE

Thomas and I walk the first half of the trail in silence. I'm quietly hating myself for the feeling of disappointment nagging at my stupid heart that Gabriel isn't the one next to me.

Have I pulled the rope too tight? Has it finally broken, and he has tired of running after me? And isn't that exactly what I wanted?

In theory, yes.

In practice, I'm not so sure anymore.

Thomas breaks the silence as we round a bend, now leading the way down the narrow path. "I had fun tonight. Thank you for joining us, Blake."

"Thank you for having me. You saved me from a boring night discussing wealth management and portfolio performances."

He chuckles. "I take it the dinner wasn't too business-like for your taste."

"No, it felt more like a verbal beer pong session accompanied by very fancy food."

Thomas slows down a beat.

Uh-oh. I've got a hunch I'm about to see a less clownish side to this Mercer brother. "You know, I've never seen my brother make such a fool of himself to get a woman's attention." Before I can say anything, he squeezes my arm, adding, "And I was living with him through his teenage years. Boys can do really, *really* stupid things to get a girl's attention at that age."

"Like what?"

"Like the time he got stuck in a storm drain after his then-girl-friend had dropped her phone down it. He had to be airlifted out."

"Let me guess, the cheerleading captain?"

"No, the mathletes club prodigy girl." Thomas smirks. "He's always been more about the brain. But he dated a cheerleader sophomore year, got drunk on cheap beer, and jumped off a high rise into the pool below, shouting his undying love to the wind."

"Why?"

"We were summering in the Hamptons and she was in Provence. He wanted to send her the video as a love token, but then someone posted it online. Our father saw it, and he got grounded for the rest of that summer."

"Is that why he hates social media so much?"

"Could be. And I know he can be an overbearing control freak with a savior complex from time to time..."

I nod, thinking of the way Gabriel swooped in to rescue me from Justin last night.

"But I take full responsibility for that," Thomas continues.

"How come?"

"When I was fourteen, I thought it'd be a good idea to steal my dad's Ferrari and take it for a ride in the backyard of our summer house while our parents were visiting friends."

I refrain from commenting on the fact that their *summer* house had a backyard so vast they could drive a car across it. "And?"

"Gabriel tried to talk me out of it. When he couldn't, he jumped into the passenger seat, agreeing to give me a driving lesson. But of course the Ferrari wasn't exactly your typical starter car. I crashed it hard within ten minutes and passed out from the airbag whiplash."

I bring a hand to cover my mouth.

"Gabriel broke his hipbone, but he still somehow managed to get out of the car and pull me out just before the Ferrari tumbled down a ditch. He's hated not being in control ever since; he can't get into a car he's not driving without getting a panic attack, and he feels like it's his responsibility to save everyone he cares about."

I frown. "Then why does he have a driver?"

Thomas scoffs. "Ah, because he also wants to control his fear, master it." He shakes his head. "But my point is, I can see he likes you." Thomas waggles his brows. "Like, *likes* you if you catch my meaning. So, please cut him some slack if he seems a little over-bearing sometimes."

"Please, we barely know each other."

We follow the shadowed trail below a canopy of gnarled roots and branches. Nothing but the occasional owl hoot cuts through the thick blanket of silence until Thomas speaks again. "Sometimes all it takes is one moment, one night, one kiss, to know when you've found that special connection."

"Would you have me believe you're secretly a romantic?"

"Me and my brother as well."

Finally, we turn a bend, and the clearing with my cabin appears at the end. Thomas leads me to the front steps and halts, gesturing toward the door. "Here you are."

"Thanks. See you tomorrow."

"Goodnight, Blake."

"Night."

I pause on the doorstep, watching him go. His words about his brother vibrate against my soul. Making my walls shake. Threatening to tear down all my barriers.

Good thing tomorrow Gabriel and I will be separated for most of the day. I close the door and kick off my heels. I slip out of my dress and pull on Gabriel's sweater—my new favorite PJs; I know, I know I'm shooting myself in the foot here—and drop onto the bed.

I check on my phone who my partner for the scavenger hunt is. A certain Horace Hodge. What a name. The dude must've had truly mean parents. I don't know the guy by reputation, so I do a quick google search on him. Forty-five, married with two kids, a real estate mogul of the Midwest. He has salt-and-pepper hair and errs on the portly side. He seems harmless enough.

Lightning flashes outside my window, closely followed by booming thunder and rain pattering the glass. I love to sleep lulled by the sound of a storm. It's sure better than being caught unaware in the woods. Even so... would I rather be warm and safe here, or wet and cold on my way to his cabin?

*Warm and safe here. Warm and safe here*, I chant to convince myself.

I cozy up under the covers and I'm about to put my phone down when a message pops up on the screen.

FROM GABRIEL

I forgot to wish you goodnight

The explosion of butterflies in my belly seems totally dispro-portionate to the relative tameness of the message.

TO GABRIEL

Already done with your secret business?

FROM GABRIEL

Should I remind you curiosity killed the cat?

**TO GABRIEL**

So the mice are ready to play?

**FROM GABRIEL**

Unless we're the mice in this scenario, I don't think so

I feel like a mouse about to be snared in a gilded cage.

**TO GABRIEL**

I'm NOT going to banter with you

**FROM GABRIEL**

You're adorable when you use all caps

And the word you're looking for is FLIRT

**TO GABRIEL**

We're not flirting

**FROM GABRIEL**

Speak for yourself

And I was only going to say goodnight

You're the one who asked about my business

Tell the truth, you missed me on the stroll home

**TO GABRIEL**

I SO didn't

A tree branch slams against my window, making me jolt.

**TO GABRIEL**

Why did Westwood have to host the conference in the creepiest patch of woods on this Earth?

FROM GABRIEL

Don't worry, Thomas already made me do a
sweep of the premises for rabid raccoons

We're safe

Afraid of the dark?

TO GABRIEL

A little

I type, not sure why I offered that nugget of truth. That little
piece of myself.

FROM GABRIEL:

I'd offer to come spoon you, but I'm afraid the
offer would be rejected

Right?

TO GABRIEL

RIGHT!

FROM GABRIEL

If you change your mind, I'll have you know I'm an
excellent cuddler

TO GABRIEL

You're a pain in my side, that's what you are

FROM GABRIEL

I believe the right expression is "you're a thorn in
my side" while the idiom for pain is reserved for
another anatomical region

TO GABRIEL

The foot?

FROM GABRIEL

No, not the foot

> Your not-the-foot looked spectacular in that dress tonight, BTW

I can't help but smile like an idiot and do a little teasing of my own:

> TO GABRIEL
>
> I thought the selling point for that dress was the midriff portion

> FROM GABRIEL
>
> That part was just mean

> TO GABRIEL
>
> Oh?

> FROM GABRIEL
>
> You've no idea how much I itched to slide those spaghetti straps off your shoulders

I shiver under the touch of phantom hands brushing against the skin of my shoulders.

I close my eyes and hold the phone to my chest, not sure how to answer that. Until it pings again.

> FROM GABRIEL
>
> Please don't bolt like you always do whenever things get interesting

> TO GABRIEL
>
> Okay, but no more allusive talk

> FROM GABRIEL
>
> Gotcha

> What do you want to talk about, other than my desire to relieve you of your clothes?

I shake my head. I ignore the second half of the question and concentrate on the first.

> TO GABRIEL
>
> You seem quieter around Thomas, like you let him bring home all the jokes… Why?

FROM GABRIEL

> Because when I take the bait it usually ends with one of us getting a nose bleed

> To Gabriel
>
> Was your childhood happy?

FROM GABRIEL

> Very. Yours?

> TO GABRIEL
>
> Short

There… I've just given up a part of myself I've never shared with anyone before. Everybody always seems so proud of me for being the prodigy child. For starting my business when I was only sixteen. And I'm not saying I'd change anything in my life. Even if I could turn back time, I'd do everything exactly the same. Only sometimes, I wish I'd got to be a carefree teenager for a little longer. Go to senior prom as normal kids do instead of having to skip town to meet with potential investors. But I never talk about it with anyone. Not even Marissa. I'm afraid she wouldn't understand. That everyone would say giving up a few school dances for a billion-dollar company is not that big of a deal. And now I'm afraid Gabriel won't understand either.

FROM GABRIEL

> I'm sorry

He texts back instead.

FROM GABRIEL

It must've been hard to grow up that fast

He understands. The walls around my heart fill with cracks.

FROM GABRIEL

If you're into role-playing, I could dust off my old football jacket and take you to a school dance

It's as if he read my mind. How did he say the exact thing that would make me feel better without dismissing my pain?

TO GABRIEL

Should I dress like a cheerleader or a mathlete?

FROM GABRIEL

I see my brother has been running his mouth again

But you could be dressed as Cinderella's ugly stepsister and I wouldn't care

TO GABRIEL

Aww, why would you say something so viciously sweet?

FROM GABRIEL

I'm sweet, period. No vicious in the mix

And to prove it to you, I'm going to let you sleep now

Sweet dreams

TO GABRIEL

As if I'm going to sleep after those earlier texts you sent

FROM GABRIEL

I could sing you a lullaby

The next message is a voice note. I'm kind of scared as I press play. Then laugh my head off as I listen to a terrible rendition of "Rock-a-Bye Baby." I reply:

TO GABRIEL

Thank you for that

I'll listen to it whenever I'm down

Sweet dreams to you, too

I put the phone down and sigh into the void of my room, "Goodnight Gabriel 'You Surprise Me More Every Day' Mercer."

\* \* \*

When a knock sounds on my door the next morning, an unbidden smile stretches my lips. Nothing I can do to stop it. I'm still in bed, even if I should've probably gotten up a while ago.

Not caring one bit, I go to open the door, wearing only Gabriel's sweater. The happy fluttering in my chest dies down when I find Justin waiting on my porch instead of Gabriel.

In my head, a sad trombone wah-wah-wah fail sound effect goes off. Talk about lowering expectations.

I wouldn't have minded if Thomas were here, too, instead of just Gabriel. But Justin? Eek. I thought he got the message he was persona non grata the first night, given how I didn't see him all of yesterday. But apparently, his emotional intelligence is just as challenged as it used to be.

"Justin," I say, suddenly unable to smile without effort.

"You don't seem too happy to see me."

I ignore the comment. "You have a reason to be here?"

He looks taken aback by my being curt. "We never finished talking the other night after Mercer interrupted us." He lowers his sunglasses with that arrogant ease I used to find so endearing and that now only disgusts me. "I thought you two had a thing, but from the way you destroyed him yesterday at that panel, I'm pretty sure you don't."

"Why?"

"You would never humiliate your man in public like that."

Objection. I could never have that sort of gloves-off competition with a man-child with a fragile, little ego like you. One thing our panel made me realize yesterday is that Gabriel is a man who can handle a strong woman treating him like an equal.

Of course, I don't explain any of this to Justin. It'd be just wasted breath.

"Listen," I start. "Regardless of what my relationship with Gabriel is—"

"Gabriel? Aww, that sounded pretty intimate," he says with a lewd smile.

I flare my nostrils.

His smile twists, turning petty. "Oh, I see you've moved up the gold-digger ladder; aiming for the stars now, are you?"

"You're calling me a gold-digger? I remember it being the other way around."

"Relax, precious, nothing you have to offer would be worth the effort."

I'm about to yell something back, to defend myself but, no. Nope. Justin is no longer the touchstone of my self-esteem. He can do and say whatever he wants. I no longer care.

I breathe in and out slowly. I only wish he didn't have the power to still get me so angry. Justin is an insignificant speck in the universe's scale, a lower lifeform than a cockroach. But, dang, if he doesn't know how to push all the wrong buttons.

I'm about to ask him to leave, when a deep voice from behind asks, "Is there a problem here?"

I look past Justin's shoulder to see Gabriel and Thomas staring at us. Gabriel's arms are crossed over his chest and he looks positively morose. Thomas has his hands shoved in his pockets and appears *slightly* less aggressive. They look so alike as to be twins, but for the eyes.

"I'm just saying hi to my ex-girlfriend," Justin says. "As you can see, she's fine."

The men enter a staring contest, and I'm glad when Justin lowers his gaze first in defeat. He takes a step away from the Mercer brothers as if he were ready to go hide behind me.

If I weren't this mad, I'd laugh at the way Justin so easily cowered before the Mercer brothers. To be fair, both men look formidable in their dark sunglasses, black hiking get-ups, and hostile expressions.

"There's nothing wrong here," I say with a forced cheeriness I'm sure doesn't sound convincing.

Gabriel's scowl doesn't relax one-tenth of an inch.

"I didn't like the tone you were using with her," Gabriel warns Justin. Small mercy he didn't catch the ugly words accompanying the nasty tone, or no one could've saved my ex from getting punched in the face. And Gabriel from being sued for it.

Thomas comes to the rescue, unleashing one of his I-was-born-so-privileged-I-can-be-at-ease-in-any-situation smiles on the scene.

He walks up the stoop and links his arm with Justin's. "Justin, it is, right? Thomas Mercer, great to meet you. I hear you're a star in your field; you have to share a few of your tricks." Thomas nonchalantly steers my ex away from the porch.

Justin throws one last glare my way but follows the money as always.

Gabriel and I watch them go until they turn a bend. At which point, Gabriel asks me, "Are you okay?"

"Except for the fact that I was just peeved by a pathetic, whiny baby with a mean streak?" I reply. "I'm great."

He nods in understanding. "What did he want?"

"I'm not sure," I answer honestly.

"Shall we wash out the sour aftertaste of that encounter with pancakes flooded in a river of maple syrup?"

"Let me just get dressed."

Emergency passed, Gabriel's eyes roam over my body, starting at my bare legs and moving up to his sweater, the *only* thing I'm currently wearing.

He smirks. "Cute PJs."

I've been caught, but that doesn't mean I have to fess up to it. "Hey, I'm wearing your sweater only because the fabric is very soft." I rub the sleeve against my cheek as a demonstration.

His eyes twinkle. "Sure you are."

I ignore him and hurry back into the cabin to get dressed and grab my trekking backpack. I'm out again in a flash.

"How was your night?" he asks as we amble across the forest.

The soil is still damp from last night's storm. But the air is warm.

I tilt my head up to feel the heat of the sun on my skin and smile for the first time in the day. "I didn't sleep much thanks to you."

"*Moi*?" he asks, mock surprised. "I thought my lullaby would be infallible."

Now I outright laugh. "No offense, but you sounded like Scuttle, the seagull from *The Little Mermaid*."

Gabriel smirks. "I take it he was no great singer."

"No."

We reach the resort lobby and head for the buffet.

"I shouldn't have wasted my talent on you. You are an ungrateful audience."

"To the contrary, I'm very appreciative. I haven't laughed that hard in a long time."

"I wish I could've seen it." Gabriel breathes down my neck as he holds the breakfast-room door open for me.

My heart skips a beat, and I avoid answering by scooting past him into the room. I need a boatload of sugar in me before I pass out from infatuation.

The buffet is grand, offering all sorts of breakfast foods, fresh juices, and pastries. As we walk up to the self-serve station to fill our plates, I'm hyper-aware of Gabriel's powerful presence behind me.

At one point, I stop to pile mini croissants on my plate, and he bumps into me. I'm not sure if it's by accident or on purpose. But he sure takes his time backing away, leaving my back glued to his front for a few excruciatingly long and unbearably short seconds. In fact, for one of those preciously painful instants, he even places a hand on my hip to pull me back into him before he mercilessly releases me to the coldness of no body contact.

"Pardon me," he says.

I'm blushing so hard I don't dare to look back. I pile more fatty sugars on my plate and drop out of the buffet line.

Thomas waves at us from a table close to the wall-wide windows with a magnificent view of the mountains behind.

I join him and sit next to him while Gabriel takes the other free chair.

"What did you do with the scumbag?" MGM asks his brother.

"I threw the dog a million-dollar bone," Thomas proclaims as if he was talking about spare change, which in their family a million dollars probably is. "He should stay out of our way for the rest of the conference."

I roll my eyes.

"Something the matter, Blakey?" Thomas asks.

"Oh, I get a nickname, too, now?"

"You're practically part of the family. What gives?"

"The way you talk about a million dollars as if it were coffee money. You're two entitled, spoiled brats."

Unfazed, Thomas bats his lashes at me. "But we're adorable, spoiled brats, aren't we?"

"You should both go work in a mine for a month."

"You sound like our mom now." He turns to Gabriel. "Is that why you like her so much? You have mommy issues?"

"No, I like her because she has great feet." He gives me a cheeky grin, and I blush.

Thomas frowns, staring at us. "You're not really talking about feet, right?"

"Nope." Gabriel smirks and takes a ridiculously large forkful of pancakes.

Thomas shakes his head and turns to me. "Look what you did to the cruel, power-training prince of Manhattan. You've turned him into a fluffy golden retriever."

"Hey," Gabriel protests. "I'm a cat person. Worst I can do is purr."

The friendly banter proceeds throughout the rest of breakfast until, fed and caffeinated, it's time to reach our respective assigned meeting points and rendezvous with our partners for the scavenger hunt.

"Boys, it's been a pleasure like always," I say instead of goodbye. "Have a good hunt. See you tonight."

Thomas waves and heads in the opposite direction to mine. Gabriel waves as well but doesn't move.

Well...

I check the rendezvous information on my phone, orient myself, and head to the outdoor amphitheater.

"Bye," I say, awkwardly waving at MGM before I hit the road.

I sense more than hear him following me.

I turn.

Indeed, there he is.

"What are you doing?"

"I'm headed this way too," he answers with an easygoing attitude.

At every turn I take, I wait for the sound of his footsteps to abandon me. But they never do.

When I reach the amphitheater, entrance two, third row on the left, I sit on the bench and cross my arms, pouting. "Aren't you supposed to be going somewhere?"

"I'm exactly where I'm supposed to be."

I look up at him. "No. Because I'm about to meet with a certain Horace Hodge, and you're not him."

Gabriel sits next to me, eliciting too much leg bumping for my taste. "We traded spots," he reveals, grinning like a mischievous boy who just got away with stealing candy from the store.

"For the scavenger hunt?"

"Yep."

Then I understand. "Is that where you went last night?"

Gabriel nods.

Oh gosh. A full day of this. How am I going to survive a day in the woods alone with him? Images of potential make-out spots invade my mind in quick flashes: on the green grass, pressed against a tree, or even on a sunny rock.

My heart flutters—totally on board with the plan.

I am doomed.

## 33

### GABRIEL

I watch a range of emotions play on Blake's face as she processes the development, then sighs and asks me, "Do you have the first clue? My briefing said my partner would provide it."

"Just like that?" I ask. "You will not protest or try to run away?"

"I've learned when to give up around you. So the clue?"

I take out a roll of parchment and hand it to her.

Blake stares at the intentionally distressed old-looking scroll and pulls at the red ribbon keeping it folded, spreading the foil wide.

"If you can't make up your mind, I might be where you're sitting," she reads aloud. "Reach the part where I let people in, find my clue, and you will win!" She looks at me. "This is worse than I thought."

"You don't like riddles?"

"I don't see the point of this whole day. Why is Westwood making us do this?"

"Networking, team building..." With a smirk, I add, "Matchmaking?"

She blushes and looks at me. "That's all you."

"Is it working yet?"

"That's still to be seen... Wait, sitting on the fence!"

"What?"

"The clue! If you can't make up your mind, I might be where you're sitting... The fence has to be the answer!"

Okay, we're not discussing feelings yet.

"Read the next part again."

"Reach the part where I let people in, find my clue, and you will win!"

"We have to go to..."

"The gate!" we say in unison.

Blake stands up. "All right, Indiana Jones, let's go." Without waiting for me, she hops down the rows of seats of the amphitheater.

I chase her with a grin, jogging to catch up. My legs cover the distance between us in seconds.

"Trying to shake me off already?"

"I'm not holding your hand for sure."

"Come on, isn't it exciting?" I tease her as we reach the bottom of the arena. "An adventure can't be bad, right?"

After exiting the amphitheater, we take a left on the way to the resort gate.

Tied to the metal bars, another rolled-up clue waits for us.

Blake stares at it questioningly. "How many pairs are there in this treasure hunt?"

"About fifty, I think?"

"And Westwood planned individual clues for all the couples?"

"I doubt he did it himself, but his staff? Yeah, sure. Why not?"

"It seems a lot of work to keep a bunch of billionaires entertained."

I shrug. "His conference, his rules." I untie the roll of parchment from the gate and unveil the next riddle. "I have hands that move but can't hold a thing. I can sing but cannot talk, and certainly can't go for a walk. Cuckoo, find me for your next clue." I re-read it silently and ask, "Any ideas?"

"Can you read the last sentence again?" Blake asks me.

"Cuckoo, find me for your next clue." I read and look up at her.

At her fish-eating grin, I catch up that she's just messing with me.

I bark out a laugh. "You're going to pay for that later."

She smiles, pleased. "Sorry, hearing you say cuckoo was just too entertaining."

"Clock!" I say. "A clock sings cuckoo and has hands that move but can't hold stuff."

"Is there a famous clock in Jackson Hole?" she asks, already looking up the info on her phone. She turns the screen to me. "A clock tower in town." She looks down the road. "How should we get there?"

"Walk? We, contrary to the tower, can, and it's only about a mile."

She hooks her thumbs in the straps of her backpack and says, "Let's do it."

Blake sets a brisk pace and I fall into step next to her, studying her beautiful face. In the warm morning air, her cheeks are flushed and her lips are parted, giving the impression she's out of breath. Is it from walking or something else?

A million thoughts run through my head about what might happen later today if I get her to lower her walls.

"You're staring," she chides.

"Just enjoying the view." I laugh and force myself to focus on the road as we get closer to town.

It doesn't take us long to locate the clock tower. It's a tall stone-and-wood structure with a small courtyard around it.

Blake stops in its long shadow. "Do you think we have to get to the top for the next clue?"

I stare at the clock silhouetted against the blue, cloudless sky. "I'm not even sure it's open to the public. Let's circle the building first."

Blake nods, and we loop around the tower in opposite directions.

We meet again in front of a red balloon tied to a low bush and holding another clue.

I gesture to it. "I'll let you do the honors."

She frees the balloon with a teasing grin. "You're just afraid there'll be another ridiculous word for you to read aloud."

"Nope, because you're reading."

Blake sighs but unrolls the parchment all the same. "Think of a country you would go just for the SAKE of it. No, it's not yet time to eat, so don't cheat. Come meet me on Cache Street."

I stare at the map app on my phone. "Cache Street is that way."

"All right, let's go. We can figure out the riddle on the way."

As we walk down the road, Blake keeps checking the parchment to solve the riddle. "Think of a country you would go just for the SAKE of it... Sake of it..." Blake says, quietly pondering.

"Not sake, but saké! We need to find a Japanese restaurant."

We find another red balloon waiting for us tied to a street sign right in front of the restaurant.

She takes it and groans. "It's another riddle. How many of these do we have to solve?"

I raise my eyebrows. "I have no *clue*?"

"Oh, I see what you did there."

"Read on, Sherlock."

She unfolds the paper and recites, "Where does a king go to get his crown replaced? You don't have to come in. Don't look so disgraced, under the stoop I am placed." Blake sighs. "So it's definitely somewhere hateful."

"Where kings go to replace their crowns? A jeweler shop?"

"No, too obvious. Either king or crown must mean something different."

I look across the street and find where we're supposed to go. "There!" I point.

Blake turns. "A dentist studio?" She swats her forehead. "Crown replacement, oh my gosh."

Since there are no cars, we jaywalk across and, trying not to look like thieves, crawl on the ground to search under the porch steps.

We find a small, ancient wooden and leather trunk.

Blake sits on her heels, brushing a few specks of dirt off the trunk. "You think Westwood had these specially made?"

I shrug. "Let's go open it somewhere else."

We find a bench and sit in the sunlight.

"You want to open it?" Blake asks with an excited smile.

"No, you go ahead."

"I'm surprised we didn't have to search for a special key or something," she says as she undoes the clasps and then lets out a strangled curse.

"What is it?"

She hands me another ancient-looking piece of parchment. "A map."

We bend our heads close together over the chart. The typography has been embellished with mystic-looking landmarks, but it basically says we have to follow a hiking trail.

I stand up and offer Blake a hand. "Shall we see what treasures lie at the end of the road?"

She beams at me, taking my hand. "In for a penny..."

I pull her up and for a moment we are almost chest to chest.

Her pupils expand, and she takes a shaky breath, but then she steps back.

Blake clears her throat. "I just hope it's not some kind of corporate shocker like Westwood wants all of us to join a let's-get-ready-for-the-end-of-the-world cult or something."

I smirk at her wild imagination. "I highly doubt it."

I know it's not.

## 34

### BLAKE

The first half of the journey is on a concrete road leading uphill. The incline is not super steep, but still hilly enough that we have little breath left to talk. Things get worse when we enter the woods and the terrain becomes less smooth.

We walk for over an hour into the forest on a dirt path with trees and bushes on both sides, the only sound being our slow footsteps and our breathing. As the sun reaches its zenith, I'm wishing I'd brought more to drink.

Finally, we reach a clearing with a modern-rustic cottage sitting in its center.

I take in the renovated mountain cottage, the cozy blanket spread on the grass in front of the house with two picnic baskets on top of it, and turn toward MGM, seething.

"This isn't the conference scavenger hunt, is it?"

His smile is shamelessly wide. "Nope. Think of it as a scavenger first date."

"I never agreed to go on a date with you."

"Hence the need for a little stealth."

"I should turn on my heel and go right back to the resort."

"But will you?"

I stay silent for a long beat. "No."

I know the concession is enough to lose the battle, possibly the entire war, but that darn impossible man has worn out my defenses.

I drop my backpack to the ground and sit on the blanket. "But I want the record to show I'm staying only because I'm thirsty and hungry."

Gabriel shrugs off his own backpack and sits next to me, our legs touching. He opens one basket and unloads a series of culinary treats: freshly baked focaccia bread, unusual cheeses, salamis and different cured meats, heirloom tomatoes, fresh berries, crisp apples, and crunchy celery sticks, along with a potato salad.

Ooooh, and there are chocolate mini cakes.

My nose twitches with interest. I'm starving.

After he's set out everything, Gabriel looks at me and winks. "Help yourself."

My stomach growls audibly, but I don't move a muscle. "How did you even organize all this?"

"I have people."

I frown at that. "So the treasure hunt was all a sham? You already knew the solution to everything?"

"No. I just told Mila where I wanted to end and she organized the how-to-get-here part."

"Poor woman. How much of a forewarning did you give her?"

MGM smirks, gesturing at the display. "Enough, as per the perfect picnic evidence. Any other questions?"

"Yeah. Where are we and whose cottage is that?"

"That'd be mine." He tilts his head backward toward the building. "I like to come up here to relax and unplug from time to time."

"And you always have food and wine stocked?"

He grins. "Yes."

My stomach growls again and I finally pluck a focaccia sandwich from the basket. "Why did you bring me here?"

"To eat, of course."

"And what's in the other basket? Your torture instruments?"

MGM lets out a barky laugh, a rollicking, sexy sound that has my toes curling up in my boots. "No, just a few refreshments." He takes a peek in. "Fresh, organic lemonade, white wine, beers, and, of course, water. What's your poison?"

"I'll take the lemonade, thank you," I say, having a look inside the basket myself.

MGM catches my gaze and quirks an eyebrow.

"Just making sure you didn't forget to mention the spare chainsaw you keep in there."

His eyes crinkle irresistibly as he uncorks the lemonade bottle. "Nothing funny in here, I promise."

I take another bite of the sandwich and it's so delicious, I scarf it down at an undignified speed.

The rest of the food is equally heavenly. We eat in silence, watching each other the whole time. I wonder if he can tell how much of the hostility I show him is really fear.

He breaks the ice by asking, "What's your favorite food?"

"I have so many, I can't pick. You?"

"Dirty water dog with sauerkraut and mustard from the cart on fifth and fifty-ninth."

"That's oddly specific."

MGM shrugs. "I'm a very decisive man. Once I find something I like, I stick with it."

I blush. "Are we still talking food?"

"Possibly."

"Can we skip the small, get-to-know-you first date talk?"

"Oh, so it's a date?"

I roll my eyes.

"We sure can skip the small talk," Gabriel says. "I just didn't think you were ready for the big questions."

"You have big questions?"

"Sure."

"Like what?"

"What happened between you and Justin?"

I pluck a grape from the fruit bowl and stare at Gabriel while I chew on it. His brown eyes are fixed on me, open and warm, showing me he cares about my answer. He's not just asking for the sake of it.

I sigh and make a decision: I'm going to give the Mighty Gabriel Mercer the benefit of the doubt.

I tear a blade of grass from the soil and twirl it between my fingers. "We met at a business conference six years ago. I know," I add, looking at MGM, "irony of ironies. My business was still a start-up in every sense, without an impressive balance sheet to show yet and my clothing line had just launched. Justin was older than me and already knee-deep into the private wealth management loop. He's a sleazeball, I can see that now, but I was twenty when we met, and I didn't know better. I fell for him. We dated for a few years, but I never felt good enough around him."

"Why?" The question is low, apparently calm, but I can feel the quiet rage simmering underneath. If Justin were anywhere close, he'd better run.

I throw the blade of grass away and pluck another one. "He'd always tell me what to wear to his business soirees, how to talk, what to say, what not to say, in what accent, not to make it *that* obvious I was from Queens. But I was young and gullible and took all the verbal abuse and gaslighting. So when Tom Cheney financed my A round at a thirty-million valuation, and Justin proposed two weeks later..." I stare at the sky, blinking back tears. "I was so naïve, it didn't even occur to me that the timing was suspicious. I was already organizing the wedding when one night…"

Gabriel takes my hand, and I don't pull away. I finish the story while he caresses my knuckles with his thumb. "We were at a party in the city. I didn't know anyone else, but he still dropped me in the middle of this grand ballroom to go talk to one of his clients. After waiting for him for an hour, I went looking and found him in one of the private lounges with a young woman— one of those Upper East Side princesses. Technically, they weren't doing anything wrong, but they were standing too close for comfort. They didn't see me come in, so pathetic as I was, I hid behind a curtain to eavesdrop on their conversation." I take a deep breath before repeating the hateful words. "'Is it true your girl-friend went to community college because she couldn't afford a real school?' the woman asked. I stupidly expected Justin to defend me. Instead, he said, 'Where did you hear that?' He sounded embarrassed, as if he was ashamed of me. She chuckled. 'Does it matter? Why do you hang out with the trash?' At which point Justin said…" My voice breaks. I stare at the unfocused trees in front of me, my vision blurred by sour tears. "He said, 'You know what's the beauty of trash? You can throw it away at any time without remorse.' And then they kissed." I wipe a few tears with the back of my hand. "I don't know if he had cheated on me before. But that night, I went home and read the prenup that I'd blindingly signed for the first time. It basically stated that if we got divorced, I'd get nothing and he'd get 50 per cent of my company."

I look at Gabriel, expecting to find pity or even disgust in his eyes, but all I see is understanding and a reflection of my pain as if he wants to take the hurt on himself and free me from the damage it wreaked.

"That's not all," I continue. "Justin didn't appreciate me calling off the wedding and did all he could to tank my B round. I almost lost everything because of him, *twice*. So, there you have it."

Gabriel shifts on the blanket, coming to my other side where there's no half-consumed food standing between us and engulfs me in a bear hug. The Earth stops, and the ground shifts. My world becomes one of warmth and muscular arms. And Gabriel's scent burns in my chest and scorches my throat as I inhale it.

"It's okay," Gabriel says, smoothing the lines on my hand with gentle caresses. His voice, while velvety, is laced with steel. "I can make sure he never does business in the city again."

I pull back, chuckling. "Now don't go mafia boss on me. You were doing well, and Justin isn't worth an act of revenge either, he's nothing. At least now. But that's why I didn't want to get involved with another rich—"

"Cutie pie?" MGM interrupts, making me downright laugh.

I give in to an instinct I have fought with for the past two days and rake my fingers through the hair at the side of his head.

The smile dies on MGM's lips as I touch him, and his stare becomes impossibly intense again.

"Let's just say that after our first meeting, I had you pegged down as an arrogant, insolent villain."

"And now?" he asks, the words coming out of his throat in a rasp.

"And now I don't know what to do with you."

A wicked grin plays on his lips. "I might have a few suggestions."

"I'm sure you do," I say, and before I can change my mind, I pull him down to me and kiss him.

## 35

GABRIEL

The kiss takes me by surprise, but I'm not about to complain. It's mind-boggling.

The moment she presses her lips to mine, I pin her against my chest and crush her to me so she can feel every breath we're sharing. Her lips are sparkling magic, and if I had to lose a million other push-up contests to kiss them, I'd do it all over again. Just for these lips. Heck, I'd go make a fool of myself in front of the president for another taste of her mouth.

I slide a hand up Blake's back and cup her neck, drawing her closer, but taking my time teasing her mouth with delicate nips. I've waited so long for this, I'm going to make it last. I taunt and tease until neither of us can take anymore, and then I deepen the kiss until she melts in my arms and I can no longer tell where I end and she begins.

She wraps her arms around my neck and clings to me like a kite in the teeth of a raging storm.

Despite all her training, her body is soft, plush, and warm under my grip and my fingers slip into her fine strands as our mouths move intensely over each other. A soft moan escapes her lips and I can feel her heartbeat thundering against my chest.

I've had my share of beautiful women, but Blake is something else. She's smarter and sexier than all the others put together. And she's real.

I break the kiss and capture her earlobe in my mouth. Blake rewards me with little mewing sounds. I inch my hands lower and lower, caressing the sides of her body, making slow circles over her hips until I become acquainted with all her delicious curves. Then I go back to kissing her mouth. Gosh, I could spend my entire life kissing her.

Blake surprises me again by putting pressure on my chest until I yield and fall down on the blanket. Then she's on top of me.

Her ocean-blue eyes are the most beautiful things I've ever seen, and I want to drink them in and swim in them forever.

A small smile curls her lips before she bends over to kiss me again.

I catch her by the back of her head and hold her in place, her lips hovering over mine, as our gazes lock. Her face is inches away and I take a moment to inhale the sweetness of her breath before I let her have her way with me.

Blake's lips feel like they're on fire, and I'm burning in the flames.

She intensifies the kiss and I grab her hips and pull her closer, the feel of her curves under my hands driving the kiss even wilder.

She's taking over the lead and I'm not fighting it. I drop my hands from her hips and slide my fingers under the hem of her tank top, caressing her waist and sides. The smooth skin is my undoing.

I want her more than anything.

Blake pulls back from my embrace as if she's read my mind.

She sits back on her heels, and with a smile playing on her lips, she looks down at me with those eyes.

I sit up to kiss her again, as desperate as a man in the desert to drink his first sip of water. But she pushes a finger to my lips.

My eyes must plead for mercy because she answers the question I cannot speak.

"I can't keep kissing you for much longer without going... further." The way she blushes as she says this is pure torture. "And I'm not sure I'm ready yet."

She frees my mouth and trails her fingers down my jaw to my collar bone, tracing the lines of my chest with the tip of her nails.

I follow their progress, rasping, "That's not helping cool me down."

"Okay," Blake says, rolling off me. "Picture a large, hairy, wet spider crawling up your leg."

"Why?"

"It'll help you cool off."

I smile, propping myself on my elbow so I can see her. "Indeed." I know that, technically, *she* kissed *me*, but I want to make sure she's okay. "Are you—I mean, are we okay?"

"Cool as cucumbers. Just taking a breather before clothes fly off."

Her words go straight to my gut, and I can't help myself. "Does that mean flying-off clothes are on the table?"

"Not yet."

"So what's next?"

"Tell me something about yourself. Something no one knows."

"Why?"

"You're the first person I've told about Justin's words that night. Even Marissa only knows about the kiss."

Talk about setting fire to the ground under a man's feet. A wave of heat and need washes over me and ignites my blood. That she would confide in me, trust me with one of her most painful memories, makes me only want her more.

"I'm afraid I'll never get what my parents have," I say without thinking.

"And what is that?"

"The certainty that you've found your person, your soulmate. I've been in love before, but my last relationship ended a long time ago. Sometimes I think I haven't found anyone because I work too much, at other times I'm afraid it's not in the cards for me."

"Why?"

"Even with all my past girlfriends it never felt *just* right. I never had that certainty, you know?"

She mock-frowns at me. "Not even with the girl you went down a sewer grate for?"

"No, not even close." The smile dies on her lips, and before I can say something even more stupid like I've never felt the stars align *until now*, I look away at the towering mountains surrounding us.

"I have a question for you," I say.

"Oh?"

I turn to her, dead serious. "Do you like the view?" I make a cute face.

She throws a bun of bread at me. "You're despicable."

"Am I?"

"One hundred per cent." She takes in the stunning scenery around us. "But at least your taste in retreats from humanity is spot-on. This is a stunning place to escape from the real world."

"There's something else I like to do up here." I extend my hand for her to take.

"Seduce unaware women?"

"No." I smirk. "Even if I've nothing against that particular activity. Come with me. I want to show you something."

She looks past me to the house, looking half curious, half terrified.

"Don't worry, it's not the bedroom."

She tilts her head, smiling again. "No, it's not that, I was just trying to gauge how much you look like Leonardo DiCaprio in that *Titanic* scene." Now she makes a mock-sweet dude voice. "Do you trust me?" And back in her normal voice. "Is there a windy railing somewhere that you want me to use as a flying prop?"

"Now who's being despicable?"

"All right, Jack Dawson, show me what you got." She finally takes my hand and I pull her up with me.

I lace our fingers as we walk up the trail. She doesn't fight me. Maybe I should've kissed some sense into her a lot sooner.

"What's this thing you want to show me?"

"You'll see. It's not that far."

"You're pretty secretive, you know that?"

"Only to build suspense. It's a pretty impressive sight."

I lead her along the edge of the mountain. The cliff is surrounded by a ridge of rocks, and on the brink, a huge tree towers above it all.

Among the thick tree branches lies my favorite place in the whole world.

"A tree house?" Blake asks, craning her neck up to admire it.

"More of a tree office."

"I thought this was your place to forget about work."

I move closer to the ladder at the base of the tree. "Oh, I don't come here to work. But to read, reflect, and think. Whenever I have a big decision to make, I always hole up here for a few days."

Blake nods. "Are we going in?"

I point to the ladder. "Ladies first."

The structure is about ten feet above us, and we have to climb a ladder to reach it. I won't lie and say I don't enjoy the view going up.

At the top, Blake hauls herself up on the main deck and doesn't wait for me before exploring the inside of the house. It's more of a tiny meditation room with wide glass windows, a rug, and plush cushions.

Just as I pull up onto the deck, Blake comes out smiling like an overexcited kid. "This is like a dream. I want to become a pirate and come live here."

I mock frown. "Don't pirates live on a ship?"

"Not when they've accumulated enough treasure, then they need a special hideout. This is going to be mine."

When I reach the end of the oak platform, I gesture for Blake to come and stand by me.

We circle the house to the edge of the platform. The wind blows in our faces, and the view is impressive. I can make out the shapes of houses, the dark green treetops, and the dirt road along the cliff.

"It's incredible," Blake murmurs, admiring the unaltered nature. "I've never seen anything so clearly."

"You can see everything from up here." I take her hand and wrap my arm around her waist, pulling her close to my chest.

Her hair is blowing in the wind and it feels so good to hold her.

"So you *were* planning a *Titanic* move," she jokes.

"Is it working?"

"Totally."

"Correct me if I'm wrong, but wasn't the next part of the scene one of the most-watched kisses in Hollywood history?"

"If I remember correctly, he sang a little song to her first."

"You want me to serenade you?"

"Please don't," she says. "Last night's performance was

enough." She turns her neck backward to look at me. "But I'll take the kiss."

I tip my face into her blowing hair, letting the scent of her wash over me until my lips are against her ear. "How could I say no when you ask so nicely?"

Blake turns her head fully until her lips are nearly on mine. I close the gap, joining our mouths again, wrapping my arms around her from behind. We kiss like in the movie, with her head turned and tilted back, surrendering to the wind, to the emotion, to the inevitable.

Only the biting cold of the air makes us pull apart. A few clouds have sprouted and, even if it's only mid-afternoon, the temperature is dropping fast.

I still have my arms around Blake from behind and she's still staring at the scenery, one hand buried at my nape like an anchor, as she asks, "It's time to go back, isn't it?"

I go a little rigid. "Technically, we could spend the night. The house is fully stocked."

Blake doesn't reply for a long time. "Maybe next time." She turns to face me. "I'd prefer to get back to the hotel tonight."

I nod and help her back down the tree house ladder.

She skips the last few steps, jumping onto the grass, waiting for me to join her. "But could I use the bathroom before we go?"

"Sure."

I unlock the main house for her and show her inside. It's a compact space. Open-space living room with annexed kitchen and four doors, one each for bathroom, bedroom, guest bedroom, and the connected garage.

"Bathroom's that way." I point to the middle door.

As soon as she gets inside, I go back out and call Mila from the patio.

"Boss," she picks up on the first ring. "Everything going

according to—"

"Abort the next part of the plan," I interrupt. "I'm taking Blake back to the hotel."

"Oh! Things didn't work out the way you hoped?"

They went beyond my wildest expectations.

"I don't have time to talk," I say. "Cancel everything and send me a confirmation text when it's done."

I hang up and put the phone away just as Blake comes out of the house.

She hugs me from behind, asking, "Should we go back the way we came?"

"If you want, but I have a car in the garage. We can drive back down the main road, and I'll have someone bring the car back tomorrow."

"Oh! So the almost two-hour hike in the woods was just for fun?"

I flash her a fish-eating grin. "Exactly." I make a beeline for the picnic blanket, saying, "Do you mind if we clear up the picnic first? I don't want a horde of raccoons to set up camp in my front yard."

I'd usually have someone come later to clear everything up, but I need to give Mila enough time to erase the next part of the plan without leaving traces.

Blake's smile is wicked as she follows me. "Or we could wait for them to show up, capture one, and release it in Thomas's room."

I cup her face and stamp a kiss on her forehead. "I like the way you think."

I more than like her, and it almost slipped my tongue earlier.

We make a quick job of collecting everything up from the lawn, but in the house, I take my time putting everything away while Blake watches me, making ridiculous comments like, "You look very domesticated when you do the dishes."

I flip her off, and she smiles.

When I have no more pretexts to delay, I excuse myself to the bathroom to check the phone for messages. There's a single one from Mila:

FROM MILA

All clear, boss. You're good to go.

I sigh in relief. In hindsight, my plan was really stupid, reckless, a step too far. I wash my hands and exit the bathroom, ready to tell Blake I'm ready when the earth shakes and a low rumble starts in the distance, picking up intensity. The noise must come from far away, but it feels like booming thunder is cracking in our ears.

I reach Blake. "Are you okay?"

"Yes, but what was that?"

"An earthquake? I'm not sure."

We hug each other and listen as the distant rumbling continues. I look out the window and stare in horror as a whole side of the mountain across from us detaches and collapses into the valley below.

Blake has her hand over her mouth, then lowers it to ask, "Was that a landslide? You think we're safe here?"

I shake my head in an *I don't know* way. The familiar lick of panic when I'm not in control of a situation rears its head, but I squish it down, ready to take charge.

At that moment, the lights in the house flicker ominously and then die out.

We wait a few more minutes, but nothing else happens.

"Is it safe to go?" Blake reaches into her pocket for her phone, angles it a few different ways but then shakes her head. "I have no signal."

"There is none here, the Wi-Fi was on before, but without electricity that's gone too."

"So we're cut off?"

"No," I say, reaching into a cabinet for my emergency satellite phone. One thing I've learned is to always plan for the worst. Never get cut off. "Let me call emergency services to make sure."

Blake eyes it skeptically. "What is that?"

"Satellite phone."

"In case of natural disasters?"

"Or power outages." I circle a finger next to my face. "Always be prepared."

A shadow of understanding crosses her face, but I dismiss it as wishful thinking. She doesn't know about the accident. She can't understand.

I call 9-1-1.

"Nine-one-one, what's the nature of your emergency?"

I explain the situation and give the operator our position.

"Please hold," she says.

The woman comes back on the line a few minutes later and I put her on speaker. "You have somewhere to spend the night, sir?"

"Yeah, we're at my house. Why?"

"The road's blocked downstream for you. Nasty business of a landslide."

"Did someone get hurt?" I ask.

"Not that we know of, sir, the brunt of the debris fell in an uninhabited area, but traffic is going to be difficult for a few days."

"What shall we do?"

"Stay put and don't get in trouble. Roads should be cleared in a couple of days tops."

"I only have a satellite phone on me, the electricity is out."

"The damage to the electrical grid is reported as minimal. It should be a quick fix. Power should be restored within a couple of hours."

"Okay, so we're all good?"

"Yes, sir, I have registered your names and your position, so should anyone enquire about you, we'll let them know you're safe."

I hang up and look at Blake. "You mind if I give Thomas a quick call?"

"No, sure, go ahead."

Once I've checked that everything is fine with my brother—he was sleeping in his bed back at the hotel and didn't feel a thing—I hand the phone to Blake. "Anyone you want to call?"

"I'd better let Evan know I'm fine but not sure when I'll be back in New York."

Just as she's about to input the number, it vibrates with an incoming call.

"It's Mila," Blake says, offering me the phone back.

An irrational panic washes over me.

Blake must read the terror on my face because she retracts the arm she had extended to give the phone back.

"Why do you have that look on your face?"

"What look?" I try to be nonchalant.

No one's buying it.

The phone stops ringing, and Blake stares at the screen. A short vibration informs me a text message just landed there.

Her brows furrow as she reads the text, then her eyes rise to meet mine like a blue fire burning straight into my heart.

If ever there was a death glare, I'm getting one at this very moment.

I'm not sure what I expect her to do. What I don't expect, is for her to leap over the coffee table with catlike agility and, phone still clutched to her chest, lock herself into the bathroom.

I rake my hands through my hair and sink to the floor, leaning my back against the couch.

I'm a dead man.

I turn the lock to the bathroom door and, with a beating heart, call MGM's assistant back.

"Boss." She picks up at once. "Didn't expect to hear back from you so soon. I have good news and bad news; which do you want first?"

I make a sort of animal grunt that I hope she'll take as a legit MGM response.

"Chipper as ever, I see. Anyway, I'm aware I'm intruding on your romantic retreat, but I just wanted to let you know the actors we'd hired to fake a blockage on the road were clear of the landslide site and made it home safe. They hadn't even placed the tree across the street when I called them to cancel." She takes a breath. "As for your current situation, it looks like you're going to be stuck up there for a couple of days. But, on the bright side, now you get to spend the night with Blake and you didn't even have to stage a natural disaster. Mother Earth put in a good word for you. And I'm not saying I'm happy there was a major landslide, but since there were no victims—"

I've had enough.

"Mila," I interrupt. "This is Blake Avery."

"B-Blake. W-what are you doing with Gabriel's phone?" She sounds terrified.

"That doesn't matter, now, does it? I'm going to need a bit more information on that fake natural disaster thingy, though."

Mila sighs. "In his defense, it really was a great romantic gesture. You know, the hero secretly whisking away his woman to a cottage in the woods, the whole forced proximity scenario... He just wanted to have a romantic dinner with you. And the tree wasn't even a live one, just timber and a few torn branches for the scene. And he called it off anyway, so literally, nothing happened."

I ask her a few more details, and, after we hang up, I take a few deep breaths in front of the mirror. I need to be calm enough not to commit manslaughter. Breathe in, breathe out.

I nod at my angry, disappointed, already regretful reflection and come out of the bathroom.

MGM is slumped on the floor, looking up at me with a guilty expression.

"I'd called it off," is all he says.

"Oh, that's not the issue." I wanted my tone to be glacial but the words come out too high-pitched. "The problem is that at any point in the past twenty-four hours, you thought it was okay to keep me here against my will. To take the choice away from me."

"That's not how it was."

"How was it then? Explain it to me."

"Since we've met, you haven't given me a fighting chance. I only wanted you to spend an evening with me to show you I'm not a monster. That I'm just a regular guy."

I scoff. "Let me get this straight. You thought the best way to show me what a chill dude you are was to hire actors to tell us a tree had fallen down the road so that we couldn't go back to the hotel and I'd be forced to spend the night with you?"

"Not the whole night. Just dinner. They would've told us they needed a few hours to clear the road and I would've driven you to the hotel afterward. The moment you said you wanted to go back I called the whole thing off."

"When? Where was I?"

"In the bathroom."

"And in this scenario of yours, what did you expect would happen if we had dinner, that I'd be so wooed I'd *want* to spend the night?"

"No, I just wanted to talk to you. For you to get to know me."

"Oh, I'm getting there. One thing I don't get though, is why you went through all the trouble of organizing a treasure hunt? I mean, you could've just roped me up, put me in the trunk of your car, and brought me here. I've been caged in before by a man, I don't care for a repeat."

"Don't be like that."

"Like what? I'm so sorry if a guy planning to kidnap me isn't the cherry on my grand-romantic-gestures cake."

"I wasn't planning on kidnapping you!" His eyes widen as if the mere notion is inconceivable. "I was just forcing the circumstances a little like I did today with the hunt. You didn't seem to mind that."

"Because it was my choice to come! Oh my gosh." I put a hand in my hair. "I can't believe I almost fell for it. For you being a nice guy."

"I *am* a nice guy. And to answer your earlier question, I wanted to make today exciting because you said you regretted your childhood being too short and I wanted you to have fun for a day without thinking about work or anything else."

His answer threatens to shake my resolve. It is actually the sweetest thought, but I can't let myself be fooled. Not again. I'm done with liars and schemers. So instead of cooling down, I lash out. "Well, thank you for the whole *Goonies* experience, but I think I'll pass on everything else. I've been in a manipulative relationship before, I won't be gaslighted again."

His eyes widen in shock as if my words have hit him like a slap to the face. After the initial shock, I can read the deep hurt in his gaze. His shoulders slump and he looks away. "Don't worry, once we get out of here, I won't bother you anymore."

"Good."

"Good."

"Which one is my room?"

He points to the right, still not looking at me. "The bed is made, and there are clean towels in the closet. The kitchen is fully stocked if you get hungry. Let me know if you need anything else. I'll head to my room and give you space."

Without another word, he turns to the door on the left and disappears behind it, closing it with a soft, anticlimactic click.

I rush across the living room, disappearing behind my door. Eyes blurry with tears, I fling myself onto the bed and quietly cry into the pillow until all my tears are spent.

Am I overreacting?

I straighten up on the bed and notice I'm still clutching the satellite phone. Without hesitating, I call Marissa.

"Hello?" She sounds sleepy.

"Did I wake you?"

"Blake? No, but I've been up since the crack of dawn, managing a crisis, so I was about to tuck in early." Yeah, in New York they're two hours ahead. "What's up? Are you still at the Billy?"

"Not exactly." I take a deep breath and try to give her the briefest account of everything that's happened in the past few days. When I'm done, I repeat the same question to her I was asking myself, "Did I overreact?"

"Honey, no, the guy sort of threw a curve ball at you. There's no right or wrong reaction. But I don't think the situation is all black or white, either."

"What do you mean?"

"He seems to be really into you and, to be fair, he had realized his mistake and called off the whole thing."

"But isn't it a little crazy that he'd planned a fake disaster to trap me here?"

"Shall we say *overzealous*? And love makes you do the craziest things; my sister once dragged me out of bed to go stalk her then-boyfriend in the middle of the night, and she's mostly a normal person."

"How old was she at the time?"

"Twenty, but it doesn't matter. What I'm saying is, do you like Gabriel? Do you think he deserves a second chance?"

"I like him." I clutch the phone at my admission. "Maybe too much. And I don't want to wake up someday and find out I'm in a relationship with a control freak who's trying to make decisions for me."

"Then double-check he understands that and take things slow. Make sure you can really trust him before you jump into anything serious."

"Is that what you'd do if you were me? You'd just give him a free pass for a kidnapping attempt?"

"You won't like my answer."

"Why not?"

"Because I have so many responsibilities in my job, so many decisions that I have to make daily that I like when a man takes control in a relationship."

"We're not talking a Christian Grey scenario, are we?"

"Gosh, no, I didn't mean any of that domineering stuff. Just that I like to be led a little. And to me, being whisked away to a beautiful, romantic cottage in the woods by a man I like wouldn't be the worst thing."

"Even if he lied to you about the circumstances."

"He lied about the scavenger hunt as well, but I didn't hear you complain about the picnic. I find the fact that he would go to such lengths just to have dinner with you kind of romantic."

"And not controlling?"

"I don't know, he seems very respectful of your boundaries in any way that matters. Even if he'd trapped you there for a few hours, nothing would've happened that you didn't want as well." Pause. "Is the problem that you fear what you want? How much you want it? Are you taking this as your excuse to bail and run for the hills?"

My heart flutters because it knows how much it wants Gabriel, and my best friend just nailed me. Two against one, I can't win. "Gosh, I hate you. And just, FYI, I'm trapped here for the next few days. I can't go anywhere."

"So use your time as a captive of the Beast wisely. Find out if he isn't really a beautiful prince. At least he didn't *literally* imprison you."

"*Hilarious.*"

"So are you going to let him stew in the west wing all night?"

"I haven't decided yet."

"All right, hon, I'm really exhausted. No matter how much I enjoy discussing your romantic captivity, I have to sleep."

"There will come a day when you'll be having men trouble, and then it'll be my turn to laugh."

"On that prophetical note, I'm going to wish you a good night."

"Night."

The moment we hang up the lights flicker back to life.

I take it as a sort of sign. I fish my phone out of my backpack and check it for a signal. There's still none, but it asks me if I want to connect to the Wi-Fi network. I tap yes and it lets me log on without asking for a password. Guess there aren't a lot of Wi-Fi thieves around these parts.

I cradle the phone in my hands for a few more minutes before I pull up the chat with MGM and type:

To Gabriel:

I'm sorry about the Goonies comment, I didn't really mean it

Gabriel replies immediately as if he, too, already had the phone in his hands.

FROM GABRIEL

You know I'm just in the next room. You don't have to text me if you want to talk

TO GABRIEL

It's easier to have this conversation with a solid wall between us

FROM GABRIEL

Why?

TO GABRIEL

Because you unsettle me and not always in a good way

FROM GABRIEL

Hijacking a scavenger hunt for a picnic is okay, felling imaginary trees to spend more time with you is not

Got the message loud and clear

TO GABRIEL

Are YOU being snippy with ME?

FROM GABRIEL

YOU called me manipulative

TO GABRIEL

And how would you define yourself?

FROM GABRIEL

Proactive? I've always liked to make my own fortune and not sit around waiting for things to happen

To Gabriel

Yeah. I also got that message loud and clear

Anyway, I already said I was sorry

FROM GABRIEL

I thought the apology was confined to the Goonies part

TO GABRIEL

No, it included everything

FROM GABRIEL

Consider me un-snippy then

A moment of silence passes, and I doubt whether he's still there. But then:

FROM GABRIEL

You mind if I come in?

I do, but I don't want to seem churlish.

TO GABRIEL

Would it matter if I said no?

FROM GABRIEL

Now who's being snippy?

And, yes, it would matter

If you don't want to see me, I'll stay in my bed

But I'd rather have this conversation face to face

TO GABRIEL

Fine

You can come in

There are a few seconds of rustling, a gentle knock, and then he enters the room. Gabriel is a mess. He has the appearance of someone who's spent the last few hours steaming in guilt. But he still looks totally beddable as he leans on the door and says, "Hey."

"Hey," I respond, still a little rough around the edges.

"I'm sorry," he says simply.

"For what part?"

"For lying about the scavenger hunt. For dragging you off into the woods. And for freaking you out this afternoon."

"I guess I shouldn't have fought against us so much, either."

His features soften. "After hearing your story about Justin earlier, I understand better where you're coming from. Why it's so hard for you to trust a man. If I'd known, or if I'd thought for a second you'd react this way, I wouldn't have pushed things so far."

"So, um, we're clear on the no-kidnapping rule?"

"Crystal," he says and his voice is pure gravel—rough with remorse.

"Okay."

He comes into the room and sits on the edge of the bed. "But there's one thing I'm not sorry for."

I stare at him interrogatively.

"I'm not sorry that you've opened up to me. And I'm definitely not sorry that we kissed. I just hope I haven't blown all my chances for one stupid mistake."

I'd want nothing more than to throw my arms around his neck

and pull him into bed with me, but I need to be cautious. Marissa is right. We need to take things slow.

So instead of jumping him like I feel most inclined to do, I only say, "Consider yourself on probation."

The smile of pure relief, joy, and hope he rewards me with is heart-shattering. "I promise I won't screw up again."

"Don't make promises you can't keep."

"Okay. I swear I won't try to abduct you again and that if I ever were to plan a romantic weekend, I'd get your full approval first."

"Romantic weekends? Aren't you getting a little ahead of yourself?"

"Am I? After the way you kissed me this afternoon, I don't think so."

"Humbleness isn't really one of your strong suits."

Gabriel stands up. "I'm going to go now. Sweet dreams," he says with the face of someone who knows my dreams will all be about him.

He pauses on the threshold, hand on the doorknob. "I'll be in the other room in case you change your mind."

I scowl.

"Sorry, had to put that out there." He winks.

"You're a real—"

"Sweetheart."

I throw a pillow at him, but he closes the door and the stuffed projectile hits the wood and slides to the floor harmlessly.

I hear his laugh on the other side. Then silence.

Is he gone?

"Blake?" His voice comes muffled from the living room.

"Yeah?" I call.

"I'm glad you're here with me tonight, even if it's in the other room."

I keep quiet for a moment and then say, "Me, too."

The temptation to go to him is strong. But I have to resist even if it means I might have to chain myself to the bed.

I'm about to undress to get under the covers when there's a knock on the door. "Are you decent?"

"Yeah, come in."

Gabriel walks into the room. He's changed into clean sweats and is holding a plate of food in one hand and a bottle of water in the other. He places both on my nightstand, coming too close for safety.

"I made you a snack in case you got hungry." He points at the plate of sliced fruit, cheeses, and crackers, which, as appetizing as it appears, doesn't look half as delicious as the man standing before me.

"There are clean PJs in the drawer."

I look at him, saying, "That sweatshirt looks really cozy."

He smirks before pulling it off. He has a white T-shirt underneath, but the move momentarily exposes a slice of his stomach, making my mouth water.

"Literally taking the clothes off my back," he protests, still surrendering the sweatshirt.

I study him. The silky hair, the toned biceps, sexy forearms, and those let's-get-naughty eyes... mmm...

"Don't look at me like that, Blake," he whispers. "Or I'm not sure I'll be able to walk out of this room."

"Then you'd better go," I say, my voice husky.

A vein on his neck pulses, but he nods. "Goodnight."

Once he's safely out of the room, I bury my face in his sweatshirt. His amber musk immediately floods my nostrils.

Oh, gosh, I'd better go fetch those chains.

## 37

### GABRIEL

After a night spent devising ways to help Blake forgive me, I decide that being spontaneous is my best option. I hate giving up control, but if I try to micro-manage every aspect of my relationship with Blake, I risk losing her. And last night was already a too-close call. Fate has gifted me another full day with her, and I won't waste it scheming or trying to pull tricks out of the hat to make her like me. Either she does or she doesn't.

She does, I think.

I get up early, and since her door is still closed, I take dibs on the shower.

Once I'm done, I towel my hair and move into the living room still wearing a white bathrobe. Outside, the sky is a stormy-gray and a dull rain has been falling ever since I got up.

Looks like we'll have to get real cozy within these four walls today. How can I help make it more pleasant for her?

A nice thing to do would probably be to get breakfast started. Pancakes never intimidated anyone. Blake doesn't strike me as a sleep-in kind of gal, so I'd better get on it right away.

I get to work, making the batter and buttering the pan. Three half-decent pancakes later, Blake finally emerges from her room.

From across the open space living room, she takes one look at me and shakes her head. "No. Just no." She goes back into her room and slams the door.

I take the pan off the stove to make sure nothing will burn and go knock on her door. "Are you coming out?"

"No."

"Why not?"

"You're cooking."

"And what's wrong with me cooking?"

"Men behind the stove are sexy."

"Well, I'm not cooking anymore; breakfast is ready. And I can even promise I made a very poor job of it."

The door opens, and she glares at me, then her gaze lowers to my chest and the door gets slammed back in my face.

"What's wrong now?"

"Go get dressed, you're basically naked in that robe."

I stare down at myself and judge her assessment rather unfair. "I'm covered down to my knees."

"Are you at least wearing underwear?"

"Yes. What's the issue?"

"I could see chest hair."

"And what's wrong with chest hair?"

The door opens again. "Everything."

For the first time, I register what *she's* wearing: my sweatshirt, white crew socks, and nothing else. I never thought white socks could be sexy, but I stand corrected.

"You're not wearing pants," I observe.

She smiles wickedly. "I'm basically covered down to my knees. What's the issue?"

The sweatshirt she borrowed reaches just *above* her knees. I swallow hard at the hint of toned thighs on display. Then I smile wickedly. "Are you at least wearing underwear?"

She smirks, brushing past me. "Maybe." She stops halfway toward the kitchen and turns to me. "Want to check?"

I stare at the few inches of thigh visible, imagine brushing my fingertips over her skin as I drag my sweatshirt up over her waist. "I would like nothing more in the world."

The smile dies on her lips. A furious, cute blush takes over her features, and she sputters, "Okay, my bad. Let's backpedal, we're trying to cool things off—"

"I'm not trying to cool things off," I protest.

"Well, I am, so I shouldn't be bantering. Sorry, I'm a very bantery person by nature."

"I like your being bantery," I say. I allow myself one last peek at her legs and then force my gaze away to meet her sparkling eyes. "Should we eat before my already mediocre pancakes become inedible?"

"Your pancakes had better suck big time," she threatens, taking a stool at the kitchen island.

I slide the plate of pancakes on the counter and take a seat next to her. "I don't know how bad they are. Maybe add a lot of syrup?" I pass her the bottle.

Her eyes narrow, but she takes it.

Everything I say and do is a step toward either her forgiving me or her crossing me off forever, so I wait with a beating heart for her to take her first bite.

I love the way her lips purse slightly as she raises the fork to her mouth. And the way her eyes close for a second as the sugar floods her senses.

Mid-chewing, she turns to me. "These are not nearly sucky enough."

"Sorry, I'll do worse next time."

She smiles, her eyes twinkling with amusement. "Do we have coffee?"

"I hope so, I'll check." I get up and go to the coffee maker. "You want a cup?"

"Can I have the entire pot?"

I get the beans out of a cabinet and, while I measure them out, I ask, "Trouble sleeping last night?"

If her night was anything like mine, it had to be haunted by regret and conflicting desires.

"I just had a lot to process," she answers noncommittally.

"I see."

I turn on the coffee maker while Blake looks around the kitchen and then fixes her gaze out the window on the pouring rain.

"That weather won't help clear the road, will it?"

I take the coffee pot over to her, filling it with water. "And I didn't even have to do a rain dance."

She frowns at me.

"Too soon?" I ask.

"You mean to joke about the fact that you wanted to trap me here against my will? Yeah, too soon."

I wait for the coffee to be done and pour her a cup. "What do you want to do today?"

She flashes me a look.

"Oh," I say. "Naughty."

"I didn't say anything."

"But you gave me *the* look." I waggle my eyebrows.

"What look?"

"The romantic-cottage-in-the-woods, storm-raging-outside, let's-spend the-entire-day-in-bed-having-fun look."

"I most definitely did not give you *that* look." Her words might be a denial, but I can see her fighting a smile.

"That's not what your eyes are saying."

"Then take another read because you're wrong."

"Mmm..."

"Don't mmm me."

"Anything else you want me to do to you?"

Her eyes widen. "You're the worst. Make another comment along those lines and I'll spend today locked in my room."

I take a sip of coffee. "I like it when you turn into Miss Bossypants."

"Final warning, Mercer."

"Okay, okay. I'll be a good boy. Pinky swear?" I offer her my little finger.

We look at each other and burst into laughter.

Her cheeks are still flushed, and I'm glad that at least I'm not the only one affected by the innuendo. Still, I change the subject.

"If you're still hungry, I can make you more pancakes, or some eggs if you want something different."

"No, I've had enough." She gets up from her stool and brings her plate to the sink.

I watch her move around my house, transfixed by the way her hips sway in my sweatshirt. "If I have to keep my good manners, you'd better go change."

"I don't suppose you have any feminine clothes lying around?"

"No, sorry."

"Not even when you had an entrapment on the schedule?"

I tap her nose. "A sleepover was never part of the plan."

She looks at me like she's one second away from kissing the life out of me, but then her eyes shift away scared, and she changes the subject. "Am I your first guest?"

"I brought Thomas here for a week a few years ago when he was nursing a bad heartbreak, but that's it."

She frowns. "It's hard to imagine Thomas taking anything seriously."

"Yep, it was pretty scary to see him so morose."

"Afraid he'd steal the scepter of family grump?"

"Are you bantering again, Miss Sass?"

"No, nope." She gathers her hair in a ponytail and wraps a rubber band around it. "I'm going to shower."

"Want company?"

She levels me with a stare, and I raise my hands. "Just kidding. I'll get you some clean clothes to wear." As I move to my bedroom to rummage in the sportswear drawer, I mutter, "Or not wear."

"I heard that," she yells.

"What?" I make an innocent face as I come out of the bedroom and hand her the clean clothes.

She pouts. "You didn't finish all the hot water, did you? Or I might have to kill you."

"Oh, harsh. But it might be a good death, depending on how you did it. What did you have in mind?"

Blake taps my forehead with a finger. "None of the nasty stuff playing around in that head of yours, perv." She takes the clothes from me and retreats into the bathroom.

I can almost imagine the petulant expression on her face as the lock clicks into place.

I bark out a laugh. "Call me if you need help shampooing."

"I'm flipping you the bird."

"Is that an invitation to grab your finger and get naughty with it?"

"Go get dressed, Gabriel. I don't want to see any chest hair when I come out."

"As the lady commands."

In my room, I pull on a pair of gray sweatpants and a long-sleeved Henley. Then, just because I'm a jerk, I stand in front of the mirror and undo the tiny buttons at the top until just the hint of chest hair is visible underneath.

## 38

### BLAKE

I come out of the bathroom looking like a gray human larva in Gabriel's oversized clothes.

MGM, on the contrary, is dressed to break hearts in a simple gray-sweatpants-white-Henley combo. He's lounging on the couch, scrolling through his phone. But when he hears the bathroom door open, I have his undivided attention.

The look he gives me threatens to melt the larva clothes right off me and turn me into a lustful butterfly. Add his tousled hair that has dried in adorable silky curls, of which I can't forget the feel between my fingers. The cocky smile. And sexy stubble. And I'm tempted to flee to my room and spend the rest of the day locked inside for real.

I paddle through to the living room, sitting on the opposite side of the couch to him at a safe distance.

"What do you want to do all day?" I ask since the storm outside doesn't look like it's about to break.

He drops his phone on the coffee table and studies me for a second. "I believe we should talk."

"About what?"

"Anything, everything. We should get to know each other better. And when am I ever going to have you all to myself again?"

Any time he snaps his fingers, if he keeps looking at me like that.

"Should I start?" he asks.

Since I'm a little choked for words at the moment, I simply nod.

He leans forward, forearms on his knees, looking at the floor. "I want to apologize for the way I behaved yesterday."

"I already said we're okay."

"I'm not." He looks up, dark eyes searing into mine. "You're the most amazing woman I've ever met, and I won't let you slip through my fingers because I didn't try hard enough."

I scoff a little at that; if he tries any harder, where are we going to end up? Secluded on the moon?

Undeterred, Gabriel continues, "I'll just lay all my cards on the table. I want to be with you. No games. I'm not in this just for the thrill of the chase. I won't get bored the moment you give in. And I'm not hiding a sleazy temperament like your ex did."

I scoot around on the couch to face him, my heart beating at an alarmingly fast pace.

"And I'm not saying I'm perfect. I have a big personality."

I can't help but smirk at that.

"And I've been on my own most of my life, so I'm settled in my ways. But also willing to change, willing to make room for the right person."

"How can you be so sure I'm that person?"

"I don't have it in writing from Cupid himself if that's what you're asking. But I'd rather hope, and be disappointed, than never expect anything."

I smile at him. "Stop being so darn sweet."

"I can see you want this too, so why are you still resisting?"

"You're older than me, more experienced, stronger..."

He smirks. "You proved the other day that's not true."

"I don't mean physically," I clarify. "I'm scared that if we got together, I'd get lost in your aura, lose myself."

"Blake, I don't want to change you or bend you to my will. One reason I like you so much is that you can stand your ground with me. You challenge me in a good way. I respect you and admire you. I love the way you call me out—"

"Even when it's in the national press?"

"Thank goodness you did, woman, or we'd never have met."

"I don't know," I say, "What if I still say no?"

"I'll be sad." A flash of a grin. "But there's no other way I can go about this. I've told you where I stand. The next move is yours."

I cover my face with my hands and shake my head.

Gabriel scoots closer to me and rests an arm behind the couch, leaning toward me. With the other hand, he gently lowers mine, gaining eye contact again. "I assure you, Blake, you'll regret it if we don't try."

"What if I end up regretting it even more if we do?" I challenge him. "What then?"

"I can't tell you how to live your life, but unless you want to spend it alone, you're going to have to open your heart again."

A flash of lightning illuminates the room as if even the storm wanted to add more drama to the moment.

"I'm scared," I admit.

He takes me into his arms. "I know. I am, too."

I snuggle into his cozy amber warmth before looking up. "You are?"

He looks at me in such a tender way my heart explodes into confetti behind my ribcage. "Yeah, I've never felt the way I feel about you about anyone before and never had the desire to share my life with someone as I do with you. And I guess I'm just more scared of letting you go than giving you the power to destroy me."

"You sound so dramatic now. Why would I want to destroy you?"

His eyes crinkle. "I don't know, my chest hair could get on your wrong side." He brushes a kiss on my forehead. "We'll face the fear together."

"Promise?"

"I promise."

I trail my fingertips down the unbuttoned neckline of his Henley. He shivers under my touch, but as I make to move my hand lower, he imprisons it in his grip and clutches it to his heart.

"We should talk more first."

I sigh, feeling his warm breath on my exposed neck. "Why?"

"You said you wanted to take things slow."

"I say the silliest things."

His chest rumbles with laughter as he hugs me tighter. "You're right, but I'm still going to listen to you."

"Can't I at least get a kiss first?"

He caresses a strand of hair behind my ear. "Baby, if I kiss you now, I won't be able to stop."

The way the word "baby" sounds on his lips has all the hair at the back of my nape standing to attention.

"What if *I* kiss *you*?"

The corner of his mouth quirks up at that. "Same thing, I'm afraid."

"Okay." I snuggle closer and smile at him. "Now, please, tell me everything about yourself. And don't take your time."

"Ask me a question."

"Significant exes, anyone, in particular, I should know about. Your Page Six profile was a long read."

"Ah. I've dated a few women."

I have to keep a very unsexy snort in check at the adjective "few."

"But they've all been superficial relationships. Mostly short. My only long relationship was in college, but I didn't care about her enough not to move to Silicon Valley, and she didn't care about me enough to follow me. So that was it. As I told you yesterday, I've never felt that special zap of *this is forever* until..."

I push two fingers to his lips. "Don't say it. Not unless you're sure."

"How do you know when you're sure?"

"You will, I promise."

"Okay, my turn to ask you something," Gabriel says. "When you said your childhood was short, what did you mean exactly? Was it just taking on the responsibility of running a business so early on that weighted on you or something else?"

"That, and I also missed out on a lot of stuff. You know, like getting my first hangover after a rowdy house party..."

"All you're missing from your childhood is a hangover? 'Cause I promise, they're not fun."

I count off my fingers. "I also missed my senior prom, graduation ceremony, senior pranks night, or, you know, just being a kid without responsibilities or sponsors to please."

"Where were you all those nights?"

I walk my index and middle finger up his chest like a pair of fictional legs until I reach his nose and tap the point. "Mostly meeting with crusty, old investors who had only looked at the bottom line of my investor pitch and were surprised Blake Avery was a teenage girl instead of a solid dude in his thirties. Remind you of someone?" I tease.

He steals my fingers and kisses my knuckles. "Best mistake of my life. Would you change anything if you could go back?"

I shake my head. "No. You? Any big regrets?"

"Other than saying you couldn't kiss me?" He rests his forehead against mine. "None."

"Are you sure?"

"Mmm, probably also not punching Justin in the face when I had the chance."

"You and me both."

"See?" He grins. "We have more in common than you think."

"What type of man is your dad?" I ask out of the blue. I met his mom, and she seems very down to earth, and his brother is next-level laid-back. But I've always been guarded against rich people, so I can't help but wonder how Mr. Mercer senior is.

"A little stern sometimes, but fair," Gabriel says. "He would love you."

"And not wrinkle his nose I'm from Queens?"

"My mom came to this country as a Cuban immigrant with just a few dollars in her pockets. We're not snobs."

"You're half Cuban?" I ask, not sure how I never noticed.

He nuzzles my neck with his lips. "Where did you think all this raw, Latino sex appeal came from?"

"How did your parents meet?"

"She worked at a bar in Miami, my father courted her until she agreed to marry him and move to New York with him."

"Poor woman. If he's anything like you, she must've had no choice."

"They've been happily married for forty years; she isn't complaining."

"No, I say poor woman because as a consequence of her lovely marriage, she had to deal with a rascal like you for thirty-three of those forty years."

"In that case, she'll be happy to know you'll take care of that from now on."

"Will I?"

"I thought that was the deal?"

"Okay, but no rabid raccoons, or I'll call it quits. Anything else you want to know?"

"Yeah." He makes the puppy dog eyes.

"Shoot."

"Can I drive the Aston Martin when we get back to the city?"

I throw my head back, laughing. "I'm not sure we're *that* serious."

His outraged face is priceless. "That, Miss Sass, I'm afraid, has earned you a visit from the tickle monster."

"No," I shriek. "Not the tickle monster."

I try to get away, but Gabriel is faster. He grabs me at the waist and traps me underneath him while mercilessly tickling my sides.

"Stop," I wail, laughing. "Please."

He does, but I'm not sure if I'm better off.

We stare into each other's eyes for a long time until I pull him down to me.

The time for words is over.

# 39

## BLAKE

Gabriel's eyes flutter closed as he lowers his head. Then his lips, full and warm, press against mine, and I melt into the kiss.

The spicy smell of Gabriel's cologne fills my nostrils. I can feel my pulse in my ears. The roaring of blood flow in my head.

My fingers dig into his strong shoulders. The scrape of his stubble on my skin is electrifying. I graze his bottom lip with my teeth, wanting more. His lips already a drug.

He draws back and grins down at me. "This is your attempt at a slow burn, huh?" he teases.

"Hush," I say, and press my lips to his again.

He rests his forehead against mine. "I want the record to show I did my best to resist you."

I nod. "Duly noted. Now shut up and kiss me."

He brings his head back up and stares at me with those penetrating dark eyes. A wolfish smile spreads on his lips. "As the lady commands." He drops a soft kiss on my jaw, then lower. "But I'm still going to take my time."

I have already lost the ability to form coherent thoughts, so I simply mmm-hmm my agreement.

"You're so beautiful," he says, worshipping with his lips every inch of my face and neck.

I love the feel of his mouth on my skin. Our bodies touch and press against each other as we kiss.

His lips trail from my neck to my ear, then along my jawline. My skin tingles under his mouth. I want more. His hands are planted firmly on my waist, so I shift mine between our bodies and roam them over the curve of his back.

His lips make their way back to my mouth, and he kisses me again. Harder than before. More demanding. The kiss deepens, becoming a sensual exploration. He tastes like maple syrup, with a hint of coffee. Enveloping me in pure bliss.

I moan at the taste of him, and my body arches against his. He pulls back momentarily and looks deep into my eyes.

"Do you want this?" he asks.

"Give me another word for yes, and I'll use it."

"Because I don't want you to feel pressured," he adds, his hands still holding me possessively at the small of my back.

With my last sentient abilities, I cup his cheek. "I want this. I've wanted it for a long time. I'm sure."

His features explode with relief, joy, and predatory instinct.

Am I making a mistake?

It doesn't feel like one.

I push the doubts away; all I can concentrate on now is the feel of his skin against mine. I run my hands through his hair and pull him back to me, pressing my lips to his.

I kiss him hungrily, and I don't stop until he matches my intensity.

He takes a breath. "I've wanted to do this from the moment our eyes met in your office." He runs his thumb across my bottom lip. "Even when I thought you were too young for me."

"Ooooh, kinky," I joke. "Should I call you Daddy?"

"I'm serious Blake." A sweet, soft smile covers his face. "I'm so happy."

He kisses me again, while his fingers slip under the hem of my shirt. Contact with his warm skin sends sparks down my spine. His hands roam my bare back, and the soft touch of his fingertips sends chills over me. His lips move to my collarbone, and I arch my back, sucking in a sharp breath when his fingertips graze over my sides as he pulls my sweatshirt over my head. His deft fingers move slowly and deliberately as they liberate me from my larva status.

The sweatpants go next, and I return the favor, liberating him from his excess of clothes.

Gosh, he's beautiful. Sculpted-like-a-marble-Greek-god-statue handsome.

His pecs are toned and firm, the dark hair on his chest leading the way to the sculpted V-line of his stomach.

I lean forward and press small kisses over the contours of his abs, marveling at their perfect symmetry.

"Blake," he says, his voice thick with desire. "You're amazing."

I pull back and look at him, but his eyes are closed. He's kneeling before me, and he's the picture of perfection. Beautiful. I get on my knees as well, and put my hands on his chest, running them over his entire torso, his arms, whatever I can reach of his back. His skin feels firm, and smooth like polished marble. His muscles twitch under my touch.

Gabriel's eyes fly open, smoldering as he glances at my hands, now lying useless at my side.

"What are you thinking about?" he whispers.

"How beautiful you are."

"Right back at you, baby."

I grin at his eagerness and then push him back to the couch.

"My turn to explore."

I crawl over his body, kissing my way from his earlobe to his collarbone. The expedition is cut short when Gabriel lets out an animal growl and flips me underneath him. The last of our garments are quickly removed and when there are no more barriers between us, leaving our souls as bare as our bodies, Gabriel looks down at me, a hurricane a thousand times stronger than the storm outside raging in his eyes.

"I love you, baby," he whispers. "I'm sure."

The world splits, lightning cracks outside the window, and I give up my entire being as we make love for the first time.

## 40

### GABRIEL

Both spent, we lie in each other's arms for a long time. I throw a blanket over us and cradle Blake close to me, stroking her back, and kissing her hair, still not able to believe what a lucky son of a gun I am.

I must doze off because suddenly I'm not in the safety of the cottage but I'm standing on the grass holding my unconscious brother, unable to move. "Thomas." I try to wake him. "Thomas."

Blake stirs on top of me. "Hey?"

My eyes flutter open and I find her peering down at me with a concerned look. "Were you dreaming about the accident?"

I frown. How does she know?

"Thomas told me about it," she responds to my unspoken question. "Says it's why you turned into such a control freak with a savior complex." I grimace at that. "You want to tell me about it?"

I try never to voluntarily re-live that day, but Blake shared with me the lowest moment of her past. And I want to do the same.

"You already know how it happened?"

She nods.

"What Thomas probably didn't tell you is that after I pulled him out of the car, we had to wait for help for hours. My pelvis was broken, I couldn't move, Thomas wouldn't wake up, I didn't have a phone to call anyone, and it was the staff's day off—why we were able to steal the Ferrari in the first place. I just lay there for hours in pain, feeling totally helpless and powerless, until our parents came back home. I vowed never to end up in a situation like that again. Then I had to spend three months in bed while the fracture healed, not able to do anything by myself. It was the worst time of my life."

"I'm sorry," she says, smoothing the creases off my forehead with a finger. "But you don't have to always control everything; you can just go with the flow sometimes."

I stare at our joined bodies under the blanket and smirk. "I like our current flow."

Her eyes follow mine to our naked chests and her cheeks flush.

"Yeah, that happened," I whisper. "Not a dream, sweetheart."

For a moment, I'm afraid she might pull away from me. But aside from the vivid blush, she doesn't hightail it.

Instead, she presses a kiss to my lips. "I know; it's been so much better than any dream could ever aspire to be."

"Now, now, that's going to stroke my male ego; are you sure you want to go down that road?"

"Despite less-than-stellar first impressions, I'm beginning to like your male ego."

"And all it took was a little kidnapping."

She playfully swats me. She's about to hit me with one of her snappy replies when her stomach lets out a loud growl.

I nuzzle her neck. "I see certain activities make you hungry."

"And I can't wait to engage in those activities again, but can a girl eat first?"

"Now that we've..." I pause. I want to say now that we've made love, but I told her that I love her and she hasn't said it back. I'm not exactly sure where I stand on that front. "Now that we've sealed the deal, is it okay if I make you a decent meal, or do I still have to be a lousy cook?"

A hint of the blush she had when she woke still colors her cheeks a delicious shade of pink. "Cook away."

"Any favorites I can rustle up?"

"I'll take whatever is served, as long as it comes with a side of you," she says, kissing me.

"Coming right up."

We get dressed and I rummage around in the kitchen, making toasted cheese sandwiches. Blake sits at the kitchen island, combing through her hair with her fingers. She looks adorably disheveled.

I place our plates on the counter and sit on the stool next to hers, thinking about how much has changed since our last meal here. Breakfast was only a few hours ago, but now the world feels like a completely different place.

We eat in silence, mostly because we're too famished to speak.

"Let me," Blake says, taking my plate once we're done. "You cooked, I can at least clean."

"That's what the dishwasher is for." I help her load it and pull her to me once the job is done.

I waggle my eyebrow. "How do you want to spend the rest of the afternoon?"

"As much as I would love to have a repeat of this morning, I should probably check in with Evan, see if the fort is holding up without me. Quick break and let's meet here again?"

I kiss her temple and retreat to my room to give her space. I sag onto the bed and check my phone. It's blown up with a million notifications. Work emails, annoying texts from Thomas, more work emails and notifications from Mila, plus about a thousand missed calls from my assistant.

I call her back.

"He lives," she says with a smile in her voice.

"What's with the million calls?"

"Sorry for disrupting your romantic retreat. How's it going? Has Blake forgiven you?"

"None of your business."

"I'll take that as a yes. When's the wedding?"

"Nice try, but we're not discussing it." I sigh. "Is there anything else besides your amateur sleuthing into my private life?"

"Actually, yes. We've just been notified the road has been cleared on your side of the valley, so you can go back to the hotel if you want to. Also, Thomas wants to know if he should wait for you, if you're going back in the jet together, and if he should add Blake to the passengers manifest. He said he doesn't mind leaving tomorrow if you want to spend tonight with Blake."

"Give me a minute and I'll call you back."

The temptation to not tell Blake we're free to go is strong. I'm afraid that if I do, she'll say she'd rather go back to work and New York as soon as possible. But keeping this from her is something the old me would've done. Not the me I want to become, that I want Blake to fall in love with.

Doing the right thing sucks. I wanted nothing more than another night with her away from the world.

I wait on the bed until I can't hear her muffled voice talking outside anymore, which takes a while, then, with a heavy heart, I step into the living room. Blake's on the couch, frowning at her phone. "Hey."

She drops the phone on the jute rug. "Oh, gosh, you scared me."

"Sorry." I sit next to her. "Mila called... The road's been cleared; we don't have to spend the night here if you don't want to."

Her blue eyes study me.

"Also, Thomas wanted to know if we're coming back to the hotel..."

"You want to go back?"

"Heck, no," I say without a second's hesitation. "I want to spend the night with you, away from everything else."

She nods. "Me, too."

"Really?"

"Hey, don't look so surprised. You've made my stay here extremely pleasant." She flashes me a fish-eating grin.

I beam back. "And would you consider me too entitled if I offered you a ride back to the city on my father's private jet?"

"Yes, but I'll take it, anyway."

I cup her cheeks and kiss her. "I—" I was about to say "I love you" again, but I don't want to smother her with too many big feelings all at once. "I'll go tell Mila. You keep working."

# 41

## BLAKE

The moment Gabriel goes to call his assistant, I hop into the bathroom and lock myself in, opening the chat with Marissa. I find a new text from her.

FROM MARISSA
How's the captivity going?

TO MARISSA
I think my next question is going to clarify a few things

FROM MARISSA
Shoot

TO MARISSA
Does it count if someone says 'I love you' mid-copulation?

FROM MARISSA
Uh, someone's been naughty

IDK. Has he said it *only* mid-copulation?

Also, how many times have you copulated?

TO MARISSA

Yes, and twice

So far

I haven't said it back

FROM MARISSA

Why?

TO MARISSA

I'm not sure how I feel yet

FROM MARISSA

And he is?

TO MARISSA

He tried to tell me BC—before copulation—but I told him not to say it unless he was sure

And then, mid-act, he went all intense on me and said, I love you, baby, I'm sure

FROM MARISSA

Gabriel Mercer doesn't seem like a guy who'd just toss stuff like that around

TO MARISSA

I know, right?

FROM MARISSA

When you say *intense* what do you mean?

TO MARISSA

Deep eye contact in solid missionary while he gently cupped my cheek and looked at me as if I'm the most beautiful woman in the world

FROM MARISSA

Aww!!!

TO MARISSA

So he loves, loves me?

FROM MARISSA

It appears he loves, loves you

You're very lovable in case I don't tell you enough

TO MARISSA

Thank you, you are, too

What about you, any more bad dates to report?

FROM MARISSA

No, I've set a date to start the IVF and I think I'm going to put the brakes on the whole dating thing until...

Well, probably forever?

TO MARISSA

Forever?

FROM MARISSA

I assume most men won't want to date a pregnant woman, and after the baby comes I just won't have time

TO MARISSA

Gabriel's brother is totally hot and vetted (once you get past the man-child act) if you want an introduction

FROM MARISSA

Thanks, but *one* child will be enough

TO MARISSA

When do you start the cycle?

FROM MARISSA

End of September as soon as my period starts

TO MARISSA

Two months from now?!

Shouldn't you make the most out of them?

FROM MARISSA

I'm honestly just too tired and fed up with it all, men especially

I send her a hug emoji.

TO MARISSA

I'm sorry

If you change your mind I'm always down for a girls' night out

Or in

Whatever you need, I'm there

She blows me a kiss emoji.

FROM MARISSA

I know, hon, thanks for the support. Now stop texting with me and go be loved

I send her a kiss and heed the advice.

When I get out of the bathroom, the sky is stormier and darker than ever, but the house is ablaze in firelight. The fireplace is lit and burning candles are scattered everywhere: on the kitchen counter, on the cabinets, and on the bookshelves. The only free surface is the large coffee table on the living room rug where Gabriel has set dinner for two. After our light lunch, I'm already hungry again.

He stands in front of the coffee table, wearing a black button-down shirt with the top two buttons undone and worn-out jeans, looking even more delicious than the food on the table.

I, on the contrary, am still in larva wear.

"Hello, beautiful."

"You're very... homely," I marvel.

"I do try." He shoots me a smile.

"This looks amazing." I point at the candlelight. "Quite the fire hazard."

He raises an eyebrow at me.

"Sorry, when I'm nervous I blab the silliest things. This is beautiful, period. I mean, thank you."

"Now, now." He casually strolls toward me and grabs me by the hips. "Exactly how nervous do I make you?"

"Oh, you know..." I try to keep my tone coherent but lose my train of thought when he nuzzles my neck.

He leans in, his warm breath tickling my ear. "Tell me."

My legs go wobbly. "You make me—"

He bites my earlobe. "Yeah?"

My chest is heaving. "I can't articulate if you keep distracting me."

His muscles flex under his shirt as he chuckles.

"Let's eat before everything goes cold; we'll resume the topic later."

Right now, gourmet food sounds like the worst thing that could happen to me. Hungry or not, I'd gladly skip dinner to have Gabriel press against me again. But I sit on the rug, legs crossed in front of me as if I'm still a functioning human being and not a messy heap of flesh, bones, and yearning.

I take in the artistically arranged food and frown. "This looks very haute cuisine; did you make it?"

He smirks. "No, I keep a few fancy meals in the freezer in case I get a craving when I'm up here."

I study his plate. Mine is fish while his is white meat. "Is that why we're having different things?"

"Yep, I only have single-serve portions since I always come alone. You can choose: sea bass or chicken breast?"

"The fish looks great."

I take a forkful and renege on everything I just said in my head. Sex can wait. This food could give me an orgasm as well. "Oh my gosh, this is the best sea bass I've ever tasted. Is it from a starred chef?"

Gabriel smirks.

"Please don't tell me you had a Michelin-starred chef come here only to cook you meals you could freeze and eat at your convenience whenever you got a foodie moment."

The smirk widens. "I won't tell you, then."

"You're so spoiled."

"Would it make you feel better if I told you that in my year in Silicon Valley, while I wasn't being a self-made entrepreneur, I survived on microwavable ramen noodle soups?"

"You're never dropping the self-made thing, are you?"

"Actually, I have a confession to make."

"Oh?"

"You were right about my father and Fidelity Credit Union."

Being right has never made me feel lousier.

"Only it happened the other way around," Gabriel continues.

"What do you mean?"

"Fidelity Credit Union strong-armed my dad into becoming their partner by threatening to drop my start-up if he didn't. It wasn't my father who bribed them."

"That's... slightly better? I guess."

"Can I ask you something?"

"Yeah, sure."

"Did you hear the rumor from Justin?"

I take a sip of water before answering, not sure fueling Gabriel's dislike for my ex is a wise choice. But I don't want to lie to him, or keep secrets, or keep my walls up. "Yeah, he was boasting about how he had played a big part in sealing the deal. But I didn't know anything about the blackmail."

Gabriel grimaces. "So, Justin is probably the one who blackmailed my dad."

I nod. "I'm sorry, when I said those things about your financing I didn't mean to—"

"Call me out?" He taps the tip of my nose. "Yes, you did, but it's one thing I love about you."

"Oh, yeah? What are the others?"

"How smart and determined you are. How stubborn, how real... and beautiful and sexy as hell..."

Heat rushes to my cheeks.

"I..." He hesitates. "I like everything about you."

Like or love? Time to man up—or woman up—and ask the hard questions.

"Earlier... while we were... mmm..."

"Yeah?" Gabriel flashes me a wicked grin.

"You like to watch me squirm, don't you?"

The grin turns feral. "More than anything."

"What I wanted to ask is... when we were... *doing stuff*, you said something..."

"Yeah, baby, yeah, just like that?"

I push his shoulder away. "Not that."

He chuckles. "Sorry, you're just so cute when you blush." Then he turns serious. Gabriel reaches over and tucks a stray lock behind my ear. He's so close I can feel his breath on my face. "Did I make it awkward?"

"No, no. But did you mean what you said or was it only in the lust of the moment?"

His fingers lace at my nape while his thumb brushes over my cheekbone. "I meant every word, baby. I love you."

I swallow. Someone call the paramedics because I'm about to swoon to unconsciousness.

Gabriel buries his other hand in my hair as well and drops his forehead to mine. "You don't have to say it back."

"Sorry," I say. "I'm just not sure where I am, yet. I am falling for you, fast, but I've only ever said it to one other person and I'm not sure I truly meant it back then. With you, I want to be 100 per cent."

"It's okay." His words are a soft, soothing whisper. "We have all the time in the world to figure it out."

He drops a kiss on my lips, and before I know it, I'm lying on the rug with him on top of me... our half-eaten dinner forgotten on the table. And I've changed my mind again; sex with Gabriel beats food now and forever.

"So I take it you two finally banged," Thomas says from his seat across from us in the Mercer family jet.

I blush, while Gabriel frowns. "Don't be crass, Thomas."

Thomas schools his features into a serious expression and in a harrowing but excellent imitation of his brother, repeats, "Don't be crass, Thomas." Then, turning to me, he adds in his normal voice, "Should I try to go more for the brooding brother vibe? Is that what did it for you?"

"No." I smirk. "It was watching him doing *grand pliés*."

Thomas guffaws. "Oh, Blake, now I'll rest better knowing someone else will amiably taunt my brother when I'm not around."

Unexpectedly, Gabriel kisses the top of my head. "You and me both."

The younger Mercer makes an outraged face. "Wait, wait. You always throw shade at me for my affectionate banter and she gets a kiss?"

Gabriel looks at his brother with a smirk. "She takes tender loving care of me, while the best you've given me is annoying teasing while asking for favors."

I lace my fingers with Gabriel's and kiss his knuckles. He responds by leaning in for a chaste smooch.

Thomas splutters. "I feel like I should leave the room and dash some cold water on my face. Do the two of you need some privacy? If you want to join the mile-high club, I could just go hide in the cockpit; I'm sure the pilot would be ecstatic to enjoy my company for the rest of the flight."

"Why are you single?" I blurt.

"Okay." Thomas raises his hands. "Now, I might actually have to leave."

"No, come on." Gabriel flashes him a grin. "Tell us about yourself."

Thomas flips him. Gabriel flips him back. And the question goes unanswered. Guess that, for how open and laid-back Thomas acts, he also has his demons.

* * *

We land in New York in the humid heat of the early afternoon. Compared to the cool temperatures of Jackson Hole, the change in climate is a quick reminder that we're back in the real world. Work, the city, busy schedules, everyday hustle. I'm a little nervous to see how—*if*—Gabriel and I will function away from his fairy cottage in the woods.

Both Gabriel and Thomas have a black SUV and uniformed driver waiting to pick them up. Now that I know about the accident, I can detect the slight tension in Gabriel's body language as he guides me toward the car he won't be driving. He greets Tobias and lets his driver drop his carry-on into the SUV trunk.

"Is someone picking you up?" he asks me.

"No, I thought I'd just get a taxi or something."

Gabriel smiles. "Nonsense. Tobias can drop you off after he drops me; you're going to the office, right?"

"Yes."

Before I can say more, Gabriel grabs my suitcase and hands it to Tobias.

I feel a bit off-kilter letting someone else take care of me and spoil me. The private jetting first, now the being chauffeured around... but it's a pleasant novelty.

I'm like a princess. A fitness queen who owns her own company, but still a princess.

But the atmosphere as we get into the vehicle couldn't be further from a fairy tale. Gabriel is sitting ramrod straight, jaw tense, fingers flexing.

"Tobias, my office first," he says in a tense, mechanic voice I don't recognize.

Tobias nods in the rearview mirror. "Yes, sir." Then he closes the darkened panel separating the driver's cabin from the backseat.

The moment the car starts moving, Gabriel's tension spikes.

I take his hand. "Are you nervous?"

"Yeah, I hate this."

And I could lecture him on how he really doesn't need to put himself through this ordeal day in, day out. But he doesn't need a lecture right now. He needs a distraction. So I climb onto his lap and tilt his chin up to me. "Any way I can help you let the tension loose?"

Gabriel pushes me back down and secures my seatbelt in place. "Anything you can do with your seatbelt on, I'm game."

I smile at him wickedly. "I can get creative."

His eyes sparkle. "For the first time, you make me wish traffic will be bad."

"Why?"

"Because I can get creative, too, and I intend to take my time with you."

Aw, heck, when he puts it like that... traffic never sounded better.

* * *

An hour and ten minutes of deliciously bad traffic later, we're pulling up outside the building where Gabriel's offices are located. My diverting tactics apparently worked wonders to make him forget he was a passenger and not at the wheel. He looks ten times more chill than when we got into the car.

Tobias opens his door and Gabriel exits the car. I follow him outside to say goodbye, but I don't have the time to put two words in before a pretty brunette—messy bun, fitted blouse, pencil skirt, friendly expression—greets me with a beaming smile.

"Blake, the woman of legend, we finally meet in person. I'm Mila, Gabriel's trusted executive assistant." She offers me her hand to shake. We do. "Can I have your phone?"

What? I look at Gabriel for confirmation and he gives me a subtle nod. So I fish my phone out of my bag, unlock it, and hand it to his assistant.

She types on it furiously for a few minutes before handing it back. "I've saved my direct line in your contacts, cell phone, and secret emergency line. If for whatever reason you can't get a hold of him, those are your go-to numbers. I also saved his office's direct line." She tilts her head and studies me for a second. "But I should let you know I listen in to all his private conversations in case you were in the mood for phone sex or whatnot."

I'm about to stutter that I'd never call Gabriel at work to start phone sex when, with a wink, she points at my blouse, and adds, "You've missed a button there."

Fair enough.

A few days ago, I wouldn't have imagined being partial to limo sex either. Not really a limo, and not exactly sex, but that's beside the point.

I blush fifty shades of crimson and quickly remedy the post-coital wardrobe malfunction.

"Blake." Mila smiles at me. "It's been a pleasure meeting you; I'll let you two smooch goodbye. Boss,"—she flashes him a slightly sadistic smile—"I'll be inside waiting with all the fusterclucks you've been so eagerly ignoring in the past few days."

Then she's gone.

Gabriel rakes a hand through his hair. "So, that's Mila."

"Oh my gosh, I love her."

Gabriel ruffles my hair, which needs no more ruffling, and says, "I'm glad. Can I treat you to dinner tonight or are you working late?"

I'm glad that he asked, that he didn't just assume I'd be free to dedicate all my time to him.

"Dinner sounds great, maybe a little late-ish... nine?"

"Out or in?"

No matter how good the car ride here was, I'll want more of him come night, and I'm not ready to experiment with restaurant sex, yet. So...

Heat blooms on my face as I say, "In."

My maddeningly red cheeks must reveal my thought process because Gabriel's eyes darken. "Tobias will be waiting for you out of your building at eight forty-five."

It'd be pointless to protest the private chauffeur offer, so I just nod and let Gabriel kiss me goodbye.

\* \* \*

Back at the office, Evan is awaiting me with a too-keen expression that informs me I'm about to be treated to my own brand of royal fusterclucks.

It's mostly related to the IPO, from the new SEC and SOX Act compliance expert we need to hire, to the mounting legal, accounting, and auditing services fees, plus liability insurance, and underwriting costs, to the new board of directors I need to appoint.

I have to deal with all that plus taking my first in-class training at the gym in four days, while still on Mountain Time and dealing with a mild case of jet leg.

By the time eight forty-five arrives, I'm glad Tobias will be waiting for me downstairs and that I won't have to worry about dinner.

As we pull up in front of Gabriel's building, I'm relieved MGM lives in a place with a personality. I like the limestone façade and retro look, and I try to gloss over the fact that this must be one of those fancy, old-money buildings where one isn't allowed to buy unless they can exhibit a pedigree dating back at least a couple of centuries.

After a livery-wearing doorman lets me in and directs me to the penthouse—of course—Gabriel welcomes me into his home with a kiss. I'm happy to find the apartment is not all modern, cold, and sharp surfaces. From what I can see from the entrance, the décor is a tasteful mix of cozy, elegant, artistic, and sure-to-be-pricey furniture.

"How was your day?" Gabriel asks, taking my jacket off.

"Dreadful, can we go back to the woods and pretend nothing else exists?"

He grins. "Say the word, and I'll alert the jet."

"Tempting, but I just need to get this IPO pressure behind me, and then we can take a vacation. Gosh, I'm starving."

"So the rumors are true?"

I stare at him wide-eyed. The official IPO announcement hasn't gone out yet, and for all we discussed at the cottage, our businesses were never a part of it.

"Yes, but still officially a secret."

"Got it, I won't breathe a word. I'm just glad dinner is ready and I can move your head away from the stress."

He leads me down the hallway. "I have a formal dining room, but I prefer to eat in the kitchen, I hope you don't mind."

"Dear sir, how dare you treat me to inferior dining settings," I say in my best British accent as I put a hand on my chest.

He chuckles, opens the door to the kitchen, and leads me to the solid-wooden-slate island that's set for two. He pulls out a high stool for me, and I sit, admiring the impeccable tableware.

Besides the plates and cutlery, there's a basket of what looks suspiciously like homemade bread and focaccia, a platter of pretty appetizers, and a bouquet of wild flowers.

We live in Manhattan, so I know Gabriel didn't take a stroll in a field somewhere to pick them. But I like that he chose something less pretentious than, say, a dozen red roses. The more I get to know him, the more I uncover all these different sides of his personality. Ruthless businessman but generous lover. Scary suit and adorable ruffled sweatpants wearer. Stern bossman and goofy brother. Powerful multibillionaire and down-to-earth man, with slightly expensive tastes admittedly, but still not as unattainable as I initially imagined.

I can't wait to find out the rest.

Showing no self-restraint, I grab a tartine and a piece of focaccia in quick succession, moaning, "I'm so going to steal your personal chef."

"No need to, you can come to have dinner here every night if you want to."

I raise an eyebrow. "Careful, you're diverging from the billionaire romance hero stereotype."

Gabriel pops a deviled egg in his mouth and chews on it before asking, "In which way?"

"I mean, you're rocking the brooding looks. But you're supposed to be this closed-off, gorgeous dude, who is down for lots of sex but doesn't want commitment, or big emotions involved. At least according to romance novels."

He laughs. "I'm sure in for the lots of sex part." Then turning serious, he asks, "Would you have preferred if I steered clear of the big emotions?"

"No, I like it. It's just not what I expected."

"I know what I want and I'm not afraid of going after it."

"There you go," I say. "That's the perfect, confident, all-powerful, intimidating attitude." I pat his cheek. "There's still hope of making a proper Christian Grey out of you."

Without batting an eyelash, Gabriel asks, "Should I show you my playroom now, or do you want to wait until after dinner?"

For a moment I'm not sure if he's joking. Until a grin breaks on his face. "The look on your face..." He chuckles. "Priceless. I think you're going to be fine with the soft-edged billionaire."

"Jerk."

"Shall I bring out the pasta?"

"You'd better 'cause that's the only reason I'm staying."

Dinner is delicious, and conversation between us is easy. We talk about work, we talk about family and trivial stuff like movies or music. Everything is perfect. Still at the back of my head, I can't shake this nagging devil, whispering in my ear that it's all too good to be true.

By the time the meal is over, I try to push the doubts away—or at least lock them in a dark spot of my mind where I won't hear them—as I ask, "Am I getting a tour of the apartment or what?"

Gabriel stands up, offering me his hand. "Yes, we should start with the master bedroom."

"Not leaving things up for interpretation, I see."

"As if you should talk, Miss Do I Get A Tour Of The Apartment."

I giggle. "Fair enough." I take his hand, a thrill of anticipation going through me.

The bedroom is exactly how I pictured it: big and masculine, with a high ceiling, a beautiful hardwood floor, and a stunning view.

What I didn't expect was the ball of fur curled in the middle of the king-sized bed.

"Is that Latte?" I squeal excitedly.

Gabriel rolls his eyes. "Give it to that wretched cat to steal my thunder."

At hearing his human's voice, the cat lifts his head and raises his chin in an "I grant you permission to cuddle" stance.

Gabriel sits on the bed and patiently scratches him under the chin.

"How is he with strangers? Can I pet him?"

Gabriel shrugs. "Worst that happens, he claws your hand off."

Ignoring the man, I sit on the other side of the bed and talk to the cat. "Hello, beautiful, I'm Blake. Nice to meet you." I offer him my hand to smell and when he doesn't bite it off, I pet him. Soon, he starts to purr and goes as far as strolling over into my lap and bumping his head against my chin.

"Traitor," Gabriel hisses from his corner.

"He clearly has a refined taste in humans."

Gabriel stands up and takes the cat from me. "Same as his

owner." He drops a kiss on my forehead. "I'll feed him a treat so that he'll give us some privacy."

"He wouldn't otherwise?"

"No." Gabriel cuddles Latte in his arms as if he were holding a baby. In response, my heart jump-starts, my ovaries explode, and my thighs clench. "He thinks of this as his room."

*Indeed.*

That night I fall asleep with 200 pounds of muscular naked billionaire half-rolled on top of me and 15 pounds of billionaire's cat solidly planted on my feet. I've never been more uncomfortable and happy in my entire life.

## 43

### GABRIEL

"Where are you going?"

I try to keep Blake from rolling out of bed, but she's quicker than a cheetah as she hops out from under the covers. Her alarm clock went off five seconds ago—at whatever unholy hour it is. I barely know my name, and there she is, collecting her clothes from the bedroom floor and treating me to a sexy reverse striptease.

"I need to go home before I get to the office."

After rubbing the sleep from my eyes, I can finally see the hands on my watch. "It's five in the morning," I protest.

Hopping into her leggings, she counters, "I have a 6.30 a.m. class; I need to go home, shower, change, and possibly squeeze in some breakfast."

"You can shower here."

She pauses her bunny hopping and cups my face. "I'd love to, but I still need to grab a change of clothes at home."

I steal a kiss, grab her hand, and drag Blake to the "hers" side of my closet I've never used.

Blake stares at the clothes with a slacked jaw. "What is all this?"

I smirk. "Call it the billionaire equivalent of giving you a drawer."

"You mean you had all this stuff *procured* for me?"

"Yep."

She shuffles through the sporty section and turns a few labels inside out. "How do you even know my size?"

I don't even try to take credit. "Mila has a good eye."

"And how does she know what bras I wear?"

"An educated guess and perhaps a bit of Instagram stalking." I hold out a pair of socks to her. "You can freak out about it later. In the meantime..."

She takes the socks from me and perks an eyebrow. "In the meantime?"

"Does this buy me another ten minutes in bed?"

Blake shakes her head, faux exasperated, then taking me by surprise, she jumps on me, straddling my waist with her legs and hooking her hands at my nape. "And they say money can't buy you happiness."

It ends up being a little longer than ten minutes, which earns me countless scowls as Blake, hair still wet from the quickest shower in the history of showers, gets dressed at the speed of light. "I knew you were going to make me late."

"Worth it," I say, unapologetically.

Another scowl. "I'm going. Tonight we should meet at my place."

"You have 6.30 a.m. classes every day?"

"No."

"Then why your place?"

"I didn't move closer to work to then commute from the Upper East Side. And, anyway, why not?"

"I have a private chef, and Latte would be crushed to be left alone."

Her eyes narrow. "Are you using your cat to emotionally black-mail me?"

"Possibly." I pick up Latte and squeeze him to my chest. Waving a paw in Blake's direction, I ask, "Is it working?"

"Like a charm." She kisses the cat's head, then my mouth. "See you later." She rushes to the door.

I follow her and hold it open for her. "Any wish for dinner?"

"Please tell your chef to keep it light, like soup or something. We can't eat like last night every day."

"Done." I smirk and watch her walk down the hallway, her bum swaying with each step.

* * *

Mila comes into my office two hours later holding a small black box in her hands. I can't even pretend to frown and demand what she wants. I'm sure my stupid smile gives her all the clues she needs.

She folds her arms, looks out the window, and then back at me.

"What are you doing?"

"Checking if the sky is falling. Is that a happy face, boss?"

Now I manage a little scowl.

"I take it Blake enjoyed my clothes selection?"

I grunt in the affirmative.

"I believe the words you were looking for are, great job, Mila, for putting together an entire woman's wardrobe in less than six hours. My girlfriend adored it."

At the word "girlfriend", I can't help but grin like an idiot again.

Mila sits on the edge of my desk and lets out a long whistle. "It's not the sky that's falling, it's you."

I raise my eyebrows. "Meaning?"

"You're head over heels in love with that woman."

I don't deny it.

"Pathetically adorable," Mila huffs.

I chuckle. "It's a novelty to me as well, so I'd appreciate some leniency."

Mila stomps her foot. "Boss."

I snap back. "Yes, Mila?"

She drops the small box on my desk and warns me, "Don't mess it up, okay?"

I wait for her to be gone before I open the box. Inside there's a folded note sitting on top of something lumpy. I lift the note and my heart almost stops in my chest when I find a set of car keys engraved with the Aston Martin logo.

I lift the keys, looping the ring inside my finger and read the note:

*Don't sit in the back if you want to be at the wheel.*
    *B, x*
    *P.S. This is an extended loan, not a gift*

I laugh, shake my head, and clutch the keys to my chest. That woman!

Heeding Mila's words, I vow to myself I won't mess it up.

\* \* \*

I keep true to my promise. In the following weeks, Blake gives me more access to her life. We spend most nights together, either at my place or hers. We eat. We talk. Sometimes we just sit in companionable silence. Or work late side by side. We watch movies. Do ordinary couple stuff. We make love.

The only thing missing is her actually saying she loves me. But I can wait for her. For as long as she needs. I already know how she feels. It's in the way she looks at me. In the way she holds me, in the way she says my name.

The season changes, leaves turn shades of yellow and orange and red and fall to the ground.

Blake begins to wear all sorts of oversized sweaters around the house that should keep her warm, but only make me want to get her naked and shivering.

Tonight, we're on her couch, supposedly watching a movie, when I make a sneak attack to remove one such sweater. Initial protests are sedated the moment I graze my teeth over her earlobe. Her weak spot. Works every single time. Blake quickly gets on board with my let's-ignore-the-movie-and-have-some-real-fun plan. In fact, she's busy removing my pullover when her phone rings and she stops.

"Ignore it," I plead.

"I can't, it's Marissa's ringtone." She squirms underneath me and reaches blindly behind her to grab the phone from the side table next to the couch.

She eventually grabs it, but before she can pick up, I distract her with a calculated nip to the shoulder.

Blake loses her grip on the phone, sending it flying under the couch.

It stops ringing.

Blake scowls at me, but I know just the right move to be forgiven. I'm about to deliver when the same ringtone plays again.

This time, Blake places the flat of her palm squarely on my chest and yells, "Answer phone."

"Blake?" An agitated female voice drifts up from under the

couch. "I need to see you, I-I—"

"You're on speaker," Blake interrupts. "Lost the phone under the couch and had to use vocal to pick up."

"Oh, is Gabriel with you?"

"Yes."

"Can you send him away? I need to talk to you."

I raise an eyebrow.

Blake strokes the short hair at my nape with a teasing smile. "Of course I can send him away."

Carrot and stick all rolled into a maddening female package.

"Are you okay?" Blake asks.

"No," Marissa says. "Definitely no. I'm traumatized."

The smile dies on Blake's lips. I'm unceremoniously pushed aside as she struggles to retrieve the phone and moves the conversation to private.

"What happened? You're not on speaker anymore."

I can still hear her friend's reply. "Not over the phone. I'll be there in twenty."

They hang up, and I sigh. "I guess this means I'm getting the boot."

"Sorry," Blake says, cradling the phone to her chest. "Marissa is never overdramatic. If she says it's something serious, it means it is."

I kiss her forehead. "I'll go, then."

She walks me to the door and we say goodnight. What starts like a chaste kiss soon turns into something heated and I have to force myself to back away. "If you want me to go, we have to stop."

Blake bites her lower lip. "Technically, I don't want you to go, just need you to."

"Same thing in practical terms, but I appreciate the sentiment."

Blake cups my cheek. "I..." *Say it, say that you love me.* "I'm going to miss you. Goodnight."

Feeling more disappointed than I should, I make my way to the elevator. Why won't she say it? I get that her past relationship blindsided her, but we've been together for two months now. Doesn't she know me enough to feel she can trust me?

Outside Blake's building, I consider what to do. I've already sent Tobias home because I thought I'd spend the night. I could call a cab. Or I could just walk. The fall night isn't particularly cold. Walk home it is.

As I cross the street, the shiny lights of a still-open Starbucks catch my attention. On impulse, I go in.

"Good evening, sir," the barista greets me. "What can I get you?"

"I'll take two venti hot chocolates with whipped cream, two donuts, two chocolate muffins, and two brownies. All to go."

The young man inputs my order into the cash register before giving me the total. I pay with my phone and go wait at the end of the counter.

The coffee shop is almost deserted. Only another patron is seated at a table, a woman with blue and pink hair, busy typing on her laptop.

"I have two hot chocolates for Gabriel," another barista yells uselessly.

I give him a perfunctory wave.

"Would you like a tray, sir?"

"Actually, I need these delivered across the street."

"Sorry, sir, we don't do deliveries."

I stare once again at the almost empty shop. There are no customers and two baristas.

"How about this?" I take out my wallet and slide four one-hundred-dollar bills on the counter. That also gets the attention of the other barista, who comes our way. "Say it was time for your break and you used it to do me this little favor. Your friend can cover for you and you both go home at the end of the night with two hundred dollars in your pockets."

They look at each other and shrug, sharing a nod.

The second guy turns back to me. "What was the address, sir?"

We go out together. I wait for him to walk up to Blake's building before continuing on my way north.

At home, I go straight to bed, but I don't fall asleep. I miss her. Watching TV seems pointless if I can't make silly comments with her, or come up with the wildest guesses as to where the plot is going—Blake contrives the most improbable scenarios and it's ridiculous how many times she gets it right despite her farfetched hypotheses. Guess I just don't have the imagination.

Next, I try to catch up with some reading but lack the concentration.

I turn the TV on again, shuffle a million channels, then turn it off again.

Three hours later, I'm still staring at the ceiling of my bedroom, not tired enough to pass out but too tired to do anything else. I feel completely despondent for no real reason.

*You know the reason*, a little voice whispers in my head. *You're sulking because she hasn't admitted she loves you.*

A rough pounding at my door distracts me from my woes.

I go to open it and there she is. Still dressed in the same oversized creamy sweater from before, a smudge of chocolate at the corner of her mouth, and her hair a complete mess.

"Couldn't stay away?" I ask teasingly.

She stares at me with a dazed look in her eyes, saying nothing.

"Is everything okay, are you—"

"I love you," she bursts out. Then, taking a deep breath, she steps forward and cups my cheek. "I love you," she repeats more calmly.

I wrap my arms around her waist and pull her into me. I nuzzle her neck and whisper in her ear, "It was all the chocolate, wasn't it?"

Her body shakes with laughter, but she pulls back to stare at me. "No, it was all you. You're the most amazing man I've ever met. You're sweet and considerate, goofy in a way I never expected, with a side of geek that I adore, and a completely hopeless romantic, but not in a cheesy way. You're strong enough to put up with my messy life and all my insecurities. You're patient. And you kiss like a god. I love you."

We hug again, our bodies pressed flush against each other.

"I love you, too."

I scoop her up in my arms and bring her to my bedroom.

She changes into one of my T-shirts—no matter how many PJs Mila has bought for her, Blake always steals my clothes to sleep in —and scoots under the covers with me.

"I'm glad you came," I say, brushing the hair away from her forehead.

She gives me a cheeky smile. "Don't get a big head now. I'm here only because I was missing Latte." She picks him up from his corner of the bed and cuddles him in her arms.

My cat purrs at once, and I don't blame him.

"Only reason I got him," I say, also scratching him behind the ear. "He's a ladies' magnet."

"Yes, he is," Blake agrees, stroking him. "Same as his human."

"Humans," I correct. "He has two now."

She lays Latte carefully on the bed and hugs me again, her hair tickling my face. "I love you."

We kiss, a long, sweet kiss full of promises for the future. For once, it's not sexual. It's on a deeper level. I don't try to take her clothes off. I simply pull her closer and close my eyes.

With Blake in my arms, I conk out in two seconds straight.

# 44

## BLAKE

When I wake up in Gabriel's arms the next morning, I expect my first instinct to be fear. I told him I love him, and there's no taking it back now. Not with him. Not with myself. I did what I promised myself I'd never do again. I handed control to someone else, at least partial control.

Instead, all I feel is joy, safety, trust.

In a way, I can see that what happened with Justin was my fault. I was too dependent on him for my self-esteem. I didn't stand up to him when he hurt me. I was a coward. I won't make that mistake again.

Not that I'm afraid Gabriel will hurt me as Justin did. But with him, I never feel inferior. He always treats me like his equal—well, maybe except for the first time we met when he thought I was the teenage daughter of his archenemy.

Gabriel rolls over to face me. "Good morning, beautiful." He smiles and smooths my hair away from my face.

I return his smile. "Hi. You're up early."

"Yeah, I have this annoying girlfriend who gets up at the crack of dawn every day to work out; her biorhythm has rubbed off on me."

"Gosh, she sounds awful."

"You wouldn't believe the things I have to put up with."

"I hope at least the sex is good."

"The best. Only reason I keep her around."

"Oh, really?"

"Yes, that, and the fact that I love her with all my heart."

He leans over and kisses me, a kiss that's so good it's worth risking my heart over.

"I love you, too."

He smiles. "I like hearing you say it."

"And I like saying it."

"I'm glad." We kiss again. And again.

Clothes come off, and soon we're making love. Our bodies have been saying "I love you" for a long time, and now, finally our words are too.

* * *

"Hey, what time is it?" Gabriel startles awake sometime later. After the intensity of our morning lovemaking, we both passed out again right after. "You didn't rush to work."

"I took the weekend off."

He raises an eyebrow. "You never take days off."

"It's because I'm going to be gone all of next week. The IPO is on the Monday after, and I need to concentrate 100 per cent of my energy on that. No distractions. But the good news is you have me all to yourself for the next forty-eight hours."

"We'd better make the most of it, then."

"I thought we already were," I say, referring to all the wicked things he just did to me in his bed.

We cuddle, kiss, and make love again. When the need to eat overwhelms our craving for each other, Gabriel orders breakfast as if we were at a hotel asking for room service. Only I discovered the food comes from a separate wing of the penthouse where his housekeeping staff lives. I still find it a little outdated that he has actual servants secluded away in the figurative attic, but every time I bump into one of them, they all seem incredibly fond of him and grateful for their jobs and free central-Manhattan living quarters so...

Also, I'm not about to complain about being fed restaurant-quality pancakes, French toast, and croissants.

In the kitchen, Gabriel pours me a cup of coffee from the pot the staff brought over. I watch as he adds the right amount of sugar, vanilla syrup, and foamed milk and sprinkles the whole thing with cacao powder.

"Cappuccino for the lady." He hands me a cup.

"You'd have a future as a barista, you know, in case you ever needed a career change."

"I did work at a bar once."

I have a difficult time picturing him working for minimum wage.

"How? When?"

"My summer in Europe. I ended up being short on money, didn't want to ask Dad for more, so I took up a few gigs."

I roll my eyes. "Of course your need for employment would be related to something as fancy as a summer in Europe. By the way, I didn't know the Starbucks across the street made deliveries."

Gabriel steals a berry from my plate. "They don't."

"Then how—" I stop mid-sentence. "I don't want to know, do I?"

"Let's just say I'm a very persuasive man."

"Yeah, I noticed."

"Hey, I forgot to ask." Gabriel frowns. "How is your friend?"

Oh, gosh. My conversation last night with Marissa comes back to me and I cringe.

"That bad?" Gabriel asks.

"Worse." I take another sip of cappuccino. "I told you she's decided to have a baby alone, right?"

"Yes?"

"Well, she's started her first hormone cycle, and yesterday she had a visit with the gynecologist and, guess what?"

Gabriel looks at me like he has no clue.

"The doctor turned out to be her ex-boyfriend from high school, who she hasn't seen in sixteen years, but still hates."

Gabriel low whistles. "Couldn't she ask for another doctor?"

"You'd think, right? But no, he was the only one on duty yesterday, and if she wanted to continue the cycle, she had to take the transvaginal ultrasound on that day for insurance reasons. Otherwise, she'd have had to give up the entire thing. So she had no other choice than to let her ex get all cozy in her buh-gina." I flinch again. "Can you imagine if I had to let Justin rummage around in my lady parts?"

Gabriel winces. "Please never mention Justin and your lady parts in the same sentence again."

His jaw tenses and I'm not sure he's being all banter right now.

"Yeah. I have no intention to."

"So what now? She's still going to go to the same clinic?"

"Yeah, but they're going to make sure none of her other appointments are with her ex again, so she should be fine."

"Do you want babies?" Gabriel asks out of the blue and gets rewarded with a spray of coffee out of my mouth and on his fancy robe.

I cough and sputter some more.

Gabriel, composed as ever, hands me a napkin and uses one to clean himself.

I wipe my mouth. And when I'm finally done choking on my coffee, I ask, "Excuse me?"

"Relax." Gabriel flashes me an easy smile. "I'm not saying now. I'm just asking, do you want them, ever?"

Still wary, I ask, "Why?"

He plants his palms on my knees and swivels my stool so that I'm facing him. "We love each other. We're in a serious relationship. Aren't these the things we should discuss?"

I relax. "Yes. And to answer your question, I've never really thought about babies before, other than as props for new workout sequences."

He raises an eyebrow at that.

"You know, pregnancy workouts divided by trimesters, those cute yoga classes new moms can do with their babies?"

He shakes his head.

I wave the topic off. "Anyway, I guess I've never been in the position to think about it. But..."

"But?"

"I'm not opposed to the concept, per se. I just think maybe I'm still too young... but in the future, why not? You?"

Still like a statue, he says, "I want at least five."

I almost have a heart attack before I notice the way he's fighting to keep his features set in stone, while the corner of his mouth twitches.

"Jerk."

He barks out a laugh. "I've never really given the topic much thought, never had to, same as you, and I'm equally not opposed to it happening down the line."

"Glad we cleared that."

"See, it's not that hard discussing the future."

"I guess. But now I need a refill." I pick up my cup. "Put your barista skills to good use."

"Yes, Miss Bossypants."

*  *  *

The weekend flies by like a breath of air. We make love and sleep, we talk and laugh, we go out to eat, and we spend the rest of the time either cuddling on his bed or lazing it out on the couch. When Sunday evening comes, we're both flying so high on love, sex, and happiness, I've almost left all the stress of the IPO behind me. But now it's time to go home and back to the real world. The last few miles of a marathon are always the hardest.

Gabriel drops me off at my place—no driver. "See you next week?"

I nod bravely.

He pulls me in for one last hug. "Wall Street has no idea what's coming. You're going to take it by storm, baby."

I wish I had his confidence.

"I'll text you later."

"Okay."

I exit the car and walk away, but I stop in front of the door and look back.

As though he'd read my mind, Gabriel has stepped out of the car.

I run down to him.

He opens his arms for me and I step into his embrace and kiss him. I hang on to him as if I'm never going to see him again. I know I will, but it won't be for a few days, and it might as well be forever.

"We're worse than teenagers," I mumble against his lips.

"I wanted to say goodbye properly."

"Bye." I get on the tips of my toes and kiss him again.

And again.

And again until he mumbles, "You're going to have to leave unless you want a scandal on your doorstep."

We pull apart and I run into my building before I ask him to come up with me. He's like chocolate cake for a person who can only eat green vegetables. In fact, I have an entire week of a greens-only diet ahead of me.

# 45

---

## GABRIEL

It's a long week. Blake is mostly a ghost. We exchange a few texts daily, but that's about it.

I go to work every day. I deal with tedious finance meetings and boring important people, and even more boring, decidedly unimportant people. And it's a sham of a life.

Is this really how I lived before Blake?

Work. Home. A few meaningless events. Yet more meaningless trysts. Work. Home. Rinse and repeat?

Yes.

How could I ever have believed myself happy is a mystery.

By the time Monday morning arrives, I'm equally excited for Blake and relieved today will be my last day without her.

I'd thought of making some grand plan for tonight, but I'm not sure how exhausted she's going to be. If she wants to hit the town celebrating, get drunk for the first time, try her first serious hangover, I'm game. If all she wants to do is lie on the couch and get a foot rub, I'm okay with that, too.

At 9.28 a.m., I'm positioned at my desk, monitors open on the stock exchange page.

The figurative bell rings at nine-thirty and a tiny green arrow appears next to Blake's stock, BLH.

Her initial offering is at eleven dollars per share, by ten the share price is already at twelve.

I get back to my work, while still throwing fleeting glances at the screen. The stock keeps going up all morning and by noon, it's flirting with a twenty-dollar-per-share value.

I frown. Even being overly optimistic, that seems odd. With a nine-dollar-per-share capital gain, some investors should've started selling by now.

I press the interphone button. "Mila, can you get me my contact at Goldman on the phone?"

Instead of her usual, yes, boss, right away, boss, I get total silence. I can hear the tumbleweed floating in the desert.

"Err." She finally clears her throat. "This wouldn't have anything to do with your girlfriend taking her company public today?"

"Mila, get me Haltman on the phone, *now*."

"Yes, Mr. Mercer."

Mila is notorious for taking the kill-them-with-kindness attitude to a whole different level.

"I have Haltman on line one," she says equally glacial two minutes later.

I'll deal with my EA's hurt feelings later.

"Robert," I pick up.

"Gabriel, long time no hear. What can I do for you?"

"I need a favor."

"That's even more unusual." Yeah, everyone who knows me also knows I don't like to be in anyone's debt. "How can I help?"

"Can you look into a stock for me, a new IPO going live today."

"Am I searching for anything in particular?"

"Any unusual activities that would drive the price up for no reason."

"Okay, what's the stock?"

"BHL."

"I'll look into it and let you know if I find anything."

I hang up the phone and turn to my monitor. The stock is past twenty-one.

I smell smoke. And usually, where there's smoke, there's fire.

## 46

BLAKE

As the stock price keeps rising above all brightest expectations, everybody in the office is euphoric, to the point of delirious celebration.

There's dancing, singing, and they've even started a drinking game where everyone has to take a shot of bubbly whenever the stock price increases by a dollar.

But as the share value hits twenty-six dollars, I get uneasy. It's too much, too fast.

"Evan." I pull aside my number two before he can down the seventh or eighth shot of the day.

"Hey, what's up?" he slurs.

I move us to a less crowded spot. "Evan, something isn't right."

"What do you mean?"

"The value is going up too fast. Something is off."

Evan opens his arms wide, making some of the champagne in his glass slosh over the rim. "Investors love us. What's the matter with that?"

"Why is no one selling yet?" I hiss. "Are you telling me that not even *one* investor who bought at eleven wants to take home a 200 per cent profit?"

Evan drops the glass, slightly sobered up. "And what's the alternative?"

"Someone has given an order to buy everything that comes on the market ASAP."

"And why would they do that?"

"To gain control of my company."

That sobers up Evan for good.

"Come into my office." I drag him away from the rest of my employees. "We need to get to the bottom of this."

We shut ourselves in my office where we're screened from the general chaos of the open space.

"Call the M&A team, see if they know what's going on."

"And what are you doing?"

"I'm calling Cheney. If someone is trying to take us over, his 21 per cent is the first we need to get back."

"That's going to cost us."

With my hand already on the receiver, I glare at him. "You have a better suggestion?"

"No. I'll get calling."

* * *

One hour before the market closes, the stock has reached a staggering twenty-nine-dollar value, and I'm sweating cold.

"Did you hear from Cheney?" Evan asks.

"No."

"He's stalling."

"Yep."

"Does he really think we're going to break thirty-five?"

I lean my elbows on the desk. "If I told you this morning we'd close the day at thirty dollars a share, what would you have told me?"

"That you were raving mad."

I push my chair away from the desk. "Exactly. A value of thirty-five is not unimaginable now, and he has twenty-four hours after we make the initial request to get back to us."

"So he's only waiting for the stock to reach the premium cap—"

"And screw us over, in short."

I stare at the stock value of 29.65, dread simmering in the pit of my stomach. This has Justin written all over it. I thought my ex was over trying to ruin or control me, but I guess he's still smarting from the conference. He's the only one I can think of with the power to move so much cash.

Forty minutes to go.

I follow the number's steady rise until we break the thirty-dollar barrier one minute before closure.

Outside the office, cheers erupt as everyone takes more shots.

I stare at the monitor, feeling almost empty. Whoever has been hoarding my shares is no benefactor. This isn't a friendly move, but a hostile takeover. Still, I need to have proof it's Justin.

Evan's phone rings, making me jump out of my despair.

Before picking up, he mouths to me, "It's the bank." Then he drops the phone on the desk and puts it on speaker.

"Evan," a serious voice says on the other side.

"Josh, you have news for me?"

"Yes, and I'm afraid it's not good."

I brace myself for the worst.

"Does the name Fidelity Credit Union say anything to you?"

My heart sinks; that's Justin's bank.

Evan says, "No." But then looking at me he corrects, "Maybe."

"Well, they've been buying shares since the markets opened this morning."

"How much have they accumulated?"

"Hard to say, but it could be anywhere between 28 and 30 per cent."

The number is so high that neither Evan nor I know how to respond. My ex now owns as many shares of Bloominghale as I do? If he gets his paws on Cheney's 21 per cent, Justin I'm-going-to-eviscerate-him Trémaux will gain control of my company.

"There's also another big player involved," the banker continues. "But they were a little better at covering their tracks, so we haven't been able to trace it back to an exact entity yet."

"How much do they have?"

"Again, hard to tell with precision, but anywhere between 4 and 7 per cent."

Compared to Justin's grab, that seems like small change now, but it's not negligible. "Can you trace the trades back to someone?"

"Give me time."

"Thank you, Josh; please call us back the moment you know more."

Tilly walks into the office then. My phone is off and I've told her to screen all my calls unless it's Cheney.

"I have Cheney on hold," she says.

"Well, put him through; what are you waiting for?"

She hesitates. "Gabriel called again, he said it was urgent. It's the tenth time today."

"And I already told you I'll call him later. Put Cheney through, please."

"Yes, right away."

The red light on my landline flashes red, and I pick up the receiver. "Tom, great to hear back from you."

"Hi, Blake." The tone is that of someone who has lousy news to deliver. "Listen, I'll cut straight to the chase. Someone has made me an offer I can't refuse and I'm going to sell my shares to them."

"Your shares are in lockup for 180 days after the initial offering unless you sell them back to me at our pre-negotiated premium."

"A premium that's now a good fifteen dollars below market value."

"There is no value if you can't sell."

"My shares are locked only if the value stays below thirty-five, which at the pace things are going, it doesn't look like it will."

While Tom explains the obvious to me, I watch as Evan leaves the office to pick up his phone.

"Things can change fast." In a last-ditch effort to make Cheney reconsider, I make empty threats we both know have no bite. "I can withdraw my offer at any moment. Sell to me now and you will have made a clean profit."

"Sorry, kiddo, I'm going to take my chances with the free market. This is still America after all."

Gritting my teeth, I give him the politest answer I can muster. "Thank you for being straightforward with me, Tom, much appreciated."

I hang up and look at Evan, who has come back into the office and is looking at me like he's about to tell me my dog died or something. Good thing I don't have a dog.

"Out with it," I say. "At this point, it can't get any worse."

"It was Josh calling me back; they were able to identify the other buyer."

"Who?"

I guess the name with agonizing certainty a moment before Evans says it. "It was Gabriel."

## 47

## GABRIEL

At the end of the craziest day, my intercom buzzes. "Blake is in the elevator headed up to see you."

Mila's tone is completely neutral. A sign she's still displeased with me. It's her version of the silent treatment. Usually, she'd offer a heads-up of what I should expect, but now she's making me ask.

"Any read on her mood?"

"Looks like you're getting exactly what you've asked for."

With that cryptic statement, she buzzes off the line.

I don't know what to do. I stand up, then sit down again. Then stand and circle the desk, leaning on it from the other side.

From outside the door, Mila's voice filters in. "He's expecting you."

Then my door bursts open and Blake walks in, looking like an avenging angel from a goth novel.

She's dressed in all black: black leggings, black shoes, and black fleece. Her hair is a messy cascade over her shoulders, and her eyes are blue fire scorching my soul.

Blake closes the door behind her and doesn't say a word. She doesn't come to kiss me or hug me hello either. She just paces around the office keeping a safe distance from me.

I'd go to her. But I'm a wise man; I can recognize when a woman doesn't want to be touched.

I get it. Her company is undergoing a hostile takeover, and everything she's worked for is at risk. She doesn't need cuddling right now.

"You want to talk about it or are you just here to pace?"

She looks at me and scoffs. "I'm just trying to decide if I'm calm enough not to scream."

"I know what Justin did, but—"

She stops and turns all her fury on me. "Justin? *Justin?* What about what *you* did?" She points a finger at me.

Oh, so she knows about that, too. I'd planned to keep the stock and then controllably release it back on the market when things calmed down without her ever knowing she had only me to thank for not losing her company. But I guess that train has left the station.

"He was buying all your shares, you weren't picking up the phone, so I took off the market whatever shares I could."

"How much exactly did you buy?"

"Seven per cent."

She closes her eyes as if taking a minute to digest the information. "And you couldn't have trusted I could handle my business on my own; no, you had to sweep in on your white horse and save the day." She claps her hands, sarcastically so, I suspect. "Bravo."

Well, not that I was expecting a medal, but a thank you would have been nice.

I ignore her sarcasm. "Why are you so mad?"

"Because... thanks to your meddling, I now risk losing my company."

"I don't see how my taking away stocks from Justin would facilitate that."

"Because I had a deal in place with my other investor, Tom Cheney. As a pre-IPO investor, he can't sell his shares for 180 days unless he sells them to me, or unless they reach a thirty-five-dollar-per-share value. And guess what, even with Justin buying as much as he has, the value would've stayed low enough, but not with two mad men competing for every share and driving the price through the roof. So thank you for that."

"How much stock does Cheney have?"

"He has 21 per cent. With my 30 per cent, it would've been enough to give the majority back to me, but now it looks like he's going to hand it over to Justin on a silver platter."

"Why?"

"Money? What else?" She looks down and sighs, her shoulders slumped. "I don't know what kind of ridiculous premium Justin offered him. And you know what the worst part is?"

I shake my head.

"When they told me a second player was amassing stocks, the thought that it could be you never even crossed my mind. I trusted you completely, I thought you had changed, that we understood each other and knew that our respective businesses were off-limits."

I can't help but note her use of the past tense.

"And now you've made a fool out of me again."

"Blake you're the smartest—"

I make to go to her but she stops me with a raised hand, dropping her head. "Don't."

For the first time, I see the exhaustion seep through the cracks of rage and adrenaline. I want to go to her, hug her, tell her everything will be fine. But I can't.

"I'm sorry," I say. "What can I do to help you?"

Her head snaps back up with whiplash speed, her eyes narrowing. "Nothing. You've done enough."

"Can't we at least talk about this?"

I take a step toward her, but she backtracks.

"No, I need space."

"Space to sort out your business or space from us?"

Gaze of steel, she says, "Both."

"Blake, you can't be serious. I love you, you love me. I made a mistake."

"A mistake that could cost me everything," she yells now, the façade of controlled fury finally breaking into outright rage. "I'd been very clear with you. I didn't want you to interfere with my business again or do things behind my back."

"I called you a million times and you wouldn't pick up your phone."

"I was busy running an IPO. And me not picking up my phone doesn't give you the right to go out and buy 7 per cent of my company like it's nothing. The company that I gave blood, sweat, and tears to build from nothing."

"I can sell the stock if you need to drive the price down. I never intended to keep it."

"Yeah, and give Justin the chance to gobble it up in one fell swoop. I don't think so."

"I'm sorry, I was only trying to help."

"Well, you did the opposite. By competing for every stock you drove the price through the roof, making the price almost reach the free-for-all premium that would allow my biggest investor to sell to whomever he pleases."

"I can sell all the stock back to you with an off-market transaction. That way Justin would be cut off."

"I don't have the capital to buy them at the current price, not if I have to buy out Cheney as well. And don't say you'll give them to me at any price because the only thing I need less than your help is your charity. I don't want a handout."

"What do you want me to do, then?"

"Nothing." She takes a step toward me. "When tomorrow comes, don't buy, don't sell; do absolutely nothing."

She stares me down as if she's waiting for me to acknowledge her words. And since everything I say today is wrong, I simply nod.

A moment later her eyes soften. A reckless hope rises in my chest that she's about to give me a sign that, deep down at least, we're still okay. But she doesn't take a step closer to me. She takes one back instead. "Good, I'm going."

She turns her back on me, shoulders stiff.

"Blake, wait." I rush for the door, but she's already sprinting down the hallway. I run after her as she reaches the elevator and fights with the unresponsive call button.

"Mila needs to unlock it for you to go," I explain.

Blake stares back at my assistant with the terrified expression of a trapped animal.

Mila looks at me interrogatively and I nod; if Blake wants to go, I'm not keeping her here by force. Learned *some* of my lessons.

Looking almost as awkward as I feel, Mila scoots hurriedly between us to unlock the elevator. Then she disappears back to her desk just as quickly.

"Can I ride down with you?" I ask.

"No."

"When can I see you again?"

Blake shakes her head. "I can't deal with this, too, now."

The elevator doors open, and Blake steps in. She turns to face me with teary eyes, but says nothing, she just pushes the lobby button, and the doors close.

# 48

## BLAKE

When I get out of the Mercer Enterprises headquarters, I don't even have time to wipe my tears. I need to get back to work and figure out a way to save my company.

Evan has set up a sort of war room in my office where a whiteboard with a pie chart dominates the space.

"Hello," I say as I walk in. "Thank you all for being here so late."

Legal, accounting, PR, everyone has sobered up and joined the fight.

"Where are we at?" I ask.

"Not much progress unless you could gather how much stock Gabriel has."

"Seven per cent." I take off my jacket and sit on my Pilates ball as Evan amends the chart.

There's my 30 per cent.

Gabriel's 7.

Cheney's 21.

Justin's 28–30 per cent.

And the last 12 to 14 per cent is widespread among smaller investors.

Heat creeps up my neck as I imagine Justin strolling through the door, sneering at me, "Gotcha." He'd own me, again. My worst nightmare. But I still have time to turn the tables. I must find a way.

Even if I count Gabriel's shares on my side, it doesn't give me the majority. There's not enough left on the market to gain the majority, neither for me nor Justin.

"The key to everything is Cheney's 21 per cent," I say. "Without his quota, Fidelity Credit Union can't go above 44 per cent worst case. The only way to ensure control is to buy back Cheney's shares, and he'll only sell to us if the share price doesn't reach thirty-five. Any idea how to tank our stock?"

Our financial consultant, Olivia, takes the lead. "Do we know what Mercer is planning to do with his shares?"

"Nothing. He will neither sell nor buy."

"Then Fidelity Credit Union doesn't have much leverage left. Counting Mercer's shares to our side, you're still the majority shareholder, but their position remains sizeable."

"What does that mean for us?"

"They can call for a vote of no confidence if they're already up to 30 per cent and if Cheney votes with them, they could remove you as CEO. Do you know how Cheney would vote?"

"He wants to sell and bring home a pretty buck, but he shouldn't be interested in deposing me. But we can't count on it."

"Assuming Cheney is a friend," Olivia offers. "Our best bet is to devalue the shares."

"And how do you propose we do that?"

"It's a dangerous move, but Fidelity Credit Union has a tight risk profile, if they have a large amount of a stock and the value drops more than 10 per cent in a single hour, their algorithm would issue an automatic order to sell everything."

"But won't that plunge the stock value even more?"

"They prefer to cut their losses early."

"How do you know all that?"

Olivia makes a waving gesture. "I know a buddy who knows a buddy..."

"Never mind. How can we lower the stock price?"

"We'd need a conspicuous sell-off from a source Fidelity Credit Union can't intercept and buy from, thus keeping the price stable."

"Is it possible?"

The consultant thinks for a second. "It'd have to be a coordinated dump happening all at once but spread out in many micro-transactions that Fidelity Credit Union wouldn't be able to appropriate."

"Micro-transactions." The solution suddenly hits me. "Olivia, you're a genius."

I exit the room and call my best friend. "Marissa, I need your help."

"What time is it?" comes her groggy reply.

I stare at my watch. "Past midnight, sorry, did I wake you?"

"Nah, don't worry, I had to pee anyway, darn hormones."

Even in the moment's urgency, I ask her how she's doing. I listen to her complain about daily hormone shots while she goes to the bathroom and once she's flushed, she asks, "Why are you calling me in the middle of the night?"

"Did you see my numbers today?"

"Yeah, I tried to call you to congratulate you, but your phone was off."

"Because I'm under a hostile takeover."

"No, by who?"

"Justin."

"That weasel," Marissa hisses.

"I know."

"How can I help?"

"Did you publicize my IPO at WeTrade?"

"Sure, it was bright and shiny on the homepage today."

"Can you see how much stock is still retained by your users?"

"Skimming legality, yes, let me get at my computer." I hear her move around her house, the scrape of a chair, the clicking of a keyboard.

"I can't give you a number, but I can tell you it's skimming the double digits."

Enough to cause a 10 per cent value drop.

"Can you send a recommendation to all stockholders to sell at the market opening tomorrow?"

"That could drive the price into the ground; are you sure?"

"Yes, I'm sure."

"Then, yeah, I can do it."

"How loyal is your user base? How closely do they follow your advice?"

"They're as loyal as a Labrador on steroids."

"Then I need you to stay tuned tomorrow, I have another idea in mind."

No response.

"Mari, are you still there?"

"Yeah, sorry, just really tired, I got a different shot today, and it's making me drowsy."

"I'll let you go back to bed. Sorry again for waking you. I owe you one, Mari, big time."

# 49

## GABRIEL

That night I don't sleep. I spend hours cursing at the ceiling, not even knowing who I'm most angry at, Blake or myself. Part of me thinks the way she treated me was a tad unfair. But then the other part tries to imagine how I would've felt if she'd bought 7 per cent of my company behind my back, jeopardizing my business at the same time.

Yeah, I wouldn't have been too thrilled either.

At 5 a.m. I can't stand the tossing and turning any longer; I throw the covers away from my body—severely displeasing Latte in my impetuousness—and get up.

The cat looks at me with slit green eyes.

"Well, you can join the line of complainers."

I blow off some steam in my house gym and then go to work.

Mila is waiting for me in the lobby with a cup of coffee from my favorite shop and a paper bag that must contain a croissant.

"Morning, boss," she greets me, if not exactly cheerful, at least not outright hostile anymore.

"Oh, so you're talking to me again."

She shrugs. "I figured it wouldn't be classy to rub salt in the wound."

I take the coffee and pastry and give a mock bow. "I appreciate your pity very much."

She smirks.

I open the paper bag and bite into the croissant as we walk to the elevator. "Do I have any meetings today?"

"You did, but they were mostly useless and you would've hated sitting through them, so I took the liberty of clearing your calendar."

My knees almost buckle with relief as we step into the elevator. "I know I don't say it enough, and that I can be a little gruff sometimes..." Mila arches an eyebrow as if that was the understatement of the millennium. "But I deeply appreciate you, and I would be lost without you."

She finally cracks a genuine smile. "Apology accepted, boss."

We stop at her desk, and instead of sitting right away, she looks at me like she wants to say something.

"If you're going to give me the look, you might as well say I told you so."

"Not that," she says seriously. "Whatever happens today, stay out of Blake's business. She might forgive you once, but she definitely won't if you mess with her stock again."

My jaw tightens, but I nod. Mila is right.

Still, when I sit at my desk, the first thing I do is turn on my computer, open the NYSE website, and click on Blake's stock.

The market will open in an hour, so I finish my croissant and coffee and wait.

The closure value for last night was 30.12 dollars a share.

As the market opens, immediately a red arrow appears next to the stock. The value plunges over a dollar in the first minute.

She did it.

How, I don't know, but she did it.

My elation is short-lived as the price continues to freefall. In an hour, it has dropped over 10 per cent.

She wanted to keep the price per share as far from thirty-five dollars as she could, but is this drop intentional?

I don't ask Mila to call Haltman; I'd never hear the end of it. I disconnect the interphone and dial the number myself.

"Gabriel," my friend greets me. "Twice in as many days. I could get used to being courted by you."

"And you know I'll make it worth your while."

"Say no more, I'm listening."

"Same stock as yesterday; do you know what's causing the turmoil?"

"Let me have a look."

I wait on the line as Robert works his magic.

"Ah," he says. "It looks like there were a bunch of sales from small investors at opening. The orders must've been placed last night. Makes sense people bought at fifteen, twenty dollars a share and took home the gain the next day."

"But why is it still going down?"

"Ah, that'd be Fidelity Credit Union risk management kicking in. They have a strict policy that if a stock they own big quantities of drops by 10 per cent in a single hour, they have to sell."

"All of it?"

"Yep."

"But with all the shares they accumulated yesterday that could kill the stock for good."

"I'm afraid so. You want me to place another order on it?"

I consider for a second. Did Blake know about the Fidelity Credit Union policy? Is the play intentional?

If she didn't, her company might not recover from this. If she did and the move is deliberate, I might mess with her plans again.

I'm on the cusp of telling Robert to place the order, but I stop myself, thinking of everything Blake said yesterday. I can't buy the stock. For both our sakes, it's a gamble I have to make and trust she knows what she's doing.

"No, Robert, thank you for the info, but I'll stand by today."

"Of course, Gabriel. Any time."

We hang up, and I stare at the bleak red arrow next to BLH.

Of all the things she could've asked me. To do nothing is the worst.

Couldn't she have asked me to jump into the fire for her? To vanquish her enemies? To crush Justin and his Class-B bank into smithereens?

But no.

She asked me to do nothing.

To sit here and twiddle my thumbs while she fights for her life.

My very definition of a personal hell.

I put my head in my hands and lean on my desk.

There has to be something I can do, a way to help her.

Come on Gabriel, think...

No, I can't make any move without risking interfering with her strategy. So, I'll just do the worst possible thing and sit here and do *nothing*. No matter that sitting still makes me literally want to crawl out of my skin. For her, I can do it.

Easier said than done.

Throughout the day, the stock continues to plummet.

Multiple times, I tell myself, if the stock goes below fifteen dollars, I'll buy. But then it reaches the threshold, and I don't. When it drops below eleven, I pick up the phone to call Haltman and drop it back again a million times.

By the time it reaches nine dollars, I'm losing my mind.

If her company tanks and I've played a part in its downfall, she's never going to forgive me.

I stare at the monitor; the freefall has slowed, but the stock is still going down.

I drag my hands down my face.

Blake, I hope you know what you're doing.

# 50

## BLAKE

When the share price hits nine dollars, I call Cheney.

"Blake, hi," he says as he picks up on the first ring. "It's been a blood bath."

"Yeah, I know." I cut straight to the chase. "I'm calling to renew my offer to buy you out."

"Yeah, yeah. I still have your offer on my desk; I'll get my lawyers to give it back to you signed."

"That was yesterday's offer. My lawyers have rescinded it a few hours ago. You should've seen the notification in your inbox."

"What are you proposing, then?"

"To buy your shares at half the premium I was offering yesterday, but the transaction must be concluded right away."

Silence stretches on the line. "Why aren't you low-balling me more? You must know I'd accept your offer at no premium today. Heck, I'd take it at less than the initial offering value."

"You were my first investor, Tom. I wouldn't be sitting here without you. I'm giving you what I can afford and what I feel is right. Do we have a deal?"

"Even after the way I was ready to drop you yesterday?"

"I understand business, Tom, your decision wasn't personal."

"Well, Blake, what can I say? It's been a pleasure doing business with you. If you ever need a favor, count on me."

"Thank you, Tom."

"Whatever, and Blake?"

"Yes?"

"For what it's worth, I hope you make it out of today alive."

"You and me both."

I hang up, wait for the legal team to confirm that we now control Cheney's stocks, and call Marissa. "Hey."

"Ready to pull the trigger?" she asks me instead of hello.

"Yes, tell all your users to buy, now."

"Done."

"Thank you, Mari. I will owe you one for the rest of my life."

"Careful there, I might collect one day," she replies playfully.

"I hope you do. I have to go now."

"Go, save your company. We'll talk later."

Almost at once after we hang up, the stock switches trend and begins to rise. I've checked with the legal team a thousand times before giving the go-ahead. We didn't share any privileged information. Or make up false or misleading data about Bloominghale. I'm not trading any of my stocks, so I won't be liable for insider trading or market manipulation. I bought Cheney out at a considerable loss. So I'm not liable for any crime.

Those accusations, if anything, should befall Justin and his company for driving the price up and down so quickly.

Soon, as the price keeps driving up, other investors smell a good deal and start buying. By market closure, the stock has recovered a healthy and fair value of 15.65 dollars a share—what it should've been yesterday without Justin's interference.

He will have lost a lot of money.

And so will Gabriel.

Five minutes after the closing bell, he texts me.

FROM GABRIEL

Can we talk?

Yes, we have to. Only it'll be harder than everything that has happened in the past two days. I text him back and tell him to come over to my place.

I'm about to leave the office when Evan calls me back halfway across the lobby.

"What's up?" I ask.

"Josh did some more digging, and he's found out why Justin attacked us."

"So it wasn't just a petty ex-lover spat?"

Evan shakes his head and, from the way his lips purse, I know I'm about to be hit by another freight train.

\* \* \*

Gabriel rings my bell an hour later, looking just as tired, underslept, and grim as I feel.

"I don't know what to say," he starts as soon as I let him in. "How to apologize."

I stop him right away. I know he's sorry, that he didn't mean to do my business harm, but the fact remains that he did and that he could've cost me everything. Not to mention the secrets he's been keeping from me...

"Gabriel."

"No!"

"No, what?"

"Don't say Gabriel like that, like you're about to tell me this is over."

I hug myself. "I'm sorry."

"No, Blake, don't."

I hate to hear the pleading note in his voice, but I have to stay strong.

"I can't," I say. "I can't pretend the last forty-eight hours didn't happen."

"But you're fine, Bloominghale is fine. You recovered."

"And I almost lost all of it because of my boyfriend and my ex. Maybe the fact that Justin targeted me has nothing to do with you, or maybe it has everything to do with the way you've been quietly picking off clients from his investment bank."

Gabriel pales, confirming the worst.

"Yeah, you thought I wouldn't find out? Would you have told me if I hadn't?"

"I was only trying to—"

"To what? *What?* To protect me? To avenge my honor? Or was it just a selfish vendetta? Who was it supposed to make feel better, me or you?"

"The way he treated you! And he was the one who blackmailed my father, I have confirmation of it now. He deserved to learn a lesson."

"And to hell with the consequences, right? You knew about the IPO and you knew Justin manages one of the most powerful trading floors in the city. Did the thought that he could take it out on me even cross your mind? Did you stop to think for a second?" The next word comes out in half a sob. "No. You let me go into the IPO blind to half the picture. You did the opposite of defending me."

"I couldn't just hold back and do nothing. You're the one who told me not to sit in the back if I want to drive."

"Yes, when it's *your* life. Not mine."

Gabriel's chin dips to his chest as his posture slumps. "I'm sorry."

"Yeah, me, too. But I already told you once, I won't let anything jeopardize my life's work."

"I'll stop. I've learned my lesson. Today I kept out of the fray even if it killed me every second. I can do better."

I shake my head. "You say that now, but you're a loose cannon. I can't predict what you're going to do in two days or in two months. I can't take that risk, not again, Gabriel."

Eyes red-rimmed, he stares at me. "No, you *won't* take that risk. You'll never let me in. You know how hard it was for me today to sit back and watch your stock crumble, doing nothing? I felt powerless."

"And I felt blindsided, so maybe we don't bring out the best in each other."

"You bring out the best in me. But apparently, I don't do the same if you're still so stubborn about not letting anyone in. It took you two months to say I love you when you knew it from day one. How long is it going to take you to realize that shutting me out is a mistake?"

"Well, it's *my* mistake to make. Gabriel, please just go."

He does the opposite and takes a step toward me. With both hands on my shoulders, he presses a kiss to my forehead, his lips lingering.

I keep my gaze down because I can't bear to look at him.

"I love you, Blake." He whispers the words against my skin in a broken voice.

He lets me go, turns around, and exits my apartment—my life.

The touch of his hands still lingers on my skin, the press of his lips still searing the skin between my eyebrows, and his amber smell still fills my senses—but for the last time.

As the door closes behind him, I'm finally free to shatter.

# 51

## GABRIEL

Thomas throws another pretzel at me from across the parlor. I ignore it like I ignored the ten he threw before.

"Come on," he provokes. "It's not fun if you don't fight back."

I brush the pretzel off my shirt and ignore him.

The next projectile lodges in my hair, only Thomas miscalculated his timing, and Mom, coming back from supervising the kitchen, catches him.

"Thomas," she chides, working her fingers through my hair to retrieve the wayward snack. "Stop throwing food at your brother."

Thomas shrugs. "Someone ought to do something; he's been like that for hours."

"I'm fine."

"No, you're not, dear," Mom says, squeezing my shoulders. "We're all anxious about you. It's not like you to mope around for days and do nothing."

The irony of the statement hits me in the solar plexus like a wrecking ball, and I bark out a bitter laugh. "Apparently I should've done more of that instead."

"More of what?" Mom asks, puzzled.

"Nothing."

My mother sighs and goes to sit on her armchair, asking Thomas, "Can you make sense of what he's saying? Because I sure can't."

Thomas snorts and takes a handful of chips, loudly munching them as if to annoy me. "If I had to paraphrase my brother's cryptic philosophy, I'd say he wished he would've kept out of his girlfriend's business, and not tried to bury her ex into the ground, thus instigating a reaction that almost cost Blake her company, and got him sacked from the role of beloved boyfriend."

I stand up. "Mom, I'm sorry. I can't stay for brunch today."

"Oh, Gabriel, no, don't leave. Thomas didn't mean it."

"I think he did."

My brother shrugs. "Sure I did."

I've been itching for a fight all week; if Thomas is offering to volunteer, I'm more than ready to take him up on his offer.

But for my mother's sake, I make another attempt at leaving peacefully.

"I'm going."

"No, you're not." Thomas stands up from the couch and gets in my face.

"Get out of my way before I make you."

"Bring it, old man." Thomas shoves me a little.

That's it, I'm about to raise my arm to punch him when my dad comes to stand between us. "Boys, sit down. Both of you."

My first instinct is to protest like a teenager, saying something like, *but he started it*. I think better of it and just sit back in my armchair. Thomas follows my lead and sinks back on the couch, looking nonetheless chastised.

Dad sighs. "Gabriel," he says in his wisdom-of-the-father voice. "What your brother is trying to convey, albeit in his usual aggravating way, is that there's a time to stay idle and a time to take action." Pause. "This is one time you should take action."

"And by action you mean?"

"Go after the woman you love; don't just sit back and let her slip through your fingers."

"She's told me in no uncertain tones that's exactly what she wants."

"If men always listened to what women said—"

"Dad," I interrupt. "You can't say stuff like that in this century."

"Nope." Thomas pops his lips in an annoying sound.

"Let's put it this way, then." Dad looks at Mom with an expression of such adoration my heart cracks a little—that is what I could've had with Blake—and then resumes his speech. "If I'd listened to your mother when she told me to stay away for good, neither of you boys would be here now."

All heads in the room turn to Mom.

She sighs. "I believe my exact words were: stay out of my way or I'll put your contact lens in backward, *cabron*."

"Ooooh." Thomas hollers with laughter. "Go, Mama."

He raises a hand and they high-five.

As much as I'm enjoying the family folklore, I'm not sure it applies to my situation. "Dad, I'm sure whatever you did wasn't as bad."

"No, you're right, son, it was ten times worse. Your mother still forgave me, but she sure made me work for it."

"Gosh, Dad," Thomas says. "What did you do?"

Dad looks at Mom in a permission-to-tell-the-story way, and she gives him an exasperated nod.

"What you have to understand, son, is that we Mercers are go-getters."

"Hear, hear," Thomas interjects.

Dad throws him a be-quiet glare, and continues, "But we're

also impatient idiots and sometimes, that can cloud our judgment." Mom scoffs emphatically at that. Dad gives her a you-know-you-love-me-despite-my-flaws look, and continues, "When I first met your mother in Miami and asked her to come to New York with me, she refused."

"Why?" Thomas asks.

Dad scowls at him.

Thomas raises his hands defensively. "It's a valid question."

Mom replies, "My entire life was in Miami, a job I loved, all my friends, my family... I didn't want to leave it all for a pretty boy I had just met."

I turn to Dad. "What did you do?"

He sighs, slightly shameful. "I bought the restaurant she was working at and told the manager to fire her so she'd have one less reason to stay."

"Oof," I say. That seems extreme even for me—and I'd considered kidnapping Blake so that should say a lot.

"Yeah, Dad, ouch. Not cool," Thomas adds.

I turn to Mom. "How did you find out?"

"The manager was one of my friends. He told me he had no choice but to let me go, but that he'd be damned if he didn't let me know why."

I stare at Dad. "How'd you come back from *that*?"

"I pleaded, and groveled, offered to give her old job back, heck, I offered to gift her the restaurant, but nothing worked. So I applied for a job at the taco-pizza joint she went to work for next. I didn't buy that one, in case you were wondering, I'd learned my lesson."

"Wait, wait," Thomas says. "You mean to say you worked as a server at a Taco Bell?"

Dad shrugs. "It wasn't a Taco Bell per se and all server positions were filled so I took a job as a kitchen helper."

The idea of my father washing dishes and mopping floors is so alien I'm having trouble picturing it.

"For how long?" I ask.

"An entire year. Took me two months just to get her to say hello to me again."

"Mom," Thomas says. "Remind me never to get on your wrong side."

"I'll hold you to that," Mom says.

"The moral of the story is," Dad continues. "If you've found the right woman, you gotta go all in. Throw a Hail Mary, do whatever it takes, but get her to take you back. If she loves you, she will. And if she doesn't, well, then she wasn't the right woman to begin with and you can move on."

Thomas rubs his hands together excitedly. "So, how are we going to grand gesture Blake?"

I don't know yet. But Dad is right, I can't just give up.

"Why don't we have brunch before we make extravagant plans?" Mom asks, motioning for us to move into the dining room.

I stand up and follow her, for the first time in days feeling something similar to hope rising in my chest.

## 52

### BLAKE

Saturday afternoon, two weeks post-breakup, I'm in my apartment slumped on the couch with my laptop in front of me, letting Facebook mock me with a "What's on your mind?" post prompt.

What's on my mind?

Regret.

Despair.

Loneliness.

Questions.

Lots of questions.

How did I end up here again? Why? What's he doing right now? How's Latte? Why? Why? *Why?* Why couldn't he let the Justin thing go? Why couldn't he keep his nose out of my business? Why do I still love him despite all that he did?

Of course, I can't post any of that.

In the past couple of weeks, I've kept all my socials on neutral, maintaining only minimal posting regularity not to drop off the face of the Earth with my followers. I've never been more glad to have tens of draft posts already prepared for emergencies.

At least the breakup with Justin taught me something—to plan for heartbreak. The only way relationships end, apparently. At least as long as I refuse to turn into a yes-lady who agrees to be controlled by powerful men.

On impulse, I drop my laptop on the couch and head to the fridge in search of some heavily unhealthy, comfort foods, then I remember the massive junk food purge I performed yesterday when I—*stupidly*—decided my body is a temple and that my recovery should start from within.

I'm considering the pros and cons of raiding the convenience store on the corner of all their Halloween candies—immediate reward—versus ordering a delivery from The Ice Cream Shop— slower, but doesn't require me to exit the apartment—when my doorbell rings.

My first instinct is: *it's him.*

And I don't even know if I'm more scared or excited by the idea of seeing Gabriel again.

With sweaty palms, I press the buzzer button. "Yes?"

"Hi, honey," Marissa says. "It's me. Can I come up?"

I drop my forehead against the wall, not able to hide even from myself the burning disappointment. "Yeah, sure."

I let her into the building, open the door for her, and go lie on the couch.

"Hello?" She pushes her way into the apartment five minutes later.

I raise a hand. "Here on the couch of despair."

Marissa comes into the living room, takes in my misery, and shakes her head. "Nuh-uh, this won't do. I need you to stand up and go take a shower."

"Why?"

"I'm calling in my IOU."

"To do what?"

"No questions asked. Just shower and come with me."

"But I don't want to, I've grown really fond of my germs and bacteria."

"Shower, now."

"Gosh, you're bossy," I say, sitting up. "You're going to be a scary mom."

I take a quick shower and come out of the bathroom still wearing a robe and feeling slightly less opposed to the idea of a girls' night out. Maybe I need a social outing. Maybe getting back out in the world will cure my broken heart. Yeah, and maybe pigs will fly. Still, it can do me no harm to step out of the house.

"What should I wear?"

"Comfortable clothes," Marissa says cryptically.

Oh, maybe she'll take me axe throwing or to one of those rage rooms, or somewhere else fun where I can misplace my anger and frustration.

I change into sweats, give my hair a quick dry, and I'm ready.

An Uber is waiting for us downstairs.

We get in, and the driver leaves without Marissa needing to give him an address.

"Where are we going?" I ask again.

"It's a surprise," Marissa says.

We cross over the Williamsburg bridge and from there it looks like we're going... "Are you taking me to my parents'?"

Marissa makes a zipper-over-mouth gesture.

"If this is an intervention, I don't need one," I protest. "I'm heartbroken, I'm allowed to wallow in misery for a few weeks." Or a few decades.

"No, you're not."

"Why?"

"Because you have places to be."

Like a petulant child, I cross my arms over my chest. "What places?"

"I can't tell you."

I brood and pout and morosely stare out of the window, but nothing makes Marissa waver.

Shortly afterward, we pull up in front of my parents' house. But instead of being marched into the living room and sat down for a pep talk, Marissa drags me to my old bedroom, where everything has remained frozen in time to eight years ago.

As soon as my best friend closes the door behind us, I wheel around to face her. "Can you explain what you're doing?"

"No, sorry, no time. You have to get ready."

She guides me to the dresser and invites me to sit. Still frowning, I comply.

Marissa works on my makeup, ignoring the steady stream of glares and protests I send her way. When she's done, she moves on to my hair and arranges it in a weird top knot with loose ends falling on my forehead that makes me look as if I have bangs.

I stare in the mirror and see a much younger version of myself staring back.

"Okay," I say. "Now that you've made me look eighteen again, what are we doing?"

"You still need a dress."

"Yes, fairy godmother," I say in a mock dreamy voice and bow in my sweats. "Please transform my rags into a gown, and we can use one of the Halloween pumpkins as my carriage."

Marissa smirks. "No need."

Crossing the room to the closet as if she owns the place, my friend retrieves a black garment bag and unzips it.

At the first hint of pink tulle, my pulse speeds up.

When she uncovers the full dress, I understand just how bad I've been set up.

"No," I say. "No! Why would you do this to me? What did he do to make you do his dirty work? Did he blackmail you?"

Marissa sighs. "He came to me, wearing his heart on his sleeve and explaining all the reasons he deserved a second chance. I listened and decided you should give him another shot."

"No."

"You don't have a say. This is my IOU, and what I want is for you to spend the evening with Gabriel. If at the end you want nothing to do with him, he's sworn to me he'll disappear from your life forever."

I snort. "As if you could trust such a promise. He'd promised he'd keep out of my business."

"He made a mistake. We all do."

"That's my prom dress," I protest, already half-choked by emotions seeing the dress I spent months searching for with my mom and never got to wear. "That's not playing fair. You know what he has planned?"

"Yeah, he's taking you to your senior prom, and you'd better get into the dress if you don't want to be late."

# 53

## BLAKE

When the doorbell rings, I'm ready for murder. Marissa, Gabriel, I don't know who I should off first, maybe even my parents for lending their house to this farce—even if, to be fair, I didn't exactly tell them about the breakup, so they might be innocent bystanders in all this.

Marissa ushers me out of the bedroom and leans on the threshold like a mother hen sending her chicks out to rooster alone for the first time.

"You're not coming?"

"No." She shudders. "I still bear scars from my last prom, which sixteen years of therapy haven't cured. I don't care much for the high-school scene."

"Yeah, me neither. Are you sure you don't want to switch your IOU to unicorn PJs, ice cream, and a *Gilmore Girls* marathon?"

"I'm sure. Now go, be brave, and give the man a chance. He messed up, he knows. But I still think he's one of the good ones."

"You know nothing, Marissa Mayer."

With one last glare, I walk down the stairs, stumbling over the last few steps as I catch a glance of Gabriel waiting on the porch. He's wearing an impeccable black tux, while his hair is in perfect disarray—as if he'd been messing with it non-stop. My heart stops for a moment. He's devastatingly handsome, and I've missed him. But that doesn't mean I should forgive him.

Still, my heart is beating so hard I fear it's about to jump out of my chest and run away.

Standing tall, I walk forward and go meet him on the porch.

Our eyes lock and it's like a grenade has gone off in my chest. I can't sustain eye contact for more than a few seconds, so I look at my dad instead.

Oblivious to the underlying tension between Gabriel and me, Dad is looking at me teary-eyed. "This is exactly how I'd imagined your prom night would be. You're gorgeous, sweetheart."

"Thank you, Dad."

Mom seems too choked up to even speak.

"Come, come." Dad ushers me forward. "I want to take a picture."

I go to Gabriel. Without a word, he gently grabs my hand and secures a corsage of pretty pink flowers that go perfectly with my dress.

"You look stunning," he whispers.

I just glare at him, trying to fuel my inner rage to combat the part of me that wants to forgive him and melt into his arms.

"Stand closer for the picture," Dad insists.

Gabriel loops an arm around my shoulder and pulls me to him. Having half my body suddenly pressed into his solid warmth does not help my resolve, especially not when his smell hits me in all its brutal force.

The instinct to turn around and pull him in for a kiss is so strong I have to clench my fists to keep my hands to myself.

I am so going to kill Marissa for this.

After a million pictures, my parents wave us off to the waiting limousine on the street.

I allow Gabriel to help me into the car, but the moment he steps inside with me and closes his door, I want to run back to the house screaming that this is a mistake. That somehow, I'm going to lose my mind to my memories if I don't get out.

The car's engine starts.

Gabriel and I both look at each other, and I see a hesitant hope in his eyes. Hope that this time things will be different. Hope that the mistakes of the past haven't ruined our future. His gaze shifts to the front and his jaw tenses. He's trying to keep himself in check, but I can recognize his anxiety at being in the backseat. I can see him struggle as he tries to keep still. My heart goes out to him and I have to clasp my hands together not to reach out across the seat to hold his hand through the journey. Even if it kills me.

I want to forgive him so badly. But can I? Can I forgive him for putting a petty revenge above me and my work? Will he ever be able not to meddle? He *is* a meddler by nature. Can a person really ever change?

"So..." I say when I can't bear the silence any longer. "What are you trying to prove here?"

His smile is tense but also sexily crooked, and it hits me like a punch to the gut.

"Nothing. I'm taking you to prom, that's it."

"And what happens after that?"

"We'll have to wait and see."

"And if I say I'm done?"

He sighs. "Give me tonight, Blake." The plea sinks into my heart like a knife. "If afterward, you want nothing to do with me, I'll take you home and get out of your life for good. I swear."

His eyes search mine, and I know I'm making a mistake by agreeing even to this much. I still can't trust myself around him. It's too soon. But Marissa gave me no choice. So here I am, between a rock and a hard chest, with no escape.

The car stops in front of my old high school. The driver opens our door, and Gabriel helps me out of the car, saying, "Shall we?"

"You mean you organized a dance at my actual school."

"Wouldn't be prom otherwise."

The moment I step out of the car, my resolve to act cool vanishes in a sea of missed memories.

Everything looks like the pictures of this night eight years ago that I spent weeks obsessing over, wishing I'd been able to attend.

The theme was moonlight under the stars, with crescent moon decorations scattered all over in gold, dark-blue, and silver accents, and glittering strings of lights.

The school entrance is framed by a balloon archway with a booth where Peggy Johnson and Cassandra Clark are checking people's tickets before letting them in—just like they did on the real prom night. Their hair is different, but their outfits are the same.

More people are coming up from behind us and from the lawn, all wearing slightly out-of-date clothes. The men in tuxes and boutonnieres. The women in gowns with corsages and clutch purses.

I recognize a bunch of old classmates as they pass me by.

A few even stop to say hi or tell me how excited they are about the impromptu reunion.

I sort of sleepwalk to the admission booth where Gabriel hands over our tickets.

We pass under the balloon arch, walking down the school halls where the lockers have been draped in glittery tulle and loose balloons hang on the ceiling.

When we reach the gym, I'm almost afraid to step in. When I do, the party is already in full swing. Taylor Swift's "Bad Blood" is blaring from the speakers around a DJ booth, and many circular decorated tables are arranged at the edges of the gymnasium, creating a dance floor in the middle. A white disco ball that looks like a full moon sends glimmers of light across the gym. A movie screen with scrolling photos of students from our senior year is mounted on the left wall. And there's a portable gazebo for taking photos in the corner.

A few teachers I recognize are presiding over tables of drinks and refreshments to the right.

Everything is exactly the same as my senior prom: the setting, the people, the music.

I don't know what to do or what to say. I've stepped back in time to a night I wished I could've lived so many times. And now he's giving it to me.

I should be in shock, but all I can do is smile as I look around me.

The DJ switches the music to "Cheap Thrills" and I can't stand still any longer; I recognize a few girls from my old cheerleading squad and join them on the dance floor. We cheer and jump in rhythm with the beat of the music as if we saw each other just yesterday at cheer practice instead of eight years ago on the last day of high school. I dance and dance and dance, switching partners, saying hello to so many of my old friends, laughing, singing along with the music, until I lose my voice and can't feel my feet anymore in my heels. I step to the side of the refreshment booth, where Mrs. Perrymore offers me a glass of punch.

She was one of my favorite teachers and one of the chaperones on the night.

"Mrs. Perrymore," I greet her. "What made you come out of retirement?"

"Oh, I couldn't very well leave a bunch of horny kids unsupervised on prom night, now, could I?"

I laugh and drink my punch, the music slows down switching from Calvin Harris and Rihanna's "This Is What You Came For" to Justin Bieber's "Love Yourself."

I know Gabriel is standing behind me before I even turn around.

And there he is, holding a hand out to me. "Do you have the energy for another dance?"

Yes. No. A million times yes.

I drop my glass, take his hand, and let him lead me to the dance floor.

The moment I'm in his arms, I realize just how in trouble I am. I feel myself sinking, spiraling down into a memory. The present and the past clash together. I close my eyes and lean my head into his chest.

Gabriel tucks me in and rests his cheek on my head as we sway in time to the slow music. There's no space left between our beating souls. He cradles me in his arms, one hand on the small of my back, the other holding mine. This is wrong. But it feels so right.

The final stroke is inhaling his familiar smell, of hikes in the woods, of making love in front of the fireplace, of lying in bed cuddling our cat. His warmth seeps into me, his hands move over my body.

I close my eyes and forget everything else.

"Why did you do this?" I ask.

"I wanted you to have this night," he says. "Even if it is the last thing I can give you."

I lift my head to look at him. "Are you trying to ruin prom forever for me?"

"Everyone has bittersweet memories about their senior prom."

I scoff. "I bet all you remember is taking the most beautiful girl in school and being named king."

"Taking the most beautiful girl to prom? That'll be a memory for tomorrow."

I can't look at him without my heart aching. I press my face into his chest again. "Let's just dance, Gabriel."

He pulls me closer to him until we're sharing every breath; his hand caresses my hair. Then his thumb strokes my cheek, moving lower until it's brushing my lips. I know if I look up, I'll kiss him. He always knows even before I do.

He's so warm, so familiar.

I wish I could wrap him around me and hold on to him forever.

I wish I could forget his betrayal.

I wish I could hate him.

A soft smile tugs at his lips, and he lowers his head to press a kiss to my forehead since I refuse to lift my head.

He pulls back and I can feel his eyes on me, searching my face.

I give up and look up at him, feeling my heart break all over again. "I can't do this, Gabriel. Not again."

"Can you really move on? Forget everything that we had?"

"I can try."

"I'm not letting you go."

"Don't you get it, Gabriel? This is just one more game you're playing with me."

"I'm not playing any games. I'm not going to hurt you anymore."

"I don't believe you."

"I know." He grasps my face with his hands. "But it's the truth."

"I can't just forget everything you did."

"I don't want you to forget. But can't you at least try to forgive me? I know what I did was wrong, going after Justin, buying your stocks without telling you. I was arrogant and stupid, but I swear I've learned my lesson."

Adele's "Hello" begins to play in the background and it's like the song is screaming at me, echoing Gabriel's words.

"How can I trust you really mean what you're saying?" I ask.

His thumbs brush my cheeks. "Because the past fifteen days without you have been the most miserable of my life, because I love you with all my heart, because I didn't mean to break your trust the first time and I'll be damned before I lose you a second time. You're my person, Blake. You're my forever."

Tears spill down my cheeks. I try to blink them back.

"I know I don't deserve your forgiveness," he says. "But I want to spend the rest of my life trying to earn it."

I look up and into his eyes, dark eyes that wash me with tenderness, love, and a promise I want to believe.

I don't want to think about anything else. Tonight, the past, or the future.

I only want to live in this moment with him.

I lean up and press my lips against his, tasting him, feeling the familiar warmth of his mouth and the touch of his hands on my cheek.

He kisses me back and I feel alive in his arms. This kiss is like diving into a pool of memories of tomorrow. I want to remember the trips we'll make to his cottage, the nights we'll spend in bed holding each other, the days we'll become a family, the years we'll grow old together. I want to remember everything.

And this is the moment I realize he means more than everything else. I could lose my company and still live a happy life. I've built an empire, I could build another. But I will never find another Gabriel.

Yes, he could hurt me again—willingly or not. He could die in a car accident tomorrow and leave me heartbroken for all eternity. But even a single minute with him is worth all the risks.

I pull back and look at him.

His face is relaxed; I don't even have to say what I'm thinking, he already knows.

But I still say it. "You're my person, too. I want to spend forever with you."

# EPILOGUE
## BLAKE

*Nine months later*

At 3 a.m., my phone vibrates on the nightstand. Already awake, I reach out for it.

It's Marissa.

"Hey," I pick up.

An inhuman groan greets me on the other side, followed by a quick series of breath intakes. "My waters broke," Marissa announces once she's able to talk again.

"You were supposed to be six more days, you little over-achiever, why do you always have to be first at everything?"

"Can we not do this now?"

"Are you already at the hospital?"

"No, still at home."

Another scream rips out of her and I lower the phone away from my ear until it's passed.

"Is Dr. Dishy with you?"

"No, he was called on an emergency surgery a few hours ago and he went because I said I'd be fine on my own and that the baby wasn't due for another week and everyone knows first babies come late."

I chuckle. "Guess the little bugger wanted to prove his mommy wrong right off the bat. Is Nora there?"

"No, at her grandparents."

"So you're alone. You need us to pick you up or—?"

"No, I called a car. See you at the hospital."

"All right, honey, hold tight."

I hang up, turn on the bedside lamp, and stare at the man still peacefully sleeping next to me. Cannon balls would not wake Gabriel; it's one of his superpowers.

I gently shake him. "Babe."

He rolls over and mumbles something, still sleeping. His hair is all tousled and his face perfect despite the million pillow creases on his skin.

I shake him again. "Gabriel, I need you to wake up."

His eyes blink open and focus on me, a smile spreading on his lips.

My heart flutters in response.

That smile.

The one he gives me every morning, or even in the middle of the night lately—whenever I wake him. The one where, the moment he comes back to consciousness, he realizes I'm by his side and looks at me like he's the luckiest man in the world.

I love that look. I can't believe I almost missed out on waking up to it every day.

"Hey, how you doing, baby?" He pushes up on an elbow. "What's up? You need me to give you a back rub?"

"No, we have to go to the hospital."

That wakes him all right. In two seconds flat, he's already jumped out of bed and is hopping around the room pulling up his sweatpants. "How are you feeling, is something wrong?"

"Relax, it's not me. Marissa's waters broke."

The dressing frenzy stops and Gabriel looks around our bedroom, sort of lost. "What time is it?"

"Twenty past three," I inform him.

"Are you sure we should head to the hospital given... uh, I mean, in the middle of the night?"

I can tell he's being attentive with his wording, carefully avoiding hate phrases like "in your condition."

"Marissa is having her baby and her fiancé just got called into surgery, I'm not leaving my best friend to give birth alone."

"All right, all right." Gabriel raises his hands in surrender. "We'll go."

I tug a cotton stretch dress out of the closet and do my best to squeeze into it. "Thank you."

Gabriel grabs a T-shirt from the dresser and pulls it over his head. "Let's go then. But we're taking the Aston Martin." He kisses me on the forehead. "And I'm driving."

As if we had a choice on who's driving.

Gabriel gently guides me out of the bedroom with a hand on my lower back. I let him have this bit of fussing; after all, the man is driving me to the hospital in the middle of the night to help my friend give birth. He deserves to be cut a little slack even if I detest being fussed over or treated as if I'm not at 100 per cent.

At the hospital, I march toward the information desk.

"The maternity ward is on the second floor," the receptionist says without letting me speak.

"Good evening," I reply. "I'm here to see my friend Marissa Mayer; I'm part of her birth plan."

The woman behind the counter frowns, but wisely refrains from saying anything. "Let me check." She types on her keyboard. "Yes, your friend is in room 206."

"Let's go," I tell Gabriel.

"Wait? Is he the father?"

"Yes, I mean, no, he's part of the birth plan as well."

We leave an even more confused receptionist behind and head for the elevators.

The hospital is eerily quiet in the middle of the night as we walk along a large hallway following the numbering to room 206.

A scream rips through the silence, making me jump. We follow the direction it came from until we find Marissa's room.

She's inside alone, wearing leggings and a loose, oversized T-shirt, and pacing.

She stops when she sees us. "Thank goodness you're here."

"How are you doing, honey?" I wrap an arm around her and pull her to me.

"Tired already. The pain is pretty bad."

I stare at the room devoid of personnel. "Shouldn't someone be here with you?"

"They say it's still too early."

A contraction seizes her, and she almost breaks every bone in my hand clutching it.

She grinds through another ten contractions with no one showing up to help.

Just as I'm about to ask Gabriel to go search for someone, a midwife walks in, looks at me, frowns, then stares at Gabriel. "Are you the father?"

"Nope." Gabriel points at me. "I'm with that lady."

"Then what are you doing here?" the obstetrician asks him.

"Moral support, cafeteria runs, whatever is needed."

The midwife seems a bit exasperated. She turns toward Marissa. "Honey, where is the baby's father?"

"Hopefully somewhere dying a slow death as punishment for putting me through this." She sobs a little. "Can I have my epidural now?"

The obstetrician checks her chart. "Dear, you were only at two centimeters half an hour ago; let's get you to four first."

"How long will it take?"

"At the pace you're going, an hour, possibly two."

Marissa despairs. "Another hour of this? Two? Are you crazy? This is legitimized torture. Can't you do anything?"

The obstetrician looks at Gabriel. "You, moral support, want to get some practice at back rubbing?"

Gabriel stares at the midwife with a deer-in-the-headlights expression. "I'm not sure it'd be appropriate... That Marissa would want me to—"

"If it's going to make me feel better, it's appropriate," my best friend interrupts, then looking at me she adds, "Right?"

I smirk at Gabriel. "Fine by me."

He dons a heroic I-gotta-do-what-I-gotta-do expression and goes to stand by Marissa. While the obstetrician helps Marissa get on all fours and shows Gabriel what to do, I sit on a Pilates ball, working on some hip stretches.

Half an hour later, Gabriel is getting sweaty and Marissa is in no better shape than when they started. I begin to worry. Childbirth is starting to look like too much of an uncivilized business for my taste.

"Excuse me," I ask. "Are you sure you can't give her anything for the pain?"

The midwife, more exasperated than ever, is about to reply when the door bursts open and the baby's father barges into the room, still wearing scrubs and a surgical cap. "Am I on time?"

"Doctor!" the obstetrician exclaims. "What are you doing here?"

He goes by Marissa's side, while Gabriel, looking more than a little relieved, steps back.

"I'm the father," he says, while Marissa accuses, "He's the one who did this to me."

The world-class neonatal surgeon lets out an amiable smile. "Technically speaking, I didn't."

"You really think it's wise to pick this moment to argue with— aaargh." Another contraction seizes her. "I want the epidural," Marissa whines once it's over.

"How far along is she?" Marissa's fiancé asks with an air of competence.

"She was at two centimeters an hour ago, must be at three by now."

"Let's call for the epidural; we can add some oxytocin to her IV to speed things along."

Marissa throws her arms around him. "Oh, thank goodness. That's why I agreed to marry you."

"Unconditional love?"

"No, unconditional access to drugs."

I stand up from the ball. "Well, guys, if you have everything covered, we'll go wait outside."

Marissa waves me out while grinding through another contraction.

Outside the room, Gabriel circles a hand on my lower back. "How are you?"

"That was brutal," I say, still slightly in shock.

"I thought you and Marissa watched the video in birthing class?"

Marissa stayed single for a good chunk of her pregnancy, so we went to birthing classes together. I didn't want her to have to go alone, and Gabriel didn't mind skipping the birthing videos. Now I wish I had, too.

"Yeah-ah, not even close." I feel a brief pang in my belly and wince.

"Are you okay?" Gabriel asks.

"Yeah, I'm fine."

He still looks concerned, but lets it slide. "You want to wait here, or go see if the cafeteria is open?"

"The cafeteria? I could use a walk, mmmfh." Another small spasm goes through me.

We walk our way back to the elevators, but I have to stop short as I'm seized by another cramp.

A passing nurse stops beside us. "Honey, you're going the wrong way. The reception desk is in the opposite direction."

"No, I'm fine, I was just here to support a friend."

The nurse raises a suspicious eyebrow at me, looking at her watch. "Stand five minutes with a straight face and you're good to go."

I make it to about four minutes before another spasm seizes me. "Ow."

"That's what I thought."

"No." I stare at Gabriel in a panic. "I'm fine, I swear, I'm not ready."

"Babe, why don't you let the nurse check you. If nothing is happening, we'll be on our way."

"No." I shake my head vehemently.

"It's okay," the nurse tries to reassure me. "You're in the best place to be having contractions."

"I'm not having contractions," I protest, shaking my head again in utter denial. "It must be indigestioooon—aargh."

"I'm bringing a chair," the nurse decrees.

I hold on to Gabriel for dear life. "Don't let them take me."

With the sweetest possible expression on his face, he sweeps a strand of hair behind my ear, and in the gentlest voice ever, he says, "It's okay, babe, we knew this was coming. You're going to rock."

"No, I don't want to spend hours suffering like Marissa, and I don't have an inside doctor to give me early access to drugs. Take me home."

"Are you sure? Because there'll be no drugs at all at home."

The reality that the baby is coming, now, whether or not I'm ready, hits me worse than the following contraction.

I gladly collapse in the nurse's chair and let her bring me to a room. There, she helps me onto a bed and asks Gabriel, "Could you please fill out the paperwork while I examine her?"

"Sure," he says.

At my pleading, please-don't-leave-me-alone, desperate expression, he adds, "I'll be right back."

The nurse helps me out of my underwear and looks down there, letting out a surprised, "Oh."

"What is it?"

"Did the contractions just start?"

"I felt a little off all day," I confess. "But I thought it was just the normal pregnancy discomfort, why?"

"You're at four centimeters already."

I sag back on the bed as relief washes over me. "Does that mean I can have the epidural right away?"

"Sure does, honey."

By the time Gabriel gets back, the anesthetist is already in the room prepping me.

The second the epidural hits, all the pain goes away. I recline on the bed, peacefully calm. If not for obvious reasons, I'd ask them to bring me a cocktail with a pink umbrella to sip while we wait.

Whenever the aching resurfaces, they pour a little magic liquid into the IV going into my back and all suffering is whisked away.

As the sun rises over Manhattan on the first day of summer, a strong pang hits my lower belly, and I say, "I think it's time for another top-up."

The midwife checks her watch. "You just had one."

"But it hurts."

She examines me. "The baby's crowning; I can feel the head."

"Aaaar," I scream. "This better be over fast." I crush Gabriel's hand in mine. "This is all your fault for getting me pregnant in the back of a limousine on prom night."

The midwife looks up at us from between my legs. "How old are you folks again?"

"It's a long story." Gabriel unleashes one of his no-prisoners smiles on her. "Her father still hasn't forgiven me for the shotgun wedding."

The woman who's supposed to be taking care of my painfully contracting womb blushes.

I scold them both and glare at my husband. "Less charming and more rubbing."

"At your orders." His hands work their magic on my shoulders, and I lean into the touch—not that it's helping much with the ring of fire in my nether regions, but human contact at this moment is soothing in a way I can't explain.

"Eaarrg," I let out another animal sound. "Are you sure the epidural is still working?"

"Yes, honey, it's just that you're ready to push." The obstetrician stares at us. "What do you say, are you two ready to have a baby?"

I'm most definitely not. But I look up at Gabriel, who stares down at me with the proudest glint in his eyes. "You can do it."

We exchange a nod. Yes, we're a team. Together, we can do anything.

"Come on, now," the midwife urges, "push."

# NOTE FROM THE AUTHOR

Dear Reader,

I hope you enjoyed reading *Not in a Billion Years* as much as I enjoyed writing it. If you're already missing Gabriel and Blake, I have wonderful news for you. They will have a prominent role also in the next book in the series *Baby, One More Time*.

Book two will feature Marissa and her IVF journey with lots of behind the scenes also into Blake's pregnancy. This story will be a second-chance romance with a slight enemies-to-lovers twist and lots of hilarious mishaps.

If you've been following me for a while, you might already know that my son was born through IVF and that I struggled with infertility. So this is a topic really dear to my heart that I want to destigmatize and bring more into the conversation even if in a humorous way in a romcom.

Now, I know what you're thinking—yes, I do, I'm psychic— you're mentally shouting, "But what about Thomas? He's so hot, and sexy, and charming. I want a book about him!"

Well, you and me both.

A book about Thomas wasn't initially planned, but I developed a major writer's crush on him while penning this story, and so book three in the series will feature him as the leading man. This novel will be a STEMinist office romance with only one bed, and an adorable droid sidekick who I'm already adoring—if robot romances were a thing, he'd get a story, too.

Reese, the heroine of this third book, is a mechanical engineer like me, and I'm having to dust off my old college manuals to bring her character to life and do my best to show how women in technical fields can kick ass with their intelligence, grit, and dedication. So I really hope you'll want to follow on reading the series for both Marissa's and Thomas's books.

Now, I have to ask you a big favor. If you loved my story, please consider leaving a review on your favorite retailer's website, on Goodreads, or wherever you like to post reviews (your blog, Book-Tok, in a text to your best friend...). Reviews are the best gift you can give to an author, and word of mouth is the most powerful means of book discovery.

Thank you for your constant support!

Camilla, x

PS. Read the acknowledgments to the end if you want to know where the inspiration for this book came from :)

# ACKNOWLEDGMENTS

When they say it takes a village to write a book they're not wrong. The novel you've read is a much-improved version from the first draft I initially submitted to my publisher, the amazing Boldwood Books.

I'd like to thank all the fabulous editors who helped me shape *Not in a Billion Years* into the story it is now: Rachel Faulkner-Willcocks, our back-and-forth on plot points and twists has been invaluable. Jenny Hutton, for the tough love. Candida Bradford, for ironing out the final details. And Susan Sugden for checking everything one last time.

Thanks to the entire production team at Boldwood Books for making the book as pretty on the outside as it is on the inside.

Thanks to the marketing team for helping me bring more readers to this story that I love so much.

And especially thanks to you, for reading this book, for sticking with me to the very end—if you're reading this it really means you don't want to let go.

Thanks to the BookTokers, bookstagrammers, book bloggers, and all the reviewers for helping me spread the word about my work. The reading community is so inclusive and accepting, I feel honored to be a part of it.

Last but not least, thank you to my husband for inspiring this entire story. Most often I'm asked where the inspiration for a novel came from and it's not always easy to give an unequivocal answer. But with this book, I can pinpoint the exact moment.

My husband and I were in the process of interviewing babysitters for the odd night out, and he was really concerned about the sitters potentially inviting guests over to the house while we were away. So I told him he should install the same doorbell with a camera that turns on whenever someone opens the door that a friend of ours was using, and then I added, "You know that the guy who invented that was initially on *Shark Tank* but didn't get an offer and then went on and sold the company for a billion dollars?"

To which my husband said, "So he's a unicorn!"

Me. "What's a unicorn?"

"A company that made it to one billion."

My head exploded; I immediately knew this had to become a book. I love unicorns, and the concept seemed really romantic. From that moment on, all I could think about was writing a story about a *woman* unicorn, and pitting her against an even mightier magical creature: so MGM was born. My enemies-to-lovers brain-cogs started spinning with endless possibilities and the rest is history...

Another little behind the scenes for you... Before receiving a proper title, this book had been referred to as the "unicorn" book for months. I even wanted to incorporate unicorn into the title. Then we discovered that unicorns, besides being billion-dollar companies and magical creatures, are also the third parties in menages—blushing, and so we decided to avoid confusion and not mention it.

Anyway, thank you, hubby, for being a business major and for giving me all these financial pearls that I sometimes incorporate into my books. Love, yah.

# ABOUT THE AUTHOR

**Camilla Isley** is an engineer who left science behind to write bestselling contemporary rom-coms set all around the world. She lives in Italy.

Sign up to Camilla Isley's mailing list for news, competitions and updates on future books.

Visit Camilla's website: www.camillaisley.com

Follow Camilla on social media:

# ALSO BY CAMILLA ISLEY

The Love Theorem

Love Quest

The Love Proposal

Love to Hate You

Not in a Billion Years

# Boldwood

Boldwood Books is an award-winning
fiction publishing company seeking
out the best stories from
around the world.

### Find out more at
### www.boldwoodbooks.com

Join our reader community
for brilliant books,
competitions and offers!

## Follow us
## #BoldBookClub

9 781837 519415